ABOUT THE BOOK

Despite her obvious lack of magical talent, nineteen year old Moira Bellamie apprentices with the Gendarmerie Magique, the magic police. She puts all her effort into solving a burglary at the National Museum where antique weapons have been stolen, to keep the hard won job. Falling for her partner Druidus wasn't part of the plan. When more and more people are murdered with one of the stolen weapons, Moira must tame uncontrollable magic, or the people she cares for will die, her partner first and foremost.

ABOUT THE AUTHOR

Katharina Gerlach was born in Germany in 1968. She and her three younger brothers grew up in the middle of a forest in the heart of the Luneburgian Heather. After romping through the forest with imagination as her guide, the tomboy learned to read and disappeared into magical adventures, past times or eerie fairytale woods.

She didn't stop at reading. During her training as a landscape gardener, she wrote her first novel, a manuscript full of a beginner's mistakes. Fortunately, she found books on Creative Writing and soon her stories improved. For a while, reality interfered with her writing but after finishing a degree in forestry and a PhD in Science she returned to her vocation. She likes to write Fantasy, Science Fiction and Historical Novels for all age groups.

At present, she is writing at her next project in a small house near Hildesheim, Germany, where she lives with her husband, three children and a dog.

Homepage: www.katharinagerlach.com
Twitter: @CatGerlach
Facebook: www.facebook.com/KatharinaGerlach.Autorin
Goodreads: www.goodreads.com/author/show/1168793
Wattpad: www.wattpad.com/user/KatharinaGerlach
Pinterest: pinterest.com/catgerlach/

Swordplay

Gendarmerie Magique
Volume 1

Katharina Gerlach

Swordplay, Gendarmerie Magique, Volume 1, English Edition
published by the Independent Bookworm, USA and D

this book is also available as eBook.

cover: Katharina Gerlach, Corona Zschüsschen (sjusjun.com)
editor: Ethan James Clarke
printed On-Demand Publishing LLC, 100 Enterprise Way, Suite
A200, Scotts Valley, CA 95066, USA, www.createspace.com

ISBN-13: 978-3-95681-016-9

For more information mail to katharina@katharinagerlach.com
Find more information on the author's homepage:
http://www.katharinagerlach.com

ACKNOWLEDGMENTS

Without the help of my long-term mentor, Holly Lisle, this book wouldn't have been what it is now, but without my family's support, it would still be part of my Unwritten Library. Thank you. I love you more than I can say.

Also, thank you, dear reader, for buying this book. Your enthusiasm for reading makes it possible for authors like me to live our dream. Enjoy this story.

Chapter 1

Moira yawned; it was only her second night shift and her body hadn't adjusted yet. At three in the morning, it preferred to sleep, no matter how eager she was to help examine a burglary. She blinked to get rid of her tiredness and wiped the sweat from her brow. It was even hotter inside the car than outside.

"We're nearly there." Buds turned a corner so fast, the centrifugal force pressed Moira against the door. Buds didn't care. "You'll take the cases, Moira."

"But don't go close to the scene," Semra added, clinging to the grip over the passenger door when Buds sped around the next corner.

Moira didn't answer. She had enough trouble to cling to something. Absentmindedly, she stared out of the window at the deserted streets of Salthaven. The all-round green light on the car's roof bathed the usually friendly, multi-level sandstone buildings of the city center in a haunting glow. Once in a while, Moira spotted the glowing net of a protective spell covering one of the many shops. *Luckily we won't have to pass the tavern district. The way Buds drives many of the late night guests wouldn't stand a chance.*

With squealing brakes, Buds pulled to a halt in front of the National Museum. The four-story building was illuminated from below. With its pillars that reached from the classical roof to the ground, it seemed even more intimidating than during the day. As fast as she could, Moira got out of the carpisto and opened the trunk. She took great care not to touch the flying carpet's fringe hanging down freely under the bumper. Back when she took driving lessons, she had ruined a brand-new carpisto that way, and she didn't fancy repeating it. She hoisted the heavy bags with the crime scene investigation tools while Buds and Semra already hurried up the wide staircase to the entrance of the National Museum.

A second patrol carpisto stopped and two young gendarmes got out and began to put up the obligatory barrier.

"Hurry up, Moira!" Buds didn't turn back to her.

Moira pretended she didn't mind this impolite behavior. She sucked in her lower lip and followed him, hauling the two heavy bags up the seemingly endless stairs. Sweat burned in her eyes, and she wished she could use a hovering spell. The last time she had tried, the cases had exploded. *Why does it have to be so hot?* She sighed. *And it won't be any better inside the museum due to the climate control spell.*

At the entrance, a slim but small nightwatchman waited for her. He hopped from foot to foot so the pale-blond ponytail under his red uniform cap bobbed up and down. Moira had hardly reached Buds and Semra when the nightwatchman led them through the big glass doors inside. A heat wave suffocated Moira in the National Museum's entrance hall. *I hate climate control spells.* She frowned. Still loaded with the heavy cases, she fell behind. Sweat flowed over her body like water. Her breathing sped up as she hurried along the gallery of the old masters. Due to the reduced illumination at night, most pictures in the high-ceilinged rooms were lost in the dark. The security spells' glow wasn't strong enough for Moira to see more than the shapes, but she had been to the National Museum's art gallery so often she knew the pictures hung in a seemingly unsorted manner all over the walls.

Even Mona Beth, the world famous portrait, hung hidden between several landscapes and a couple of paintings with bony, naked women. She looked for Buds and Semra. They were standing in front of a door labeled 'private,' talking to the nightwatchman without taking any notice of her. Moira dared to stop for a second to catch her breath. Although she knew exactly where Mona Beth hung,

8

it took her a while to discover the hand-sized, magically enhanced painting. The young woman in the picture winked at her and stuck out her tongue. Surprised, Moira raised her eyebrows. Until now, Mona Beth had never winked before. She set down one of the cases and wiped the sweat from her brow with the back of her hand. For a fleeting moment she envied the gendarmes for whom the climate control spell felt cooling. *Should I tell them?* She gazed at Buds and Semra again. *Better not. How am I going to explain that a magically enhanced painting sticks out her tongue at me where everybody else sees a mellow and mysterious smile?* She picked up the case again and walked to the gendarmes still waiting in front of the heavy iron door with the nightwatchman.

Asked if he'd been to the cellar, the nightwatchman shook his head. "When I noticed on the surveillance globes that the rolling gate stood open, I raised the alarm immediately and informed the director. There he is."

A slim man in a black, stylish two-piece approached. The nightwatchman introduced him as Director Professor Doctor du Mar.

The head of the National Museum bowed stiffly. "Please excuse my late arrival." He put one hand on the ID-panneau and pushed his white fringe from his face with the other. The identification spell traced his fingers with a green glow and the door to the basement opened.

When the director took a step toward it, Buds held him back. "Please stay up here until we have secured all evidence."

The director opened his mouth to complain but Semra cut him short. She pointed to a man hurrying along the gallery with flying coattails.

"Commissaire Magique Marten will have to talk to you, and our colleagues will also have questions for you."

Moira noticed the commissaire stop beside Mona Beth to bend forward before Semra pushed her through the door. Carefully she descended the steep staircase after Buds. She was grateful that it got colder the further down they went. At the bottom, Semra put a hand on her shoulder. "Stay here. We don't want to ruin this crime scene, the way it happened to the guys from the day shift, right?" She looked at Moira more threateningly than questioningly.

Moira nodded. She didn't like to remember how she had destroyed every clue within reach when she had tried to spread a stasis spell. Luckily headquarters had given them the wrong address, which had been the only fact that had saved her, but Moira could still recall the relief in her colleagues' faces when they realized they weren't at the true crime scene.

She made herself comfortable on the bottom step and watched Buds. He carried his case toward the rolling gates at the other end of the gigantic, nearly empty stockroom. Semra walked to the other side of the hall where a fireproof steel door led to the museum's archives. Patiently Moira waited, glad she wasn't asked to help. She knew that despite her enthusiasm, she had no talent for crime scene investigation; one more reason to be even more diligent with all her other tasks. She had fought too hard for her preliminary job. *I have to prove that I'm just as good as normal people. It's the only way to get a permanent job with the Gendarmerie Magique.* Mechanically, she felt for the letter with her appointment for a RealJob™ analysis in the pocket of her uniform. On one hand, she feared the interview; on the other, she could hardly wait. Whenever she thought of it, her heart beat harder. To take her mind of it, she watched the two gendarmes work. Buds had spread a stasis spell over the whole crime scene. Now, they could collect clues without changing or destroying them accidentally.

Moira wished magic would come to her as naturally. She watched Buds with great interest as he spread fingerprint powder on his palm and murmured the activating words. The powder lifted off his hand, spread through the hall, and stuck at every single fingerprint it found. Buds moaned when he realized there were hundreds. He was just pressing a sticky paper on his third print when someone called out from the top of the stairs. "Did you secure the crime scene? Can I come down?"

"All green," Semra called back, and she was right in the truest sense of the word. She had activated a marking spell that made all footprints glow neon green. From Moira's spot on the stairs, the hall resembled an oversized, futuristic painting.

"We should preserve this. It is intriguing," the head of the National Museum said. He came down the stairs behind Commissaire Magique Marten.

Moira slipped to the side to make room for them.

The commissaire looked at her and raised an eyebrow. "Are you the young woman with the stasis spell that backfired?"

Moira nodded and stared at the ground, her cheeks burning. *Does everybody know that by now?*

A strong hand warmed her shoulder. "Don't worry about it. All beginnings are difficult, and not everybody is cut out for crime scene investigation."

A butterfly of hope fluttered in her stomach as she watched the commissaire walk away. Accompanied by the director and the nightwatchman he stepped over to some boxes waiting for the morning to be unpacked. The nightwatchman took off his cap, put it on a box and wiped the sweat off his forehead while Director du Mar walked around the boxes, frowning. "At first glance, nothing seems to be missing, but I'd better compare the contents of the boxes with the bill of delivery," he said.

"Let the new girl do this." The commissaire waved for Moira to come.

She got up hesitantly, glancing at Buds. The commissaire grinned. "Buds. How much longer?"

Buds answered without looking up. "We'll be done in ten minutes."

"Good. Lift the stasis spell so Moira can come in. You can recast it before we leave."

"No problem, Commissaire Marten."

The commissaire looked at Moira. "When stasis has been lifted, you'll compare the inventory with the content of the boxes."

Moira nodded.

The nightwatchman sprinted off, fetched long folding tables from a shelf, and set them up.

Commissaire Marten turned to the director. "Did you notice something strange in the gallery?"

"No, why?" The director hurried up the stairs, and the commissaire followed. When he passed Moira, he smiled. She felt like hugging him. He was the first member of the Gendarmerie Magique who had been friendly to her. With a warm feeling in her stomach, she settled down again and waited for Buds and Semra to finish.

Half an hour later, Buds deactivated the stasis spell. "You will touch only the boxes or you'll be in trouble."

Moira nodded, slipped on a pair of latex gloves and picked up the clipboard with the inventory lying on the boxes. *Hopefully they aren't sealed with a spell.* She took an open-sesame from Buds' case and woke the thumb-sized nerl living inside. "Could you please open the boxes for me?"

The nerl opened his eyes wide with surprise, which made the warts on his green skin dance. "A polite human? That's refreshing." He zipped to the first box, and soon the lid clattered to the ground. While Moira took out bundle by bundle and placed them on the long folding tables, the nerl opened the other boxes. When he returned to Moira, he reached out with his right arm and open palm in the traditional farewell gesture of his folk. Before he could climb back into his home, she thanked him. Shaking his head with a smile, the nerl climbed back into the open-sesame. Moira grinned when she heard him snore a little later.

Luckily all bundles had been labeled carefully. Moira easily found them on the lists. Meticulously she ticked off clay fragments, hair needles, cloak clasps, pottery, gold coins, weapons, bones, and much more. When she fetched the last bundle from the last box, she found the nightwatch-man's dark red cap. She picked it up and put it on the table too before she ticked off the last few bundles. Everything was there. Satisfied, she folded back the lists. *Wait a moment.* She unclipped the lists from the clipboard and examined them. The content of each box was listed on a separate sheet. The pages had been stuck together with a glue spell and placed in the clipboard. A small scrap of paper clung to the last page. "One page is missing." Moira took the night-watchman's cap and the list and climbed the stairs, looking for Buds. When she found him, she said, "I'm done."

The burly gendarme nodded. "I'll reactivate the stasis spell."

Moira waited until he left and went to look for Commissaire Marten. She handed him the list. "Someone ripped out a page. Since there is one page per box, I believe one box is missing."

"Good work." Commissaire Marten smiled at her. His tired face with the three-day beard lit up like a cloudy sky opening to the sun.

Moira felt the warmth in her heart and smiled back.

"I'll tell Director du Mar." Commissaire Marten turned and left.

Open-mouthed, Moira watched him leave.

"He's the best, isn't he?" Semra stepped closer. "Work is twice as much fun with him. It's a pity he works with us so rarely."

"What department is he in?"

"Murder Two."

"Murder Two," Moira repeated. "Why is he here today?"

"There was a body in the yard of the museum, probably a homeless. Maybe Sabio believes that the burglary is connected to the murder. It's said he's got a sixth sense for connections."

Something occurred to Moira and she turned to Semra. "Do you know where I can find the nightwatchman? He left his cap below."

"Impossible. I interviewed him just now, and he was wearing it."

Without a word Moira showed the cap that she had discovered between the lids of the boxes to Semra.

Semra scratched her head. "Maybe the burglars had an accomplice in the house. Buds will not be pleased that you picked it up."

At this moment, the nightwatchman entered the gallery,

and he was wearing his cap on his head where it should be.

"Do you still need me?" He addressed Semra. "I've been off duty for an hour already, and my wife will be waiting for me."

"Do you know who this might belong to?" Semra showed him the second cap.

He nodded. "It's Huudien's. He was in charge of the rooms downstairs and the basement. Weird, he's not usually losing pieces of his uniform." He held out his hand. "Shall I take it along?"

"Thank you, but we'll take care of it." Semra bagged the cap and nodded at the nightwatchman. "You may go home now. If we have more questions, we know where to find you."

He thanked her and shuffled tiredly in the direction of the exit.

Moira hesitated, then asked, "Why couldn't he take the cap along for his colleague?"

Semra looked at her as if she had asked the result of two plus two. "It's evidence. We found no signs of forceful entry so far."

"Not even in the recordings of the surveillance globes?" Moira was surprised.

"We'll get an expert to look at them. Buds already packed them." She put her hands behind her and stretched. "I'll put away the cap. You take the cases back to the carpisto, so we can get going when Buds is done."

Obediently, Moira looked for the cases. Again, her gaze met the Mona Beth's, and again, the girl in the painting winked before it stuck out its tongue. Moira stepped closer to have a better look.

"Stop dawdling and take the cases to the carpisto," Semra said.

"Just a sec." Moira reached out and traced the lines of the face in the air with her finger. Hadn't the contours been slightly rounder before? Or was her memory playing tricks on her? The shrilling of a siren interrupted her thoughts, and she spun around, wide-eyed. Had she really touched the painting?

14

Commissaire Marten came running with his hair flowing, and Semra scolded, "Can't you be more careful? You're worse than a toddler."

Moira grated her teeth but endured the rebuke. She had to fight the urge to talk back, but she would give up her last chance for a permanent place in the Gendarmerie Magique if she didn't keep herself under control. *I can't hear her,* she told herself. *The words roll off me like water from a duck.*

"That's enough, Semra," Commissaire Marten's voice rang. "After all, she was the only one from your team who realized that something is wrong with Mona Beth."

Semra's eyebrows shot up. "What?"

"If you look closely, you will discover that she frowns a little before smiling. Power of observation is the key talent of a great gendarma, Semra."

Semra pressed her lips together and shot Moira an angry glance. Director du Mar arrived and stopped beside Semra. "At least now we know that the alarm is working fine."

Semra pulled up her eyebrows. "But that would mean someone in the building switched off the alarm."

"Well deduced, Semra." Commissaire Marten put his hand on Semra's arm. "You'd better pack all surveillance globes from tonight, not only those from the basement. I believe we should have a somewhat closer look."

"Right away, boss." Semra hurried away.

Moira marveled at how fast she had calmed down again. All of a sudden, she knew in which department of the Gendarmerie Magique she wanted to work, should the analysis of her magical abilities deem her worthy. Commissaire Marten was exactly the kind of superior she needed.

"Mademoiselle Bellamie?"

Moira took a while to realize that she had been addressed. It had been quite some time since anyone had used her surname.

Commissaire Marten held up a bag-safe with evidence. "Could you take this to the carpisto and keep it in sight until we arrive at the gendarmerie? I don't want our proof to become invalid because we can't keep to the rules."

Beaming, Moira took the bag and the responsibility and carried it and the two cases to the carpisto. She put the cases in the trunk, settled on the backseat with the bag of evidence on her knees, and waited. To her surprise, Buds and Semra not only returned with two more bag-safes full of evidence, but also with Director du Mar. They had spelled him into a cocoon of silence, so Moira was squeezed in between the cocoon and the three safes on the whole flight back to the station.

Chapter 2

Buds and Semra left it to Moira to take the safes to the court exhibit archive.

"When you're done, get started on the report." Buds took the director's elbow and led him to one of the interrogation rooms.

"Three copies," Semra added before following her colleague.

Moira set out for the court exhibit archive in the building's vaulted cellar. She felt a bit used, although she knew that due to the rules, two gendarmes had to be present at every interrogation.

On her way back, Commissaire Marten stopped her on the stairway. "I was pleasantly surprised that you identified Mona Beth as a forgery. Even Director du Mar didn't see it right away."

Moira blushed and stared at her feet.

"I'd like you to have a look at the surveillance globes with my expert."

Moira's eyes widened and she looked up. "But I'm only an aspirant."

Commissaire Marten smiled. "With very good eyes. Maybe you'll discover something my expert misses."

Moira's ears burned. The praise made her feel foolish although it was nice not to be considered a moron all the time. "I will have to write a report first," she said hoarsely.

"I will tell Grub that you'll join him later." Commissaire Marten nodded and proceeded down the stairs toward the archive.

An hour later, Moira opened the door to the dark-room and slipped in. A surveillance globe flickered in front of her, projecting the museum's big basement hall onto the wall.

"There you are." The voice came from the dark. "Make yourself comfortable. I just got started, so you haven't missed anything."

Moira felt her way forward until she found a chair that allowed her a good view of the picture on the wall.

"This globe starts at 10 p.m. and runs to the point where Semra packed it. We should be able to view the whole burglary. I'll speed it up for a while, so watch closely."

For a long time there was nothing but the empty hall with the boxes. Moira was already pondering how she could extract herself in time for the end of her shift when a nightwatchman appeared, coming down the long stairs. He walked through a door and returned a little later in plain clothes carrying his uniform in a bag. Moira watched him set it on a box to tie his shoelaces. *He probably lost his cap there.*

The nightwatchman walked over to the two big rolling gates and lifted his hands in a conjuring gesture. Since the globe's surveillance eye didn't record sound, Moira couldn't hear the activation words, but the left gate opened obediently. A white arrow shot out of the darkness behind it toward the surveillance eye, and the picture splintered to white snow.

"That's all," Grub said. "Seems to have been a put-up affair with the nightwatchman as spy."

"What about the arrow?" Moira asked.

"Buds found it, a Cupido26^E. You can get boxes of them at every carpisto-chargerie. Next globe?"

"I'd like to see this one again, if you don't mind."

"No problem." The projected image whirled for a moment and the short scene began anew.

When the nightwatchman put the bag on the box to tie his laces, Moira bent forward. She wanted to see the emblem on his shoulder, but the globe blurred it, *Dnu*. She wanted to know whether the nightwatchman was an employee of the National Museum or someone from one of the many security companies that had sprung up like mushrooms recently. She squinted but the picture didn't clear. Maybe it was a faulty recording or a badly smoothed patch on the wall the picture was projected on. The nightwatchman straightened up and walked toward the two rolling gates, but the blurry patch remained.

"Is it possible to zoom in on the man?" she asked into the darkness.

"Sure, no problem." Immediately, the focus of the surveillance eye changed.

Moira felt as if she were flying toward the man. She clung to the armrest involuntarily. When the picture refocused, she recognized the National Museum's logo on the man's shoulder. She had expected as much. But the blurry patch over his shoulder was still there, and it looked bigger than before. Moira frowned.

"What's that?"

Grub whistled approvingly. "It's an elveshield. Sabio was right. You really do have a keen eye."

Moira ignored the praise. "Do you think an elf crept in and forced the nightwatchman to open the gate?" She was surprised, since elves were hardly ever criminals.

"Or the nightwatchman smuggled him in. I believe Semra and Buds have a new prime suspect." Light flared up, and the globe switched itself off. "That's it for today. I'll get back to it tomorrow. I want to go home in half an hour. Thanks for your help."

"A pleasure." Moira turned to look for Grub, but the room seemed empty. Finally she discovered a toddler-sized nerl on a high seat beside the globe-reading device. When he noticed Moira's surprise, he beamed a toothy smile and his big, pointed ears perked up. "What did you expect?" Grub asked. "Admin can't afford a centaur."

"No, I…" Moira blushed. "I am awed by your size."

"You should see my cousin. He almost reaches Sabio's thigh." Grub hugged the box with the surveillance globe and climbed down from his seat. "I'm off-duty now. You too?"

Moira nodded.

"Why don't you hop along? The colleagues and I will go for a drink now."

"I have an important appointment at RealJob™ later today, and I really should get some sleep before it."

"A pity." On his short legs, Grub flitted to the door, which opened for him automatically. "Don't let the Realos talk you into a job. You're going to be a great gendarma, I know it."

Moira pressed her lips together. She'd rather not talk about this subject. Although she was pleased by the nerl's praise, most of her colleagues thought differently. She was sure her file at RealJob™ was filling several binders by now.

She watched Grub as he shot away on a self-made wagon after a farewell. Lost in thought, she set out too.

Back home she slipped her shoes off tiredly, hung her shoulder bag and her jacket up at the coat rack, and slumped into a comfortable seat near the window. Three lights danced on the rim of a blue glass bowl on her sideboard, but Moira didn't want to listen to the calls right now. She enjoyed doing nothing for a few minutes. Finally, she pulled herself up, ate, took a warm shower, and crawled into bed. Her wake-up nerl barely managed to extract the time she needed to wake before she fell asleep.

She woke well rested. Amused, she watched her wake-up nerl dance on the bedcover and sing "Sortie du sommeil, sortie du sommeil." After the traditional farewell, she set him back on her nightstand and walked into the kitchen. It felt weird to eat breakfast in the afternoon. She went into the bathroom where she had laid out the unobtrusive, dark blue costume with the white flouncy blouse and the straight-cut trousers the day before. Only the shoes took somewhat longer to choose. She finally settled on the dark blue ballerinas.

After applying only very little make-up, she looked at herself in the mirror in the hall. *I look as if I'm still going to school*, she thought, and applied a darker lipstick. A melodious triad vibrated through the tiny flat.

"It's Franka," the parlebol's voice said.

With a sigh Moira walked over to the blue speaking bowl on the sideboard. She requested her nerl to activate the bowl, leaned over it and accepted the call. In the lens of water at the bowl's bottom, the round, ebony face of her best friend appeared. Her short, white-blond curls had been tied into two pigtails on either side of her head. They resembled plush balls.

"Honey, I've been trying to reach you for days," Franka said after the greetings.

"I've been in the night shift since Monday. Midnight to nine a.m."

"That's no reason to ignore me for weeks." Franka's eyes sparkled. "I will pick you up at half past eight tomorrow evening whether you like it or not."

"I've got to be at work on time."

"I'll drive, Cinderella."

Moira suppressed further protest. If Franka decided to take her out tomorrow evening, she'd waltz her hundred kilos through Moira's two-room apartment until the neighbors complained, and would leave Moira no chance but to go. She sighed again.

"Moira!" Franka threatened her playfully with her index finger. "I know you've always wanted to join the Gendarmerie Magique, but ever since you got the preliminary job, you've been obsessed about it. You have to relax once in a while or you'll go crazy."

Reluctantly, Moira admitted her friend was right. She shrugged. "All right, I'll get up in time."

"Make yourself presentable." Franka frowned. "You look sixteen, not nineteen."

Moira grinned. "I will dress up if you promise not to pair me off with someone."

Franka's face lit up. "I didn't mean to anyway. We'll go to the unofficial reunion party of our residential home. Do you remember?"

Moira remembered very well. After all, it hadn't been that long since she shared one level of a house with a grimy kitchen, two living rooms, and two semi-dark halls with fifteen comrades. Both girls giggled, and all of a sudden

Moira was looking forward to the evening. Her gaze brushed the clock. Half past four. "I got to hurry," she said.

"Where are you going?"

"To RealJob™ again. My magical potential has to be assessed by a specialist."

Franka rolled her eyes. "Don't forget to take your handicapped ID."

Moira frowned. "I want to do without. After all, it shouldn't matter that I can't use magic the way everyone else does."

"Girl!" Franka's face grew bigger as if she bent closer over her bowl. "As a challenged person, you've got right you can claim. And if people won't understand, you've got to make them. I bet you'll be just as good a gendarma as a magically healthy woman."

"Maybe you're right." Grudgingly, Moira fetched the yellow, bank-card-sized handicapped ID card from the sideboard's top drawer and put it in her shoulder bag. "But I'll only use it if nothing else helps."

Franka rang off with a laugh.

Moira shifted her position for the umpteenth time on the red plastic chair in the waiting room of RealJob™. Since they had taken a blood sample and her temperature an hour ago, she had been waiting to be called. It took all her strength not to pace. Instead, she chewed her lower lip and tried to think of something nice.

"Moira Bellamie, room five," the nerl in the loudspeaker announced and his amplified voice echoed through the waiting room.

In her excitement, Moira missed the door with the five and had to turn back. Finally, she entered the small but classily furnished bureau. A panorama window offering a breathtaking view over the town's roofs and the nearby ocean dominated the office.

"Do you like the view?"

Only then did Moira notice a slim woman with blond curls and an expensive designer costume at the desk. She blushed and sat on the offered chair in a hurry. "Sorry."

The woman held out a slender, manicured hand with purple fingernail-tattoos. "I am Aparta de Frees, registered auralogist." She opened the folder on her table and stared at two colored diagrams. "You have been presented with several job options that would better suit your talents. Why do you insist on joining the Gendarmerie Magique?"

Moira wondered if she should tell the truth. *What do I have to lose? The whole story has probably long found its way into the file anyway.* She crossed her legs and said, "My parents were both gendarmes, my mother with internal affairs and my father with the drug division. When I turned eight, he was suspended and accused of corruption but my mother managed to clear his name."

"I understand. Have you ever considered a different line of work at all?"

Moira shook her head.

The auralogist pointed to a paragraph in the file. "It says you did an internship in archeology after you finished school."

Moira shrugged. "That was only an interim solution since I didn't know whether I would get a place at the Forensic Institute."

"It is surprising they accepted you with your limited magical talent." Madame de Frees looked at her. "Well, my task is to find out if you can focus the necessary minimum of magical energy needed for a job at the Gendarmerie Magique."

Moira bent forward. "I got the best marks in all exams."

Madame de Frees smiled. "I know that the results of your final exam were impressive. But since you didn't get the advanced proficiency certificate in magic, we need an auravaluation to judge your magical qualifications." She pointed to her file again. "As far as I can see, previous tests haven't been conclusive."

Moira nodded. One device had judged her magic aura as way above average, and all the others had attributed to her no magical abilities to speak of. Since Moira's magical abilities had been tested countless times during her childhood, she already knew all the emotions underlying the voices of the auralogists requested to examine her. Some were full of sympathy, others dismissive or even hostile. Sometimes, she felt as if it was a sin to be born without the ability to channel magic. Because of this, Aparta de Frees' friendly tone surprised her all the more.

"I will now examine your aura more closely than it's even been done before. Would you please take off everything made of metal?"

Secretly relieved that she was wearing a bra with hook and eyelet made of plastic, Moira took off her grandmother's bracelet and the earrings and slipped out of the trousers with the metal button.

The auralogist placed the jewelry in a colorful box and closed it. Then she led Moira to an archway that sparkled from the spell it held. If the colors didn't change all the time, it could have been wound with colorful ribbons.

Madame de Frees pushed Moira below the arch and adjusted her position. "Current reading devices analyze the test subject's aura as a whole, resulting in a bias in the data and often a misjudgment. A little while back, a friend of my husband developed this gadget. With it I can filter out individual parts of your aura." She smiled but gazed past Moira as if she weren't there. "He's a bright guy."

Moira's palms sweated when she noticed the longing in Madame de Frees' eyes, so she stared at the ground until the auralogist pulled a transparent curtain from the upper rim of the arch and turned away. The material of the curtain glittered like water reflecting light. It seemed magical. Fascinated, Moira reached for it.

"Please don't touch it. The filter is quite sensitive." Madame de Frees' voice sounded hard. She waited until Moira had lowered her hands before she vanished behind a black curtain. "I will calibrate the device with your health data, then I'll take a look at your aura."

So, that's the reason for the blood sample and temperature. Moira closed her eyes and tried to relax. She didn't believe the gadget would find anything different from what the other auravaluations had found, but at least Madame de Frees seemed willing to give her a chance

"Your Santé spectrum glows strongly. You're quite healthy." The curtain damped Madame de Frees's voice. "Let's have a look at your magical base-immunity."

"Base-immunity?" Moira raised her eyebrows.

"I wish schools would prepare their graduates better for life." Aparta de Frees sighed. "Without a healthy base-immunity, a human's magic field conflicts with the natural magic surrounding us. A human with conflicting magics will change his appearance periodically in a very radical way."

"Like werewolves?"

"Similar, but there's no cure, not even a blocker like Lupilin, which helps werewolves get through the difficult times at full moon. Children without a healthy base-immunity usually die within a few days."

"That would mean my base-immunity is fine, right?"

"Except for the rather unusual colors. But that doesn't have to mean anything. It could be due to the filter or a setting on my dials that is slightly off."

Moira breathed with relief.

"Can you summon a Lumière Magique?"

"More often than not." Moira's ears burned.

Creating a magic light was the first thing kids learned in school.

"Go ahead, please."

Moira held her hands in front of her belly as if holding a ball and concentrated. With closed eyes, she imagined light condensing into a sphere. When her mind held the correct picture, she opened her eyes and whispered the spell. A tiny spark crackled between her fingers.

"Oh, that was interesting. Again, please," Madame de Frees said.

Moira concentrated once more, and this time she managed to call up a small ball of light between her hands. She breathed a sigh of relief.

"The control-spectrum of your aura is fluctuating," Madame de Frees said.

I could have told you that. Moira dissolved the ball of light. After all, she didn't want to start a fire in the room like she did in third grade.

A little later, Madame de Frees stepped from behind the dark curtain and walked over to Moira. Carefully she tugged at the lower rim of the filter and it snapped up like a roller blind. She pointed at Moira's trousers. "You can get dressed again."

While Moira slipped back into her trousers and donned her jewelry, Madame de Frees fetched a folder with assessment sheets from behind the black curtain and put it on her desk. "Your aura sports a couple of very interesting color variations. One could say it fluoresces like a soap bubble."

Moira sat down. "Is that bad?"

"I don't think the aura's color is of importance but it's kind of beautiful. Aside from this variation, my analysis agrees mostly with those of my colleagues. You have little to no control of magical energy. Worse, you seem to influence magic aimed at you in a way that triggers unpredictable reactions." She looked up from her sheets. "Admittedly, there were a few very interesting readings of your first try creating the Lumière Magique. Still, your magical control is too low to work for the Gendarmerie Magique."

Moira's heart fell. Was this the end of her dream? Aparta de Frees' friendliness had given her hope. There had to be a way to join the Gendarmerie Magique even with less than stellar results in magical control. Her disappointment turned to anger. She pressed her lips together, clenched her fists, and didn't listen to the alternative jobs Madame de Frees suggested. Finally she remembered something. Breathing deeply, she forced herself to relax. "I want to join the Gendarmerie Magique, and there is nothing in the job description that says magical control is obligatory. I know I'm none too good with spells, but I'm excellent with everything else. Really excellent!" She got up, placed her hands on the desk, and bent forward. "I'm fed up. Ever since I've been a child, I've been considered disabled just because I can't do spells the way others do. As far as I know there is a rule in public service that disabled people have to be favored if the other qualifications are equal." She pulled out her yellow handicapped ID card from her bag and slammed it on the desk in front of Aparta de Frees. "Here you've got it black on yellow. I am handicapped. I do not like to be favored, but I will get hired."

Madame de Frees held out her hands defensively. "I will make a copy and add it to my report."

"That's not enough. For all my life, I never wanted anything else but to join the Gendarmerie Magique."

Madame de Frees smiled, and Moira thought there was pity in her voice. "I am only testing your abilities. The decision to keep you or not will be made by the staff manager of the Gendarmerie Magique."

"Well, write a recommendation, then."

"It's impossible. I am only allowed to analyze facts in my report."

Moira stared at Madame de Frees without words. Tiny pearls of sweat formed on her upper lip.

"I can offer you a practical examination to which I will invite the staff manager of the Gendarmerie Magique. That way, he gets a better impression of you, and you could tell him your arguments."

Moira nodded and stuffed the ID card back into her handbag. This was the best she could hope for at the moment.

Madame de Frees breathed with obvious relief. "I will contact you as soon as I have a date for you."

Chapter 3

Moira left the bureau without an answer. On the one hand, she was still angry, but on the other she felt ashamed about her outburst. When she stood in the open, she forced herself to breathe deeply a couple of times. It calmed her a little but she still felt too agitated to take the bus home for a couple of hours of sleep.

To let off steam, she set out to walk the long way to the station. She enjoyed ambling through the crowded streets and to gaze into the shop windows. The heat wave had finally subsided a little and a gentle wind blew from the ocean into town, cooling the air and her temper. She bought a jacket potato with salad and sat on a bench in the park in the heart of the city. By and by, the paths emptied; skaters, cyclists, and walkers went home. For a long time, Moira sat on her bench with her eyes closed and enjoyed the serene silence of the park. She heard people with dogs walk the paths, and lovers hiding away from curious onlookers in the bushes. Birds twittered in the trees and a squirrel chattered angrily somewhere nearby. Moira wished life could always be this peaceful.

When the sun set behind the houses with colorful ribbons, she got up to walk the final distance to her work. She hadn't quite reached the park's exit yet when the trees in front of her reflected the green sheen of all-round green lights. She evaded a patrol car that floated past her silently. It stopped beside several more patrol cars on a meadow where a sizable shrubbery had been fenced off. Behind it, Moira could just about see the sparkling of a stasis spell. A broad-shouldered young man got out of the patrol car and stepped through the fencing spell. He talked quietly to a gendarma.

Curious, Moira stepped closer but didn't touch the fencing spell. She didn't want to complicate the gendarmes' work by destroying their magical barrier. An elderly woman with a dachshund on her arm pressed her nose against the spell.

She asked the old lady, "What happened?"

"A pair of lovers found a body. I think he might have lived in the park somewhere. I never thought that possible. Living in the park, I mean. I tell you. Something like that never happened in my time." The woman answered as if someone had pressed the play button on a dicta-nerl. "When they still had work houses, no one had to live in the streets. But the way things have been lately, something like this had to happen sooner or later. It's said someone cut the guy's throat." The woman's eyes glittered. "Imagine that. What a mess. I just hope the park warden will wash away the blood when the Gendarmeric has left. I'm flabbergasted that something like this happened in my park. I will…"

Moira mumbled a short thank you and left in a hurry, leaving the woman to her babbling. She didn't like being near a person who didn't have a single word of pity for the victim. Slowly she walked along the barrier and watched the gendarmes search the area for evidence. Her heart longed to help. Near the park's exit, the barrier ended. Two strong gendarmes carried the coffin with the victim and loaded it into a black carpisto with an extra-long boot and floral drapes in the windows.

Moira had half passed the carpisto, when she recognized an approaching voice.

Semra said, "Come on, Dru. Your mother behaves as if you belong to her. Tell her she can't call you when you're on duty."

"She only wants to protect me." The man's voice was low and deep. A warm sensation rose from Moira's stomach and her heartbeat accelerated. *What a sexy voice.* Hoping she could hear it again, she stopped and pretended to tie her shoelaces. She wasn't disappointed.

"My mother loves me, and I'm happy about it even if it's slightly annoying from time to time," the voice said. The door of the carpisto groaned as it was opened.

Semra snorted. "I would use a different word for a mother who's interfering with my life all the time. You will have to get away from her apron strings, Dru, or you will be nothing but her son for the rest of your life." The door slammed shut again.

"I know." The man sighed. "It's just hard to affront someone who loves you this much."

"You'll have to find something worth fighting for." By the sound of Semra's voice, Moira realized they were on their way back to the crime scene. She retreated into the dark hastily. She didn't want to be caught listening in on a private talk. Biting her lower lip, she suppressed an urge to pant.

Only when she reached the street that led around the park, could she breathe freely. Her gaze fell on a clock hanging over a shop window. A nerl was just pushing the minute hand to half past nine. She'd have to hurry to reach the Gendarmerie in time. She tried to forget the talk she had overheard but the voice seemed to run on in her heart and didn't let go.

Buds glanced up from his desk. "I've got an interesting task for you," he said.

Moira interrupted him. "Did you know that a homeless was murdered in the park?"

"Sure. Semra is supervising the crime scene investigation but should be back soon. Until then, you can make yourself useful." He pointed to a thick folder balancing on the edge of his overflowing desk. It was a wonder that it hadn't toppled yet. "The nightwatchmen in the museum are tagged magically in each room they pass and the times are noted. This is a compilation of the last few months. Have a look if there have been unusual or irregular occurrences, who was on holiday and when and so on."

"May I ask why that's important?"

"Why?"

"I have to get my report folder up to date on the weekend and thought I'd write an essay about this case."

"Trying to make a good impression, are you?" Buds grinned. "Very well. The day shift didn't find Pete Huudien in his flat. It seems he bolted. Now we're examining his movements." He pointed at the thick folder.

Moira didn't dare to sigh although the task promised to be more tedious than exciting. Again, Buds left an unwanted problem to her. Without hesitation she took the folder and retreated into one of the interrogation rooms. She sat facing the one-way glass window. Even with no one in the other room, she felt watched. She opened the folder, took out a pile of paper covered with tight writing and scanned the first page. *At least the print-nerl has neat handwriting.* She stretched and delved into the lists.

Three hours later, she flattened the floor plan of the National Museum she had drawn from memory and upon which she had noted the routes and times of the two nightwatchmen. Discrepancies in the individual time-notations were less than half a minute. *Well, if that hasn't been a complete waste of time.* She picked up the last list and checked the bottommost entries.

Nightwatchman Huudien's tour went like it always did, ending with him clocking out in the basement shortly before the burglary. But the other nightwatchman had changed his tour. Moira sucked in air with a sharp hiss. She hadn't expected this. Every day, Joes van Gro went from the foyer through the gallery of the old masters to the Egyptian exhibit. On the day of the burglary, however, he'd made a short trip to the cellar even though the store rooms and the archive belonged to Huudien's tour. *Why did he do that?* Moira indicated the anomaly in red. *Did he do that before?* She took the lists of earlier weeks and scanned them. He had! Once a month, Joes van Gro changed his tour and went into the basement from the gallery of the old masters. *I wonder what he's doing there.*

Moira noted the dates of the anomalies on her diagram, put the lists neatly back into the folder, and carried everything back to Buds.

Of course, he made her wait, talking to different informants on his parlebol and dictating the information into his dicta-nerl. Just as he reached for the documents, Semra returned.

"Let me see." She took the floor plan from Buds' hands, unfolded it, and studied it. "Great idea to present the data like this." Moira was happy about the praise but tried not to let it show.

Buds stood beside Semra and looked at the map. "I think we should talk to Monsieur van Gro."

Semra looked at the clock over the door to their tiny room. It was a quarter to three in the morning. "He should be on duty."

The parlebol rang. Buds accepted the call and the pale face of a young plainclothes gendarme appeared on the water's surface. "The light in his flat went on half an hour ago, Sir. It seems he's at home."

"We're coming." Buds ended the call and reached for his jacket. "The second nightwatchman has reappeared. We'll have to get him first before he vanishes again."

Semra and Moira followed him. They drove along dark roads to a quiet but none too reputable neighborhood. Moira discovered a pair of vampires huddling in an entrance and smooching. She preferred to live in a neighborhood free of vampires – even if that increased the risk of burglary – because she didn't feel comfortable near vampires.

Buds halted the carpisto in front of a building in need of repair. He handed Moira a clipboard and a pen. "You'll write."

Moira frowned. *Why doesn't he use a dicta-nerl? He could print the conversation right after.* Annoyed, she followed her colleagues into the building. The stairs smelled of cooked white cabbage and piss. Moira wrinkled her nose and hurried up the stairs after Semra. A little later Buds knocked at a door on the fifth floor. When no one came, he knocked harder.

Reluctantly, the door opened a crack with the restraining chain still hooked in. A part of a face with a red-rimmed, gray eye and shoulder-length brown hair appeared.

"Who are you? What do you want?"

Buds and Semra showed their ID cards. "We have to talk to you, Monsieur Huudien."

"Pete isn't here. Piss off."

Semra pulled up her eyebrows. "If you are not Pete Huudien, what are you doing in his flat, Monsieur?"

"Please go away." The gray eye flickered to the flat at the other side of the landing that had opened a crack, too. "I can't tell you anything."

"Let us in, damn you! You are hindering our investigation." Buds was losing his patience.

Semra put her hand on his arm soothingly. "It would be better if you'd let us in, really. Otherwise you risk a warrant."

"Merde!"

The door closed, and the restraining chain rattled. A small, thin woman with stringy hair opened. Moira grinned when she realized her colleagues had mistaken the woman's gender. The woman with the red-rimmed eyes pointed to a door at the other end of the apartment.

"In there." She sniffed, and Moira knew the redness of her eyes was from crying. She wondered about the reason while she followed Buds and Semra along the narrow hall into the living room.

It was nearly as empty as the museum's storage room. In the middle of the room stood a bright yellow couch with a multi-colored woolen blanket in front of a big cardboard box. The woman sat down on the sofa, covered her knees with the blanket and suppressed a yawn. She glared at Semra and Buds.

"What do you want with my fiancé?"

Moira wrote shorthand. Secretly she wondered at the woman's suspicion. *She behaves as if she has to protect Pete Huudien from something.*

Irritated, the woman gazed at Buds who examined every corner of the room thoroughly.

"We need your name and address," he said.

The woman only answered reluctantly. "I'm Rosina Ardappelen, and I live one floor down."

Semra crouched until her face was level with the woman. "We are investigating a burglary in the National Museum where Pete works."

"He is their nightwatchman." Frau Ardappelen spoke with a low voice. "Did something happen to him?"

Buds stepped up beside Semra and looked down at the woman. "We suspect him of stealing a box with valuable artifacts."

"He'd never do something like that. Never!"

Semra put a hand on the woman's knee. "At the very least he's an important witness. Where is he?"

"If only I knew." Madame Ardappelen wiped her eyes.

Moira was sure she wasn't telling the whole truth, although she didn't know where the certainty came from. There were no clues. Rosina sat up straight and looked at Semra.

"I have not seen Pete since last night, and I did not talk to him. Usually he even lets me know when he's only a few minutes late. You have no idea how worried I am."

Moira would have loved to ask Madame Ardappelen why she didn't tell them all she knew but she also worried about Buds' reaction. *Would he allow me to speak although I'm only here on probation?* She glanced at Buds, who bent down to Madame Ardappelen with a frown.

"Don't tell fibs," he said. "If you were really worried you would have reported him missing yesterday. Now, where is he?"

Rosina Ardappelen burst into tears. For a moment, Moira thought her a superb actress but then she realized the tears were real. Semra growled at Buds, sat down beside Rosina and patted her back. After a while, Pete's fiancée calmed.

"Just tell us what you remember," Semra said.

Rosina blew her nose and wiped away her tears, but her voice still shook. "Pete and I had dinner together yesterday. Then he went to work. He was very excited because the director had enforced a pay raise for nightwatchmen, janitors and cleaners. Pete meant to go by his bank to see if the money had already arrived."

Moira was surprised that the woman talked so much all of a sudden. Semra must have found the right words.

"With a higher pay, we would finally be able to get married and move into a joint apartment," Rosina continued. "But then he didn't come home the whole day. For a while, I thought he had left me for someone else. Maybe he didn't really want to marry me after all. Maybe he took his money and…" Rosina's gaze wandered through the room and her lower lip trembled. "He wouldn't leave much."

"So, he's got financial problems." Buds signaled for Moira to keep writing, as if she hadn't so far. "At which bank does he have his account?"

"Why do you need to know? What's that to you?"

Semra put her hand on Rosina's knee again. "We will have to ask whether he had been there before or after work. Maybe someone talked to him and can tell us where he went."

Rosina lowered her head and stared at her hands for a while. Finally, she sighed. "His account is with the West-Friesian. But they don't have a branch here, only an auto-nerled teller. I don't think anyone saw him there."

"If he's visible in one of the surveillance globes, we might find a clue as to his whereabouts," Semra said.

The woman's face lit up for a second but clouded again. "I just hope nothing happened to him."

Although Rosina Ardappelen was obviously worried about Pete Huudien, Moira still had the feeling she was hiding something. She wondered what made her think like this but couldn't find an explanation. *Maybe it's the so-called gut instinct Mom kept talking about.*

Buds scratched his forehead and pointed to several lighter patches on the worn carpet.

"Why did Pete sell his furniture? Did he have debts?"

Rosina Ardappelen winced as if someone had hit her. Her tear-filled eyes glared at Buds. "That's none of your business."

Buds lifted his hands defensively. "I was just wondering where the stuff went that still stood here a few days ago. Are the other rooms this empty too?"

35

Rosina didn't answer.

"I believe Pete had a bigger problem than you care to admit."

"Up yours!"

Buds raised his eyebrows. "So that's the way you want it. Well, then we'll take you to the station for interrogation." He took handcuffs from his pocket and approached the sofa.

"Wait." Semra held him back and kept talking to Rosina. "We only want to help."

"I can do without. No matter what you say or do, you don't really care about Pete." Rosina jumped up and pointed to the door. "Go away and leave me alone."

"But Madame Ardappelen!" Semra got up and reached for the furious woman but she wouldn't calm down.

"Go, now. I haven't got the slightest clue where Pete is and that's the truth." Rosina's voice cracked.

Buds and Semra exchanged glances, and Buds nodded. Moira interpreted it as 'we can't do more at the moment.'

"We'll come back in a few days," Semra said. "Should Pete return before then, ask him to contact us, please."

Rosina Ardappelen didn't accompany them to the door. She stared after them with tightly pursed lips until they had left the flat. When Moira closed the door behind her, she still felt as if Rosina hadn't told them everything. An important part of the puzzle was missing. Deep in thought, she set out to follow Buds and Semra downstairs. A parlebol rang in Pete's flat. She stopped to listen but the sound didn't repeat. *I must have been mistaken.* She shook her head and walked faster to catch up with the gendarmes.

In the carpisto, Buds turned to her. "I need the report in triplicate on my desk before the end of the shift. Don't forget to emphasize that Madame Ardappelen reacted very suspiciously when I asked about the furniture."

Moira ground her teeth. She hated to write reports, but her mood improved when she remembered Franka's call. If she hurried and finished early, she could have a shower at work. In that case, she could sleep a little longer before her best friend would drag her out of bed. She smiled.

Chapter 4

In the early evening, Moira's wake-up nerl tugged at her nose until she climbed out of bed reluctantly. Bleary-eyed, she shuffled to the bathroom and got ready for the outing. Right on time at half past eight, she stood in front of a mirror, clean and nicely dressed, and put up her freshly washed, shoulder-length, brown hair. She was wondering whether she should put on make-up when the door-nerl slipped through his tube and announced Franka. She gave him permission to open and a little later her best friend stormed in.

Like always, her hug hurt a little. Also, her new hairdo pricked Moira's face. She had colored her short, white-blond curls and used gel to make them stand up in all directions. "Put on some make-up or you'll resemble a vampire beside me." The sofa groaned when she slumped into it. "You can't imagine the day I had. People bought shoes as if the world is ending tomorrow and they'll have to walk to heaven on foot." She put her feet – clad in bright red cowboy boots – on the table. "I'm so glad Tord will be back tomorrow."

"I didn't know he was gone." Moira walked back to the mirror to apply enough make-up to look her age.

"No wonder. You holed yourself up in this flat for months, cramming for some test or other that you might never get a chance to take, and you don't even call." Franka took a dark chocolate praline and pushed it between her dark red lips that stood out from her dark skin like bloody diamonds. "It's about time you'll see some people again. When was the last time you had a boyfriend?"

Moira shrugged. "It's been a while."

Franka clasped her hands behind her head and gazed over her shoulder back at Moira. "There is nothing better than love."

"In my opinion, love is thoroughly overrated." Moira cleared away the make-up into the drawer, where it could stay for the next few years if she got a say in it. When she looked up, Franka stood behind her with a stern face.

"Do you think I could be the kind of happy soul you see without Tord? Look at me." She indicated her massive body dressed in a loose, light green summer dress. "I look like a dressed-up hippo on land. But he loves me – not despite the way I look but because of it, and because he likes my personality." She pushed out her rounded belly, placed her hands on her wide hips and shook her impressive breasts. "Whatever I do, he loves it, and he still stands by me when I goof up. He's a male Moira, so to speak, with a healthy appetite for sex."

Moira thought of the lanky young man who adored Franka, and smiled. "You are lucky. That breed of men is rare."

Franka shook her head. "That's no fault of the men, it's you! You expect that they'll leave you like your dad did, so you're only attracting that kind of guy." She tapped Moira's shoulder with an index finger. "You'll have to start believing that someone loves you enough to stay with you forever and a day. Not every man is like your dad."

Moira pressed her lips together. She didn't want to talk about her father.

Franka sighed. "Fine. No hard feelings." She grabbed her handbag and walked to the door. "Will you still come?"

Moira glanced at the mirror a last time. Everything looked great, and she knew Franka's harsh words were only meant to help her even though they hurt. She nodded and followed.

Half an hour later they entered the festively decorated dining hall of their former residential home. Music thundered from big boxes, drowned out by talking party guests.

Moira wished for earplugs. She stopped and looked around for familiar faces. Behind the guests, the same old photo prints hung at the same old pastel green walls. *Dear me. I've sat here every day a short while back and it feels like an eternity.*

"Moira! You're here, what a treat." A former floor-mate stormed toward her with outstretched arms. He put both hands on her shoulders and kissed her cheeks left and right. "You look great."

Franka put her hands on her hips and grinned. "And what about me?"

He laughed. "You aren't easily overlooked, like always." He kissed Franka on both cheeks too. "Get yourself something to drink and mix with the folks. The Archies have come back a day early. Everybody is in a great mood." He pointed to a group of youngsters besieging the buffet, laughing and talking. "I'll be with you in a minute." He hurried toward the next arrivals.

Franka looked at the group of archeologists. "Can you see Tord?"

Moira shook her head. She only recognized Lif Borson, Tord's former fellow student and ex-floor mate of Moira's. His shoulders had become even wider from his work on the dig, emphasized by the tight shirt he wore. His strong back muscles ended in a firm bottom and strong legs.

He's as sexy as ever. Moira's mouth felt dry, blood roared in her ears, and her feet refused to walk even though Franka pulled at her arm. Lif always had this effect on her although he had never even acknowledged her. She enjoyed the view of his backside and ignored the rest.

At that moment he left the group and walked toward them. When he saw Moira, his eyebrows rose and his mouth fell open. He caught himself and laughed. "Moira? What a surprise. You look great. I'd never thought you could ever look so... so appetizing." He ignored Franka, put his hands on Moira's shoulders and kissed her cheeks.

A tingling went through Moira's body from her cheeks over her shoulders to her feet, making it impossible to answer.

Lif didn't seem to notice. He put an arm around her shoulders and whispered in her ear. "Tell me when you're free to go, and I'll put the world at your feet, my Venus."

His warm breath caressed Moira's cheek, and her knees threatened to buckle. It took all her strength to speak. "I don't work this weekend."

"I'd prefer tonight." He planted a kiss on her cheek. "But first, I'll have to show the world to my little man down there. After that, he and I will be all yours."

Moira watched him leave the dining hall. Only then she realized she was holding her breath.

Franka frowned. "Why are you gazing after that idiot like a lovestruck moron? He's only chatting you up because I'm too fat for him and all the other women in the room have already shared his bed."

"You're not fat, more like cuddly." Moira sighed. "And I know that Lif is a heartbreaker. But I wouldn't shove him off the edge of my bed, should he be there." She didn't consider Lif Borson boyfriend material for a second, but he'd be a nice alibi to evade Franka's matchmaking for a while.

Franka grabbed her arm and pulled her along. "Forget him. He's an idiot. Better help me to find Tord. I wonder why he didn't tell me they'd be back early."

Moira pulled herself together and pushed thoughts of Lif aside. "I bet he meant to surprise you. He knew you'd be here tonight, right?"

"Yeah, but I can't see him anywhere."

Moira looked around. Franka was right. Tord's head didn't tower over the other guests like it usually did. "Maybe he had to go to the toilet and will be back any minute."

Franka shook her head. She had paled. "Something happened to him."

"Balderdash." Moira took Franka's elbow and pulled her toward the group of archeologists. "He's probably got a good reason for not being here. Come, we'll ask."

When they reached the group, the talking stopped and everybody stared at Franka.

"Where is Tord?" Her voice sounded hoarse and her body shook from head to toe.

Embarrassed silence descended. Finally, a suntanned girl said, "Did no one tell you? He's in hospital."

With a silent sigh, Franka crumpled to the floor.

Moira grabbed her just in time to prevent her head slamming into the ground. She put one arm between her legs and shoved the unconscious body over her shoulders. Her knees wobbled under her friend's weight, but she managed to stand. The first-aid course she had taken would pay off after all. "I need a sofa and a healer." Breathing hard, she looked around for the young man who had greeted them. He came running, pale as a corpse.

A little later, Franka rested on a narrow bed in the medical room with her legs put up and her face turned to the side. Moira ordered the suntanned girl to get a wet cloth. *Learning so much is good, after all.* She put the cloth on Franka's forehead and watched her eyes flutter in waking.

"Tord? What happened to Tord?" Franka's usually energetic voice sounded feeble.

The suntanned girl answered. "The healer said he'll survive."

Two paramedics shouldered their way through the crowd of party guests that had assembled in front of the room. The stocky paramedic took Franka's wrist and nodded at Moira with respect. "Very good shock position."

The other one pulled out a hand-sized parlebol from his case where the water had been fixed with a special spell so it couldn't flow out. The connection to the hospital was already established. "Patient gained consciousness, but is weak." He looked at Moira. "Has something like this happened before?"

"No."

"Good. Make the people go away." He turned to the gadgets in his case and to the parlebol while his colleague examined Franka.

Moira pushed the onlookers out and closed the door to the medical room behind her. "Go back to the party, guys. There is nothing left to see here."

It took a while but finally most guests went back to the dining hall. Only the suntanned girl stayed with Moira. Silently they waited until the paramedics carried Franka out of the room on a stretcher.

The girl took Franka's hand and whispered, "I'm sorry."

"Don't," Franka said. "Bad weeds grow tall."

The girl wiped away a couple of tears and left, but Moira accompanied the paramedics with the stretcher to the ambulance. Luckily, Franka was already able to smile again. "They promised I could share a room with Tord."

Secretly, Moira sighed with relief. It was good to see her friend feel better. "I'll visit you tomorrow."

"Could you feed my cat?"

"Sure." Moira took Franka's handbag from the rear end just as the paramedics pushed the stretcher into the big carpisto. "See you tomorrow."

She waved after the ambulance until the flickering of the all-round neon red lights vanished beyond the next junction. All fun she had at going to the party was lost, so she entered Franka's car and drove home despite the fact that she hated driving.

She parked the car in the garage below her building, took the nerlift to her apartment, and settled into her favorite chair. When she reached for the 'Handbook for Gendarmerie Magique Staff,' she remembered that she had neither given Lif her new address nor the number of her parlebol.

When Moira left the nerl-U-railway station near the Gendarmerie, it was raining cats and dogs. She arrived at her office with wet shoes despite her protective clothing. Everyone else was dry – another reminder of how untalented she was magic-wise. She hadn't even managed a parapluie spell. Her mood got even worse when she heard Buds rant in the corridor outside. Hurriedly she poured coffee into the Nerlaroma 2000. She had already learned that it was usually easy to calm Buds with a good-sized cup.

"Why don't we have it? Can someone please explain how that happened?" He stormed into the office behind

Semra and slammed the door so hard the glass window in the door rattled. "We're having a first-rate suspect and no one thought to take his address? Which idiot interrogated him?"

Semra stopped and turned to him. Her nostrils flared and her eyes glittered. "Never call me an idiot again or you can find yourself another partner."

Buds paled. Subdued, he sank onto the chair behind his desk, picked up a file, and pretended to read.

"Anyway, that's easily remedied with a simple call." Semra activated the parlebol and asked for the National Museum.

Secretly, Moira was relieved that for once Buds wasn't angry with *her*. Without a word, she filled his mug with coffee. Then she waited for Semra to finish talking and filled her mug too. Semra nodded her thanks and turned to Buds. "I've got his address, but he isn't home just now. He's at work."

Buds got up. "What are we waiting for? We've got to arrest a potential burglar."

Semra sipped from her coffee. "First, he won't run away as long as he's at work. Second, due to the drug department's raid there isn't a free interrogation room in the building. And third, Commissaire Marten is still waiting for the report you promised."

Grumbling, Buds sat down again. "Will we leave when I finish writing?"

"Sure." Semra winked at Moira. "Would you be so kind to fetch the report from analytics? They called to let us know they're done."

Moira sped off and returned with the report soon after. She would have loved to read it, but it was in a sealed envelope that she handed to Semra.

"Do you know what it says already?"

"Why do you think Buds got so upset?"

"I wasn't upset. I'm always like that." Buds got up and reached for his jacket. "I'm done. We can go."

Semra and Moira followed him and took two more gendarmes along as reinforcements. Fifteen minutes later they reached the National Museum. A security-nerl was sitting in a box beside the main entrance. Buds whispered the password the director had given him for the duration of the investigation into the creature's ear, and the nerl opened the doors for him. Buds walked straight to the porter's office where the nightwatchmen stayed when they didn't tour the building.

Surprised, Joes van Gro looked up from an Art magazine. "Yes? What can I do for you?"

Buds pulled him up from his chair, turned him around, and snapped handcuffs on his arms, grinning. "Joes van Gro. You are hereby arrested. All you say or do can and will be used against you in court. Please do not talk until your lawyer arrives. Should you not be able to afford a lawyer, you can request a dicta-nerl as temporary substitute who will record the interrogation relevant to court."

"But I didn't do anything. Really."

Buds meant to answer but Semra held him back. "Wait for his lawyer or the dicta-nerl or he can claim a formal defect against his arrest."

"You are right." Buds pushed the nightwatchman toward the door.

Joes wriggled in his grip. "Please, you will have to inform Director du Mar. There is irreplaceable art at stake in here that may never be without supervision."

"Don't worry, we thought about that," Semra tried to calm him. She explained to the gendarmes who accompanied them that they were to stay and watch the museum until the director arrived. Joes breathed with visible relief and allowed himself to be led to the carpisto without further trouble.

Chapter 5

Moira wondered about what his role had been in the burglary, because he didn't behave like she imagined a guilty person would. Hesitantly, she sat in the backseat with him. He smiled at her.

"I'm sure this will be cleared up soon enough."

"I hope so," Moira said. She knew how uncomfortable the pallets in the rooms for the detainees were since it was part of her duty to put new sheets on them in cells where the residents had been transferred.

When they returned to the station, one of the interrogation rooms was free. Buds pushed the arrested man inside and asked for his lawyer again.

"I don't need one. This is all a big misunderstanding. I didn't do anything."

With a quiet sigh, Buds fetched the dicta-nerl from a drawer and opened the recording flap. "Wakie, wakie. Time to work."

Immediately, the head of a tiny nerl shot out. "Are you nuts? To wake me this late at night? Have you never heard of regular hours?"

Buds glared. "Shut up and do what you're paid for."

"Paid?" The nerl jumped from one foot to the other. "With that kind of pay I'll be just as tiny in a hundred years as I am now."

Buds lifted his hand as if he meant to hit the mite.

Semra held him back. "Let Moira try. She's got a knack with nerls."

Moira was surprised that Semra had noticed, and she agreed to Buds' request without hesitation. She crouched beside the table until her face was level with the nerl and fluttered her eyelashes. "Please, dear dicta-nerl, would you be so kind and record the interview? It is vital for our investigation."

The nerl's bulging eyebrows shot up. "Oh! Finally they got a polite person in this pigsty." He bent forward, and his eyes widened. For a moment, Moira feared they'd pop out of his head. Instead, he clapped his hands with obvious delight. "For you, I'll do anything, fair maiden." He vanished into his recording box without another word but with the traditional farewell gesture.

"Fair maiden!" Buds bent over with laughter. "What a compliment."

"Shut up and do what you're paid for." Semra used his own words.

The nerl popped out of his recording box again.

"Shall I record that too?" He vanished when he noticed Semra glaring at Buds.

"A compliment is a compliment, regardless from whom. And as you should know, nerls see our auras better than our physical selves. How can you judge Moira's aura? In that regard, we're all blind fish. So, shut up and get back to work."

Moira was surprised by the force of Semra's anger but before she could say something, Joes van Gro butted in. "I thought this was supposed to be an interrogation, but so far, it was better than any kind of entertainment show I know. You should get on stage with this."

Buds snubbed him. "Shut it. You will only talk when I ask you a question."

"Fine." Joes lifted his hands defensively. "Could you tell me first what you are accusing me of?"

Semra pushed Buds down on a chair and sat beside him. Then she made sure the dicta-nerl wrote along. After that, she addressed the detainee.

"The analysis of the magical functions at the crime scene proved that you turned off the alarm during the night in question. There were traces of your magical signature on the deactivation spell trigger."

"That's correct."

Buds' mouth fell open and he stared at Joes. Moira had to suppress a grin. Obviously, he had expected the night-watchman to lie.

"So you admit to switching off the alarm the night the burglary happened?" Semra asked.

Joes nodded. "I also changed my usual route that night, just in case you haven't noticed."

"We know. Why did you do that?" Semra seemed confused. "Did you know the burglars would come?"

"I would hardly have called the Gendarmerie Magique in that case, now, would I?"

"Why then?"

At that moment the door slammed open and a lanky, pale man in a dark blue suit stormed in, followed by Director du Mar.

"Don't say another word," the wearer of the dark blue suit ordered as he slammed a briefcase on the table. "I hereby declare the interrogation over. It shouldn't have started without me in the first place, and I will complain about this in court."

Hurriedly, Semra took the dicta-nerl and shoved it into Moira's hands. "This will stay in our safekeeping. Your client has refrained from using a lawyer explicitly before the interrogation, so everything the dicta-nerl recorded is legal and usable in court."

The lawyer opened his mouth to contradict, but Semra was faster. "We will send you a copy. Good evening."

The lawyer snorted but couldn't do anything.

"Come." He pulled Joes van Gro up from his chair.

The nightwatchman looked at his employer. "How did you know I had been arrested?"

"By chance, I was in the house when they came for you. It just took a while to wake my lawyer." Director du Mar patted Gro's shoulder. "Everything will be fine now."

The lawyer took Joes' elbow and led him from the interrogation room. Buds followed with measured steps, trying hard to look intimidating. Moira and Semra looked at each other and smirked.

"Sometimes, he's like a bull in a china shop," Semra said. "Still, I like him." She looked at Director du Mar. "Why were you in the museum tonight?"

"Professor Solveigh, the head of the dig where the boxes with artifacts came from, sent me a copy of the missing page from the inventory. I left them in the bureau and went over after dinner. It's not that far." He handed Semra a sheet of paper.

"Thank you. Now we know what has been stolen." She pointed to one of the chairs in the interrogation room. "Would you like some coffee or tea?"

"Tea, please." He sat.

Semra followed his example and studied the list. "It's all weapons."

"The aim of the dig was to find Hern's smithy. The most valuable items of the find were in the stolen box." Du Mar put his face in his hands. "Professor Solveigh is very indignant."

Unasked, Moira set the dicta-nerl on the tabletop and hurried into the bureau to fetch a mug of coffee and another one with tea. Joes van Gro was waiting near the exit for his lawyer, and she remembered that he hadn't answered an important question during questioning. Even if a statement he made to her didn't hold up in court, she thought it her duty to ask. Surprised by her own courage, she walked over and spoke to him. "I was the one who analyzed the protocols, and I noticed that you changed your route once a month, roughly at the same time. You went into the basement before you checked the Egyptian section. Why?"

"The archive is in the basement."

"I told you to stay silent!" The lawyer pushed Moira aside and dragged Joes along. The nightwatchman winked at her conspiratorially.

Shaking her head, she fetched the drinks and walked back to the interrogation room where Semra and the director were chatting amiably. She set down the mugs on the table and chose a seat. Semra sipped her coffee and watched Du Mar pensively. "Why are you so sure Joes van

Gro isn't connected to the burglary? All evidence points to him, and he even admitted that he switched off the alarm."

"To steal the heavy box from the storage hall, the thieves needed at least half an hour. But I spoke to Joes hardly five minutes after the alarm was turned off, and he was already heading out of the Egyptian exhibit. Of course, I didn't know the alarm was off, back then, or I would have taken him to task."

"Didn't you find it at all suspicious that he turned off the alarm?"

Director du Mar forced a smile. "I am sure he had a very good reason to do so."

Semra smiled as well. "What a pity he can't tell us because of his lawyer."

For a while, they drank in silence.

Moira wondered if she could ask something as well. It didn't seem to be an interrogation, more an informal get-together. Finally, she braced herself. "Are you often in the museum at night?"

"More than I'd like care for," the director answered with a sad smile.

Semra perked up. "Why?"

Director du Mar frowned and got up. "I don't think I owe you an explanation. It has nothing to do with your case. Good-bye."

Semra got up too and held out her hand. "Can Moira take you home?"

Director du Mar accepted the offer with thanks and walked out of the room.

Semra handed Moira the keys to her official carpisto, bent forward, and whispered in her ear. "Try to find out why he was in the museum the night of the burglary."

Grumbling, Moira followed the director. *How am I supposed to do that? I've got enough on my plate to maintain the flying spell.* She didn't like driving carpistos. It was too easy to accidentally touch the flying carpet that lay bare in the driver's foot space, which would crash the carpisto immediately.

Reluctantly, she slipped into the vehicle and her muscles tensed. A quick glance at the area below the steering wheel revealed a pleasantly small area of carpet around the speed pedal. She waited for Director du Mar to fasten the seat belt, activated the carpet, and drove off carefully. It was easier than she had feared.

"Won't your wife wonder if you are delivered by a police carpisto?" she asked with a sideways glance at Director du Mar's silver armband of marriage.

He gazed at her pensively. "You know what, take me to the museum," he said. Then he kept silent for the rest of the trip.

Moira didn't wonder. *Dad also never talked about his work with Mom although they were both in the Gendarmerie Magique. Maybe it was part of the reason why their marriage didn't work out despite his rehabilitation. The world would be a better place if people would communicate more often and truthfully.* She stopped at the last streetlight near the museum and glanced at her passenger. He sat there with his lips pressed tight, staring out the window without moving a muscle. But he looked so sad as if he'd just lost a family member. Moira's heart melted. *It's really not my business but if I don't say a thing, I'll be a coward like Dad.*

When Du Mar unfastened the seat belt, she mustered all her courage and put her hand on his arm. "I understand why you don't want to say anything to the gendarmes, but your wife is an entirely different matter. You should explain to her why you are spending so much time at the museum, or you might lose her. A partnership needs trust… on both sides. Believe me."

Director du Mar snorted and got out.

"Thank you for the list," she called after him. Unhappy with herself and with the world, she drove back to the station where several gendarmes bustled about hurriedly. Moira made room and watched them drive off full speed with flashing green lights. When she reached Buds, she asked, "What happened?"

"A man found another murdered homeless when he took his rubbish to the bins."

Moira's eyebrows rose. "Did he die the same way as the other?"

Buds shrugged and told her to sort reports for the rest of her shift. "Take the files with the settled cases to Excelsior van Steen in the archive."

Moira took a pile of folders from his desk and sat down to work.

Some time later, Semra tapped her shoulder. "Are you coming? Sabio wants us to talk to the nightwatchman's fiancée again. You can finish the files afterward."

Moira was surprised. "No one took care of the woman until now?"

"When could we? Staff is following clues in two cases of murder. There is hardly any time to bother with something as trivial as the fiancée of a thief." Semra smirked. "Sabio hopes she's heard of Pete Huudien by now. He thinks the nightwatchman might be an important witness."

"Let's go." Moira donned her jacket and followed Semra.

The gendarma said, "We'll have another look at Pete's flat. Maybe, she'll be there today, too."

Moira nodded. "We could try to find out why Madame Ardappelen reacted so strongly to Bud's questions about the furniture."

After they showed their IDs to the janitor, he opened the door to Pete Huudien's flat even without a search warrant. The rooms were completely empty. Even the sofa Semra and Madame Ardappelen had been seated on was gone. Only some traces in the dust indicated that there had been furniture a short while ago. Semra pursed her lips into a thin line. Wordlessly, she pushed the janitor down one set of stairs to the flat of Madame Ardappelen.

The door hardly opened before she stormed inside. Moira asked the janitor to wait in the corridor before she followed Semra into the living room. It was just as empty as Huudien's except for a few cardboard boxes.

Semra clenched her fists. "Merde! The birds have flown."

"I don't think so." Moira entered the tiny kitchenette. "It looks as if she's still using this." She pointed to a couple of sturdy cardboard boxes covered with a tablecloth. Beside it, a second cardboard box had been used as a chair judging by the deformations. In the sink, dirty dishes were piled up, and a minidrac lay curled up and snoring in the oven-nest.

"But what did she do with the furniture?" Semra wondered out loud.

Moira shrugged. Then she remembered something Madame Ardappelen had said about Pete Huudien's pay raise. "Maybe her fiancé has returned after all and they began to move. After all, she said they had planned this for quite a while."

"Let's have a look in the other rooms." Semra opened the door to the bathroom. On the rim of the basin stood a toothbrush and paste in a plastic mug, and a towel hung on a hook. Everything else was gone.

Moira went into the bedroom. It was stuffed with cardboard boxes and the curtains were drawn. Using the light switch proved fruitless, so she snaked past the boxes to let in light from the streetlamps in front of the house.

"Ouch!" Pain shot through her foot. Carefully, she felt the obstacle she had hit her toe on. It was a wide bed standing in the middle of the room. Shaking her head, she proceeded to the window and opened the curtains. With the light streaming in, she noticed someone lying in the bed. Hopefully it wasn't another corpse. Her knees shook but she went over to the person lying motionless under the cover. She reached out and touched the shoulder.

"Pete?" Rosina Ardappelen crawled out and sat up. When she recognized Moira and Semra, the hope left her face. "Go away." She fell back into the cushions and pulled the cover over her head again.

Semra pulled it off. "Get up. We've got some questions for you."

Instead of obeying, Rosina curled up and cried silently. Moira waved Semra out of the room. "I'll take care of her," she mouthed. Semra nodded but stopped in the door frame.

Moira sat on the edge of the bed and stroked Rosina's back until the crying subsided. "You can't imagine how glad I am that you're still alive," she said. "All those vanished furniture made me fear the worst."

"I sold the stuff." Rosina's voice sounded hoarse from crying.

"Pete's too? In his flat there's even less stuff left than in yours."

"It was the only way to get all that money."

Moira looked over to Semra and pulled up her eyebrows in an unspoken question. She wanted to know if the gendarma could hear Rosina. Semra answered with a nod and held up a portable dicta-nerl.

Moira spoke gently. "What did you need the money for?"

With a jerk, Rosina sat up. Her eyes fixed Moira with an accusing stare. "Why are you asking? You know what I value most in this world."

All of a sudden, Moira understood what it was that Rosina couldn't tell them during their first talk. "Someone kidnapped Pete Hundien and blackmailed you?"

Rosina nodded. Tears ran down her cheeks. "The caller said Pete would go free if I didn't contact the Gendarmerie and if I paid."

"Did you recognize the person?"

Rosina shook her head. "The picture was too dark and the voice sounded somehow twisted. But I'm sure it was a man."

Semra barged in. "When? Where? And to whom did you hand the money?"

Rosina ignored the question. "I found this when I came back from the delivery." She handed Moira a crumpled letter. It had been glued from words and letters cut from the same text, seeing as the font was the same all over. Due to the crossed-out words and word-parts, Moira suspected they came from an advertising brochure of one of the big newspapers or a regional ad-flyer. She smoothed out the paper and studied it.

STUPID COW~~BOY BOOTS~~. YOU WILL NEVER SEE HIM AGAIN. LIVE~~R~~ THE PAIN OF MY HEAR~~INGT~~. PETE WILL LOVE ME~~AL~~, OR HE'LL DECOMPOST~~ER~~ IN THE DARK-~~CHOCOLATE~~.

"It stuck in the public parlebol hut where I had to leave the money," Rosina whispered. "I blame myself, but what else could I have done? I fear I'll never, that he... That she..." She covered her face with her hands.

Moira put her arm around Rosina's shaking shoulders. "We will find Pete, I promise. Until then, you shouldn't be alone. Do you know someone who can take care of you for a while?"

Rosina shook her head.

"In that case, we'll inform Victims Unit. They will help. Financially too." She saw Semra reach for her mobile parlebol and vanish into the hall.

"What if the letter tells the truth? I can't live without Pete."

Moira wanted to tell her no man was worth suffering for like this, but she caught herself in time.

"I'm sure he's still alive."

"Really?"

"According to the letter, the kidnapper wants to force Pete to love her. So, she'll give him some time to change his mind." Moira hated herself for these words. The longing and hope in Rosina's face made her stomach ache. How much worse would she feel if Pete really didn't come back? Did Pete stage the kidnapping to press as much money out of his fiancée as possible before breaking up? Was he ruthless enough to ruin her? Moira suspected that some men were capable of this and more. She let go of Rosina's shoulder, got up, and followed Semra into the hall. The gendarma was just pocketing her parlebol.

"The Victims Unit will send someone any moment, and Sabio is sending an artist to draw Pete's picture. We'll start a manhunt with it. I think Huudien really is a key figure in the burglary."

Moira leaned against the wall.

"Do you believe that he was kidnapped?"

"All I know is that Madame Ardappelen believes this. If Pete doesn't appreciate her love, he's an idiot."

Ten minutes later, a small, fat man in a pinstripe suit stomped in and held up an ID card. "Victims Unit." He raised an eyebrow and glared at Moira and Semra. "You don't look like victims." His high-pitched voice sounded accusatory.

"Madame Ardappelen is in her bedroom." Moira pointed him to the correct door.

"Thank you. I won't need you any more then," he said.

With that voice, he could sing in a woman's choir. To keep from laughing, she bit her lower lip. An idea flashed through her mind and she turned to Semra. "If there really was a kidnapping, wouldn't we believe in two kidnappers due to Rosina's statements?"

Semra nodded. "If there was a kidnapping, the chance is high that there were two people involved. One would be the man who called, and the second is the woman who wrote the letter."

"But what if it was a single person? Look at that guy there." Moira pointed with her thumb over her shoulder to the bedroom door. "He's male but if you'd only hear his voice, especially if magically disturbed, you could take him for a woman."

Semra understood immediately. "You think we'll have to look for a woman with a man's voice?"

"I would think so." Moira made room for the artist who pushed past them wordlessly with his drawing tablet. "If the letter isn't a clever diversion by Pete Huudien himself, then there must be a woman who is very much in love with him and passionately envious of Rosina."

Semra took her arm and pulled her out of the flat. "In that case, there is the question of why someone would kidnap Pete Huudien exactly on the day of the burglary."

"And why Pete opened the gate to the burglars, and why an elf was flying beside him." Moira sighed. "Why easy if it can be complicated?"

Semra laughed.

When they showed Rosina's statement to Sabio, he rubbed his chin. His beard stubble crackled audibly.

"Another lead we'll have to follow. I might have to call in a couple of men from patrol duty. Someone has to question Huudien's friends and the museum stuff about

Pete's secret admirer." He folded his hands behind his head and stretched. "Good work. Keep it up." He waved for them to go. Satisfied, Moira returned to organize the last few files.

Chapter 6

When her shift was over, she slept a few hours. Then she hurried to the hospital to visit Franka and Tord. She found them in good spirits.

"Oh, Moira!" Franka, sitting upright in her bed, hugged Moira vehemently and nearly choked her. "Promise you'll be my bridesmaid."

"Why do you want to get married so soon? You've barely known each other for more than eight months." Confused, Moira looked at Tord, who was grinning from one ear to the other despite the head bandage and the heavily wrapped chest.

"The events on the dig woke me," he said. "Life is too short to waste it."

Franka grabbed her hand. "And I want you to become the godmother of our first child."

"Whoa, don't rush it. There will be enough time later." Moira felt the world crumble under her feet. She bent down to Franka and whispered in her ear. "I like Tord and know how much he loves you, but maybe you should enjoy married life before you begin thinking about kids."

Franka laughed. "Too late. And you sound like my mother. Come on, be happy for us."

Moira raised an eyebrow and looked from Tord to Franka and back. Tord's grin had grown even wider. Her knees turned to jelly. "That's not true, is it? You're kidding me."

Tord and Franka shook their heads simultaneously.

"You are really pregnant?"

A united nod.

"Dear me. And I thought you became unconscious due to shock." Moira slumped on a chair beside Franka's bed because her legs wouldn't carry her any more. This news was hard to digest.

"That too." Franka beamed at her just as happily as Tord. "Imagine. I didn't even notice although I'm already three months along."

"How wonderful for you." Moira noticed her congratulations sounded hollow, but she didn't know whether she should cry or laugh. When Franka became a wife and mother, she'd have even less time for Moira. The only consolation was that no one would nag her again when she got lost in her books. She tried not to let the lovers know her true feelings. *Why does everything have to be so complicated?* All the same, she liked Franka enough not to be envious of her happiness. *At least, Tord isn't like Dad.* With a crooked smile, she hugged Franka.

"Please excuse that I can't be really happy just now. I have to grasp the concept of being a godmother first."

Franka held her tight. "I am sooooo looking forward to the kid, and you will surely be the best auntie in the world."

Moira freed herself from the hug. "Why do you have to stay? A pregnancy is no illness."

"They want to make sure the child didn't suffer from the fall. I may go home tomorrow after the docs visit. Will you have the time to go shopping for a wedding gown?"

"Tomorrow? How soon do you plan to wed?"

Tord and Franka laughed.

"What a pity that you haven't found the right one yet. I would have loved a double wedding. Do you remember how we promised each other to get married together?" While Franka began to tell anecdotes of their childhood, Moira remembered what had happened after the oath.

It had been the Saturday after her eight birthday, and she had celebrated merrily the whole afternoon. Franka was the last to leave seeing as she lived next door.

"See you tomorrow," Moira called after her. Then she hurried into the sitting room, where her mother was clearing the party leftovers from the table. Moira pressed her nose against the windowpane, waiting for her dad. Her breath condensed on the glass, and she drew the logo of the Gendarmerie Magique with her finger. After hesitating for a moment, she drew the logo of her dad's new security firm beside it. "Why does he always have to work that long, Mom?"

"That's the way it is when you try to build up something new." Her mother stroked her hair. "You'd better get ready for bed. I'll call you when he comes home."

Reluctantly Moira went to the bathroom. While she brushed her teeth and changed, she listened intently for the slamming of a carpisto door in front of the house. Nothing. Moira sat in her bed to wait and tried unsuccessfully to concentrate on the book that had been one of her gifts. Finally she heard her father's footsteps on the stairs. She jumped out of bed and ran to him. Her tummy bursting with love, she threw her arms around his muscular belly and pressed her face into him. He smelled of cigars and leather.

"Did you have a nice day, princess?" He put his hands on her head. "Happy birthday, dear." He kissed her cheek and vanished into his study.

Moira crawled back into bed. In vain she waited for him to come in for a goodnight kiss. She heard him pace up and down in his room, and then the stairs creaked. On tiptoes she followed him and from the top of the stairs she watched him stop in front of the kitchen. He was carrying a small suitcase.

"Well then," he said. "I'll fetch the rest later. Don't you think I should tell her at least…?"

"No." Her mother's voice cut him short. Without a word, he turned and left the house.

As quietly as she could, Moira slipped into the sitting room. She was just in time to watch his carpisto roll down the driveway, turn at the next crossing, and vanish.

"Dad." The whispered word rang through the empty room like a shout.

She bit her lip to keep from crying. Why didn't he say goodbye when he had to go on a trip? Hesitantly she went into the kitchen. Her mother sat at the table with stony features and clung to a steaming mug of coffee.

"He's gone," she said with a flat voice.

"But he'll come back, won't he?"

Moira's mother sipped and stared at her feet. For a long time, she didn't speak. Moira's heart burned, and the longer her mother stayed silent, the more she feared her answer.

"Your father has a new family now. He doesn't need us anymore." Moira's mother looked up into her daughter's eyes. "Now, it's only the two of us."

Moira felt as if hit on the head and whirled around for hours. She was dizzy and ill. Wordlessly she turned, staggered back into her room, and slumped down on her bed. Her heart hurt as if someone was cutting it with a sharp knife, but she couldn't cry. At the same time, anger boiled in her veins.

She stayed awake for a long time. Only when morning dawned did she feel her tiredness. "No one's gonna hurt me like that again," she said to Cuddly Ted. "Never, ever."

His black button eyes seemed to ask, "How will you do that?"

"I will stop loving people. I won't even love you." She hurled Cuddly Ted into a big box of toys and curled up. When the church bells in the distance rang six times, she fell asleep without dreaming.

And I've been successful in keeping the promise all these years, Moira thought. Only Franka didn't let her withdraw from their friendship. She had forced herself into her life until Moira simply accepted her as a given. Now, Franka wanted to get married. Would she lose her best friend now? Her only friend? Why did the thought scare her so much?

She breathed deeply and swallowed her tears. *I knew this would happen sooner or later.* Faking a smile she hoped looked sincere, she inquired about the couple's plans. "Will you have enough room for another family member?"

The door opened and a nurse with a clinical thermometer entered, but Franka ignored her. "We had already planned to move into a bigger flat Tord's professor asked him to become his assistant, and offered a four-room flat in the archeology branch of the dorm, right under the roof where the professors live."

"I hope you've got plenty of friends for the move," the nurse said. "Your fiancé will not be able to lift anything heavy for the next four to six weeks." She took the clinical thermometer from Tord's mouth. "A male nurse will change the dressing in a minute." She hurried off.

"Why don't the two of you go downstairs into the café and have a piece of cake on me?" said Tord to Franka. "My wallet is under the bag of dirty laundry in the wardrobe."

Franka raised her eyebrows and looked at him. Then she blushed, crawled out of bed and donned a bathrobe. "Of course. We're already gone."

"Wait a moment." Moira walked over to Tord's bed. There was something she urgently needed to know. "Did you know that someone broke into the museum?"

Tord's eyes widened. "Was a lot stolen?"

"One box with weapons from Professor Solveigh's last dig. It looked as if the thieves knew exactly what they wanted. Didn't you work for the professor?"

"The box with the most valuable finds?" Tord paled and clenched his fists. "That's getting me down. Now we can't examine the artifacts, and science will lose insight in a long forgotten time." He ground his teeth.

Moira swallowed. Her next question was hard to ask. She bent forward and whispered so Franka couldn't hear her. "You weren't part of it, were you?"

Tord sat up with a jerk. "I'm no thief. What are you thinking? I didn't even know about the burglary before you told me!"

Moira sighed with relief. He knees wobbled and her voice was hoarse. "I'm glad about that."

Franka stepped up beside the bed and pressed Tord gently back into the cushions. "You are not allowed to get excited, honey. We need you safe and sound back home in a few days." She patted her belly. Then she grabbed Moira's arm and dragged her along out into the corridor. "Come."

Chapter 7

Moira wondered about the need to hurry. "I didn't mean to upset Tord. Really."

When a male nurse hurried past them into the room they had just left, Franka let go of her arm. "I know."

"Why the hurry, then? I don't fancy a piece of cake."

"Me neither. We'll wait in the lounge."

"Why can't we wait in the room until the nurse is done?"

"Tord has a rather deep gash on the inside of his thigh. He doesn't like people watch when they change the dressing." Determined, Franka stormed along the U-shaped corridor. Her voice echoed eerily through the long, empty hall. "Our unborn very nearly had to stay a single child. Worse, it nearly would have had to grow up without a dad."

"Wow. What happened?" Moira opened the door to the empty lounge.

"He didn't tell me all. Maybe he didn't want to scare me." Franka sighed with relief when she sat in a comfy chair near the window.

"He hasn't got a clue how resilient you are." Moira looked out the window to the parking lot – an exhilarating view for those who enjoyed paved areas, stunted bush monocultures, and carpistos in all colors and shapes. The only pleasantness was a muscular, young man in jeans and t-Shirt with short-cut, black hair and slightly longer bangs, who hurried over the parking lot.

Moira was surprised that she found him even more attractive than Lif. Most likely, the list of his love affairs was as long as Lif's. Dissatisfied with herself, she shook out her brown hair and turned to Franka. "At least, Tord isn't really sexy. With guys like the one down there, a divorce would be pre-programmed."

"Well, I think Tord's very sexy." Franka looked down at the man and shook her head. "He looks quite nice, too. Don't be so pessimistic all the time."

The young man vanished through the hospital's entrance and Moira grinned at Franka. "I think you should reconsider if you really want to get married to a man who nearly unmanned himself at work. If something like that happens more often, you won't have much fun during your married life."

Franka shrugged. "Tord insisted it was an accident. Lif played with a sword and mishandled it, so it happened."

"Weird. As foreman of Professor Solveigh's digs, Lif always put a lot of effort into security."

"He wasn't foreman this time. Since Tord found the important details about Hern's smithy during his research for his thesis, he got the job on this dig. You know how long Professor Solveigh has been looking for Hern's smithy." Franka gazed out of the window as if she was looking at the archeological camp. "Of course, Lif didn't like it. He did his best to boycott Tord. My sweet even had to lock up his records because Lif spilled ink on his drawings. The closer they got to the end of the digging period, the worse he got."

Moira didn't wonder about Lif playing tricks on Tord. He had never grown up; a big, sexy youngster pretending to be grown. It was part of his charm.

"Well," Franka pushed a strand of hair from her face. "At the end, he overdid it and played around with the most valuable find. Poor Tord found out the hard way that the sword's blade was still quite sharp after all these centuries it had been buried."

"I can't believe that Lif did it on purpose."

"It was an accident. Tord thinks so too." Franka looked at her watch. "They should have had enough time to change the dressings. If the wound keeps healing this well, he can come home on Monday or Tuesday. Isn't that great?" She heaved herself out of the chair. "Let's go back, or he'll put me on the list of missing people."

"Maybe he should adore you a little less." Moira followed her.

In the corridor, Franka patted her belly. "Oh, he will when I look like a pregnant hippo."

"I don't think so." Moira didn't say that to ease her friend's mind, but because she knew that her words were wrong. Tord had been deeply in love with Franka from the day they met and, as far as she could tell, he was one of the few faithful men in this world. Sometimes, she envied her friend, but never longer than one or two heartbeats.

"Does that mean I can eat what I want at the wedding buffet?" Franka grinned at her, and Moira's good mood returned.

"I'm slowly getting used to the idea of you being part of a family soon."

Franka threatened playfully with her index finger. "If you don't come around at least once a week, I'll not invite you to the wedding."

Laughing, Moira turned the corner and walked straight to the door to Tord's and Franka's hospital room. She was reaching out her hand for the doorknob when the massive wooden door opened and slammed into her face. The pain made her eyes water.

"Drat. Can't you be more careful?" She pressed both hands to her nose and tried to stop the blood dripping on her white t-shirt. Through her tears she didn't see more than a blurred figure. Still, she recognized the man immediately. It was the one she had seen in the parking lot.

"Sorry about that." He took Moira's arm to support her.

His voice seemed awfully familiar but the pain made it impossible for Moira to remember. Her nose throbbed so much she hardly heard his apology. As he held her and talked to her, Franka ran to fetch a nurse. Calmly, the nurse pressed a cold cloth to Moira's neck and handed her another one to wipe her face.

Franka pulled Moira into her room and sat her down on the chair beside her bed. "Will you be fine?"

"I hope the idiot didn't break my nose." Moira's voice sounded dull due to the swelling. At least the pain had subsided a little allowing her to blink away the tears.

"The idiot is really, really sorry." The young man stepped up beside her chair.

The voice. Moira's heart fluttered. She had heard this voice before, she was absolutely certain of that. The warm, dark timbre of it warmed her from the inside out.

"I didn't mean to." The young man put a hand on Moira's back. She tried hard to ignore the warmth spreading from his fingers through her body. From the corners of her eyes, she noticed Tord trying to get up. The nurse stopped him.

"You should look after Tord," Moira said to Franka.

He friend patted her shoulder and walked over to her fiancé. "I think all gendarmes should have a broken nose – if only for image reasons."

The young man put his hand on his mouth and shook his head. "A colleague. That's even worse." The longer it took to stop the bleeding, the more worried he looked.

Finally Moira remembered where she had heard his voice. It belonged to the gendarme Semra had talked to near the crime scene in the park after the second dead homeless had been found. Relieved her memory still worked, she endured the flood of excuses and simply enjoyed the voice.

When the blood stopped dripping, she looked up at the nurse. "Thank you for not using a cooling spell."

"Your friend said they wouldn't work on you. If you want me to, I'll call Doctor Tauber to have a look at your nose."

Moira agreed.

"You have apologized more than enough." Franka pushed the young man out of the room energetically, ignoring his protest. "My friend needs some peace now."

Luckily, the nose proved to be fine. The swelling would abate in one or two days.

"It's a good thing I've got a long weekend before my next shift," Moira said.

"That's good. By Monday you'll hardly see the swelling anymore." The healer packed up his instruments and left.

Moira stayed until the painkillers she got did their job. When it grew dark, she said farewell and left.

The young man stood in the corridor. He seemed to be waiting for her, holding a gigantic bunch of flowers in his hands.

"What a pity you can't smell them. May I invite you to a small snack by way of apology?" He pushed the slightly too long fringe from his face and looked at her with dark blue, puppy-dog eyes. "Please."

He seemed so hopeful that Moira couldn't refuse.

Immediately, his face brightened. "I don't mind reacting to 'Idiot,' but just in case you want to use something different sometime... my name is Druidus."

Moira's stomach filled with fluttering butterflies. She shrugged with forced indifference. "'Idiot' is good enough for me."

Druidus led her to the cafeteria and paid for the tea and sandwiches they chose. They sat at a table standing slightly to the side and ate and drank silently for a while. Druidus' gaze flickered from his food to her face and back.

Moira thought he wanted to say something but didn't quite dare.

Finally, she took pity on him and asked, "Which division of the Gendarmerie Magique are you working for?"

"Murder Two."

"With Commissaire Sabio Marten?"

"You know him?" Druidus seemed glad about it.

"I met him a few days ago after a burglary."

He nodded. "So you are the aspirant with the great power of observation that impressed Sabio so much? In that case, I'm threefold sorry for the accident."

Moira blushed. Commissaire Marten's praise felt good even if heard second-hand.

Druidus bit into his sandwich and spoke around it. "Sabio is the only one worth working for. I even put in overtime when he asks me to."

"Did he send you?"

He bent over the table. "Tord Mutelen's injuries come from the weirdest accident we ever heard about. Sabio thought it better to get every single detail about it."

"What was so weird about the accident? Or aren't you allowed to talk about it?" Moira pushed her teacup away and bent forward too, so Druidus could lower his voice.

"I can, with a colleague." Druidus stared at his hands as if pondering where to start. Then he looked at her, and his blue eyes made the butterflies in her stomach try summersaults. "He had a colleague who was jealous of his job of leading archeologist."

"Lif Borson."

Druidus looked at her with surprise. "My, you are well informed."

Moira waved him aside. "Tord's fiancée is my best friend, and I know Lif from the dorm. Franka, Tord and I have talked about him a lot."

"Then you know the basics." He didn't recount Lif's pranks but got to the meat of the story right away. "On the day the accident happened, the professor had asked Tord to pack the valuable artifacts safely."

Druidus' soft voice woke Moira's imagination. In her mind's eye she saw the archaeological camp, and the cafeteria around her faded. She saw Tord standing under the pavilion shading a narrow but very long table holding the artifacts.

Everything was labeled and numbered. Paper, wood shavings, puffed maize and other packing materials were piled under the table. Beside it, several wooden boxes waited. Tord was just checking his list with items for the last time. Everything was where it should be.

At this moment, Lif approached him. "I wanted to have another look at the beauty." He took the surprisingly clean short-sword from the table.

"Careful. It's got a sharp edge. Everyone who held it already cut themselves." He showed the Band-Aid on his palm.

Lif shrugged and studied a bubble of glass set into the sword's hilt holding a blue liquid that sloshed around. "It's surprising that so much is left after more than two thousand years. I wonder what it is."

"Please put the sword down." Tord reached out for it. "It's too valuable to play around with it."

Lif grinned and held the weapon closer to his body. "What do you think the professor might say if it went missing?" Lif poised the sword in his hand. "Fairly well balanced." He let the blade cut though air. "And you're right. It's still quite dangerous."

Tord jumped aside to avoid being hit. "Put it down."

Lif swung the sword around, and Tord stumbled backward, leading him away from the table with the other artifacts.

"I could probably hurt you a lot with this." Lif's eyes sparkled as he followed Tord. "If I wanted to, that is." He giggled.

Tord paled. In all the time he had known Lif, he had never giggled.

"Be reasonable, Lif. We can talk about everything."

"Not today. Today, we'll leave him in one piece." It didn't sound as if Lif was talking to Tord. He giggled once more and turned away.

Tord shivered all over. Something was exceedingly wrong with Lif. He followed him at a safe distance down the hill toward the dig.

By now Lif didn't giggle any more. He cried and pleaded with someone Tord couldn't see. All the while, he swung the sword through the air as if decapitating an army, without caring what he hit. Close to the dig, he stopped. The faces of several students, preparing the area for the winter, turned to him.

For a moment, he stared at them, then he shouted. "I'm not gonna do that, ass. I'd rather kill myself." He hurled the sword vertically up and watched it fly with a strangely empty smile. On the highest point of the arc, the weapon seemed to stand still before it turned and plummeted. The sharp blade sped toward Lif.

"Go!" Tord jumped forward and pushed Lif over the rim of the dig, using his momentum to push himself back to get as far out of the way as he could. The blade sliced open his abdomen and groin and the handle slammed into his head. Numbed, he sat on the ground and stared at the blood pulsing out of his body. It drained away so fast, as if the soil was a sponge. Tord had hardly enough time to wonder about it before the world turned dark.

"Luckily, one of the students had swapped over from medicine," Druidus said to wrap up the events. "She crimped his femoral artery with her fingers, saving his life. The ambulance healer gave him three bottles of blood on the flight to the hospital."

Moira leaned back and set aside the rest of her bread. Her appetite was gone. To think how close Franka had come to be a single mum. She shivered. "What a strange story."

"It is, isn't it? All witnesses agree on the fact that Lif is an idiot, and that some of his pranks bordered on the dangerous. But they also insist that he's never been violent." Druidus grabbed his cup and drank the now-cold tea. "If I believe that, the only explanation would be drugs, but all tests were negative."

"No wonder. You should listen to his 'my-body-is-my-temple' speeches for only five minutes."

"I did."

"What about the liquid in the sword's pommel? Maybe it's a little known drug. If some of it seeped out, Lif might accidentally have been exposed to it." Moira thought out loud. "As far as I know, the legends often tell about a secret elixir for the berserkers. Maybe the blue liquid is some of it? All of those legends are from the time of Hern's smithy."

"That's a great idea. I will talk to Professor Solveigh first thing on Monday. It's his specialty." Druidus drank the rest of his tea. "It's getting late. May I take you home? It would be the least I could do to make amends for my attack."

Moira though for a moment. After all, she hardly knew Druidus. Did she really want to let him know where she lived? He was as sexy as Lif, and she remembered his reaction to her new hairstyle and the make-up all too well. On the other hand, Druidus was neither as pushy nor seemed to be as full of himself as Lif. And without carpisto it would take her at least an hour to get home. *He's a gendarme, and he works for Commissaire Marten.* She came to a decision and got up. "Very well, you may take me home."

"Fantastic." Druidus offered her his arm and led her out of the hospital to a dented carpisto in the parking lot. Gallantly, he held the passenger's door open. Moira entered suppressing a grin, and soon they were on their way.

Chapter 8

The trip took less than three quarters of an hour. They chatted animatedly about colleagues, interesting cases, and imminent tests. Moira learned that Commissaire Marten had suggested Druidus for advancement, and she told him about her friends and their plans.

When Druidus stopped in front of her door, Moira felt as if she'd known him for years. She had never gotten on this well with a man since her father left, and it scared her to the marrow.

"I'd love to see you again, if I may." Druidus took her hand and looked at her. He gazed into her eyes until she blushed and turned away, pulling her fingers free.

Wiping her wet palms on her pants, she cleared her throat. "Thank you for the drive." The ringing of her mobile parlebol rose from the pocket of her jeans. She pulled out the hand-sized bowl with the magically secured water and waited for her mini-nerl to accept the call for her. She had learned to work around her disabilities – at least partly. Curious, she bent over the mobile parlebol.

It was Lif. "Hi, sweets. Where have you been? I tried all afternoon to phone you at home."

"I've been in the hospital to see Franka." Moira frowned in annoyance. "How did you get my number?"

"From the dean's office. All the information I need is stored there. And I've known for quite a while how to get them."

Moira shook her head. Minor inconveniences like data protection and personal privacy didn't seem to bother Lif. "Why are you calling?"

"I ordered a table for two at the Ritzisi. I'll pick you up at half past seven."

Moira opened her mouth to protest, but Lif didn't let her. "See you tomorrow, sweets." He ended the call, and his face vanished from her parlebol.

Druidus clenched the steering wheel with both hands and didn't look at her. "I'm sorry. I should have known a wonderful girl like you has a boyfriend already."

On first impulse, Moira wanted to tell him the truth about her meeting with Lif, but she reconsidered. *It's better he doesn't have false expectations.* She put away her parlebol, thanked Druidus once more, and got out. With a strange sort of sadness in her heart, she watched the carpisto drive away until it turned a corner and she wondered why all of a sudden she wasn't looking forward to the time with Lif. A nice date and sex without the commitment of a long-term relationship were the things she wanted, weren't they?

Moira pondered this the whole evening. Even in her dreams, the questions didn't let her rest.

She sat in a bar. The stale air smelled of cheap schnapps and smoke. When she looked around, she saw her father with Lif and Druidus on a nearby table. All the three of them were stark naked.

"On escapades." Her father lifted his glass.

"I care not whether fat or slim, I fuck all women on a whim," Lif rhymed badly and knocked back his schnapps.

Moira's father patted his shoulder jovially and waved the waitress closer. Before she arrived, Druidus put his head on his arms, began to snore, and dissolved.

Lif licked his lips and stared into the blonde's buxom neckline. "Wicked!" His eyes widened when the woman's dress vanished. He reached out with both hands, grabbing her breasts. His tongue shot out, long and sticky like a frog's. It slid over the waitress' skin, and she laughed.

The woman hung her breast into Lif's wide open mouth and rubbed his manhood with one hand.

Moira fought not to watch but her gaze couldn't leave Lif's ecstatically twisted face. His moaning and his growing greed filled her vision, pink and wet, until her father addressed her.

"Hi, honey," he said and laughed.

Moira shot up. Sweat soaked her nightdress and she panted. It took her a long time to calm down. When she felt better, she went into the bathroom, had a shower, slipped into a fresh nightie, and crawled back into bed. But try as she might, she couldn't sleep.

Finally she picked up her sleeping aid, the book "Techniques for Ascertaining the Truth" by Excelsior van Steen. According to the subtitle, it contained "Significant and Useful Inventions for the Daily Work of the Gendarmerie Magique," but it was written in a very boring style. Still, she needed three chapters before her eyes closed.

When she woke close to midday, she still remembered the dream. While she cooked, tidied her flat, and took a walk in the nearby park like she did every Sunday, she tried not to think about it. In fact, the warm, slightly windy late summer day was made for forgetting everything and for enjoying the beauty of the big parks in the city center, but the dream wouldn't leave her. Moira wondered why, in retrospection, Lif's sexual greed neither shocked nor surprised her. She had always known he couldn't resist a willing woman.

She pushed her hair from her face and breathed the park's fresh air consciously. The trees around her looked parched, and the benches, usually filled with countless people, were now mostly empty. Surely the families normally filling the park frequented the city's swimming pools. Moira sat on a bench beside a small lake and watched the ducks play. She didn't understand why her father and Druidus appeared in her dream. Were they the reason why she couldn't forget about it? Especially the Druidus part was weird. Why did he fall asleep and vanish the minute the temptress appeared? *Does that mean my subconscious refuses to judge him? Or isn't he interested in big-bosomed beauties, and my subconscious noticed?* She leaned back, enjoyed the warm sun on her skin, and pondered the questions until a shadow fell on her. She opened her eyes and realized the sun was on its way down behind the multi-story houses. It wouldn't be much longer until Lif would pick her up. *Oh, well,* she thought. *At least there won't be any unpleasant surprises with him. Since I already know he's only true to himself, I won't shed a tear when he's gone in the morning. A relationship isn't important anyway.*

She went home to get dressed. Deliberately, she chose a dress with a very low neckline and short skirt, then added the full-length velvet cape with the hood and her low-heeled dancing shoes. She used little make-up, except for the dark red lipstick, which she applied generously. Then she settled into her favorite comfy chair and grabbed the newspaper. An article with the headline UNSOLVED MURDERS caught her attention. Curious, she read.

THREE MURDERED HOMELESS PEOPLE ARE CURRENTLY WORRYING THE GENDARMERIE MAGIQUE. AS AFFIRMED BY A SPOKESMAN, SEVERAL FACTS ARE STILL UNCLEAR ALTHOUGH FIRST CLUES HAVE BEEN FOUND AND ARE CURRENTLY BEING EXPLORED. IT WOULD BE TOO EARLY TO TALK ABOUT A SERIAL KILLER, SAID THE SPOKESMAN. HE EMPHASIZED THAT ALL VICTIMS HAD BEEN FOUND SOON AFTER THE VICIOUS DEED. DUE TO THIS LUCKY CIRCUMSTANCE, THE EVIDENCE WAS STILL FRESH. THE LAST VICTIM WAS FOUND THIS MORNING IN A PRIVATE BOWER WITH THE SAME WOUNDS LIKE THE OTHER TWO BODIES. THE GENDARMERIE'S SPOKESMAN WAS CONFIDENT THAT THEY WOULD CATCH THE MURDERER SOON. STILL, IT IS FEARED IN THE GENERAL PUBLIC THAT MORE PEOPLE WILL DIE BEFORE THIS HAPPENS.

Moira lowered the paper. *Three already,* she thought. *How awful.* Since she was sure that Sabio was doing his utmost to catch the murderer, she put newspaper and thoughts aside. She wanted to enjoy her weekend this time, so she grabbed a book to free her mind. Reading to pass the time, she waited for Lif.

The clock on the wall struck nine, and it was already dark outside. Moira was furious. Did Lif forget about her? It wasn't impossible that he had fun with a different woman, but it was also possible that he was waiting for her to come by despite his words. She reached for her parlebol and woke the nerl living in a glass box attached to the bowl. "Can you establish a connection to the person who rang last although I wasn't in to catch the call?"

"Sure." The nerl started to work immediately without grumbling. When the surface of the water lit up, he held out his tiny arm in greeting, climbed back into his box, curled up on a pile of rubble, and fell asleep again.

The surface of the water showed a nerl's face. "This is an automatic voice recorder. What can I do for you?"

"I want to talk to Lif Borson," Moira said.

"He is in but currently unavailable, I'd say. Are you the lady he meant to see tonight?"

Moira nodded.

"Well, I'm sorry. Usually, he doesn't let his conquests wait, but in this particular case, it was probably unavoidable. I wish you a wonderful evening." The nerl ended the call before Moira could stop him.

She frowned. *Something's fishy here. I've been waiting for hours, and the idiot gets rid of me through a voicemail-nerl. You've got it coming, pal.* She woke her parlebol-nerl again and called a taxi. A few minutes later, the driver rang at her door. The trip to Lif's apartment complex didn't take much longer. When she entered the hallway, her heartbeat accelerated. What should she do if she found him in bed with another woman? It wasn't worth making a scene.

In front of the nerlift, a concierge in a green fantasy uniform stopped her. "Who have you come to see, mademoiselle?"

"Lif Borson is waiting for me."

"Your name?"

"Moira Bellamie."

"One moment, please." The concierge took a funnel from the wall and shook out a small nerl. He whispered in his ear, and the tiny creature zipped away through a narrow tube that led vertically through the ceiling.

One minute later, he returned. He gasped for air. "No one's there."

The concierge frowned. "Strange. I didn't see him leave." He turned to Moira. "I am very sorry, mademoiselle, but the monsieur seems to be out."

Moira wondered at this, seeing as the voicemail-nerl had told her that Lif was at home. "Do you know if he took his carpisto?"

"Monsieur Borson never walks."

Moira cocked her head and fluttered her eyelashes like she had seen in the cheap romance movies Franka insisted on dragging her to. "Oh, please? Couldn't you have a look?"

The concierge shrugged and ordered the nerl to run. He sped away, this time through a tube leading down. Moira guessed it was leading to the vehicle hall. A few heartbeats later, he returned and announced, "The carpisto is in its place. It doesn't look as if it has been moved today."

"That's even stranger." The concierge took off his cap and scratched his scalp with the sparse, white hair.

Maybe Lif hadn't let her down for another woman after all. Moira began to worry. She put her hand on the concierge's arm. "We should have a look. Maybe he fell and hurt himself."

He shook his head. "I can't just waltz into the flat of a lodger."

"I will take the responsibility on me. Come." She entered the nerlift and waited impatiently until the concierge joined her. Then she told the nerls to close the doors.

"Fourth," the concierge said reluctantly, and eight nerls sped through a tiny trapdoor in the ceiling to pull on their hauling cables. Soon, they reached the fourth floor. Lif's apartment was directly opposite the nerlift. Impatiently Moira waited for the concierge to finish knocking on the door and to open it. While he stopped in the frame, twisting his cap in his hands and calling for Lif, she walked along the narrow corridor into the living room. The first thing she saw sticking out from behind an L-shaped white leather couch was a wooden box with the logo of the National Museum. *Where does that come from? Is it an original one?* She stepped closer. An arm hung over the box's side, unmoving, palm up. The line of fine, red splashes on wall and ceiling probably wouldn't be paint.

Moira's eyes widened, and she pressed both hands on her mouth to keep herself from screaming. She remembered that no one was to enter a crime scene until all evidence had been secured, so she stumbled back to the entrance to hold back the concierge.

"What's wrong?" The concierge tried to squeeze past Moira.

She pushed him toward the exit with both arms. "Lif was murdered. Call the Gendarmerie. Hurry!" She waited until he obeyed and walked back to block the living room door. As she stared at the lifeless arm, she chewed on her lower lip. There! Did it twitch? What if Lif was still alive?

Reluctantly she entered the room again. She walked around the couch to the box that was placed in front of it like a table. Lif's head hung over the edge and his sightless eyes stared at the window's drawn curtains. He lay with his lower back on the box and a wide, deep cut cleaved into his chest. The breastbone was shattered, and Moira could see the cleft heart.

She retched. With shaking knees, she bent forward and supported herself with both hands on the couch's armrest to fight her nausea. From the ceiling came a shrill whistling. Instinctively she looked up. Countless razors sped toward her – a Charme Securité.

She screamed, her eyes closed and her arms raised to protect her head. Soft petals stroked her exposed skin. She looked around in surprise. Instead of razors, the ground around her was covered with flower petals. Her knees buckled and she sank to the ground beside the box. Her body shook with sobs. For the first time in her life, she was grateful for her freaky talent that twisted every spell aimed at her.

She sat for a long time, crying with relief. When the shock subsided, she felt something dig into her knee. She changed her position and stared at a small pin, lying beside the couch leg. It was decorated with the plain diagrammed letters 'LB,' held by two hands. She knew the logo, but her brain refused to think about it. Instead, her gaze wouldn't leave the puddle of blood the pin was lying in. Lif's blood.

Lif! Alive a short while ago, and now... *The poor guy. Womanizer or not – he didn't deserve this.* She put her hands on her arms and let her tears run free.

After a while, a hand touched her shoulder. "Come away, girl, this is not good for you." Commissaire Marten pulled her up and led her to the door.

Moira's legs were leaden. *Lif is dead, and I escaped only narrowly.* Every step cost her dearly, as if her body had forgotten how to move.

Sabio Marten led her to the nerlift, from which Druidus was just emerging.

"There you are." Sabio shoved Moira into his arms. "Take her home and make sure a healer looks at her. As soon as she has recovered – and only then – will you take her statement."

"My pleasure." When Druidus noticed how much difficulty Moira had with walking, he picked her up wordlessly and carried her into the nerlift like she was a small child. He smelled of tobacco and leather, just like her father. Although she fought the feeling, the smell woke a sense of warmth and protection. Memories that she had suppressed for so long flooded her mind. She felt Druidus' hands on her back and under her legs, but it didn't really register in her mind. To forget about her father Moira tried to think of somebody, anybody, who could have had a reason to kill Lif in such a brutal way. She couldn't think of anyone.

Druidus carried her into his carpisto and a little while later into the bedroom of her flat. There he very gently lowered her onto the bed, as if she was made of glass, and covered her. With gentle fingers, he stroked her cheek. "I will call a healer." His vice reached Moira's ear from far away, and his steps, as he went into the living room, faded away.

Moira curled up under the covers like a fetus and tried to push the horrible images of Lif's mangled body and the flying razors from her mind. Some part of her brain registered her shivering, but she couldn't stop. Lost in fear and pain, she forgot about time. At one point, Druidus pulled the cover from her face, took her hand, and stroked it. The spicy smell of burnt incense drifted into her nose, as someone started to chant. A deep voice repeated a simple melody that made Moira very tired, but it carried a tone that ripped her from her lethargy. All of a sudden, her mind was wide awake and alert as if she had swallowed a stimulant drug. She sat up and stared at the shaman who sat in the middle of her room, waving burning incense through the air and singing.

"The blood," she said. "There wasn't enough blood."

Druidus's eyes widened. "What do you mean by that?"

"Every grown human holds five to six liters of blood, men usually some more than women. The room should have been swimming in blood but there were only the splashes on the wall and ceiling and a few small puddles on the floor."

"That's not important. Lay down and try to forget about it. At least until tomorrow."

Moira obeyed. The shaman's persistent, monotonous sing-song tone helped her to push aside any thought of the murder. Her eyelids drooped, and she felt Morpheus creep closer on silent soles. "One more thing," she murmured. "I know who the pin belongs to." Druidus' answer didn't reach her any more.

Chapter 9

When she woke the next morning, Druidus sat on a chair beside her bed with his head sunk on his chest. He snored gently. Moira watched him for a while. His fringe hung into his eyes, but the rest of his black hair was cropped much shorter. His shirt and pants were crumpled, but made from expensive material. She suspected both to be custom-made because the clothes fit like a second skin. Asleep, he resembled a boy. His care made her feel good until she remembered that he was only waiting for her statement. With this thought, her memory returned, and pain cut through her heart again even though she didn't truly miss Lif. The way he died was too brutal not to be sorry for him. She curled up and cried for him once more. A small part of her mind wondered about this since she hadn't shed a single tear when her beloved grandfather had died. Back then, she had been too numb.

When she felt better, she climbed out of bed and tiptoed into the kitchen to make some coffee without waking Druidus. But she had forgotten about her wake-up nerl. Just as she meant to close the door silently, the nerl jumped from the nightstand onto her bed and danced around singing. "Sortie du sommeil, sortie du sommeil."

Druidus' head shot up. When he saw Moira standing in the door, a big smile lit up his face. "You're better."

"Bad weeds grow tall."

"I was worried." He stepped close to her and hugged her tightly. Then he held her at arm's length and gazed into her eyes. "Shall I call someone you can talk to? A friend? A priestess?"

Moira shook her head.

Druidus bent forward and kissed her cheek. Brotherly. "You really are someone special."

For a moment Moira was distracted from Lif's brutal death. She had to calm the butterflies somersaulting in her stomach. She chided herself. *How can I forget Lif this fast?*

Fighting to smooth her features, she asked, "Do you want coffee too?"

He nodded. "And a statement for Sabio, if possible."

She fetched two mugs from the cupboard.

A little later they sat at the kitchen table and Moira dictated her statement to the dicta-nerl Druidus had brought. Meanwhile, the coffee dripped through a filter the old-fashioned way, since Moira's coffee-machine-nerl was on holiday for a few days.

When she finished her statement, Druidus said, "Last night you indicated that you know the pin's owner. Could you explain?"

"Oh, the pin." Moira tried to win time by getting up and pouring coffee into the two mugs. Then she pulled herself together. "More than eleven years ago, my father founded a security firm he called P&OS: Personal and Operational Security. If you look at the logo closely, you can see that the hands holding the letters are made of this abbreviation."

"We found the enterprise but didn't know the owner is your father."

Moira wanted to tell Druidus that she hadn't seen her father in years, but she stopped herself at the last moment. It was none of his business what kind of relationship she had with her parents.

"Last night, you made it sound as if you knew the exact person the pin belongs to."

"My father designed it so the letters between the hands are its owner's initials." Moira sighed. "LB stands for Lavant Bellamie. The pin belongs to my father." Even if she was at odds with him, she hated to tell on him.

Druidus stared at her with surprise.

Moira was sure she knew what he was thinking and shook her head. "He didn't know I was meeting Lif."

Druidus waved her comment aside. "Your father is Lavant Bellamie? *That* Lavant Bellamie?"

"Is it important?"

He set his mug aside. "We have to tell Sabio. Do you feel well enough to come along?"

As an answer, Moira went into the hall to fetch her summer jacket.

Druidus watched her with a dreamy expression on his face. "Has someone ever told you that you're very beautiful?"

Moira's mouth went dry and her heart skipped a beat. With her hand on the doorknob and her back turned to him, she said, "We've got work to do. Are you coming?"

Three quarters of an hour later, they entered the Gendarmerie. Halfway to Sabio's office Semra approached them. She looked tired and annoyed.

"There you are. Today of all days, you're late." She took Moira's elbow and pulled her toward the exit.

Druidus stopped her. "Moira reports ill today."

"She can't. I need her urgently." Semra put her hands on her hips and frowned. "I've got to question fifteen women from the cleaning service and two secretaries to find out who has been pining for Pete Huudien."

Druidus pushed Moira behind himself and bent down to Semra. "Her boyfriend was murdered, and she found him. I will take her home the minute we finish talking to Sabio." He glared at Semra.

"Work is the best medicine."

Semra and Druidus faced each other like two dogs fighting for the same bone.

"Stop it! It is my decision to say if I'm going to work today or not." Moira hated being treated like a minor. "I will go to Sabio now, to repeat my statement. And then, I'll start working as usual." She left the two squabblers and walked away.

Druidus caught up with her near the door to Sabio's office. He put a hand on her arm. "The healer said you're to go easy on yourself for a few days."

Her hand on the doorknob, Moira looked at him. "First, I'm feeling much better. Second, I'd get cabin fever without work. And third, I'm not like my father. *I* do believe that the Gendarmerie catches criminals, and I want to be part of it."

Without waiting for Druidus' answer, she opened the door and entered Sabio's bureau. It was small and overflowing with bookshelves and filing cabinets. On the few free places on the walls, pictures showing the sea gave the room a personal note, and two chairs with a floral pattern stood in front of the fastidiously tidy desk.

The Commissaire seemed glad to see her and offered her a chair. "Hadn't you better stayed at home? After this kind of loss?"

Moira sighed. "Everybody assumes that Lif and I were lovers, but we weren't. We had a date because both of us wanted some fun. He is… He was sexy." It was hard to use past tense in connection with Lif. She pushed her hair back and stared at the desktop. "I got to know him when I lived in the dorm. He did his last year for his archaeology degree when I participated in the preliminary course for the Gendarmerie. He was a womanizer with a new girlfriend every week." She looked up at Sabio. "When he asked me out, I knew he wouldn't be interested in long-term commitment. Lif only loved himself."

"Thank you for your trust." Sabio smiled before looking at Druidus, who stood beside Moira. "Did you record her statement?"

Druidus nodded and summarized Moira's report in a few words. He placed the dicta-nerl on the desk. "You can listen to the details later. The most important fact is that the pin we found at the crime scene belongs to Moira's father."

"Well done." Sabio rubbed his hands. "In that case, you two should talk to him."

Moira raised her eyebrows and stared at the Commissaire. "Me too? But I'm aspirant of the burglary department."

"Someone who doesn't lose his power of observation even when in shock is a most valuable addition for my department," Sabio Marten said. "Druidus will look after you."

"Sabio is known for getting people into his team that others don't believe in." Druidus winked at Sabio.

The Commissaire smiled knowingly. "I've never been wrong so far."

Moira feared that she would be his first misjudgment, but her heart still thumped in her chest with joy. *I can join Murder Two.*

Sabio seemed amused by her silence. He leaned back and stretched. "It will take a few hours to sort out the paperwork. You can come here after lunch."

Druidus patted her shoulder. "Welcome to the team."

Sabio reached for the parlebol, and a little later Moira's temporary relocation to the department of murder had been granted. If the memories of Lif's brutal murder had been less haunting, she would have been singing on her way to Semra.

"Done already?" Semra looked up from her file. "Let's go then. Buds insists that we visit the museum again. He's sure the director is hiding something from us."

Moira lifted an eyebrow. "I thought we were meant to question service personnel and secretaries."

"Already done. They all knew immediately who we meant. Are you coming?" She grabbed her jacket and went to the carpisto with Moira.

"Why doesn't Buds come along?"

"He's picking up the unhappy paramour. Also, an informant said he'd seen the second nightwatchman, and Buds wants to try to catch up with him. He's convinced that Pete Huudien is the key to the burglary. "

"Does he think he's one of the burglars?"

"A good gendarme never draws conclusions without all the facts and statements. It would be wrong to take someone off the list just because your gut tells you he or she wouldn't be able to commit a crime. With this credo, Buds and I made it to Maréchal after all."

She found Director du Mar in his bureau, where he was staring at his planar of his magicuter. He deactivated the planar and greeted them cordially.

"What can I do for you?" he asked when they had settled on the comfy chairs in a corner of his room.

Semra slipped to the edge of her seat and poised a pen over the notepad on her knees. "I ensure you that this meeting will remain confidential, but we have to understand why you were in the building the night of the burglary."

"Is that necessary?"

Semra frowned. "We could go to the station and have an official interrogation. But in that case, I can't guarantee privacy."

The director's shoulders sagged, and he sighed. After a while, he sat up straight once more. "I've been working late for a couple of months. Financing Professor Solveigh's latest dig has been quite a burden for the museum's budget, and I have had to find new sponsors." Director du Mar stared at the wall, rubbing his palms on his knees. "Two weeks ago, one of our patronesses got so drunk I had to carry her to a taxi. Since my clothes smelled strongly of perfume and my collar was smeared with lipstick, my wife assumed I had an affair and threw me out. I've been sleeping in my office ever since." He pointed at two leather suitcases standing beside the sofa. "My wife will attest to that if you ask her."

Although he sounded very convincing, Moira couldn't shake the feeling that he was still hiding part of the truth. But she was sure he wouldn't tell anyone, not even under pressure.

Luckily, Semra seemed satisfied. She wrote a single word on her notepad. "You do have to understand that we need to know all facts to solve the case."

The director nodded. "Is that all? I've got a lot to do."

Semra put away her notepad and pen and got up. "Sorry. We didn't mean to keep you long. May we look around some more?"

"Of course. As I already told your partner, you've got free access to all parts of the museum." Visibly relieved, the director handed her the keys to the service rooms and connecting doors. "Please be considerate with our visitors. At the moment, negative publicity is something we don't need at all."

"We are aware of that." Semra turned to Moira. "You start with the basement. I am sure we didn't miss anything there, but like my gran used to say, twice is the charm."

Moira nodded and turned to the director. "May I have a look at the archive too?"

"Sure. But it's a little confusing for someone who doesn't know the way around. And our registrar is... Well, let's say it's not always easy to motivate him."

Semra handed Moira the key to the archive. "I'll walk through the upper levels of the building to take a few more samples for the lab."

"I will be in here all day long in case you need me again." The director returned to his work.

Moira was glad about the permission to rummage in the archive. She had always enjoyed going to a museum, and each time she had wondered about the things that couldn't be exhibited in the displays. On her way to the basement, she imagined what kind of hidden treasure she'd find in the archive.

With a fluttering heart, she approached the archive's fire-proof security door, unlocked it, and entered. Inside, the light burned; the registrar had to be somewhere. She looked around. The whitewashed ceiling was rather low but arched like the vaults of a cloister. A Lumière Magique hovered in each dome and illuminated the room. It was hard to say how big the archive was since it was stuffed with a riot of shelves, boxes, cartons, bags, covered paintings, and baskets.

Hesitantly she walked the only unobstructed path right into a cobweb. She screamed, shuddered, and wiped the sticky strands from her face.

A hairy hand picked something from her shoulder. "Careful. You'll hurt her." The voice was deep and so low that Moira wasn't alarmed. She turned. At first, she thought she was facing a human, but then she noticed the green skin, the pointed ears, and the scent of forest soil. The nerl was as big as she was, the biggest one she'd ever seen.

He watched a little spider on his gnarly palm. "Do not come back, right? I cannot allow you to weave webs in my archive." He walked to the door, opened it, and put the spider down outside. Then he turned to Moira. "What can I do for you…? Oh, you're not part of the museum's staff. I'm sorry. In that case, I can't…" His eyes widened, and the hand he held out to her trembled. "Wrong. I'll do anything for you." His fingers stopped an inch from her shoulder before he pulled them back. He beamed at her. "So, what are you looking for?"

Moira was thrown off guard. She had never experienced such a weird reaction with any nerl before. Clearing her throat, she tried to concentrate on her task. "I am from the Gendarmerie Magique, and I'm supposed to look around."

The smile vanished from the nerl's face. "What a pity. I would have loved to help you."

He seemed really disappointed, so Moira hurried to reassure him. "If I don't keep you from more important work, I would be honored to have you come with me. The archive seems rather big."

"Oh yes. It's easy to get lost here," the nerl said. "Except for me. I've been earning my energy for far too long down here." He followed her into a side corridor that led past countless display cases. Paintings, carefully wrapped in covers, leaned against them. "What are you looking for, anyway?"

Thoughtfully, Moira looked at the carefully labeled skulls, stone weapons, pottery and jewelry in the showcases. "I'm not sure, but I think I'll know when I see it. One thing's for sure: If there is something here, it couldn't have been here long. After all, the burglary was less than a week ago."

Chapter 10

The nerl clapped his hands. "A week ago, Joes van Gro brought something. Shall I show you?"

Moira remembered Joes' answer when she had asked him why he had changed his usual route. *"The archive is in the basement."* His voice still rang in her ear. She nodded and followed the nerl.

He led her through passages barely wide enough to squeeze through until they stood in front of a door with a low table beside it.

Moira cocked her head. "I didn't know there was a back door to the archive."

The nerl laughed. It sounded like the cracking of wood. "That's no back door. It's the entrance to my living quarters."

"Oh!" Moira would have loved to peek inside but she didn't want to appear impolite. The nerl pulled her to the low table. On it, piled one above the other and wrapped in linen or blankets, lay five paintings. Not one was bigger than Moira's hand.

"These are the paintings Joes van Gro brought me in the last few months. He told me to take special care of them, so I put them right here. This was the last one." He picked up the one on top, handed it to her, and pulled away the linen wrapped around it.

Moira sucked the air through her teeth. A brown-haired girl stuck out her tongue. Without winking first.

The Mona Beth! Even though Moira wasn't an expert, she was sure that this was the original Mona Beth. Did Joes store the painting here to smuggle it out later unnoticed?

Maybe he'd even be asked to do so by Director du Mar. Hadn't he told them about the museum's financial difficulties? She forced herself to stay calm. *Facts first, conclusions later.* She turned to the nerl. "I will take the paintings along. They are important evidence."

The nerl folded his arms in front of his chest. "That's impossible. You are not a staff member of the museum."

"I will bring the paintings back the minute we don't need them anymore."

"Very well. But I need a receipt, and you've got to pay for the lending."

"No problem." Moira was sure that the Gendarmerie's accounting department would refund the costs in this case.

After the nerl had wrapped the valuable painting again, he handed her a clipboard with a form and told her which line to sign. When she was done, he reached out in the traditional greeting, passing his hand through the air above her arm without touching. Moira blinked and fought off a wave of vertigo. She had to steady herself on the small table to keep from falling.

"What was that?" She looked at the nerl.

His hands covered his mouth, and he stared at her wide-eyed. "Sorry! I took way too much… I'm so sorry. I didn't know… It flowed far too fast." His skin was more gray than green all of a sudden, and he seemed bigger than before.

Moira breathed deeply a couple of times and felt better. When the dizziness subsided, she stood straight and looked at the nerl. He had grown, hadn't he? "What happened just now?"

"Are you really well again?" The green color returned to the nerl's face, but he still seemed to be very worried.

Moira cocked her head and tried to look stern. "I want an answer."

"This has never happened to you before?"

"No, never."

"Maybe it's due to my size." The nerl wrung his hands as if someone had caught him cheating. "I only meant to take my payment, really. I didn't know that so much would flow into me. It was an accident. Luckily, your aura healed all by itself."

Moira shook her head. She didn't understand a word. Maybe the auralogist would be able to explain what had just happened to her. She decided to ask her at the next meeting. Felling much better, she took the paintings. "How do I get back to the exit?"

"Come this way." The nerl went first but turned every so often. All the time, he kept murmuring, "It's surprising, absolutely surprising."

On the way to the exit, Moira noticed several piled crates. Each had a number burned beside the logo on its side. With a shiver, she remembered that Lif's had held a number too. "I don't understand why someone can use a box like that as a living room table."

"No one can," the nerl said. "Every single one is numbered and the contents are catalogued. Also, the logo is copyright protected and can only be used for property of the museum."

Moira's eyes widened, the strange occurrence from before having been all but forgotten. "Does that mean no one outside this museum can own one quite like this?"

The nerl shrugged. "You can get fakes everywhere. But there is just one from our stock that's currently missing. And the Gendarmerie is already working on it as far as I know."

Moira felt first hot, then cold. If the logo on the crate in Lif's living room was the real one, his murder was directly connected to the burglary Semra and Buds were investigating.

"I have to tell Sabio... I mean, Commissaire Marten." She walked faster.

The nerl accompanied her to the door and watched her for a long time. When she turned at the top of the stairs, he was still standing there. Shaking her head, she went to find Semra. She found the gendarma in the foyer where she was kneeling in the dirt on the ground behind the coffee-nerl-o-mat.

"What are you doing there?" Moira asked.

Semra wiped her sweaty fringe from her forehead and replaced the safety over the lens of the foto-nerl. "Someone deposited a narrow object here. Considering my measurements, it could have been the missing painting."

"Maybe it was a different painting, because more than one has been swapped. Look what I found." Moira put her left foot against her right leg, the way she had learned at ballet as a kid. She balanced the pile of paintings on her knee, holding them with her left forearm. In her left hand, she held the Mona Beth. Wordlessly she lifted the linen that covered the valuable painting. The slightly twisted posture was exhausting but the reward was an unforgettable expression of shock and surprise on Semra's face.

The gendarma got up and kicked the coffee-nerl-o-mat back to its usual place. "I believe we will have to talk to Du Mar a little more earnestly." She took the Mona Beth from Moira's hands and stormed along the corridor toward the director's office.

Moira followed her with the four other paintings. They entered without knocking.

Director du Mar looked up and raised his eyebrows. When he saw the Mona Beth Semra showed him, his jaw dropped and his eyes widened. Shaking, he half stood and reached for the painting without touching it.

"It's the real one. It's truly the real one. I knew it'd reappear." He sank back in his chair, closed his eyes, and breathed deeply. Then he smiled at Semra. "Where did you find her?"

"I think you know this better than we do." Semra pulled a couple of handcuffs from a pouch on her belt, pointed them at the director and said the activating spell. "Director du Mar. You are hereby under arrest in the name of the Gendarmerie Magique. You are accused of attempted robbery of public property." The cuffs closed around his forearms with a click.

He gasped for air like a fish on land, and it took him a while to regain his composure. His voice sounded feeble and tired. "You are making a mistake. I never stole any paintings. On the contrary, I tried to get them back."

Semra ignored his words. She rattled off the obligatory instructions and left it to Moira to lead the captive to the carpisto, but she stayed right behind them.

Moira sat in the back with the director, although it wasn't usually approved. Still, she didn't think him dangerous and she believed his protest of innocence. He couldn't have faked his surprise and relief at the reappearance of the paintings. That's why she had a couple of questions for him that Buds and Semra surely wouldn't ask him during his interrogation.

Before Semra drove off, she phoned Buds on his mobile parlebol. "You should fetch Joes van Gro again, too. They could be accomplices." She listened. "He's probably at home. Go and have a look." Ending the call, she activated the carpet.

When the carpisto began to move, Moira turned to the captive. "I would like to know why you got a lawyer for Joes van Gro even though you believed him to be the thief of the paintings."

The director smiled at her but his eyes remained sad. "He never took anything without replacing it with a wonderful copy. I am absolutely sure that he hasn't got anything to do with the burglary."

Moira had come to the same conclusion, but she insisted. "Why didn't you contact the Gendarmerie about the missing paintings?"

"Did you notice the quality of the copies? They are incredible and I didn't want to get their creator into trouble."

Moira remembered the winking of the fake Mona Beth. "But they were faulty."

"Correct. With each picture he swapped, the creator built in a fault deliberately. So tiny and so fitting that only an expert or a very good observer would notice. That's not something a common thief does who's only interested in the financial value of art."

Moira shook her head at the thought of so much naivety in a learned man like him. "What if he had sold the originals already?"

The director leaned back and closed his eyes. "Over the last few years I have built up a virtual alter ego that's known as a rich collector without scruples. I expose fencers and get stolen art back. None of my pictures have been offered on the black market." He sat up, pulled a card from his pocket and handed it to her. "Here is my Infonet information. You can check it."

Moira pocketed the card. "I wonder why Joes van Gro didn't take the copies to you directly."

"Sorry, but I can't help you there. I don't understand it myself." He turned to her and took her hand. "Could you please tell my wife where I am?"

"Are you sure she wants to know?"

"I never betrayed her trust. I didn't even think of it. I love only her." Du Mar looked hurt.

"Aren't you lying to yourself there?" Moira pulled her fingers free. "Did you ever consider that your wife might not be jealous of other women but of your work?" Amused, she watched Du Mar open and close his mouth without finding the words to speak. "Maybe that's why she sent you packing." As a sign that she didn't want to talk any more, she folded her arms in front of her chest, stared out her window, and lost herself in her thoughts.

In the station, Buds approached them. "Well, at least you were successful," he said to Semra. "My bird had left the nest."

Semra cocked her head. "Who are you talking about?"

"Samantha Belz. The woman who worked in the museum's cleaning team and who is madly in love with Huudien. Her flat is empty and no one knows where she went." He took the director's free elbow and led him into an interrogation room with Semra.

Moira went into Sabio's office and told him what she had learned about the museum's boxes.

"So we can safely assume that Lif Borson was somehow involved in the burglary. Good work," Sabio said.

Moira's ears turned hot, and she didn't know what to say.

Luckily Druidus popped in at that moment. "I'm going to the canteen for lunch. Anyone interested?"

Sabio pointed to several files neatly lined up on his desk. "I've got plenty of work, but I'm sure Moira wouldn't mind."

Moira followed Druidus into an uninviting green room with many tables and one long counter with glass displays. At least the food looked good. She chose a casserole with salad, and Druidus took some soup. He insisted on paying for both of them.

"As a first day treat, so to speak, since we'll be partners from now on." Druidus walked straight to a table where Grub and some more gendarmes sat. He introduced Moira as a new colleague, and everybody greeted her cordially.

Druidus sat beside her. During lunch, the group discussed the murders of the homeless.

"Sabio has assigned four teams already," Grub said. "But they haven't got much to go on."

"I thought they'd found this footprint at the last crime scene." The dainty brunette beside him looked surprised.

"It was from the gendarme who found it. Typical newbie mistake," a stout man on the other side of the table said. "Also, it's quite possible that we haven't found all the bodies yet. Especially homeless often lie around for several days because no one's missing them."

Grub shook his head. "So far, we found each one the day after the murder. To me, it seems the murderer wants them to be found."

"Maybe he likes playing cat and mouse with the Gendarmerie." Druidus stole a couple of fries from Grub's untouched plate.

The nerl didn't complain.

"Headquarters increased the number of patrols," the brunette said. "Maybe someone will see the murderer next time."

"He's a professional. They'll never catch him that way." The stout gendarme wiped his mouth and leaned back. "I wouldn't mind if someone would come up with a really useful plan though. One that proves to be effective."

Everybody pondered this but no one came up with a new idea how to catch the serial killer.

After a while, Druidus said to Moira, "By the way, Sabio announced us at your dad's for one o clock."

Moira looked at the clock on the wall; a quarter past twelve. "Oh dear." The prospect of having to speak with her father affected her stomach and she couldn't eat another bite. She pushed her plate aside. A little later, Druidus finished too.

On their way to the official carpistos, they met Buds leading Joes van Gro, whose hands were handcuffed behind his back.

"Wait a moment," Moira said to Buds. "I need to ask him something really important."

"Piss off. The guy is on his way to jail, and until he tells us where to find the stolen crate, he's not getting out again." He tried to walk past her, but Moira didn't make way.

The knowledge of belonging to Commissaire Marten's team now gave her the strength to oppose him. "The crate is a piece of evidence in a murder, and it should be with Excelsior van Steen in the archive right now."

"How would you know?"

"Because I found both, crate and corpse. And now, let me talk to him. It's only one question."

Buds ground his teeth, but gave in after a glance at Druidus. "But hurry."

Moira nodded and turned to the captive. "I would like to know why you placed the stolen paintings into the archive, even though you could have made millions with them on the black market."

Joes van Gro straightened up and glared at her. "How could you assume even for a second that I would hawk masters like Leon del Vacca or Marc Franz-Cheval and keep them from the public for good? I am an honorable man, an artist, a—"

"A thief," Buds interjected.

Joes van Gro snorted derisively. "I just wanted to see if Director du Mar would live up to his name as art connoisseur. Had the burglary not happened, I would have returned the paintings already. Nevertheless, they haven't been in danger for a single moment."

"You can tell that to your lawyer when he arrives." Buds pushed Joes van Gro past Moira. Seeing as she had learned what she wanted to know, she didn't stop him again.

"Do you believe him?" Druidus asked.

Moira shrugged. "His indignation seemed genuine, but we can only be sure when we know who was responsible for the burglary."

"You sound like Sabio." Druidus laughed and held out his arm. "May I invite you to a short outing, my lady? I know a cozy security firm."

Moira wondered about his turn to silliness but had to admit to herself that she found it charming. For the first time since Lif's death, she smiled, and she felt surprisingly good.

Chapter 11

Half an hour later, Druidus stopped in a no-parking zone in front of P&OS, the firm of Moira's father.

Moira got out and looked up. The skyscraper's front was covered in mirroring panes. As modern as they were, they made the building look forbidding to Moira. *Like a mirror of my father.* She followed Druidus into the entrance hall.

"Please take a seat for a short moment." The young receptionist pointed to a group of seats in the back of the hall and dispatched a message-nerl.

Druidus sat on a black sofa, but Moira paced up and down. She felt Druidus' gaze which made her even more nervous.

To take her mind off the coming meeting, she stopped at a metal display rack with advertising brochures. On one title, five of the seven staff members had been made visible with magic retroactively. They were inhumanly pale. Vampires seemed to be favored as security personnel. Moira shivered at the thought of living in the same house as a blood-sucker. She had grown up in a vampire-free village. Of course, she knew that none of the so-called night-actives were so barbaric these days as to hunt their own meal; still, she felt uncomfortable near these pale and tired-looking creatures. Hopefully she wouldn't have to interrogate one of them.

At this moment, a stocky fifty-something came toward them with outstretched arms.

"Welcome at P&OS. We awaited you. Please follow me." He ushered Druidus to the nerlift, pretending he hadn't seen Moira. Druidus let Moira go first. Secretly grinning inside, no muscle moved in her face as she entered the nerlift. They sped upward to the top floor.

"You will surely understand that I cannot let you meet Monsieur Bellamie without sufficient reason." The man marched along the corridor in front of them with fast steps. He didn't turn while talking. Moira felt as if he was trying to get rid of them. They passed a bureau with a small brass plate with her father's name beside the door. One look at the curly-blond secretary in the antechamber made clear that it wouldn't be easy to get past her should it prove necessary. For a moment, Moira was glad about having an excuse not to face her father. Then she remembered that the only clue from Lif's murder incriminated him. She wouldn't get out of this easily.

Diagonally opposite her father's office, the round man opened a door to another office with a view on the sea and the city's harbor. He sat down in a comfy chair behind a chunky desk and pointed to a chair in front of it. "Please. Let us discuss your wishes."

Moira stopped at the door to keep the corridor in view, where a young man was delivering mail from a dolly into the offices. Druidus passed her when he entered the room.

When he sat, the man steepled his fingers and leaned his elbows on the desktop. "Now, what can I do for you?"

The chair was deliberately low so Druidus had to look up at the man despite his stately size. "We have to talk to Lavant Bellamie personally."

"I assumed that much but as I said, a meeting on such short notice is not feasible. Monsieur Bellamie is much in demand." The man bent forward and smiled jovially. "It has already been a hassle to free half an hour on my schedule. But it shows you that we're always cooperating with the Gendarmerie. Now, what do you have to talk about?"

"That's for Monsieur Bellamie's ears only."

Moira only half listened to the polite battle of wills. She watched her father's blond secretary step from the office to flirt with the young man. *Opportunity makes a thief*, she thought, although she had always hated this saying. She hurried across the corridor.

The stout man shouted after her. "Stop!"

She slipped past the dumbfounded secretary into the antechamber of her father's office, but at the last moment, the young man managed to get hold of the seam of her jacket. The jerk nearly toppled her. She slipped from the sleeves but the delay was long enough for the secretary to gather her wits. With open arms, she stood in front of her employer's office door. Without getting rough, Moira wouldn't be able to pass her.

"Please step aside. I don't want to hurt you."

The secretary didn't move. The stout man shot into the room. From the corners of her eyes, Moira noticed the sweat running down his face.

"You can't go in there," he screamed.

"Go ahead." Druidus nodded at Moira over the stout man's head.

Before Moira could do anything, the door to the office opened. A giant with close-cropped hair stepped out. His chest muscles threatened to burst the custom crafted shirt. After he took in the scene, his frown made way for amazement.

"Moira!" Lavant Bellamie pushed aside the secretary and wrapped his strong arms around his daughter. "Honey, why didn't you say you'd be coming?"

Moira wriggled in his embrace.

"Let go."

Lavant obeyed, excusing himself. He pushed her into his office. "Come in, darling. I am so happy to see you."

Before he could close the door, Druidus squeezed in and showed his ID.

"I doubt your daughter's pleasure equals yours."

"We're only here on official business," Moira folded her arms in front of her chest, "father." Her last word dripped contempt.

The glow left her father's face.

"Oh. And I thought…" With his head lowered, he walked around the desk and sat.

Only now did Moira realize that his office looked very different from what she had expected. When she was a child, he had told her of generous rooms with wooden floors, mahogany furniture and leather sofas. Instead, she stood in a small room with the same old wobbly pine furniture she remembered from back then. A magnet board framed with photographs, pictures of her at every age – school photos, snapshots – dominated the only free wall. Even the picture she had used to apply for the Gendarmerie was there.

Moira swallowed. Her voice shook.

"Why did you never visit? Not even once?" She pointed to the pictures. "It looks as if you did miss me after all."

Lavant pressed his lips together and looked at Druidus.

"You said you've got business?"

Druidus pulled a photo of the pin from the breast pocket of his jacket.

"Do you recognize this?"

Lavant didn't answer right away. He pulled a magnifier from a drawer in his desk and examined the picture. Then he nodded.

"It's one of our Ident-pins. Why?"

"Can you tell me who it belongs to?"

"If you give it to me for a second."

Druidus raised his eyebrows.

"Don't the letters on the pin tell you anything about its wearer?"

"Are you accusing me of obfuscation?" Lavant frowned. "I am under legal obligation to protect the personal data of my staff."

"Not if it obstructs the inquiries in a case of murder. Do we have to return with a warrant?"

The two men stared at each other wordlessly for a moment, then Lavant forced a smile.

"Including myself, we've currently got three staff members with the initials LB, and each of them owns a single pin. The Ident-needles contain a micro-nerl who remembers the personal data." He held up a flat box reminding Moira of a packet of glowstalks. "I can call up the information any time with this reader." He pointed to the collar of his own shirt. "Just to ease your mind, I am wearing my pin, as you can see. Is that enough to get me off your list of suspects?"

"Would it have sufficed when you were still a gendarme?" Druidus reached out. "May I use the reader?"

Wordlessly Lavant handed him the black box. Druidus pulled the pin from a special compartment in his wallet and placed it gently into the reader.

Without further ado, the box recited the required information. "This Ident-pin belongs to Leclerque Bastide, resident of Elveholme, currently on duty with project 19/643K North York."

Moira was relieved that her father's name was cleared. Her legs trembled so much, she had to lean against one of the shelves.

"What is project 19/643K North York?" Druidus handed the reader back and replaced the pin in the security compartment of his wallet.

"As you might know, the Great Carnival resides there." Lavant searched the chaos on his desk and pulled out a file triumphantly. "In the last few weeks, many valuable items went missing from the Carnival people, and I sent Bastide to find the culprit."

"Why him?"

"Bastide is one of my best men."

Druidus picked up the file and got up.

"The Gendarmerie thanks you for your cooperation."

"My pleasure." Lavant leaned back and folded his hands behind his head. "If there is nothing else, I'd like you to leave."

With her knees under control again, Moira stepped forward and asked, "How long has Leclerque Bastide been in North York?"

Lavant shrugged.

"He was supposed to start working at seven this morning. I assume he left on the weekend."

Druidus thanked him again and walked to the door. Moira followed him hesitantly. In vain, she waited for her father to call her back to cheer her up or explain some-thing… anything. The door closed without another word from him, and she fought her tears. Druidus put his arm around her shoulders and handed her a handkerchief.

She shook her head and blinked away her tears.

"I'm fine."

Druidus stroked her cheek with his index finger.

"If you need me, I'll be there for you any time."

"Thanks." All of a sudden, Moira realized his arm was still around her shoulders. Careful but decisively, she freed herself. Then she walked swiftly to the nerlift. From the corners of her eyes, she observed Druidus following her.

At the station they reported to Sabio. "And the best thing is," Druidus said, "that Leclerque Bastide resides in Elveholme."

The Commissaire scratched his chin. "So we would have to assume that he might be an elf. There are hardly any humans living in the vicinity of the elves."

Druidus remained skeptical. "A criminal elf? Isn't that a bit far-fetched?"

Moira shook her head. "Since the box in Lif's room implies that he had been involved in the burglary, it makes sense. There was an elf that night, and it seems as if Lif and Bastide had been friends."

Sabio nodded. "It's possible. But it's also possible that Bastide didn't lose the pin himself at the crime scene or at a different point in time. I'll send Lel and Buster to Elveholme. Maybe they can find out when he left."

Moira was disappointed. She longed to help with the investigation.

"Aside from that, I think Leclerque Bastide is an important witness," Druidus said. "Don't you think we should talk to him?"

"You only want to ride the Tapisrapide." Sabio grinned. "Fine, let's try it. Maybe he really is the elf on the surveillance globe. In that case I'd love to ask him where the other nightwatchman went to." He glanced at the clock. The shift was nearly over. He turned to Moira. "I'd like you to accompany him. Otherwise, he will try all the fairground carousels at the expense of the Gendarmerie."

Moira beamed. She only knew the Great Carnival from magazines. The high price for admittance and a six-hour drive with the trainerl-way had always put her off. Also, she had never been in a Tapisrapide either. "Shouldn't we take along a couple more gendarmes? In the Great Carnival, a single elf might be hard to find."

"We'll take a traceball." Druidus rubbed his hands. "I love it when fun and work are the same. I'll be back in ten minutes." He ran from Sabio's office.

Obviously, Sabio had noticed the confusion with which Moira gazed after her colleague, because he said, "He's fetching his Tapisrapide."

"His?" Moira's eyebrows shot up.

"Truth be told, it belongs to his father, but Druidus can use it for work any time. The Gendarmerie refunds only the usual flat rate for official journeys." Sabio put his feet on his tabletop and reached for the parlebol. "You didn't think the Gendarmerie could afford their own high-speed carpisto, did you?" He turned to the bowl, called the inventory department, and ordered a traceball and an elf-net.

Chapter 12

The first quarter of an hour of the trip flew by. Moira couldn't get enough of the world speeding past down below, and she was a little ashamed for feeling like a small child. When they had left the mainland behind, Druidus switched over to auto-nerl. He turned his seat to face hers. "Finally, we're alone with you awake."

Moira looked up at him. His gaze made her blush.

He bent forward and took one of her hands. "I know this isn't the best moment to tell you this, but I fell in love with you head over heels." He pulled her hand to his mouth.

The gentle touch of his lips shot through Moira's arm like a lightning strike. Her jaw dropped and her arm muscles refused to work, so she couldn't pull away her hand. Was she trembling from excitement or from fear? She didn't know.

Druidus slipped closer until she felt his breath on her face. "I knew from our first run-in that you are the woman I'll fight for. I want to grow old with you."

Moira swallowed. Heat waves pulsated from her fingers through her body, and her heart thumped so hard, she felt it in her throat. Her mouth opened and closed but not a single word came out.

"I know Lif's death was a downer for you, and there is probably no room in your life for me just now. But I will always be there for you," Druidus said. "I would be incredibly happy if you'd agree to have a date with me some time soon. Will you give me a chance?" His big, dark blue eyes begged her.

Moira nodded wordlessly, and then shook her head. She pulled her hand away and cleared her throat but again, didn't know what to say. Embarrassed, she stared at her fingers.

"Just think about it. Please." Druidus' voice soothed her soul. Something inside wanted her to say "yes" but she couldn't utter the word. Without his declaration, she would have had fewer problems to go on a date with him.

Druidus breathed deeply. "I'm sorry for being so persistent. I have never been in love like this, and I'm scared. I'm probably blabbing."

Moira realized he understood her confusion, which made it even more difficult. How could she turn him down without hurting his feelings? Druidus had made it clear enough that he wanted more than a one-night stand, but any thought of long term commitment froze her blood. She stared at the clouds that resembled cotton wool balls from up here and struggled for words.

"Don't say anything, just think about it." Druidus turned his seat back and grabbed the steering wheel. "I love you, and I can wait."

In silence, they flew on. Moira's thoughts were in turmoil. *How can I be so cold to such a wonderful and attractive man? And he seems to be well off too. Am I crazy? Franka will kick my ass if I don't date him at least once.* She still felt his strong fingers, smelled his scent of leather and tobacco. And he didn't even smoke. He seemed to be using the same after-shave as her father used to. The scent reminded her so much of her childhood, and it resulted in a feeling of security which also woke the old pain. She did believe he was earnest, and her heart longed for him. Feelings Moira had suppressed for so long threatened to overwhelm her. *What if we really grow old together? What if our wishes and dreams change? Will his love for me die the way my parents' love died?* There was no way she could stand another blow like the one when her dad left. After all these years, she was still mourning. She stared out of the window, trying to calm down again, but her feelings churned even when Druidus made the Tapisrapide sink into the clouds.

"What do you know about elves?" he asked out of the blue.

Moira forced her feelings back under the shell where they had been for the last several years, and concentrated on his question. "Elves are to be taken with care, since they like to play tricks on humans. But ever since the Contract of Compatibility, they don't swap children for changelings any more, and they are never criminal."

"Nearly true." He smiled at her sideways.

"Elves only obey the rules of the Contract of Compatibility because their queen issues punishments that even the most conservative human finds excessive and unfair. So, most elves are nitpicky about keeping the rules. But that's not what I was asking about." He switched on windscreen wipers because it had begun to rain when they broke through the lower rim of the cloud cover. "Did they teach you Theoretical Magic in school or during the prep-course?"

Moira shook her head.

"Sabio would be horrified. Theoretical Magic is his hobbyhorse. He could explain things much better than I can." He sighed. "But I'll try. As we know, light and wild magic are our only energy sources."

"And we can't use either directly," Moira added.

"So you do know some things after all." Druidus smiled. "And you are right. Humans cannot use wild magic. But elves, sprites, nymphs and many more thrive on it. Their metabolism is adapted to this form of magic." He toggled several switches, and the Tapisrapide hung in the air. "The problem is that our magic isn't compatible with elf-magic. Or to put it differently, if an elf throws a spell at a human, there are unexpected and usually very… let's say, unpredictable results. Therefore we need special equipment like the traceballs and elf-nets made by elves, in case an elf resists interrogation or capture." Druidus turned his seat toward her again. "Although I don't think Bastide will start any mischief, I want you to stay behind me when we find him. If necessary, I can neutralize him in less than a second with an elf-net. Will you promise?"

Moira nodded. To fetch an elf for questioning seemed to be more dangerous than she had expected. "Shouldn't we have taken more men?"

"No." Druidus pressed a final button, and the Tapis-rapide sank so fast Moira's stomach felt as if it wanted to squeeze through her throat. "Elves cooperate best if humans face them in pairs."

A little later, the Tapisrapide landed on the flat roof of a house. The lights of castles, the giant's wheel, the roller-coaster and countless other attractions covering the area in front of them like a colorful carpet sparkled through the front window. Though it wasn't yet dark, the sea of lights glowed in the dusk like a multi-colored jewel. The paths between the attractions were stuffed with people that looked like dolls from this height. The noise reached them hardly dampened.

Moira was awed. "Oh my. There are a lot of people."

When they exited, the manager of the Great Carnival met them. He handed them his direct parlebol number and two VIP-passports for free entries on every attraction. While he told them what he suspected of Bastidc's where-abouts, he led them down.

After that, they were on their own in the churning masses. The noise was deafening. The visitors of the carnival all talked at once, trying to drown out the attractions' melodies and the ringing and shouting of the ticket sellers.

"This is worse than a closing sale," Moira shouted in Druidus' ear.

He nodded and took her hand. "So we won't be separated."

They squeezed through the crowd. It was so full, Moira had to walk very close to Druidus to stay with him. She felt the warmth of his body through the thin fabric of her jacket. When she realized she longed for his embrace, she moved a little bit away. Luckily the crowd thinned a bit more the further they went from the entrance.

Finally, Druidus let go of her hand again. "I suggest we walk the whole carnival before we free the traceball. That way, we'll get an overview of the area in case something un-expected happens."

Moira agreed, so they walked side by side, without touching, through the carnival. Several times, Druidus cajoled her into trying a ride. They rode high above the crowd in the giant's wheel turned by the cloddish creature, and sat on a giant caterpillar with saddles attached to it which ran at an incredible speed on a circular trail. They had fun like teenagers, and Moira relaxed.

"Will we have to book this as working time or spare time?" Druidus smirked.

Moira countered. "Don't they pay a flat fee for business trips?"

He laughed and bought her cotton candy and a ginger-bread heart with "Always Yours" written on it. Moira wanted to hide it under her jacket or in her handbag. Instead, he hung it around her neck, and she wore it with smarting ears.

Although Moira enjoyed the fun, she kept watching out for Leclerque Bastide. She was surprised to see that most visitors of the carnival were human. She noticed a few elves and only three families of centaurs, but a lot of the fair's folk were magical creatures. The most prominent were two giants taking turns moving the giant's wheel. The most popular was an artificial forest where children could ride a unicorn. It took them two hours to walk the whole area once, but afterward they had a good overview of the stalls distribution, the paths and the most favored attractions.

"I will now free the traceball so it can take us to Bastide," Druidus said. "If possible, we should try to ad-dress him in a less frequented area of the carnival where there aren't so many people." He pulled out a small ball that looked like a soap bubble, and tapped it three times with his index finger. "Find Leclerque Bastide and indicate. Do not make contact."

On either side of the ball, pearly butterfly wings un-furled. They moved up and down majestically, losing glittery dust. A glittering trail remained hanging in the air when the ball took off.

"Come." Druidus took her hand and pulled her along. He kept his gaze on the track and the ball blinking red in set intervals. Due to their haste, they kept bumping into visitors. Each time, Moira mumbled an apology, but Druidus was fixated on the ball. With surprise, Moira noticed that the blinking slowly changed color. It turned from red through orange to yellow. Finally, the traceball turned green and hovered over a tent motionlessly.

Relieved, Moira stopped, gasped for air, and looked at the tent. Below a generous roof of black fabric and concrete pillars stood a tent painted over and over with golden flowers. It looked as if it belonged to a Sindhu Maharaja. Beside the entrance, a big sign read:

MME SUZANKA

CLAIRVOYANTE

INTERPRETATION OF HAND LINES

ANALYSIS OF AURAS

TAROT READING

A TRUE GAZE INTO THE FUTURE.

Don't you believe it. Moira shook her head over the countless people waiting for admittance. "What is Bastide doing in there?"

Druidus shrugged. "Didn't your father say he was searching for stolen goods? Maybe he's got a lead already." He walked up to a dwarf guarding the entrance, held his hand in front of the small man's eyes, and the Gendarmerie's logo sparkled. The dwarf threw his long beard over his shoulder, pounded his fist into Druidus' stomach and ran. As he hurried directly past Moira, she stuck out her leg. The dwarf slammed into one of the concrete pillars with his head and lost consciousness. Just in case, Moira put handcuffs on his hands and feet.

While she waited for Druidus to recover, she told the waiting people that Madame Suzanka would be closed until further notice and convinced them to try different attracttions. The area in front of the tent slowly emptied, and by the time Druidus patted her shoulder approvingly, the dwarf had regained his consciousness. Wordlessly, he pulled at the cuffs, glaring at Moira.

"I wonder why this reaction," Druidus said, but the dwarf didn't answer. "I am hereby arresting you for resistance against an official in a less severe case." Druidus picked him up, sat him behind the advertising sign so he couldn't be seen easily, and explained his rights to him. Then he linked arms with Moira and lifted the tarpaulin that covered the entrance to Madame Suzanka's tent.

Inside, it was quite dark. Moira and Druidus stopped close to the entrance and waited for their eyes to adjust. Three small balls of Lumière Magique illuminated the more or less bare room. Their light fell on two low chairs and an octagonal table with a long, white cover. Madame Suzanka sat with her back to the door. Long, black hair flowed over her back, held together just above the ground by a golden ribbon. She was whispering. On the other chair stood an elf, hardly bigger than a three-year-old. He bent far over the table, and his wings shimmered in the low light. Druidus cleared his throat, and Madame Suzanka turned around.

She frowned at him. "Why did Roche let you in? I'm not done yet." Her gaze fell on Moira, and her eyes widened.

"Katie Féroce!" She paled.

The elf stood straight and held out both arms. Blue-white fire shot toward Moira.

For her, it looked as if it was in slow motion. The individual flames toppled over each other, blazed, billowed, swelled toward her. She pulled up her hands in defense, stumbling backward. Her movements seemed awfully slow to her. Equally slowly, her mouth opened to scream. Through the gaps in her fingers, she saw Madame Suzanka. Their gazes met, and the clairvoyant formed the sign against evil with index and middle finger. Her face was a mask of fear.

From the corners of her eyes, Moira saw Druidus fling the elf-net. It sailed graciously through the air, its pink blossoms fluttering. The closer the ball of fire came, the more blue the world around Moira got. She tried to move faster to avoid the fireball, but her body was caught in the molasses of slowed down time while her senses grasped everything in split seconds.

The fireball hit Moira, hugged her in a cloud of flames. Everything, even the net settling on Bastide, was tinged blue. Her flesh vanished, leaving nothing but bones surrounded by blue fire and pain eating into her arms. She knew she was screaming but she couldn't hear.

A power surged though her body like a cooling wave. All of a sudden, she remembered playing with this power as a toddler. The wave rose higher and higher, soothing the vanished tissue, making it visible again. In the end, the wave broke over her head. The blue flames died with a hiss, and steam shot away to all sides. Chairs, table, tarpaulin, elf, and humans were scattered like grains of sand.

Only Moira stood confused and with shaking hands in the chaos, her mind empty as if the steam explosion had wiped away every thought. Numbed, she stared at her hands. Very slowly, the world returned to normal. Moira wondered what had happened and how she had done whatever she had done. Under the tent's debris, someone moved, and Druidus rose slowly.

His face was a mixture of awe and excitement. "Dear me, your reaction was superb. I've never seen anyone activate a shield this fast."

It was no shield, Moira meant to say but couldn't speak.

"It must have been an Anti-Elf-Special." Druidus patted the dust from his jacket and pants. "Where did you get it? From your father?"

Moira shook her head. She couldn't believe that she had created a shield spell out of nothing. It was impossible. There had to be another explanation.

"You should tell Sabio where you got the shield spell." Druidus didn't give up. "The Gendarmerie could use good protection against elf magic."

Moira wondered why they would need protection against elves with their alleged peacefulness. Anyway, she couldn't help, so she decided to keep her confusion to herself to try to figure out what had happened.

She looked around. Not too far away, Madame Suzanka sat on the ground with her hands in front of her face, whimpering.

With shaking knees, Moira walked over and bent down. "Can I help you?"

Madame Suzanka flinched and looked up. When she recognized Moira, she scrambled backwards trying to get away, her face twisted with fear. "Roche forced me," she croaked. "He hit me when I refused him. Please don't hurt me, Katie Féroce."

"I'm not..." Moira began and reached out for the clairvoyant. She stopped when Madame Suzanka closed her eyes tightly and put her arms protectively over her head. Slowly, Moira withdrew, leaving it to Druidus to calm the distraught woman. Instead, she searched the debris for Bastide and the dwarf. Valuables lay scattered everywhere. Moira found necklaces, rings, parlebol-specials, musi-nerls, and much more. *So, Bastide was onto something after all*, she thought.

She found the elf unhurt under the net. He was snoring. Next, she looked for the dwarf. He had crawled away and was already most of the way to the next attraction. Moira caught him trying to convince a lottery seller to cut his bonds.

"I'm sorry, but this guy is under arrest." Moira shouldered the little man and her knees buckled under his weight. Despite his small size, he weighed easily as much as a fully grown man. Panting, she carried him back and dropped him unceremoniously beside Bastide.

"Thank you." Druidus nodded and put away his parlebol. "The manager was glad to learn that the theft had been cleared up. He informed the local Gendarmerie station and will arrive with his security team soon. Until then, we'll have to wait."

"And we'll have to make the onlookers move on." Moira pointed at the people standing in growing groups taking in the chaos.

Chapter 13

When they returned close to three a.m. Sabio was waiting for them in the station's parking lot. He handed them two mugs of strong coffee. Without a word he took the doped elf and unwrapped him from the net.

"How long has he been asleep?"

"Five and a half hours."

Sabio frowned. "That's very long. Let's hope he can remember everything."

"There was no other way. The North York station interrogated us for three hours, and I didn't want to risk a second attack." Druidus downed his coffee with one gulp and shivered.

"Attack?" Sabio raised an eyebrow. "Tell me."

Moira drank the disgusting brew much slower. It tasted like dishwater but helped against her fatigue.

Sabio put the elf over his shoulder like a baby and patted his back carefully. Bastide coughed, and his arms twitched. Sabio sighed with relief.

"We need a blanket, a bottle of morning dew and honey."

"I'll drop his fingerprint card in the lab and bring everything to interrogation room three." Druidus hurried off.

Sabio turned to Moira. "I know your shift is long over but would you mind listening to the interrogation? Maybe you will hear something Druidus and I don't."

Moira nodded and followed Sabio, who carried the elf to the interrogation room. In fact, she was tired enough to go home and drop dead, but she was very interested in Bastide's statement, and she didn't want to disappoint Sabio.

While he took the captive into the interrogation room, Moira walked into the room beside it. Through a big one-way mirror, she could see two gray chairs and an equally gray table with Bastide on it. When Druidus returned, he wrapped the elf tenderly in the blanket he had brought. Moira saw him talk to Sabio without understanding a word. After a while, Sabio came into the observing room and put his hand on her shoulder. "Druidus told me what happened. Very well done." He pointed to the glass pane, missing her blush. "As long as you don't turn on the light, Bastide can neither hear nor see you. Also, the interrogation room has been built in a way that makes it impervious against any sort of magic, even elf magic. He won't be able to harm you."

"Can I hear what's being said on the other side?" Moira sat on a chair close to the one-way glass, glad she didn't have to stand.

"Sure. The mirror holds a speech transfer spell." Sabio activated it for her.

Immediately, Druidus' voice carried through. "...think he's regaining consciousness."

Moira put her hand on Sabio's arm. "How long will the interrogation take?"

"It's difficult to say, but I'll try to keep it short. Druidus looked rather tired too." He turned to go but stopped in the doorframe. "If it's too much for you, knock on the glass once and we'll call it a day."

Of course, Moira couldn't knock on the pane without destroying the speech transfer spell, but she nodded. Then she concentrated on the scene in the other room.

Sabio entered and bent over Leclerque Bastide. The elf came to very slowly and looked around in confusion. Sabio fed him honey and dew, alternating between the two. When Bastide was looking better, Sabio activated the dicta-nerl and noted the date and time of the interrogation.

Then he turned to Bastide. "The manager of the Great Carnival will send you the promised bonus. How did you know Madame Suzanka's dwarf was responsible for the thefts?"

Bastide pressed his lips together and didn't answer.

"Why are you interested in the thefts on the Great Carnival? We're investigating a murder." Druidus put both hands on the tabletop and bent down to the elf. "Where were you Saturday, let's say from eight p.m. on?"

Again, the elf stayed silent.

Sabio put a hand on Druidus' shoulder, but kept looking at Bastide as he spoke. "Come on. You're... Surely you're just as tired as we are."

"Let go." Druidus shook off Sabio's hand.

Moira wondered. Was he really angry? Or did they act out good cop, bad cop? She couldn't decide. To her, Druidus' anger seemed real. She noticed beads of sweat forming on Bastide's forehead.

Druidus stared at Sabio, hands clenched, slightly bent forward and frowning. "If he doesn't speak up soon, I'll call the elf queen."

Bastide paled but still didn't talk.

Sabio shook his head. "Let's stay reasonable." He pulled a chair closer and sat opposite from Bastide with Druidus standing behind him and glaring at the elf.

Sabio pushed the Ident-needle Moira had found at the crime scene toward the elf. "Do you know this?"

Bastide nodded. "It belongs to the company. Every employee has one."

"Your boss confirmed that this one belongs to you." Druidus' voice still sounded hostile.

Bastide shrugged. "So what?"

Sabio bent over the table. "How well do you know Lif Borson?"

"Who?" Bastide's hands moved in a confused gesture.

Moira noticed easily that the elf's surprise was fake.

Druidus took a step forward, grabbed the elf's collar, and bent so far over the table that his nose was only inches from Bastide's face. "I will give you one more chance, but if you don't spill it, then... one spell will be enough and the elf queen will send her men."

Bastide slumped. "I met Lif two years ago at the New Year's celebration of the company. Some of our employees had worked on one of his digs. The stuff the students drag from the soil can be quite valuable. Lif and I often imagined what we could earn if we nicked a piece or two." Bastide lifted his gaze and looked at Sabio pleadingly. "But we never did. You have to believe me. We only talked about it."

Moira noticed that his hands under the table were visible neither to Sabio nor to Druidus.

"This Sunday too?" Sabio asked.

"No."

"Stop lying," Druidus barked at him. "We found your fingerprints on a glass and on the window in his flat."

Moira knew Druidus was bluffing. He did take Bastide's fingerprints right after his capture but he'd only taken the prints to the lab a few minutes ago. Not even the best analytics could process them this fast. But his bluff seemed to work.

Bastide's eyes widened, and he seemed genuinely devastated. "Lif is involved in a murder? I mean, he's rather dominated by hormones, and he can get quite rough if a cuckolded husband follows him. But he'd never kill anyone."

"*He* did not kill anyone." Druidus folded his arms in front of his chest.

Bastide frowned at him, then seemed to understand. His jaw dropped, and he paled so much his skin lost its greenish sheen and looked gray. He choked.

Sabio handed him the bottle with morning dew. "Drink."

After a few gulps, color returned to Bastide's face. His eyes swam in tears, and his voice had a pleading undertone. "You're making fun of me, right? Lif isn't really dead. It's a bad joke, isn't it?"

Sabio shook his head. "Late Sunday evening, someone sliced his chest open with a very sharp tool."

Bastide put his hands over his face. He shivered all over and needed a long time to compose himself. Then he looked directly into Sabio's face. "When I left him on Sunday evening, he was still alive. I told him about my new job and about the bonus I would get for a speedy clarifycation of the thefts. We planned to get drunk on the bonus upon my return." The elf's gaze flickered form Druidus to Sabio and back. To Moira, he resembled a hunted rabbit.

"I stayed until he made it clear that he had to pick up his newest sugar baby. Maybe she mur... murd..." He didn't manage to finish the word. "He changed his girlfriends daily, you know. But I can't tell you whom he meant to fuck that night. I never bothered to keep track of his affairs."

Moira was fairly sure Bastide truly didn't know who killed Lif. Still, she observed each of his movements, listened to every word intently. During the remainder of the interview, Sabio and Druidus didn't win any new insights, and Moira didn't discover anything unusual either.

After another hour, Sabio ended the interview. "Thank you for your statement. We will have to insist that you don't leave town, though, because a charge about the attack on one of my officers is still pending."

Bastide nodded. "I'm sorry for attacking her. Madame Suzanka's shock made me overreact. Luckily no one was hurt."

"You will still have to bear the consequences."

"Of course. May I go now?"

Wordlessly, Druidus opened the door. Bastide seemed relieved that he could fly off unhindered. Moira went to the corridor and watched him until he was gone.

Sabio stepped beside her. "What does your gut feeling say?"

She shrugged. "I'm sure Lif's death shocked him. But when he insisted that he and Lif never stole anything from the digs, he was probably lying."

Sabio looked at her with surprise. "How do you know?"

"I can't prove it, but he rubbed his hands on his thighs under the table. Many people do that when they are lying."

"We'll interview him again soon." Sabio put a hand on her arm. "It's time to end our shift. Have a good night's sleep. It's enough if you come in around lunchtime today."

Moira thanked him and walked to the exit. She faltered due to her tiredness.

Druidus ran after her. "May I take you home?"

She nodded without thinking twice. A trip with public transport would take far too long at this time of day.

On the way to Druidus' parking lot, two patrol carpistos with green lights and sirens sped off. It took a moment until the importance of it managed to penetrate her muddled brain. "Another homeless?"

Druidus sighed. "I hope not. It would be a real gift for the press. I can see the headlines already. 'Serial Killer in Salthaven - Gendarmerie useless.' "

Moira also hoped that no more homeless were killed. It was so unfair that someone preyed on those people that had the greatest difficulties in life already. Gratefully, she got into Druidus' carpisto, leaned her head against the headrest, and fought to keep her eyes open. In vain. She fell asleep before Druidus left the parking lot.

She woke because someone gently caressed her cheek and called her name. The voice was familiar and tender. "Papa?" Moira opened her eyes.

"Sorry, it's only me," Druidus said with a loopy smile. "We're there."

The warm feeling in Moira's stomach dwindled, and instead her ears began to smart. She forced herself to smile and thank Druidus before she got out.

"Shall I accompany you upstairs?" Hope filled Druidus' gaze.

Moira shook her head. When she noticed his disappointment, she bent down into the carpisto and kissed his cheek. "You may pick me up around lunchtime."

Druidus's face lit up immediately. "See you later."

Moira waved after him for a while, then she climbed the stairs to her flat. After the shortest possible wash and seconds of cleaning her teeth, she fell into bed. Just before she fell asleep again, she realized that she still didn't know what Madame Suzanka had meant when she had called her "Katie Féroce."

Half past nine, the parlebol rang until Moira woke. Still tired, she shuffled into the living room and asked her nerl to accept the call. Franka's face appeared on the water's surface.

"We've been waiting for you for two hours, Moira. The movers will arrive any moment."

Moira blinked. Her brain seemed to work in slow motion. Movers?

"What's wrong with you?" Franka's voice sounded concerned.

"I'm just tired. I only came back at five this morning."

"Really?" Franka's eyes widened. "When are we going to get to know him?"

"Who?"

"Well, the young man you spent the night with."

Moira smiled. "I worked. But if you insist, I'll introduce you to my colleagues."

"You're hopeless." Franka snorted. "Now, hurry back to bed."

"No way. I promised to help you move and that's what I'll do."

"Don't you dare. If someone looks as knackered as you do, she has to sleep. We'll talk later." Franka ended the call.

Gratefully, Moira climbed back into bed even though she felt a little guilty for forgetting about the move. Franka would tease her for years to come. Moira's head hardly hit the pillow before she slept again.

Shortly before eleven, she woke fresh and well rested. After a short jog in the nearby park, a long bath and a late breakfast, she felt great. She looked at the clock. There wasn't enough time to visit Franka and Tord before her next shift started.

"I could try to find out why Madame Suzanka was so afraid of me." She had a nerl activate her magicuter, opened the worldwide Infonet, and searched for "Katie Féroce."

She was very surprised when her Surfer found only eight entries, none of them helpful. All took her to spam sites, useless forums or non-existent pages. But Moira didn't give up easily. She tried translations. "Ferocious Katie" got her no results but "Wild Katie" rendered two useful articles.

The first one was from a hobby author introducing his newest writing project. With interest, Moira read the few lines he had posted about his main character.

"According to legend, Wild Katie was the princess of a wandering clan of the early Iron Age. It is said that she could tame wild magic and was therefore banned from her clan. According to legend, she beheaded her whole tribe in a bout of craziness and killed herself right after.

Historically, the legend cannot be proven, but in traditional stories of today's Wanderers, Wild Katie shows up again and again. Many mothers use it as a warning for their children, similar to the boogeyman in our culture."

Moira ignored the rest of the page, which was dedicated to other characters of the novel. The second article was hardly more than a side-note on the website about the dig of Hern's smithy.

"Romanic Historic Turodot stated that legendary Wild Katie had been Hern's lover, and that she banned a monster with his help. Since no other source backs up his claim, the existence of Wild Katie stays unconfirmed."

Moira leaned back and stretched. *Hern's smithy is Tord's specialty. Maybe he knows something about Wild Katie. I should talk to him.*

As if she had read Moira's thoughts, Franka called at just that moment. She was agitated. "Imagine, Tord has hardly been released from hospital when the Gendarmerie fetched him. And we were meaning to organize the chaos in the new flat."

Moira waited until Franka calmed down. Simultaneously, she turned off the magicuter. When her friend felt better, she asked, "Do you know why they fetched him?"

"It's got to do with some theft, but Tord is no thief."

"I know. I'll take care of it. Promise."

Franka seemed slightly more optimistic. "In two hours, the movers will have emptied the van. I meant to unpack Tord's boxes then. It would be nice if he could be home by then."

The doorbell rang. "I'm getting picked up for duty. Don't worry. I'll send Tord off early enough so he can tell you where he wants his stuff." Moira ended the call and opened the door. Surprised, she looked at the young gendarme who was waiting for her, cap in hand.

"Druidus asks you to forgive him. He had to help Commissaire Marten with another murder. The fourth homeless this week."

"Poor guy." Moira didn't know whom she meant, the homeless or Druidus. She grabbed her jacket and followed the young gendarme downstairs to his carpisto which he had parked in the no-parking zone right in front of her building. When she got into the front seat, she was surprised that she could honor her promise to Franka much faster than expected.

On the backseat, Tord slid to and fro impatiently. He greeted her with a crooked smile. "Don't be alarmed. I'm supposed to identify the content of a box that might have come from my dig. The professor thought I'd know best."

Moira laughed. "Franka thought they'd arrested you."

Tord paled. "Dear me. I hope that isn't bad for her, in her state." Immediately he pulled out his mobile parlebol and called Franka, who was very relieved about his explanation. When they had finished talking, Moira asked him about Wild Katie.

Tord scratched his head. "Why are you interested in a legend from the Wanderers?"

"Because someone called me by that name yesterday, and I found hardly anything about her on the Infonet."

"I see." Tord slid forward and rested his arms on the back of Moira's seat. "You know, there isn't a single scientifically sound proof for her existence, and her legend is only passed on by the Wanderers."

"I don't care." Moira pushed her hair from her face. "I only want to understand why the woman was so afraid of me. After all, I didn't do anything."

"Fair enough, but keep in mind, it's only legends. I only worked with them because one unconfirmed source claims Katie had been Hern's lover."

"Thank you, Tord." Moira leaned her back against the window and listened closely.

"According to the old stories, Wild Katie or Katie Féroce, like the Wanderers call her, was born as the eldest daughter to a clan-queen. Even as a child, she used magic that scared her people. Both the child and her magic were wild and untamable. Still, Katie was accepted as the crown princess. The clan's elders thought it better to use her powers for the tribe than to disinherit her. They didn't want to risk Katie getting picked up by an enemy clan to be used against them. Thus she grew up with her family, always on the move as is their custom.

It is said that they passed the village where Hern lived with his parents on their travels. The elders worried when they noticed that Katie fell in love with him. In their eyes, the young smith was an unbeliever and a settler, no candidate for a princess of their clan. But the lovers wouldn't give each other up. Around the time Hern discovered how to forge magic into his weapons, Katie abandoned her tribe. For a while the pair lived happily in the smithy of Hern's father. Although Katie's magic was very different from Hern's, they managed to unite their powers, creating weapons the world still knows today."

"So far, it doesn't sound very scary," Moira said when the carpisto stopped in front of the station.

"I'm not done yet."

Chapter 14

They got out, and Moira promised the driver she would take Tord down to the archive. The young gendarme drove off to park the carpisto and she led Tord though the long corridors. He didn't get to tell her more, because Semra approached them.

"Good to see you," she said to Moira. "Sabio isn't back from the crime scene yet. He said you should look at the evidence in case HnP 25/19 again. His gut feeling tells him that they overlooked something crucial. You know Sabio thinks highly of his gut feeling."

Moira frowned. "Case HnP 25/19?"

"The twenty-fifth homicide among natural persons in the year 3019," Semra translated the file reference. "It's Lif Borson's murder."

Moira paled but caught herself in time. After all, she only had to look at the evidence. She wouldn't see Lif's body again before the funeral.

"You've got to fetch the evidence from Excelsior van Steen," Semra said.

"That's great. Tord's headed there too." Moira pulled the silent archeologist along to the staircase leading down to the archive. She looked up at Tord. "What else happened with Katie Féroce and Hern?"

"You never change a subject, do you?" He laughed. While they descended the endless steps, he kept talking. "Of course, the Wanderers didn't give up their princess easily. One night, they ambushed the village and kidnapped Katie. It is said Hern was devastated and went searching for the kidnappers immediately. The culprits fled into the mountains with their princess, trying to remind her of her duty. More than once, Katie managed to free herself with her special kind of magic, but she was captured again each time. Finally her clan put her into a sacred cave in the hope she'd reconsider there.

Instead, she went overboard entirely. Crazed, she magicked herself a sword, and when the clan came to lead her home in triumph, she beheaded everyone, women and men, children and elders. Not a single member of her clan survived. She didn't even spare her own family. Only Hern managed to stop her crazed haze. When he appeared, she realized what she had done. In a bout of remorse, she plunged the sword into her own chest and died in his arms. It is said Hern built his smithy over her grave."

Moira's curiosity was endless. "And? Did you find something during your dig?"

Tord grinned. "Didn't you see the boxes? But we didn't find a grave."

Moira snorted and opened the steel door to the archive. Bells chimed. She looked around. The front part of the gigantic vaulted cellar was brightly lit and dominated by a big desk. A mesh wire fence separated the area behind it where long rows of shelves led into the semi-darkness. Beside a fireplace in a side wall stood a white-haired man with his back to them. When the chiming faded, he turned to them. Holding out his hand, he approached Tord. "You must be Tord Mutelen. Come, I prepared everything already."

With surprise, Moira noticed that Excelsior van Steen was wearing the full safety armor. The long, midnight blue coat with the silver symbols went very well with his white beard. Moira stared at his pointy hat. Although she knew the hat focused magic, she struggled not to laugh. Obviously, Excelsior van Steen was one of the few people using magic directly without the help of nerls. Maybe that's why he reminded her of a magician from times gone by.

Van Steen led Tord to the desk where the box from the burglary in the museum waited. He looked at Moira and raised an eyebrow. "Thank you. You may go now."

Moira felt herself blush. "Commissaire Marten sends me. I am to examine the evidence of case HnP 25/19 once more."

Van Steen nodded. "Excuse my ignorance. The box is already here, as it needs to be identified by Monsieur Mutelen. I will fetch the rest." He hurried off.

Moira stared at the box with the museum's logo and swallowed. Her memories threatened to overwhelm her when she noticed Lif's dried blood still staining the lid. Breathing consciously, she turned away and bit her lower lip not to cry. When Tord had set the lid aside, she helped him. Inside lay a long, narrow container of stone and iron. Nothing else.

Tord pulled the plug off the stone container and looked in. It was empty. "Gone! What a loss." He looked devastated, so Moira put her hand on his shoulder.

He looked at her with tears in his eyes. "The thought that greedy thieves are selling valuable artifacts to sleazy private collectors makes my blood boil."

To take Tord's mind off things, she looked closer at the stone container. "What was it for?" It was about as long as her arm and both ends were wound tightly with metal bands.

At first, Tord didn't answer. He still frowned. But when Moira traced the runes cut into the stone with her index finger and asked for their meaning, he relented.

"We don't yet know what the runes say. They are very old and magical. Put your hand here." He pointed to a bit where the runes were placed around a hand-shaped depression.

Reluctantly, Moira put her hand in the print and flinched. "Ouch! I got zapped."

"Impossible." Tord shook his head. "I put my hand on the stone often. There is only a voice talking in an unknown tongue. It's completely harmless."

Moira swallowed and reached out again. Pain shot through her body. Every fiber of her self burned. An unknown voice whispered words into her ear in a strange language. She pulled back her hand. "What's that?"

"I think it's Hern's voice but I can't prove it yet." Tord grinned from one ear to the other. "Impressive, isn't it?"

Moira stared at the hand-shaped depression in the stone. It was obviously magical, because it glittered. Despite her fear of feeling the pain again, her hand was pulled inevitably toward it. She didn't struggle because she had the feeling the message might be important for her. This time, the pain was less severe. Her hand merged with the stone. Slowly, the babbling changed until the words began to make sense.

"TakeCare. TakeCare. TakeCare," the voice murmured. It was decidedly female. A face appeared, transparent and vague, as if the spell had trouble to reconstruct it after all these years. Only her black eyes burned into Moira's soul. "NotOpen. YouListen? NotOpen!"

"Who are you?" Moira's throat felt sore, so she thought her question more than whispering it.

"TheSeal. SeeTheSeal." The voice ebbed away, the face dissipated, and Moira's hand dropped off the stone. She sank to the ground like an empty bag. Just before she lost consciousness, she felt Tord's arms around her.

When she came to, she lay on the ground with her head in Tord's lap. His eyes were full of worry. "Praise and thanks, you're better." He caressed her face. "Franka would have killed me."

"Don't be upset." Excelsior van Steen put a hand on Tord's shoulder. "You couldn't know that our colleague reacts differently to magic than other people. As far as I know she's always had problems with magic." With his free hand he gave Tord a wet cloth. "The paramedics will be here any minute."

Moira sat up. Even without the cloth she felt well rested and fresh. "What happened?"

"You glowed like a lamp and collapsed," Tord said. "I thought I had killed you."

At that moment, the young gendarme who had picked them up entered the archive. "I can take you home now if you're done," he told Tord.

Tord took Moira's hands and looked deeply into her eyes.

"Are you really feeling better? No side effects? Shouldn't I rather stay?"

Moira shook her head. "You'd better go. Franka is waiting and you know her patience."

"I will only leave if I have proof that I didn't harm you permanently."

Moira got up and waved Tord's help aside. "I'm fine. Really."

The paramedics Excelsior van Steen had called attested the same when they arrived a little later. This convinced Tord but he left reluctantly, looking back at her every so often.

When the door closed behind him, the archivist sighed. "Wonderful. Finally you can tackle Sabio's request, and I will be able to concentrate on my work. What a day." He pointed to a cardboard box with thick black letters saying 'HnP 25/19.' Without another word he left her and went back into the fenced part of the archive.

As Moira took the evidence from the box, she contemplated her experience. *I didn't see Hern but Katie.* She was absolutely sure. She was less sure why the legendary woman had appeared to her and not the others who had touched the stone before. Also, she wondered why Tord and the archivist hadn't seen the face. *It must have been a sort of magic that isn't compatible with the others. Either that or someone has gone to a lot of trouble to... do what? Pretend Katie existed? Attack someone who hasn't much magic for defense? But why?* She pondered this while sorting the evidence. When she began to examine each clue thoroughly, she pushed all thoughts of Wild Katie aside.

An hour later she was done but hadn't found anything new. She called the archivist but had to wait quite a while before Van Steen stepped through the mesh wire door to inspect the content of the cardboard box.

"Here is your receipt." He handed her a paper attesting that she had given back all evidence. Then he took the carton and returned to his work.

Moira shook her head at his unfriendly behavior. While she climbed the stairs, she wondered how he had managed to convince anyone to buy his book. At her desk she took the files Buds had left for her and began to sort reports, photos, and analyses.

She was so engrossed in her work that she didn't notice Druidus before he stood beside her. He put a hand on her shoulder and bent down until his breath caressed her cheek. "Did you consider my request? I will fulfill every wish I find in your eyes if you agree on a single date."

Moira's heart fluttered. His dry aftershave muddled her head, and his lips beckoned her, sensual and moist. She closed her eyes to see if he would kiss her unbidden, but he only stood there waiting for her answer.

"Very well," she said. "You can pick me up for dinner tonight. Eight o'clock. Separate bills."

He beamed and squeezed her shoulder gently before hurrying away.

When she returned home, a packet lay in front of her door without address or sender. It definitely hadn't come by regular mail. Moira took it into the kitchen and opened it, and found herself staring at a bundle of letters all addressed to her. All were marked 'Return to Sender.' A folded note lay on top. She read.

Dear Moira,

Please read these letters. They are sorted chronologically. I know you won't forgive me any time soon, but maybe you'll learn to understand. I'm sorry I can't give us back the time lost.

Lavant

Moira let the note sink and breathed deeply. She didn't know whether she should be angry or touched. Hadn't she made it clear enough that she didn't want anything to do with her father? She put the letters aside and dressed up for the evening with Druidus but it was hard to concentrate on makeup or dress.

"Very well," she said to the letters. "But only one." She took the topmost, opened it, and read.

My favorite daughter,

I miss you so much and wish I had said farewell to you despite the doubts. Now, your picture is hanging above my desk. The one with the islands full of butterflies, do you remember? Each time I look at it, I want to cry. My interior designer insists I should get rid of the old furniture, but I just can't. How often did you sit on this desk keeping me from my work? I can't remember if I indulged you or if I got angry often. I only know you're no longer sitting here - and it hurts. More than you can imagine.

If you want, you can come visit. I'll show you my new work and my office (it's bigger than my old one and there is plenty of room on the wall for your pictures). I've got so much more to do than I anticipated, but I'll always have time for you.

Please excuse your old idiot of a father.

Below the words a heart sticker glittered.

Moira bit her lip to keep from crying. She read the next and the next and the next. Between the lines, she saw Lavant's growing despair even though he mostly wrote about his work. Tears ran over her face, leaving black mascara lines. She wondered why her mother had never accepted the letters. Maybe, she would have been able to forgive her father. Snuffling, she read letter by letter. She hardly noticed the time fly by. The doorbell pulled her from her thoughts.

"There is a man claiming to be Druidus van Steen," the nerl said. *Van Steen? Druidus is related to Excelsior?* Moira told the nerl to let him in, stacked the letter on top of the others on the table, and hurried into the bathroom to wash her face and reapply the mascara.

Still, Druidus noticed immediately that she had cried. He put his hand against her cheek. "Can I help you in any way?"

Moira shook her head and dashed past him down the stairs, glad that he didn't insist on learning more.

Chapter 15

They left Druidus' carpisto and walked to a restaurant Moira visited regularly. Silently, Druidus held the chair for her to sit. Then he read the menu. Moira was grateful that he didn't force her to talk. She ordered and sorted her thoughts until the waiter brought the appetizer.

"That looks delicious." Druidus stirred his soup.

"Yes, I…," Moira's lip trembled, "loved this as a child."

Druidus put his hand on hers and looked at her face. "Shall we go? We could sit in the park and talk."

Moira watched Druidus silently. Countless thoughts whirled through her head. Finally she pulled herself together. "I received a whole pile of letters from my father today." Tears dropped into her soup as she told him everything – right from the beginning. It was as if a dam had burst. She even told him some things she hadn't shared with Franka. The warmth of his hand on hers soothed her feelings, but she didn't look at him. "It still hurts that he left us for another woman," she finished.

"There are no guaranties in relationships. It's a pity the kids always suffer the most." Druidus put his other hand on hers too. "On the other hand, without a relationship between your parents, you wouldn't exist. So, for me, it was a good outcome."

"Why did he never visit? I'm scared that my kids will have to suffer like that too, one day."

For a long time, Druidus stayed silent. Finally he spoke with a hoarse voice.

"You're not the only one who is afraid." Both hands on hers, he stared at the tabletop while speaking. "Ever since

I've been old enough, Mom has been dragging girls she wants to see as my girlfriends to my door. Each one was hand-picked by her after a diligent financial check, all of them with great pedigree, of course. Each one of them was as boring as a joke without a punch line. And each one of them was driven away by my father's attitude. I didn't mind. In high school, I fell deeply in love with a girl and eventually introduced her to my parents – after I had warned her. Two days later, she packed all her belongings to move to a different high school. Father had arranged this by giving her a lot of money for a new start. When I confronted her about it, she laughed. Do you know what she said?" He looked up into Moira's eyes. Although he didn't cry, she saw the pain. Seeing as she didn't speak, Druidus answered his own question. "She said a bird in the hand is worth two in the bush. I thought I'd die." He bent forward. "And I didn't love her as much as I love you. Yes, I'm terrified at the thought of getting hurt again. But I'm no longer hiding behind my fear. If you want me, I'm ready to take the risk."

Suddenly, the pain in Moira's heart felt only half as bad as before. Warmth spread from Druidus' hands through her body, and although she didn't want to jubilate, she felt comfortable. That was better than anything she had ever had with a man before.

"By the way," he said and pulled his hands away, "I've known Lavant for many years. He has been visiting my parents often, but I never saw a woman with him."

Moira's head shot up. That was impossible. Hadn't her mother told her over and over again that he had a new love? "But …"

"Maybe you should talk to him one day."

The waiter approached, bent down to Moira, and whispered, "If I have to keep the dishes warm for much longer, it will not be very tasty anymore."

"You may serve." Druidus leaned back to make room.

The food was delicious although the meat had gone a bit dry. They ate in silence, but Moira felt comfortable. She came to a decision before dessert. Her heart thumped in her throat as she spoke. "Well, I won't allow your father to drive me away, and I won't be bribed either."

Druidus' eyes widened.

"Does that mean… Are you… Are we…"

"Let's give it a try. It can't get worse than failing another relationship, right?" A tingle started in her stomach and spread through her body. She beamed – Druidus too. They paid and left.

Druidus stopped in front of the restaurant.

"How about a little walk in the dark?"

Wordlessly, Moira turned toward the park. They strolled along the streets, hand in hand. This late in the evening the park was nearly empty. They sat on a bench near the lake, and Moira rested her head against Druidus' shoulder. He put an arm around her, and they enjoyed the summer evening.

After a while, Druidus bent over and kissed her gently. Moira's lips prickled. She put her hands around his neck, so the kiss would go on.

Something wet and cold slapped around her ears, and an uncomfortably high voice screamed at them.

"Damned vermin. Get off my bench. This is a kiss-free zone." The woman attacked Druidus with bare hands.

Moira flung away the wet shoulder cloth, and Druidus grabbed both the woman's wrists. He got up and forced her to sit on the bench. All fight went out of her, and he let go.

Moira shook her head.

"What was that about? You can't just attack visitors of the park for no reason."

"No reason?" The woman laughed, and a cloud of alcoholic breath surrounded Moira. "You were smooching on my bench. My bench!" She pointed to a brass plate screwed to the backrest. It read, "Donated by Samantha Belz in memory of her beloved father."

Moira's eyes widened.

"You are Samantha Belz? The one Samantha Belz, who knows Pete Huudien?"

"Pete, oh my Pete." The woman put her hands over her face and cried.

"What about him?"

"He's go-ho-hone. Gone like a bird that slipped from the cage." Samantha pulled a bottle from a pocket in her wide coat, put it to her lips and drank deeply. Then she waved Moira and Druidus aside. "Piss off. Leave me alone." She curled up on the bench and fell asleep.

Moira looked at Druidus. She didn't know whether to laugh or cry. "I believe we have found the woman who is madly in love with Huudien," she said.

Druidus nodded. "We should get her into a drunk tank so we can get some sense out of her in the morning." He pulled out his mobile parlebol and called his colleagues from the night shift.

They didn't have to wait for long before a patrol carpisto stopped beside them. Two gendarmes carefully transferred the drunken woman to the back seat and drove off again.

"I want to go home," Moira said.

"Understandable." Druidus linked arms with her. "What a pity the evening had to end like this."

"We'll catch up on it another time." Moira held his arm with both hands and huddled close. "Promise."

The next morning Moira reached her desk just in time before her shift started. She had been sitting in her living room for quite a while, reading her father's letters and wondering why her mother had deprived her of them. She stifled a yawn.

Semra peeked out from interrogation room three and waved her over. "Didn't you want to be here for the questioning?"

Moira hurried into the room and sat beside Semra.

In daylight, Samantha looked even worse for wear than at night. The coat was way too big and dangled around her angular body over in several layers of T-Shirts and pullovers. Her long, blond hair hung limply in her face, and her eyes were red. Samantha snuffled and wiped her nose on the sleeve of her coat. "What do you want with me? I didn't do anything."

"Does this tell you something?" Semra put a drawing with Pete Huudien's face on the table.

Samantha spit on the ground. "Asshole. Like all of them."

"Just because he didn't fall in love with you?"

"What does this Rose tart have that I can't surpass? My love for him is much bigger than hers, and my tits are, too. But the dickhead just didn't want to understand. Not even when I had him all to my self. He only cried. Rosine here, Rosine there. Puke-tastic."

"So you admit to having kidnapped Pete Huudien?" Semra cocked her head.

"That was no kidnapping. I only invited him to my place. Anyway, this Lif so-and-so and his elf friend helped. I thought that if I showed him how much I loved him, he'd stay for good."

"With 'elf friend,' do you mean Bastide Leclerque?"

"Basti, sure."

Moira asked, "Where is Pete Huudien now?"

"Haven't got a clue. He went nuts when I showed him the money Rosi-posy got for us. He pushed me against the table, and when I came to my senses, he was gone. With the money." Samantha wiped her nose on her sleeve again. "I called Lif right away. He took care of everything, Basti said."

Moira paled. She bent to Semra and whispered in her ear. "Does one of the murdered homeless resemble Pete Huudien?"

"Not that I know of. But that might mean we just haven't found his body yet," Semra whispered back." Get Druidus or Buds and fetch Bastide, so we can press him for details. I'll try to get some more information from Mademoiselle Belz." While Moira got up and walked to the door, Semra turned back to Samantha. "Where did you last see Bastide Leclerque?"

"He was on his way to the rail-nerl station because of his job."

In the corridor, Moira found Druidus coming from Sabio's office. She ran to him. "The drunken woman from last night really was the one we've been looking for. She accuses Bastide Leclerque. Semra thinks we should fetch him for more questioning. Do you have time?"

"I am already on my way to Leclerque. The lab identified his fingerprints with some found at the burglary." Druidus grinned. "I think it's about time we ask our elf what happened to the weapons."

"And he might know what Lif did to Pete. If he was the elf in the surveillance globe, he had close contact with both." Moira was happy. Finally there was a clue she could follow, especially together with Druidus. Despite the gray sky, she hopped down the stairs. Druidus followed a little slower. His mobile parlebol rang. When he realized who was calling, his eyebrows shot up. "Oh." He waved Moira over but held the parlebol away from her. "It's your father. He wants to talk to you."

She shook her head, mouthing, "I'm not here."

"I'm sorry, sir. I cannot find her." Druidus ended the call and opened the carpisto. "It's quite difficult to get my number. So why does he phone me and not you?"

"He knows we're working together, and I left my mobile parlebol at home."

"Call him back." He held out his parlebol.

"Sorry, but if I touch it, the water in it will do crazy things. My first one turned into a miniature water fountain, and another one soaked my best friend. Now, I've got a special model." Moira got in. "I'll call him when I'm back home."

"You should talk to Sabio about your magic-related problems. He's got some very weird ideas sometimes, but he might be able to help you." Druidus drove off.

While he threaded through the crowded streets, Moira thought about his suggestion. She liked Sabio. A lot. But could he know more than the numerous doctors her mother had dragged her to?

"We're nearly there," Druidus said.

Moira started and looked around. She hadn't noticed how dark it had grown due to the rain clouds. The wet roads glittered in the light of the Lumières Magiques that were placed in regular intervals along the sidewalks. Only the road they traveled on led into twilight.

Druidus stopped in a parking lot. "We've got to walk from here."

He offered Moira his arm gallantly. She put up the hood of her raincoat and linked arms. Together they walked along the cobbled path to Elveholme. Like most humans, Moira had never been to the elves' quarter. She marveled all the more. Trees stood close to each other like in a wood. From their branches, trunks, and roots, windows of different size blinked. Aside from the cobbled path, there were no roads. Everybody walked or flew where they wanted.

Moira stopped to look at a hand-sized female elf, who pressed both hands and her forehead against the tree with her living quarters. A little later, a baldachin of branches and leaves grew out of the wood above the door to her flat keeping the rain away.

Druidus put his arm around Moira's shoulders. "Impressive, isn't it? It's due to the kind of magic they use. Sometimes I wish I could do this as well." He pulled her along. "It's not far to Bastide's home."

Before Moira could decide whether to shrug off his arm or not, they stopped in front of a gigantic oak. "It's up there." He pointed to a staircase that had grown from the trunk leading round and round. Between the branches, Moira spotted the entrance of a flat also grown from living wood.

One after the other, they climbed the stairs. At the top, an elf stood that was barely smaller than Druidus. "I'm sorry, but no admittance," he said. His light green clothes with the yellow crown stitched on the chest identified him as a member of the Royal Guard.

Druidus pushed past her and showed his ID. "Gendarmerie Magique. What happened?"

The guard didn't move. "You have no jurisdiction here."

Druidus didn't let him say more. "We are making inquiries in a kidnapping, a murder, and a burglary. Leclerque Bastide is strongly suspected of having committed at least one of the crimes."

"It doesn't matter. He's dead." The guard lowered his spear. "And now, you'd better leave." Another guard landed beside Druidus, a female this time.

"Surprise, surprise, our favorite human." The elf kissed Druidus' cheek. Her uniform turned into an evening dress with a very low neckline. "What are you doing here, my sweets?"

"Your Majesty." Druidus lowered himself to one knee. "Please excuse my appearance but it is of utmost importance that we may examine the crime scene too. Methinks Leclerque Bastides's demise is connected to two cases we are investigating. I appeal to your immeasurable benevolence."

"Charmer." The queen laughed, and it sounded like the singing of a bird. Then her gaze became hard. "What will you give Us?"

"Your Majesty knows that I do not own anything of importance."

"Not you, but maybe your companion." The elf queen turned around.

Moira noticed a craving in her eyes that made her worry, and she felt her palms grow hot and wet. Clumsily, she tried to curtsy.

The queen took Moira's chin in her hand and stared into her eyes. "Let Us have your aura, girl. You can't use it anyway. Without it, you'll be able to use magic like every other human."

The suggestion was tempting. For a moment, Moira imagined how she would enjoy using all the things others took for granted. But then she remembered the stories she had heard about the elf queen. Most people regretted their bargains later. Also, her greedy gaze made Moira shiver all over, and the royal fingers burned on her skin. She cleared her throat, but before she could talk, Druidus spoke.

"She is an aspirant of the Gendarmerie. You may not ask her for compensation yet because her contract is not finalized."

Moira ignored his excuse. *There has to be something we can give the queen beside my aura.* She closed her eyes and thought.

Deep inside, she felt the gentle swell of the waves that had created the weird shield on the carnival. She remembered that she had often used these waves as a kid to create illusions she could play with. *If only I knew how I did that back then.* She opened her eyes again.

The queen had pulled Druidus to his feet and leaned against his wide chest. A pang of jealousy shot through Moira like a lightning bolt.

The queen's voice was low and hoarse. "My offer still stands, sweets. Gift Us one night, and you shall have whatever takes your fancy."

"We all know that none of your lovers fared truly well, your Majesty." Druidus stood stiff as a rod, not moving one muscle.

The queen pursed her lips and turned away. "In that case We will not allow you to enter."

The wave inside of Moira surged and spilled out of her. Like a fountain of multi-colored water, it shot up high and returned. Beside herself, no one took notice of the colorful show. When the tingling in her body subsided, she discovered an egg in her hands. It glowed from the inside and pulsed in shades of green. A tiny golden crown was engraved into the shell at the top.

"Good catch, and there was no warning even," Druidus said. "What is it?"

"An egg." The admiration in his eyes made her blush, especially since she didn't know where the green wonder had come from. Had it been the wave again? At least, Moira knew who it was meant for, because to the crown. She held it out to the queen who had already spread her wings, ready to take off. "Your Majesty, might this please your heart?"

The queen gazed at the egg once and paled. With shaking hands, she took it, lifted it to her face, and examined it thoroughly. Then she kissed it and bundled it against her chest. The gaze she used on Moira was icy. "Where did you get this?"

A shiver ran down Moira's spine. She had to answer as truthfully as she could because the elf queen was able to spot lies. Also, she didn't know where the egg had come from, and there was no way she could explain the wavy power inside of her. While she was still searching for words, Druidus answered.

"It fell from the tree's crown. Luckily she caught it or it would have smashed."

The queen paled even more. Her green face seemed nearly white. The egg pressed against her chest, she waved the guard aside. "Allow the gendarme and his assistant access to the crime scene once Our guards finish working. And keep them updated about any progress you make, as long as it concerns their investigations."

The guard bowed, and the queen took off. She melted into the canopy so fast, Moira's gaze couldn't follow.

"I'm wondering where the egg came from." Druidus looked up into the tree's crown.

Moira shrugged. "I rather wonder why it seemed so important to her. It was only an egg, if a rather beautiful one."

"You humans are so ignorant!" The guard shook his head. "You gift Our most gracious queen the child she has been awaiting for centuries, and you don't even know it. How stupid is that?"

Moira looked at the ground. She hadn't known that elves got their children in an egg.

The guard pointed to a bench at the rim of the platform in front of the flat. "You can wait there."

Chapter 16

Druidus and Moira sat. While they waited, Moira pondered the strange power that had helped her twice already. Secretly she wondered why Druidus hadn't noticed her strange skills. *Could it be that I'm not as magically challenged as everyone believes? Could I have hidden my magic away subconsciously and forced people not to notice? But why does everything change right now?* Although it took the team of elfin investigators a long time to finish, she didn't find answers. *I just wish I had someone I could talk to about this.* The whole situation felt unreal to Moira until the wooden coffin with Leclerque Bastide's body was carried past them. At that point, she realized that another life had ended violently. Again they hadn't come in time to save him. She wondered if that had been the reason why her father had turned his back on the gendarmerie.

Finally, the guard waved. "You've got the whole flat to yourself. Should you find something we didn't, let me know. I'll wait out here."

"How did Bastide die?" Druidus slipped on a pair of cotton gloves he took from the emergency packet on his belt.

"We haven't got a final diagnosis." The guard shrugged. "Although we haven't found anything, it seems as if he touched Cold Iron unprotected. His right arm has been completely charred, not to mention the hole in his chest."

Moira felt ill by the description alone. She pressed her lips together. Druidus thanked the guard and entered Bastide's flat. If he lowered his head a little, the door was just big enough to let him in.

Moira pulled herself together and followed him. While she put on the rubber gloves Druidus handed to her, she looked around. Bastide seemed to have a foible for big rooms. The flat was one big room used as kitchen, living and sleeping quarters simultaneously. Only the bathroom was separated by a door that stood slightly ajar now. The walls and the ground were covered in blue stains marked with yellow flags.

"What's that?" Moira pointed at the stains.

"Blue blood. Bastide must have been related to the royals. So, that's why the queen came personally." Druidus went into the bathroom and lowered himself to his knees. "Let's get started." He began to search the ground.

Moira swallowed. She couldn't take her gaze from the blue blood. It reminded her too much of the way she had found Lif's body. She even thought the pattern of the stains was similar. She closed her eyes and clenched her fist. *Stop looking and do your work*, she ordered herself. *Do not think about Lif or Bastide. You can't help either.*

Reluctantly she walked to the sleeping area and let her hand glide over the few pieces of furniture. They grew directly from the tree's wood that also formed walls and roof. Table and bed were covered in leaves, and the windowless back wall was covered in a decorative mosaic of different plants in pots of living wood. Moira was reaching out to pluck a withered leave from the mosaic when she froze. Between the tendrils, leaves, and flowers stuck a dagger. The grip, wrapped with rusty wire, melted into the mosaic in a way that made it difficult to discover. Moira called for Druidus.

"You really are astounding. I would never have found this." He looked at her with so much admiration, she felt uncomfortable.

"Shall I pull it out?" she asked.

"Let's see if we can find fingerprints first." He pulled a small box from his emergency pack and asked her to step back. "This makes prints visible that have been there for less than four hours." He took a pinch of red powder from the box, blew it on the hilt, and said the activation spell.

Immediately, fiery lines flashed and showed two prints in red.

"What luck I took my photo-nerl," Moira said. She pulled out the hand-sized gadget and took some zoomed pictures.

Druidus laughed. "I got one too. It's part of the standard emergency pack." He repeated the procedure with a second powder, blue this time, which made older prints visible. He got four blue prints that became visible under the red ones. Moira took their picture too.

Druidus examined the dagger as thoroughly as possible without pulling it from the wall. "It looks quite old. Do you think it could be from among the missing artifacts from the museum?"

"I think so." Moira pointed to a couple of runes carved into the lower end of the handle. "There were several engraved daggers on the list. Maybe we can find this one. Tord will know for sure."

"We'd better take a picture of the whole dagger, since we'll have to leave this one for the elves until they close their investigation."

"What a pity." Moira took another picture of the dagger. Then she plucked some more leaves and took more pictures. The edge was jagged and covered in black rust. Still, it had cut into the wood for nearly half an inch.

"The deepness of the cut makes me think it was thrown." Druidus took a cord from his bag and pressed one end into Moira's hand. "Let's see where it came from." He explained to Moira what she had to do. Then he pressed the nail at his end of the cord against the wall right above the dagger. Holding her end and led by his commands, Moira walked into the room until blade, hilt, and cord were aligned. Then he said the activation spell. The cord stiffened and stood in the air except for the bit Moira held in her hand. It stiffened too when she let it go.

"Wonderful." Druidus covered the ground below the cord with his red powder and activated it. Footprints became visible. Moira took overlapping pictures of the whole area. The tracks showed exactly what had happened.

"He was visited by a human." Moira examined the prints of sneakers leading from the door into the room. Bastide's smaller prints started at the bed. Obviously, he had been asleep when his visitor came.

"It seems as if he didn't expect anyone." Druidus gazed at a circle where one half consisted of Bastide's prints and the other half of the human's. Right where Bastides's footprints met the line marked by the cord, he had stepped forward. "Looks like he threw the dagger but missed his target."

"The pain from the metal on the hilt must have been terrible," said Moira. "Still, he clung to it all the way from the bed. Why didn't he throw it right away?"

"Maybe he had hoped to get away. See, his footprints are not fully formed. He probably tiptoed. Elves can be surprisingly quiet."

"But if he intended to flee, why did he put up with the pain from the dagger?"

"It's valuable, isn't it? Also, it was at least something he could use to defend himself somehow. Poor sod." Druidus put his arm around Moira's shoulders. With tears in her eyes, she stared at the place where the trail of bloodstains began. As much as she felt sorry for Bastide, her brain was alert.

"There is very little blood; only the splashes, no puddles. Don't you think that's strange?"

Druidus shrugged.

"First, Bastide wasn't very big, and second, he was killed by Cold Iron according to the guard's assessment. It probably burned the wound so much that hardly any blood escaped. The murder weapon could have been a long knife."

They stood silently. Moira leaned her head against Druidus' shoulder feeling consoled and protected. It made bearable the sense of deficiency she had when she thought about Lif or the dead elf.

"It's not easy to work for the department of serious crimes," Druidus said. "Maybe you should reconsider if you really want to work with us."

As if I'm the one to decide. Moira didn't want to think about her problem, since she was still teetering between hope and anger when she thought of her appointment with the auralogist. She straightened up and wound herself out of Druidus' arm. "Let's keep going."

Half an hour later, they finished without new clues. The glowing footprints had faded and the cord had been packed. Druidus called the guard and showed him the dagger. Then he pulled it out and handed it to the elf in a padded evidence bag. "We also took pictures of the footprints. We will send copies."

The guard thanked them with a short nod and waved them out of the flat. Moira and Druidus watched him seal the entrance before they returned to their carpisto.

At the station, Moira took the photo-nerl to the lab immediately. They developed the pictures faster than she expected, and the result of the fingerprint analysis was equally speedy. As expected, the red prints were those of Leclerque Bastide. The blue ones were Lif Borson's.

Moira wasn't surprised but it was satisfying to finally have proof for one of their many theories. She hurried to Sabio's office where Druidus already waited. They entered together.

Commissaire Marten looked tired, and his hair stood up in all directions, but at least he had shaved. Photos of the dead homeless covered the desk in front of him. He focused on Moira completely, however, when she told him about Bastide's murder and the evidence they had found. When she was done, he leaned back and sighed.

"Let's recap the whole mess. We've got two men, Borson and Bastide, who broke into the National Museum to steal a box of freshly excavated antiques. Both have been murdered by an unknown third person, and the only proof we've got is a dagger that might be part of the stolen goods, but which is currently under lock and key with the elf queen's Royal Guard."

"Also, we're still missing the second nightwatchman, who might have been kidnapped or not," Druidus said.

A flash of inspiration hit Moira. "What if there isn't an unknown third? Huudien could have staged his kidnapping to cover his tracks."

Sabio cocked his head. "Does that fit in with Samantha Belz's statement?"

"I think so," Moira said. "Samantha insists she invited Pete to her place with Lif's and Bastide's help. From there, he eventually fled. If Pete were in league with the two, it would have been easy to use this situation for a staged kidnapping."

Sabio nodded. "That's possible." He turned to Druidus. "Take Buds and Semra and try to find out where Pete Huudien is right now. Use every contact and informant we've got, and talk to his fiancée again, too."

Druidus nodded. "And Moira?"

"I've got a different task for her." Sabio waited until Druidus had left before he turned to Moira. "This came by Internal Mail." He handed her a letter with the RealJob™ logo, and Moira read.

DEAR COMMISSAIRE MARTEN,

AFTER CONSULTING WITH THE PERSONNEL OFFICE, WE SCHEDULED A PRACTICAL QUALIFICATION TEST FOR MADEMOISELLE BELLAMIE ON MONDAY, 27TH OF DRALLOR 3019, WHERE SHE CAN GIVE PROOF OF HER MAGICAL TALENTS AS FAR AS EXISTENT.

THERE, SHE WILL ALSO HAVE THE CHANCE TO ARGUE HER CASE REGARDING THE HANDICAPPED PEOPLE'S EQUALITY LAW. HOWEVER, SHE IS NO LONGER AUTHORIZED TO PARTICIPATE IN EXTERNAL DUTY UNTIL THIS POINT.

SINCERELY,

APARTA DE FREES

Moira looked up. "What does that mean?"

"I can neither let you run with Buds and Semra, nor with Druidus in the next few days."

Moira pressed her lips together.

"Don't look like that. It's only three days and a weekend." Sabio took the letter back. "I think it might be for insurance reasons. That's the norm."

"What shall I do until next Monday?" Moira put her hands into the pockets of her trousers and clenched them.

"I want you to go into the archive to help Excelsior van Steen with his work. Due to these serial murders," he pointed at the photos on his desk, "he's got so much to do that he asked for an assistant. Unfortunately, all personnel are needed for investigations."

The familiar cold feeling of disappointment seeped through Moira's body. She had enjoyed participating actively.

"Don't be sad. The archive is really fascinating. I have tried several times myself to get transferred," Sabio said. "And on Tuesday, you can go with Druidus again. After all, you're the first partner ever that he didn't complain about."

Moira swallowed her negative feelings and smiled as best she could. "I'm not surprised." She remembered the kiss in the park.

"Wonderful. You know, Excelsior's work is likely the most important part of the Gendarmerie." Sabio bent forward and pushed the pictures into a pile. "Every piece of evidence goes over his table. The files of every single case, be it solved or not, rest in his catacombs. You can learn a lot from him, and maybe you will stumble on a clue we have overlooked." He put his left hand on the pile of pictures. "So many dead homeless, and we're not a step closer to the murderer. And the press is increasing the strain. The public wants to see results."

"Don't we have any hints to the identity of the killer?"

Sabio shook his head. "We can't even say for sure whether it's one or several culprits. There are no links between the murdered people except for the fact that all were homeless."

"How did they... I mean, what was the murder weapon?"

"They were stabbed with a very sharp blade, about ten centimeters wide. After that, the murderer bled them. The most curious fact is that the murderer or murderers took the blood along. I wonder why?" He pushed back his hair with his fingers. "An illegal blood bank for vampires doesn't make sense as long as there are shops with free blood sales. It's driving me crazy. But the worst thing is that I've got the feeling I overlooked something important." He slammed his fist down on the table before spreading the photos anew.

Moira understood him much better than he could know. Since she didn't want to keep him from work, she said goodbye and left.

Excelsior van Steen frowned when she reported for duty. "Very well, if you're all Sabio can spare..." He pointed to a pile of files on a table beside a half-filled shelf. "They need to be sorted by case number and put into the correct compartment."

Resigned, Moira set to work.

Chapter 17

The next day, she sorted files. That wasn't very satisfying but she got the chance to ponder the relationships with her father and Druidus.

When the clock-nerl called out the end of her shift, she dropped everything. She reached the desk in the entrance area where Excelsior van Steen worked precisely at the same moment that Druidus entered.

Excelsior frowned. "Would it be too much to ask to leave me alone during work hours, son?"

Druidus grinned. "First, my shift is over, and second, I haven't come for you." He offered Moira his arm and pulled her along to the exit.

Moira felt Excelsior's gaze like daggers on her back. It took a load off her mind when the fireproof iron door closed behind them. On the way up, she looked at Druidus questioningly.

"Are you sure he loves you?"

Druidus' laugh echoed through the stairway. "He hates being disturbed when he's working. Just wait what he'll say when I tell him about us."

Moira swallowed. All of a sudden, her father seemed comparably nice. She came to a decision and asked, "Can you take me to my father's company?"

Wordlessly, Druidus opened the door to the parking lot.

In front of the company's building, Druidus got out of the carpisto and accompanied her to the door.

Moira put her hand on his arm. "Please, Druidus. I need to talk to him alone."

He opened his mouth as if to object, closed it, and nodded. "I'll see you later." He kissed her cheek and went back to his vehicle.

Moira watched him drive away until the carpisto was lost in the traffic. A little later, she stood in front of her father's office.

The secretary pointed to a chair. "Monsieur Bellamie will be free soon. If you would wait a little moment."

Moira sat. When the little moment had stretched into half an hour, she was fed up. "I want to see my father now," she said and got up.

The secretary hurried around her desk and grabbed Moira's arm to hold her back.

"You can't go in like that. Your father is working with highly sensitive data."

Moira thought of the pile of files on her desk in the archive and grinned. "So am I. I will not get them tangled." She freed herself, knocked, and entered without waiting for an answer.

"It's not eight yet," Lavant said. Only then did he look up from his papers. His face lost all color, and Moira suspected his legs wouldn't have carried him if he had tried to stand. He moved his lips as if he wanted to talk but no sound came out.

"Good evening, Father."

"Father?" The word seemed to cost Lavant incredible strength. "I haven't been much of a father to you. I was a coward and an idiot."

With surprise, Moira noticed tears in his eyes. She struggled not to cry herself. "Why did you leave like that? Why did you start a new life?"

"It wasn't as easy as you make it out. I left because your mother couldn't bear the changes in my life."

"With changes you mean the new woman?"

"Your mother has always been the only woman for me." Lavant stared at his hands. "And my work. It was my company she hated, and she didn't want anything to do with it."

"You could have visited me at least." Moira's lower lip trembled but she couldn't stop it.

"Your mother asked me not to. She thought I'd be too preoccupied to be a good father for you, and that I'd make it harder for you to accept the situation. I wasn't even allowed to say goodbye."

Moira was taken aback. Had her mother lied to her?

Lavant got up, walked around the desk, and took her hands. "How I longed to talk to you or hold your hand in all those years. Your mother and I decided this because we thought it'd be best for you. But it hurt me so much."

"It hurt you? You?" Moira didn't feel the tears burn on her cheeks. "What about me? I thought someone cut out my heart alive. I thought you didn't love me anymore."

Lavant hugged her wordlessly. He pressed her close as if he'd never let her go again. His arms shook, and his voice too. "We meant to spare you sorrow, not cause you pain. You were supposed to have a home without having to choose between your parents."

Moira cried into his chest like a small child. "I missed you so terribly."

Lavant kissed her crown and held her until she recovered. "Can you forgive your mother and me?"

"I don't know." Moira stepped back and wiped away her tears. "I really don't know, but I'll try."

"Thank you." Lavant kissed her hands. "From now on, I'll always be there for you. I promise I will never leave you again."

The kind of warmth Moira had missed since her childhood spread through her body. It was a wonderful feeling, much like what she felt when thinking of Druidus. *Maybe everything will come right after all*, she thought.

Lavant straightened up. "You know what? I'll finish early today, and we'll have a bite to eat together, all right?"

They left the office arm in arm. The secretary's eyebrows shot up. "You're leaving already?"

"Some things are more important than work." He smiled down at Moira. "You can go home now, too."

They entered the nerlift. Moira leaned against the wall and waited for the nerls to start working before she asked, "Why does mother hate your company so much?"

Lavant stroked his smooth shaved chin and sighed before he answered. "Your mother needs a regulated family life to be happy, and I couldn't give her that after I left the Gendarmerie. To work freelance means to work all the time with hardly any break. I hardly ever go home before nine in the evenings."

"Even now?" Moira cocked her head. "What's so important you can't leave it to your secretary?"

"My clients." Lavant smirked which made him look years younger. "The files we have for our cases can only be reviewed by the one working on the case and by me. When the case is solved, I control the paperwork to make sure the work was top notch. I have a reputation to protect."

Moira had an idea.

"Did Bastide keep files too?"

"Sure. In that regard, he was perfect. Funnily enough, he enjoyed writing reports."

They reached the cellar, and the nerlift's doors slid open.

"May I have a look at them?" Moira linked arms with Lavant and allowed him to lead her through the badly lit underground garage.

"None of his cases were directly related to his death or the Gendarmerie would have appeared with a search warrant right away."

"But maybe he wrote a diary about his friendship with Lif. You said yourself he enjoyed stuff like that."

"Come back tomorrow, and you can have my office for the evening, my dear. But only because you will inherit the whole shenanigan anyway one day." With a wide gesture encompassing the whole building, Lavant opened the door to his luxurious carpisto. "No more talk about work now. I want to know everything you do in your spare time. Do you still meet with Franka?"

The next morning Druidus waited in front of her door when she came down. He hugged her and kissed her gently. "I thought I'd show you around the archive before father arrives. He keeps forgetting that not everyone knows their way around as well as he does."

Moira was glad for the offer, so they walked along the shelves hand in hand some time later. The vaulted cellar was gigantic, and the deeper they ventured the darker it got. Only the glowing of the cursed weapons' magic lit the semidarkness. Moira felt like she was in a horror movie.

Druidus pointed to the many corridors. "All in all, the structure of the archive is rather simple. There are four main corridors parallel to each other that lead from the entrance desk to the outside walls. From there, crossways lead past the shelves." He pointed to the faraway outside wall on the right of the vault. "This section contains cursed weapons. Father and Sabio are working on a method to destroy them without harm. The rest," his arm swept around in a big arc, "hold all the files. Come, I'll show you something." He pulled her along to a corridor near the back of the cellar. The files were dusty and the cardboard covers looked as if they'd crumble any moment. Many files weren't bound in cardboard but in leather. The air smelled of dust and tannic acid. Moira held her breath as best she could.

"Careful, this is really scary." Druidus took a file from the shelf and opened the lid. A scream echoed through the vault, never seeming to end. It chilled Moira to the bone and she pressed her hand on her ears. The scream ended abruptly when Druidus closed the file. "Up to roughly forty years ago, the death screams of the victims were magically recreated and stored to convict and punish the murderers. It was stopped when psychiatrists realized that the relatives of the victims suffered far more under this method than the killers." He put the file back.

"I'm relieved." Moira imagined what a strain the noise must have been for the gendarmes of that time. "Can we leave now?" She couldn't stand the smell much longer. "Why do we have to keep the files for so long?"

"The law dictates fifty years but many files are much older. Father thinks we should keep the Gendarmerie's past alive for following generations." Druidus led her back to the more modern part of the vault. "Sabio would like to move part of the files into a different room, but Father refuses, and so far, he's got what he wants."

His gaze fell on the clock over Excelsior's workbench. "I think I'd better leave. Father will be here soon." He kissed her and hurried away.

Moira was sitting on the chair at the desk assigned to her when she heard Excelsior enter the archive. Without a greeting, he handed her a new pile of files to sort. With a sigh, she set to work. The only ray of hope was the fact that she could study Bastide's private files this evening.

Finally time to quit. Moira sped up the stairs and wondered if Druidus would take her to Lavant's company again. She was just about to hurry through the entrance door when she noticed Druidus waiting beside his carpisto. She hesitated when she saw a woman with blond curls hurry toward him. The expensive designer costume seemed familiar. She stood rooted as Druidus hugged Aparta de Frees and kissed her heartily on the mouth. All of a sudden, her throat was parched, and her knees shook.

So, he did lie after all. Tears shot into her eyes. She stumbled toward a bench in the hall and sank onto it. *I wonder if he ever truly loved me. Or did he only playact? I'm such an idiot.* She put her hands on her knees, closed her eyes, and forced herself not to cry. She wouldn't let Druidus see her desperation. After a while, she had her feelings under control again. She pushed her chin out and walked to the door. Druidus and Aparta had left.

No problem, I'm not going to see him again anyway. She bit her lower lip and went to stop a taxi.

Lavant led her into a small office filled with plants. The walls were covered in creepers, and the low desk was a single massive plank of oak. A cardboard box stood on top.

"These are the last few cases Bastide worked on," Lavant said. "The older cases are in the archive just in case you need them. I couldn't find anything else but you can have a look for yourself." He kissed Moira's cheek and left her alone.

Moira crouched in front of the desk, unpacked the files, and opened the first one. She caught herself thinking of

Druidus. With a frown, she pressed her lips together and forced herself to read the tiny script. Bastide had recorded every detail of the case, but there was nothing about Lif – and not in the next one or the one after. Still, she read every single file thoroughly. When she opened the second to last folder, a name jumped out at her.

EXCELSIOR VAN STEEN AGAINST UNKNOWN.

What did Bastide have to do with Druidus' father? She delved into the words. Soon, she realized that Excelsior had suspected his wife of having an affair. According to his own statement, he feared more that his good name would suffer than considering his wife's lover a problem. He had hired the elf to find out the man's identity so he could remove him from his wife's life with a generous sum of money.

Just like he did with Druidus' girlfriend, Moira thought. *He probably thinks he can buy everything with his money. I just hope his wife's lover won't fall for this.*

The last letter Bastide had written to Excelsior asked for the payment of the agreed sum. After reception of the money, Bastide had meant to tell him the name of the lover. The letter had been dated to the day of Bastide's death. That meant that Excelsior didn't know the result of Bastide's research. And it wasn't in the file either. *Serves him right.* Moira closed the file. The last folder contained a detailed report about the happenings on the carnival and about Bastide's arrest. Moira put it aside and wondered if he had hidden a diary somewhere. She looked for hidden drawers in the desk and secret compartments under the floorboards or in the walls without success. Finally she gave up and went to her father to say goodbye.

He didn't let her keep him from taking her home personally. When they stopped in front of her house, he turned and looked into her eyes. "You've been under a dark cloud the whole evening. Don't you want to tell me what's wrong?"

Moira froze. Was she so easy to read? She couldn't tell him about Druidus. The wound was too raw. She needed an excuse, and fast.

"They shunted me into the archive to sort files."

"That's not all, is it?" Lavant cocked his head.

Moira folded her arms in front of her chest and stared at the dashboard. Lavant waited. She really couldn't tell him. He'd been the first man who deserted her. How could she? She glanced at him sideways, but he just sat there, silent and strong. His presence eased her mind like it used to do when she had problems as a kid. Still, her pain was none of his business anyway.

"There's nothing else."

"Honey, I'm a good judge of sorrow. I've had years of practice, and I know what went wrong in my case. Maybe I can help?" His eyes pleaded with her, so she looked away again.

Fiddling with her fingers, she considered his offer. Maybe he was right and talking about the betrayal would soothe her feelings. But what if she bared her soul and there was no help? A part of her longed to tell him all her problems and another part fought against that feeling. After a long struggle, her feeling won out.

"The man I thought loved me kissed someone else."

"That's not the end of the world." Lavant put his hand on her arm. "Talk to him. There might be a good reason for the kiss. You won't find a perfect partner but you will not find the best there is if you jump to conclusions."

"You sound like Franka."

"Really? Maybe I should revive our contact." Lavant grinned.

Suddenly, the world didn't seem half as dark as before. It was possible that she misjudged the kiss. She tried to think whether it had been a passionate one or not, but she couldn't tell. At the thought of talking to Druidus about the situation, her stomach plummeted. She smiled wearily.

"Thank you," she said and kissed his cheek. "I will think about it."

Chapter 18

She pondered the whole night whether to talk to Druidus or not. She even thought about it the next day at work. Sorting and filing the folders was so monotonous she nearly fell asleep, but at least it soothed her troubled mind a little. When the end of her shift drew near, there was a single folder left on her table. Relieved, she patted the cardboard cover. It was the file on the burglary of the National Museum.

Since Excelsior was nowhere in sight, she opened it. Beside the report she had written, there were several copies of drawings labeled by Tord and dated with the day and time of the find. Interested, Moira examined the pictures. The box had only held weapons. There were knives, lances, arrow- and spearheads, hunting knives and swords, as well as a drawing of the dagger that had stuck in Bastide's wall. *I knew it.* Satisfied, she nodded and turned the page. The next drawing pictured the metal-bound stone urn. It was the only drawing with Lif's handwriting on it. Moira recognized his letters immediately. With a lot of attention to detail, he described the seal. He had also added a drawing of it. In the middle, there was a stylized anvil with a hammer standing vertically over it. Seven parallel semicircular lines led around Hern's hammer. They reminded Moira of a rainbow without the color.

A shiver ran down her spine when she remembered the warning she got when she had touched the urn. According to Lif, a leather-wrapped sword had been inside the stone's cavity. Before Moira could search for the drawing of the sword, footsteps approached from behind.

"You're supposed to put the files away, not read them." Excelsior sounded annoyed.

Moira pushed the drawings back into the file and placed it in the appropriate shelf.

Excelsior was already on his way back to the front. "Bring the mace from shelf seven, compartment one hundred and fifteen, to the desk at the entrance. Under no circumstances are you to take it out of the safety bag. There is a homicide spell on it."

"What is a homicide spell?"

"Don't they teach you anything at the academy anymore?" The archivist sighed. Moira opened her mouth to explain that the university had not employed an academic for Magical Theory in many years, but Excelsior didn't give her a chance to speak. "It is a spell forcing the user of the mace to kill someone with it. As long as the weapon is inside the protective cover, the spell is neutralized."

Moira thanked him for the explanation and left to find the shelf. The vault got darker the farther in she went. Despite trying hard, she didn't manage to create a sufficiently big Lumière Magique. The tiny ball of light over her head only illuminated a short stretch of the corridor in front of her.

When she reached shelf seven, she walked more slowly. Weapons filled the whole construction. Where was compartment one hundred and fifteen? She squinted at the numbers on the uprights. Her light flickered and died. Annoyed, she created a new one. The constant concentration made her sweat. It took her a while to find the correct compartment. She took the mace – including the cover – and hurried back to the entrance desk. When she saw the light, she let hers die with a sigh of relief. She was drenched in sweat. *The doctors and auralogists are right after all. I am magically handicapped. The few spells I do get right are hardly more than flukes.* She placed the mace on the desk and looked around for Excelsior. He stood near the fireplace together with Sabio. They stood in front of a glass casket the length of an arm that stood on a platform of wood with wheels.

"And you're sure it works?" Excelsior looked skeptical.

"I tried it half a dozen times. The burning box works without a fault." Sabio put a hand on the archivist's shoulder. "But I have to prepare it since it can't be transported over longer distances when the fire spell is in place. It'd be too dangerous."

Excelsior looked at Moira and waved. "Bring the weapon."

Moira obeyed. Fascinated, she watched Sabio raise a ward standing in the hall like an oversized hemisphere of faceted crystal.

In the middle, he drew a pentagram with red crayon. Around the five-pointed star, he placed symbolic items: one candle on every point of the star, and in between he put a skull, a dried paw of a rabbit, a potted four-leaved clover, a few drops of blood, and a bow with eternal fire. The blue flames flickered and shadows danced over the vault's walls. In front of the eternal fire, he drew a circle with blue crayon. He put on the obligatory safety coat and donned the pointy hat that focused magic.

Moira thought he looked like an apprentice magician from an old painting with his dark blue star-spangled safety clothes.

"You'd better stand back. I raised a ward and it might be better to stay outside of it just in case." Sabio opened the glass casket's lid.

Moira and Excelsior withdrew until they stood outside his ward. Sabio stepped into the blue circle and murmured a spell. Then, he reached his hands upward to the vaulted ceiling and called, "En Feu! Semera Magique! Rougisse! Lumière!"

It hissed. Sabio's knees trembled when the magic swept through his body like a whirl of stars. Sabio sparkled and glittered. The spell he had to control had to be a very strong one. Impressed, Moira stared at the Commissaire. She has thought that the direct use of magic was only employed in laboratories and factories.

Sabio's spell shot through the eternal fire and ripped it along into the open glass box. A glaringly bright flame lit up the vault. Blue flames wavered in the burning box.

"Lumière." Sabio called the activation word once more, and the flames died. He left the circle and walked over to Excelsior. "Go ahead, try it."

The archivist pushed a white lock of hair from his face, put on a pair of safety gloves, and picked up the mace with its cover. Hesitantly, he put it into the glass box, which closed automatically. He activated the spell, and a blue flame pulverized the weapon.

He beamed at Sabio. "Your invention is incredible. Finally, we can destroy the cursed weapons without danger. Sometimes I think you're much better suited to work down here than I am."

Moira had never seen the archivist this happy. She raced off immediately when he asked her in a rather friendly tone to fetch coffee. When she returned Sabio leaned against the desk, touching the signature field of a return form for files with his left hand. A purple flame ran around all of his fingers and condensed into his initials while the men discussed the murders of the homeless.

Sabio shook his head. "No, there are no leads on the killer. The murders continue. There's one nearly every night."

"At least the press is holding back." Excelsior took the form and examined the signature.

"It's because I begged them during the press conference." Sabio took the coffee with a grateful smile. "But they won't hold out much longer."

"What about the burglary at the museum?" Excelsior filed the form and took a coffee too.

Sabio shrugged. "There is no trace of our main suspect, Pete Huudien. I've got men observing his flat and his fiancée, so far without any result."

"Is the burglary related to the murders?"

"I can't prove it nor can I exclude it. The only sure fact is that Lif Borson's and Bastide Leclerque's deaths are connected to the theft."

Moira fell in. "We should work together with Director du Mar. He..."

Excelsior frowned at her with obvious disdain. "Haven't you learned that it's impolite to interrupt grown-ups?"

"Let her." Sabio turned to Moira. "Your idea is good, generally. Unfortunately his wife has managed to obtain a court order that doesn't allow us to talk to him."

Excelsior shook his head. "You're much too nice, Sabio. The greenhorns from the academy have to learn discipline first and foremost." He waved Moira aside. "I put more files out for you. Get to work."

With a shrug, Moira returned to her desk. *At least I will be able to have a look at the sword from the stone urn as long as they talk.* She took the last file from the shelf. It was the wrong one. *That's impossible.* Frantically, Moira searched the archived documents, but the file she was looking for was missing. *Did Sabio ask for it?* She thought hard but couldn't remember if there had been a folder on the entrance desk or not. *Maybe Excelsior hid it away so I can't read it.* She sighed and returned to sorting the folders.

A little later, Excelsior dropped more files on her desk. "I hope you can manage without supervision for a while. I have to go to court for a few hours." When he noticed Moira's questioning look, he added, "As authorized expert," and left.

The clock in the entrance hall rang six. End of shift. Moira dropped everything and went into the entrance hall. She looked for Excelsior van Steen because she didn't want to leave the archive unattended but couldn't lock it without a key. She looked over to his personal desk on the side behind the fence near the fireplace. A couple of gadgets stood on half of the big wooden table and papers covered the other half. Since she thought Excelsior close, she walked over and called for him.

"Monsieur van Steen?" Her gaze took in the chaos on his desk. Right on top, she noticed a sheaf of paper with the patent office logo. Curious, she picked it up and read. It was a patent application for the burning box. Moira's eyes widened when she noticed Excelsior had given his own name as inventor. *What a twerp! He adorns himself with borrowed plumes. Just you wait until I tell Sabio.* She replaced the application exactly where she had found it and walked back into the entrance area of the vaults. She had hardly closed the mesh wire door when Excelsior came in.

"Shouldn't you be at work?" His voice cut the air like a knife.

"It's past six."

"Oh. Well, then." He walked past her without looking at her. "Don't be late tomorrow."

Moira didn't think it her duty to remind him that she wouldn't be working on the weekend due to her status as aspirant on probation. *He'll find out eventually.* As fast as she could, she ran to Sabio's office but it was locked. *Drat, he's gone already.* She was wondering who might know Sabio's private parlebol number when Semra walked along the corridor.

"What luck to meet you," Moira said. "Do you know how I can reach Commissaire Marten? It's important."

"I don't think you'll get him today any more. He's been called to another murder. That's the sixth homeless." Semra shook her head. "Poor Sabio. He hardly gets time to rest. I don't know when he's going to take the days off that he's accumulated in overtime."

Moira thanked her for the information. Sure, she was miffed that she couldn't tell Sabio about Excelsior's betrayal immediately, but she understood that his work came first. She could tell him the next time she saw him. She wished Semra a good weekend and left. In the exit door, she slammed into Druidus.

Before she caught herself, he kissed her cheek. "Moira! There you are. I wanted to ask you if you would go out with me tonight."

Moira's nostrils flared. He was the last person she had wanted to see today. "I'd rather go out with your father. With him, at least I know he can't stand me." She pushed past him without taking in his surprised face. Pain shot through her heart and it shocked her to realize how much her own words had upset her. *Why does it hurt so much to know that Druidus is a typical male?* She bit her lip to keep from crying and walked faster. Footsteps echoed behind her, and Druidus grabbed her arm.

"Moira, I love you. I would never lie to you."

She turned. "Is that so? And because you love me so much, you smooch with another woman right in front of my eyes?" She ripped her arm from his grip.

"What are you talking about? I didn't smooch with another woman."

"Stop lying! I saw you very well yesterday. I'm not blind."

He slapped his hand against his forehead and laughed. "Oh, that."

Moira turned wordlessly and walked away.

Again, Druidus grabbed her arm. "Wait, I can explain."

"No more lies."

Druidus' gaze hardened. "Do you really think I'm an ass like that?"

"All men are like that." Moira forced herself to look into his eyes. "Exceptions like Tord only emphasize the rule."

Druidus pressed his lips together. For an endless second they stared at each other. Blood roared in Moira's ears. Suddenly, Druidus grinned, and before Moira could react, he grabbed her and threw her over his shoulder. "Those who won't listen will have to see." He carried her back to the station. Moira struggled in vain. He was much stronger than she was. Relentlessly he carried her through the gendarmerie's corridors. She was glad they didn't meet anyone. In front of the display cabinets with the awards for special feats, he put her down and pointed to the picture of a faded newspaper article.

"Look closely at that. If you still think I'm cheating on you afterwards, I'll go."

"You'd better." Moira looked closer. The people in the picture looked familiar. She stepped closer and squinted. The picture showed Excelsior, Druidus and the auralogist Aparta de Frees. There was a description below which read, "18 Sedar 3013 – In the comfort of his home and surrounded by his family, Excelsior van Steen celebrates his well-earned promotion."

Moira blushed. "Aparta de Frees is your mother?"

"The picture was taken six years ago," Druidus said.

"She seems way too young to be your mother."

"She keeps fit."

Moira felt Druidus breathe in her neck.

He whispered, "Aparta is a good mother who loves me very much. Do you believe me now?"

Moira's heart raced. Her father had been right. Again, she had misjudged a situation because she didn't know all the facts. The thought that Druidus had only kissed his mother made her dizzy. Her knees trembled, and her voice sounded hoarse. "Can you forgive me?"

Sunshine lit up Druidus' face. "Only if you go on an official date with me."

Moira looked at him sternly but in her stomach, butterflies somersaulted. "The last time someone wanted to date me, I found him dead in his apartment."

"That's why we'll go right to the restaurant. You are perfect even without an evening dress." Druidus bent forward and kissed her gently on the mouth.

A prickle spread from Moira's lips that she had never felt before. It turned her knees to jelly. She wrapped her arms around his neck and, since his mouth was tantalizingly close, she paid him back with a passionate kiss. A storm of emotions coursed through her leaving no room for thoughts, fears, or sorrow.

When they stopped to catch their breath, Druidus said, "Let's go to eat something or I can't guarantee anything."

The evening was wonderful, although Moira was secretly disappointed that Druidus didn't want to accompany her into her flat.

"We've got all the time in the world for that," he whispered in her ear.

In front of the door to her block, they kissed for a long time and it still wasn't enough for Moira when he left. She waved until Druidus' carpisto turned a corner.

Chapter 19

Then she glided up the stairs as if on clouds. Although it was rather late, she was too exhilarated to sleep. *Should I call Franka to tell her about Druidus?* She shook her head. At the moment, she didn't want to share her happiness with anyone. Not even with her best friend. She thought for a while and decided to ask Tord for a copy of the drawings of the dig. She still smarted because Excelsior had hidden the file from her. Unfortunately, Tord didn't answer her call. After a while, she gave up and put the parlebol back in its place. *I wonder if Director du Mar has copies of the drawings?* She called the museum, but the central parlebol station had long closed for the night and the operator didn't know his dial-through number. She remembered the card with Du Mar's Infonet-data. She found it in the pocket of her summer jacket where it had stayed ever since the director gave it to her. She switched on her magicuter and wrote a note. Director du Mar answered immediately, and they fell into an animated exchange of notes.

CdM: It's so nice you called. I'd like to use the chance to thank you. After pondering your advice for a while, I did as you suggested and told my wife more about my work. I could dispel any worries about a mistress, and I got a second chance.

MB: I'm glad to hear that. What a pity that you can't work together with the Gendarmerie.

CdM: If it helps you, I'll always be there.

MB: Thank you. I'll use that offer right away. Do you have copies of the drawings Tord Mutelen did at the dig?

CdM: Of course. I'll mail them right away.

A little later, the magicuter spit out the pictures Moira had already seen in the file in the archive. She thanked him.

CdM: One hand washes the other. If you need more help, please let me know. I'll be there for you.

MB: Can you tell me more about the weapons they found? I'm fascinated by the sword from the stone urn.

CdM: Tord Mutelen knows more about that than me.

MB: True, but he's so involved in preparing for his wedding, the move isn't finished yet, and his injury needs time to heal too.

CdM: In that case, I'll find out more. Tomorrow, I'll take my wife out for lunch. Should Emily agree, I'd like to meet you at the same place. Wait, I'll ask her.

CdM: She agreed.

He gave her the address of a restaurant in a respectable neighborhood, and Moira promised to be there on time. They talked some more about digs and private small talk items, until the director said good night because his wife was waiting for him.

Moira was glad her advice had helped him. And she was delighted to have the drawings. She turned off the magicuter and studied them. The sword from the stone urn was the only find that hadn't rusted. The blade was wide and obviously quite sharp. Moira was amazed that a weapon that was more than two and a half thousand years old could be this well preserved. Disregarding the great preservation, it looked rather similar to the other swords of the find. Moira wondered why someone had thought it important to warn finders about this sword in particular. But as much as she stared at the drawing, she found no answer.

Chapter 20

The next day, she arrived at the restaurant five minutes before the appointed time. She walked through a row of small, bright rooms decorated with prints from paintings of well-known artists and countless green plants. Most of the dark oak tables were occupied, so it took her a while to find the director.

He sat close to his wife in a round bench in a corner. She leaned against him as they studied the menu. When Du Mar noticed Moira, he greeted her and introduced his wife.

Emily du Mar took Moira's hand. "I'm so happy to get to know you. Charles told me a lot about you. Please take a seat."

Moira sat on a chair on the side of the table. That way, she could see a good part of the restaurant and still chat comfortably with the Du Mars. After some small talk, Director du Mar addressed the dig.

"There isn't much information on the weapons," he said. "Due to circumstances, they haven't been analyzed yet. So far, we assume that Hern forged them, since all carry his seal." He showed her a drawing with a hammer floating vertically over an anvil.

Moira recognized it immediately. "The same seal is on the stone urn, but there's a semicircle with seven lines around the hammer."

"It's not clear why he changed the sigil for the stone urn. Maybe he added the sigil of the potter. I'm sure Tord will find the explanation." The director waited until the waiter set down their drinks before he continued. "By the way, the sword inside the urn did not bear Hern's seal. It seems to be much older. Ever since we got the first few sketches, Professor Solveigh and I have searched more sources than I've ever done since before I got my degree."

Moira bent forward. "And? Did you find something?"

The director nodded. "If it really is the sword we think it might be, the discovery would be a sensation. The weapon would be invaluable." He fell silent because the waiter brought their food. When he had left, the director went on. "Historic sources call it the Sword of Tears. It is said its bearer becomes an invincible fighter who will kill all his enemies but goes insane eventually."

"That fits the legend of Wild Katie."

"At least, it's not contradicting it." Director du Mar handed the sauce to his wife and took some potatoes. They ate silently. After a while, Emily went to the bathroom and Du Mar put his cutlery aside. "I got an offer for some of the stolen weapons. Anonymously."

Moira's finger itched with excitement. "The sword too?"

He shook his head. "I arranged a meeting but it was canceled at the last moment."

"Wouldn't it be better to involve the Gendarmerie?"

"I will, once I've got a set date for another meeting. I indicated that I'm especially interested in swords and made it clear that I will pay very well."

Moira frowned at him. "Please be careful. People like that are unpredictable."

He nodded. "Promise. When I have news, I'll tell you."

"Moira?" Druidus hurried toward her. He glanced at Director du Mar angrily before he turned to Moira. "I've been trying all morning to reach you."

"Why? Did we have a date?"

"Yes. No. I mean… My mother wanted to take me out for lunch and I thought I'd take you along."

"How nice of you." Secretly, Moira was quite relieved she didn't have to talk to Aparta de Frees right now.

"Will you at least come to the barbeque tomorrow afternoon?" He lifted his hands in a defensive gesture. "Don't worry, we'll not be alone. My parents invited a bunch of their closest friends."

"I don't know." Moira enjoyed frustrating him.

Druidus cocked his head slightly and begged with his eyes. Moira's heartbeat accelerated.

"Sabio will come too," he said.

Moira pulled a face as if she had to think about it. "All right." She got up. "See you tomorrow, then." She kissed Druidus' cheek, which smelled of eau de cologne as always. She would have liked to breathe the smell forever. Instead, she turned and walked to the restroom. She thanked Madame du Mar, who held the door open for her, and turned to Druidus once more. A satisfied smile crossed her face when Druidus' face relaxed as Madame du Mar cuddled close to her husband. She grinned. It was great to see that he was a tiny bit jealous – not so much as to make a scene but enough to give her the feeling of being loved. *I never thought I'd feel like this ever, and so fast.*

When she washed her hands later, the door behind her opened. In the mirror, she recognized Aparta de Frees and turned, but she didn't get to greet Druidus' mother.

"Listen well. I'm only going to say this once." Suppressed rage reverberated in Aparta de Frees' voice, and she fixed Moira with a cold stare. "I will not allow you to be more than a fleeting affair for my son. He doesn't need a magical zero like you. Should you try to worm yourself into our family, I'll take measures." She emphasized the word 'measures' in a way that made a shiver run down Moira's back.

Without another word, Aparta de Frees left. Moira breathed deeply, shocked by the hostility. She wondered what she had done to the woman. She needed a long time to digest the scene, and she pondered it for a long time that day.

On Sunday, she didn't know whether to follow the invitation or not, but her longing for Druidus was too strong. When he rang to fetch her, she wore her best costume, comfortable shoes, and little make-up.

"You look beautiful." He kissed her for a long time, and Moira regretted that they had to leave.

When they reached Van Steen's property, Moira marveled at the luxury. The house stood on a generous piece of land in the most expensive part of town surrounded by a high wall. The entrance hall was decorated with paintings of different time periods. The few Moira recognized would bring a lot of money if sold.

Moira whispered to Druidus. "Are they genuine?"

"Mother's inheritance." He helped her out of her coat. Wordlessly, he handed it to the butler along with his own jacket and pulled Moira past a row of visitors waiting to greet Excelsior van Steen and his wife. A dry and pungent smell cut though the air into Moira's nose. At first, she thought Druidus had tried a new aftershave, until she noticed the smell came from Aparta. She wondered why she didn't use a perfume for women, but had to admit the scent suited the dainty woman well. She was just greeting the President of the Gendarmerie Magique.

Smiling, Druidus waited until she was done. He kissed her cheek and introduced Moira. "She is the love of my life."

Moira felt the truth in the way he spoke. Her heart thundered with happiness. But when she remembered Aparta's threat, her throat constricted.

"Aren't you exaggerating a little, darling?" Aparta took Moira's hand. "What a treat to finally get to know you. Druidus told us so much about you. We will have to talk later." Her voice sounded so friendly, as if the scene in the restroom had never happened.

Moira admired her talent for playacting, but she wondered why Aparta pretended not to know her. She curtsied as best she could.

Excelsior watched her with a frown. "So, it's you. Very well." He patted Druidus' shoulder. "At least she's beautiful enough. Well, show her around." He turned to the next guest.

Moira felt as if she hadn't passed the test.

Druidus put his arm around her and whispered in her ear. "Don't think twice about it. They will get used to it. If not, I will force them." He pulled her aside, and for a while they watched Druidus' parents receive their friends. He explained where his parents knew the guests from, but Moira only had eyes for Aparta's strained smile and Excelsior's jovial gestures.

"Are they always so... so cold?" Moira shivered.

Druidus looked at her with surprise. "Cold?"

"I've got the feeling they dislike most of their guests."

Druidus smiled. "That's true. Sabio really knew what he was saying when he told me about your excellent perception. Come on, let's go." He led her to the garden.

On the terrace, Moira stopped, rooted to the ground. A broad-shouldered man with close-cropped hair stood there with his back to her, but even from behind Moira recognized her father.

Lavant Bellamie turned before she could pull Druidus in a different direction. He smiled at Druidus. "I should have known you'd bring her, lad. The way you looked at her..."

Druidus hugged Moira close. His voice sounded defensive. "I love her."

"One thing." Lavant bent forward and lowered his voice. "I haven't been a good father but if you hurt my daughter, I'll take it out on you."

Druidus stared at him open-mouthed, and Moira found it hard to suppress her rising anger. "Will you please excuse us for a moment?" Before Druidus could say a thing, she took her father's arm and pulled him to the edge of the terrace past the guests standing in groups.

"How dare you talk to Druidus like that? You have no right even though we're getting along again." She tapped Lavant's wide chest with her index finger. "It's my life. And if I get problems, they are mine to cope with. If Druidus and I will ever part, it'll surely not be his fault alone."

"I'm sorry. I only meant to tease him." Lavant took his daughter's hands. "I like Druidus. Really. And I'm glad you gave him a chance."

Moira sighed with relief. For a moment, she had thought Lavant might be as opposed to Druidus as Aparta was to her. She looked around for Druidus. "I'll better find him. He meant to show me around."

Lavant nodded, and she ran off.

Druidus was nowhere on the terrace. Excelsior was missing too. Only Aparta talked animatedly with the President of the Gendarmerie Magique and the mayor. Moira took a different direction. In passing, she grabbed several canapés handed around by muscle-packed, sparsely dressed servants. She went into the house but saw neither Druidus nor his father. Moira hoped they had mixed with the guests. At last Sabio hurried through the wide open entrance door. *Finally, I can tell him about Excelsior's betrayal.*

He smiled, when he met her. "So, Druidus did manage to convince you."

Moira didn't know what to say to that but she was glad she got Sabio alone. It wouldn't be easy but she didn't hesitate. "Can I talk to you in private?"

Sabio nodded and opened a door to a side room.

"Wow!" Moira's eyes widened as she took in the luxurious interior. The walls were upholstered with light-blue spider silk, and several seats of matching dragon leather stood on the smooth parquet.

"What can I do for you?"

Sabio's voice pulled Moira from her reverie. *All this should belong to him, not Excelsior.* She breathed deeply before she spoke. "Excelsior van Steen pretends he's the creator of your inventions. That's why he can afford this luxury."

"And?" Sabio shrugged. "I already know that."

Moira's eyes widened. "You don't mind? But he's stealing your intellectual property."

"There are more important things in life than luxury. Also, I stole from him something far more valuable." Sabio's smile was tired. "Let it be, Moira. Ex and I have known each other way too long to quarrel over a few stolen ideas." He turned to leave. "You'd better enjoy the party. The Van Steens know how to have fun."

Numbed, Moira stared after him. She couldn't believe that he didn't feel anger toward Excelsior. If she were in his place, she would have dragged the thief of her ideas through all levels of jurisdiction.

Chapter 21

Before she managed to calm down completely, Excelsior entered the room. "Oh, here you are." He closed the door behind him and stood in front of it with his arms crossed. His strained expression scared Moira, and her palms grew wet and hot. She tried hard to appear unbothered.

"My son is looking for you," Excelsior said, "and I want it to remain that way."

Moira's mouth felt dry. "Druidus loves me."

"He'll get over it when you stay away from him. It wouldn't be the first time." He pulled out his purse and pulled out a bundle of notes. "How much do you want?"

Moira's heartbeat accelerated. She clenched her fists. "I refuse to be bought. You don't have the right to decide who Druidus may love and who he might not. He's of age."

Excelsior frowned. "He's my son, and he deserves better than a slut like you. You wouldn't even be an option if you had a spark of magical talent."

Moira was hurt, but she had a weapon of her own she could use. "I would rather live without magic than live as a thief. Sabio may ignore that you're living off his ideas, but that doesn't legalize it."

To her surprise, Excelsior took her accusations seriously. His eyes shot daggers at her. "Without me, all his inventions would have remained prototypes. He's got no talent to market them, and where would the Gendarmerie be today without fingerprint powder or stasis spells?"

"You could have offered him a partnership." Moira stomped toward him. "I, for my part, will not allow a thief to bar me from meeting Druidus."

He grabbed her arm, and his voice dropped to a level of controlled anger. "And what will you do about it?"

"I will press charges. Stealing ideas is just as illegal as other kinds of theft."

Excelsior laughed but it didn't sound merry. "Save yourself the trouble. There isn't a single proof that I'm not the inventor, and Sabio will not testify against me." He bent forward until Moira felt his sour breath on her face. "I'm in the better situation. So, you'd better vanish from Druidus' life or I'll turn yours into hell."

Moira felt like crying. Was there nothing she could use to fight back? Her gaze went through the window where Druidus pushed through the guests, searching. An idea occurred to her. She freed her arm. "Druidus will surely love to hear that you fleeced Sabio."

"He won't believe you."

"He loves me. Do you really want to bet on that?"

Excelsior paled.

Wordlessly, Moira turned her back on him and left. As fast as she could, she ran outside to the place she had seen Druidus a few heartbeats ago. She wanted to go home. Unfortunately, she couldn't find him, and her father and Sabio seemed to have left already. Annoyed, she realized she didn't have money for a taxi seeing as she hadn't brought her purse because it didn't go with her dress. Druidus had to be somewhere. She asked a couple of the guests. One suggested she should look deeper in the garden.

She walked through the park-like garden until she reached a lake where a huge weeping willow trailed its long, mourning branches in the water. From here, the house was difficult to see. Close to the willow, a bench for two stood at the bank of the lake. It was a romantic place but Moira had no mind for it. Annoyed, she sat on the bench. Where was Druidus? She looked back to the house. Its lights lit up the clouds in the darkening sky. A few raindrops fell but Moira didn't want to go back. She wasn't interested in the guests' small talk, and without Druidus, she didn't want to meet his parents again. When the rain grew stronger, she took off her high heels and climbed into the willow.

Halfway up, she found a sturdy branch she made herself comfortable on. While the rain ran off the willow's dense canopy, Moira thought. She didn't doubt for one minute that she had fallen in love with Druidus. But was it enough for a long-term relationship, especially since both his parents didn't like her one bit? She sighed. It was a fact she couldn't dismiss: if she wanted Druidus, she'd have to get along with his family.

Before she could decide on a course of action, she heard voices come along the path. Peering through the leaves, she noticed a super-sized umbrella. Since she didn't want to be seen, she tried to be as silent as possible. She held her breath when she recognized Sabio's voice.

"I can't stand it any longer," he said. "It wears me down to deceive my best friend."

A low, female voice answered but Moira couldn't understand the words.

"Why should I be interested in the money? I need you!" They stopped beside the lake, and the umbrella sank to the side. They kissed.

Moira suppressed a surprised scream at the last possible moment. The woman in Sabio's arms was Aparta de Frees.

"Did you hear something?" Aparta looked around.

Sabio pulled her closer and lifted the umbrella back up. "Not in this rain."

They sat on the bench and vanished completely under the umbrella's cover, so Moira only heard their voices.

Sabio sounded desperate. "Why can't you get a divorce?"

"I'm going to get one soon," Aparta said. "My office is firmly established, and I'm finally earning enough to be independent. But I need some time to prepare Druidus. Under no circumstances will I leave him."

"Druidus is of age. Let him find his own way."

"I can't bear the thought of losing him."

"You won't. He loves you way too much for that."

Silence, but Moira knew they were kissing again. *How can I get away without them noticing me?* She looked around but no escape route presented itself.

"I could sit like this forever," Aparta said.

"That's no option. Someone is coming," Sabio whispered. The umbrella rose. Fast, but without running, the lovers left the lake.

Moira looked toward the house. Sabio was right. A shape with another umbrella was running toward the lake. It was Druidus. *Finally.*

She climbed out of the tree and landed right in front of him. He jumped back in surprise.

"It's about time," she said.

"Moira! I've been looking for you all over the place. Where have you been?" He wrapped his arms around her as best he could with the umbrella in his hand, hugged her, and spoke without waiting for an answer. "I was afraid my parents might have bullied you out. They are much too good at that."

"I had a couple of – let's say – very interesting conversations with them. But I wouldn't have left without a farewell anyway." She breathed in his fresh scent and relaxed.

Despite the rain he pulled her to the bench where Aparta and Sabio had been seated a few minutes before. "Don't take it personally. Father believes I have to obey his every whim as long as I'm living at home, and Mother treats me as if I'm still her little boy. All the while, both want what's best for me. It's just that their ideas about what's best for me don't get along with mine."

Moira leaned her head against his shoulder. "Your father said you have never kept a girl he didn't like."

"So far, I have kept no girlfriend at all." He laughed but it didn't sound happy. He took her hands. "Most didn't mean enough to me to start a fight with my parents. With you, it's different. I want to marry you and grow old with you whether my parents like it or not."

Moira gasped and freed her hands. "Not so fast. I'm not really known for long-term relationships. How can you talk about marriage?"

"Don't worry. I won't push. I just wanted you to know that I'm prepared to fight my parents for your sake. I will not allow them to hurt you."

Moira was touched. She sat up straight and offered him her lips. He kissed her tenderly. When she was able to breathe again after long minutes, she closed her eyes and leaned against his shoulder. "I've had enough for one day. Can you take me home?"

"Sure." He didn't stand up, but Moira didn't mind. In silence they watched the sinking sun break though the clouds until the lake reflected the light.

Finally, Druidus sighed and got up. "Let's go and pay our respect."

"I think you should do that without me. At the moment, neither of your parents is keen on talking to me." Moira linked arms with him and together they walked toward the house.

Soon they saw the other guests that had found refuge from the rain in the big conservatory and were slowly returned into the open again now that the rain had subsided.

"It seems as if my parents are inside," Druidus said.

"I'll fetch my coat." Moira kissed him. "They'll probably be delighted to see me go." She hurried into the house, found a servant who handed her the coat, and waited patiently for Druidus.

Through the living room's wide open gullwing doors, she watched the guests standing around the ample buffet in small groups, talking and eating. The conversations blurred to a monotonous mumble until Druidus' voice rose over it.

"I don't care what you think of her. She is my life."

Excelsior's answer was too low to be heard in the hall, but Moira recognized his voice.

"Another remark like that and you'll be a dead duck for me. Dead. For ever!" Druidus stormed toward her. He pushed the guests aside that didn't get out of his way fast enough.

"Come, let's go."

At that moment Sabio entered from the garden. His hair hung down in wet, limp strands, making his face even more solemn than usual. With his mobile parlebol in his hand, he took Druidus' elbow and pulled him toward the exit.

"Independence Road seventeen," he said.

Druidus paled. "Another one?" He matched his step to Sabio's, looked back at Moira, and waved her to come.

"Several, and this time they are not homeless." Sabio created a green, blinking Lumière Magique and put it on the roof of Druidus' carpisto. "From all Semra said I gathered that we'll have to take a closer look before we can eliminate a connection to the murders of the homeless." He put both hands against the roof and stared at the ground between his arms.

"I'm so fed up." When he had entered, he slammed the door. Moira, who already sat in the back seat, flinched.

A few minutes later they stopped in front of a single-story house with a well-kept but small front garden. Patrol carpistos had been parked in such a way that they blocked the brightly lit stone path to the entrance. The pattern of a protective spell glittered over the lawn.

Druidus swallowed and got out. "The Ramasseurs are living here. Mother once worked for Monsieur and tried to force his daughter on me."

Moira thought he looked pale. She followed him and Sabio, who wove past the carpistos and walked into the house.

At the door, Druidus stopped. "You should probably not come along. It's not for sensitive people."

Anger rose in Moira. Did Druidus think she didn't have it in her too? She looked into his eyes to give him a piece of her mind and recognized the worry in his gaze. Her anger evaporated. "That's fine. This time, it's no one I meant to take on a date," she said.

Sabio pulled Druidus along. "Let her. She has proven more than once that she can observe under pressure. She will cope with the rest."

They walked along a hallway that swarmed with gendarmes. Through a door leading to the kitchen, Moira saw Semra talk soothingly to a young girl with a black dress, white pinafore, and bonnet. In the dining room, Buds was just spreading a stasis spell. He frowned when he saw her. Moira hurried to catch up with Druidus and Sabio, who had entered the generous living room. Near the big double doors she stopped, since she didn't want to destroy the stasis spell in the room. Its pattern of blue and yellow threads contrasted nicely with the dark wooden floor.

Sabio bent over an unmoving figure and lifted a blanket that someone had spread over it. "Are the pictures done?"

One of the gendarmes nodded. "Also, Doc has released the bodies."

"Great. Take them to the lab." Sabio crouched and examined the ground around the victim while Druidus walked over to the parlebol, activated the display of connections and noted the numbers.

Moira longed to help but as long as the stasis spell hadn't been lifted, she didn't dare to enter the room. Under no circumstances did she want to destroy evidence. Impatiently, she waited for the investigation of the crime scene to be over. She concentrated on the pattern of blood splashes on the ground, the wall, and the ceiling. Gendarmes hurried past her, and some of them glanced at her questioningly.

Only Buds stopped and grinned. "I noticed you've learned from your mistakes."

Moira didn't answer.

"Maybe we'll make a decent gendarma out of you yet." Buds left.

In his place, a gaunt man with thick glasses and a heavy, black handbag stopped. He watched Buds and shook his head. "Well, he wasn't exactly nice, now was he?" he said to Moira.

"Once, I nearly destroyed one of his crime scenes." She wondered at how easy it was to talk about this to a stranger. It felt as if Druidus' love for her had strengthened her resistance in this respect.

He smiled. "In that case, you've got to be Moira Bellamie. Sabio thinks the world of you." He set down his bag and took her hand. "I'm Doc."

"Doc?"

"No one uses my full name, but that's fine by me. I think most don't even know it."

Moira stared at him. "I think it's very impolite."

He shrugged. "No way. Everybody knows me as Doc. At least that leaves no confusion as to what I do."

Only now did Moira realize that Doc was the head of the forensic lab despite his boyish face. She blushed. "I took you for one of your staff."

Doc laughed. "Dear me! I won't leave an intriguing crime scene like this to the infantry."

Sabio stopped beside them. "Whom are you calling infantry?"

"Not you, of course." Doc patted Sabio's shoulder. "I bet you'd love to have my report on your table before I reach the lab, am I right?"

"A preliminary cause of death would suffice for the moment." Sabio made room for two gendarmes carrying a metal coffin with a semi-transparent lid into the room.

Silently they watched the two take the blanket off the dead woman and place her gently, one could say tenderly, into the coffin. When the gendarmes passed them again, Doc held them up. "Take her into storeroom four. I'll be there in half an hour. By then, room one had better be ready."

"No problem, boss." The gendarmes carried the coffin away.

Moira watched them leave with tears in her eyes. She had seen the dead woman though the lid, slightly blurred by the frosted glass. She was hardly older than Moira herself. Surprised, she saw the gendarmes return with a second coffin. She turned to Sabio. "Isn't she the only one?"

He shook his head, his lips pressed into a narrow line.

"How many are there?"

"The owner of the house, his wife and daughter, as well as the housekeeper and the assistant." He pointed to the door of the kitchen with his thumb. "The service girl survived because she had gone shopping. The gardener discovered the family shortly before she returned." He pulled Moira and Doc a little to the side to make room for the bearers of yet another coffin. "Now, Doc, what killed them?"

"I'm not sure." Doc squirmed and kneaded his hands as if sitting for a test. "It's fairly obvious with the husband. The blade goes right through his heart and exits at the back. But don't nail me down to that. You know very well that things might not be as straightforward as they seem."

"What about the others?"

"I can't say without an autopsy."

"How so?" Sabio frowned. Moira had never seen him this confused.

Doc nodded his head while he thought out loud. "They have shallow cuts all over their arms, legs, and necks. But the time from the start of the attack to the return of the servant was too short to bleed to death. Also, there would have been much more blood."

Sabio scratched his head. "Does that mean we can eliminate a killing spree?"

"No. It only means that I cannot give you a conclusive explanation before I finish the autopsy. And that's why I'll go right back to work." Doc picked up his bag and followed the last coffin out of the house.

"There was just as little blood at the crime scene as with the homeless murders," Sabio said.

Moira's eyes widened. "Who needs that much blood? Even vampires don't drink more than a glass or two a day."

"It can't have been vampires. The supervising offices would have noticed if sold amounts or blood bank storage had changed significantly over the last few weeks. Although, we can't completely rule out this option."

Sabio wiped his eyes. "Let's keep at it. Will you help me question the gardener?"

"I'm not allowed to. It's not Monday yet."

"I don't care. I need your opinion. We'll just keep you out of the protocol." Sabio cocked his head. When she nodded, he walked back along the hallway.

Chapter 22

Moira followed him into a room filled with antique music instruments. Even the paintings on the walls depicted scenes of musical entertainment. When Moira stepped closer to a painting of a piano player, she heard a simple melody played by a beginner on a violin. For a moment, she wished she could hear the correct music that was magically bound into the painting.

"Monsieur Ramasseur was an avid collector. This," Sabio pointed at the items displayed in the room, "apparently is only a small part of his collection." He walked to the window where a folding table with three chairs waited. A thin file lay on the desktop, and beside it stood a dicta-nerl.

Moira thought the furniture looked misplaced. She had hardly sat down beside Sabio when the door opened and a gendarme led a young man in a green apron in. He introduced him as Monsieur Ramasseur's gardener.

Surprised, Moira stared at the muscle-packed torso. The man was naked, aside from an apron and very tight, black swimming pants. When he sat down, the muscles played under his tanned skin.

He looked at Sabio, then at Moira, and she noticed fear in his eyes. His smoothly shaved face was as open and innocent as that of a child. Nervously, he kneaded his apron to a ball and smoothed it out again. Only when pearls of sweat appeared on his forehead did Sabio look up from the folder he seemed to have been studying.

He nodded at Moira and waited for her to activate the dicta-nerl. "Well, Monsieur..."

"Sauté. Frederic Sauté." The gardener slipped on his chair to the front until he bumped into the edge of the table. He blushed and slipped back.

Dear me, he's nervous. Still, Moira didn't smile at him. She understood that Sabio wanted to use the big man's insecurity as a weapon.

"Monsieur Sauté, you are working as a gardener for Monsieur Ramasseur?" Sabio asked.

The young man nodded. "He pays me so I make his garden beautiful. But his wife tells me what I have to do. I think she knows more about flowers than Monsieur does."

"If you're in charge of the garden, why were you inside the house this afternoon?"

"I... ehm... I..." Frederic looked around for an escape route and slipped to and fro on the chair. "I'm here every Sunday. Luisa gives me some cake for my mother then."

"Luisa is the housemaid?"

Frederic nodded again.

"Do you like Luisa?" Moira asked.

"She is much, much nicer than Madame. I love her, and she loves me too." Frederic beamed and looked so happy that Moira longed to hug him for comfort.

But Sabio didn't give up easily. "So, you met secretly with Luisa."

"No, I didn't."

"Don't lie to me." Sabio's voice thundered. "No gardener goes to work on a Sunday afternoon just to get some cake. Tell me, what did you do here?"

Frederic's eyes filled with tears. "I can't say."

"Why not? Who forbade you?"

"I can't tell you that either." Tears ran over Frederic's cheeks but he didn't seem to notice.

Sabio clenched his fists. "Let's think this through again slowly. You came here this afternoon to do something you can't tell anyone."

Frederic nodded.

Sabio slammed both fists on the table, but his voice stayed dangerously low. "You do know I can put you into jail if you don't tell me the truth?"

Frederic's eyes widened in panic. He slipped as far back on his chair as he could.

When Sabio opened his mouth to continue the interrogation, Moira put her hand on his arm. She had an idea. Slipping closer to the table, she bent forward. "Does Luisa know why you're here on Sundays?"

Frederic shook his head, blinked away his tears, sniffed, and nodded.

"Does she like it?"

"She says I'm expo–something ... expotited. I should better be home with my Mama on Sundays. No matter how much extra money I get."

"Did Monsieur ask you to come?"

Frederic shook his head so hard, his hair flew. "He's the last one who should know, says Ma..." In the middle of the word, he slammed his hand in front of his mouth.

Moira lowered her voice to a whisper. "It was Madame Ramasseur, wasn't it? She asked you to come on Sundays."

Frederic bit his lower lip and stared at the ground.

Sabio gave Moira a satisfied nod. He also spoke quietly. "What did she want you to do, Monsieur Sauté?"

The young gardener put his face in his hands and didn't answer. Tears welled through his fingers and ran over the backs of his hands. Moira reached out and touched his shoulder. "You wear more clothes the other days, right?"

Frederic nodded. "The other days, Monsieur is at home," he whispered. "She says if I tell anyone, I get locked away, and no one will ever like me again."

"Luisa likes you. You said so yourself." Moira squeezed his shoulder. His muscles felt warm and strong.

"But she'll fire Luisa and write a horrible recommend-dation."

"She can't harm you any more. She's dead."

Frederic lowered his hands. "Did Monsieur cut her dead with the sword?"

Sabio's eyebrows shot up. "How is it that you know about the sword?"

"I can tell you that. Monsieur only begged me not to say anything to Madame." Frederic wiped his tears away with his sleeve. "He had bought a something, an item. That's what he always called it. Usually, Luisa helps him to place the new pieces. Monsieur said she's got an eye for compo-ehm."

"Composition," Moira suggested.

"That's it!"

"So, he bought something new for his collection," Sabio said. "And then?"

"The parcel was delivered this morning. That's why Monsieur was at home when I came. He made me carry the box into the library. It was rather heavy."

"Was Luisa there too?"

"She waited in the library for Monsieur because she meant to tell him about Madame and me. But I didn't stay because Monsieur would have been angry with me."

"So, he knew his wife cheated on him." Sabio leaned back and folded his arms in front of his chest. "What did you do?"

"I waited in the Café du Paradi for Luisa. We talked for a long time. Luisa wanted me to help Monsieur when he talked to his wife. She promised he wouldn't be angry with me, and she wanted to come along to protect me. But I didn't want to go, so she went alone." He chewed his lip for a moment. "I was so afraid for her. Madame can be really nasty when she gets angry. And I knew she'd be really angry with Luisa. So I followed her when my cocoa was empty. But she was in the house already and I don't have a key for the front. So I went through the garden and over the ter-race."

He wiped the sweat from his face with his apron. "You can get into the library right from there. Monsieur was lying on the ground, and the sword stuck in his chest. I screamed and ran away and hid in the tool shed. I called the Gendarmerie from there."

"It fits the tracks Buds has found." Sabio seemed satis-fied. He thanked Frederic for his statement and closed the dicta-nerl.

"Can I go now?" Frederic still hunched on his chair like a scared rabbit.

"You should join Luisa," Sabio suggested. "Her interrogation should be over by now. And if we've got more questions, we've got your addresses."

Frederic got up so fast the chair left scratches in the wooden floorboards.

Smiling, Sabio watched him leave, and then turned to Moira. "A killing spree of Monsieur becomes more and more likely, don't you agree?"

Moira supported her head with both hands. "I don't know. I always thought killers on a rampage were really violent, but from what Doc said, the victims only had shallow cuts. I think that doesn't fit together very well."

"Yes, that's one aspect that doesn't really fit. Tomorrow, when I get Doc's reports, we'll know more." Sabio looked at his watch. "The boys should be finished by now. Do you want to have a look at the crime scene?"

"If I may."

"As if I would forgo your observing talent." Sabio got up and walked back to the hall. Relieved, Moira realized that the stasis spell in the living room had been canceled. She entered and looked around thoroughly. There were hardly any signs of a fight; very little blood on the walls, no toppled furniture, and the tube was running. Everything looked as if the owners would return any moment to enjoy a cozy evening. Beside the parlebol Moira discovered a deep cut in the wood of the sideboard as if someone had jammed a knife into it from above. Something around the scratch glittered like golden sand. Moira didn't know what it was. She wondered how no one seemed to have noticed. "Did something stand here?" she asked Sabio.

"The voice-nerl. A rather new model."

"Where is it?"

"Buds probably packed it with the evidence so he can listen to the messages later."

Moira went into the library where Buds was just packing his case. She asked him, "May I see the voice-nerl, please?"

"But don't take it out of the bag."

Moira nodded and took the bag containing a black lacquered box. A cut went through it as if someone had

185

skewered it on a blade. Carefully, Moira lifted the lid. She flinched. In a corner of the box, a tiny nerl crouched. His left arm was cut off and sparkling blood ran unhindered from the wound. His naturally ugly face was twisted so badly due to the pain, Moira needed a while to realize he was still breathing. She ripped the bag. "We need a healer. Hurry. Get a specialist for nerls," she yelled at Buds, who ran off immediately.

Carefully, she pressed her index finger on the wound. Since the nerl was rather small, she could easily reach his other shoulder with her thumb. Like this she could apply slight pressure on the wound. The bleeding stopped immediately. The nerl whimpered and Moira gently stroked his shaggy, purple hair with her free hand.

"Everything will be fine," she whispered while around her chaos broke loose. People came and went, Semra tried unsuccessfully to pry the wounded nerl from her fingers, and Druidus put his arm around Moira protectively.

A little later the emergency healer arrived. On his shoulder sat a nerl not much longer than a cubit who was also wearing the white-red striped lab coat of a healer. Both praised Moira for her fast reaction and hurried away with the severely injured nerl after they had taken care of his wound as best they could. When they were gone, Moira's knees buckled. Druidus dropped the case with the evidence and caught her. The case opened, and the meticulously numbered bags spilled out.

Open-mouthed Moira stared at a sword in a super-sized bag lying between the other pieces of evidence. The bag glowed with a dull red, suggesting danger.

"But that is…" She freed herself from Druidus' grip, crouched, and reached for the weapon. It was true. The decorations on the hilt and blade were the same she had seen on the pictures in the file of the burglary. There was no doubt; this sword was the one from the stone urn. "The cases are connected!"

"Which cases?" Druidus asked.

"The burglary in the museum, Lif's and Bastide's death, and this slaughter."

186

Sabio appeared beside her as if from thin air. He pulled her up, and his eyes sparkled. "How did you figure that out?"

"The box from the burglary was found at Lif's apartment, a dagger at Bastide's," Moira pointed at the sword, "and this was part of the booty too."

"I think it rather unlikely that Monsieur Ramasseur took part in the burglary," Sabio said.

Druidus reminded him that some collectors didn't always make sure the item they wanted to buy was available legally. Sabio nodded and patted Moira's shoulder.

"Thanks to you we're one step closer. Now, it gets more and more important to find Pete Huudien. I am sure he's the key to these cases."

Moira pulled back her hand. She wasn't sure whether the red glow came from the bag or the sword, so she didn't dare touch the bag. "We have to be careful with the sword. I'm sure it carries a dangerous spell."

"That's why we put it into the protective bag," Druidus said. "It is encased with a very strong spell that counters all suicide or homicide spells."

Moira sighed with relief.

Buds entered. He paled when he saw the spilled evidence. "What have you done now?" He pushed Moira aside and began to examine the bags and replace them in the case. "Luckily none of the seals broke."

"Sorry, but it was me," Druidus said. Buds didn't listen.

Moira pulled Druidus aside. "Will it take much longer?" She was so tired she could barely keep her eyes open.

He looked at Sabio and raised an eyebrow.

"You can go," Sabio said. "I'll take care of the evidence until Excelsior reports for duty."

Moira and Druidus said their farewells and took the shortest route to Moira's flat. By some miracle, there was a free parking space right in front of the building.

"I'll accompany you upstairs if I may," Druidus said.

Moira nodded. In the stairwell she took her post from the box. There was a single letter – no sender address. While they waited for the nerlift, she opened it and read.

"Dear Moira, enclosed as promised a list of all collectors who bought illegal wares last week. Please keep me anonymous. CdM." Wordlessly she handed the letter to Druidus and scanned the list of names. The dead collector was the last. "It looks as if you were right. Monsieur Ramasseur illegally bought art for his collection," she said.

Druidus handed the letter back. "Who is CdM?"

"I'm not at liberty to tell you." Moira knew well that CdM stood for Charles du Mar, but a promise was a promise. She entered the nerlift and looked up at him. "Are you angry?"

"Why should I be? There are many things we can talk about and some we can't. That's the way with our job." He told the nerls the floor number of Moira's flat and put his arm around her shoulders.

Moira leaned her head against his chest and watched the nerls hurry to their cables. She felt incredibly secure and protected, as if she had come home after a long journey. Was this love? Druidus' breath caressed her cheek, and a warm tingle spread throughout her body. *Should I risk asking him in?* Moira ignored her mind's alarm bells. She was sure Druidus loved her truly. With a pounding heart, she waited until they reached the door to her flat.

Druidus bent forward and kissed her. "Good night, darling."

"Would you like some coffee?" Moira's voice trembled but she didn't miss the happy glitter in Druidus' eyes.

"Very much," he said. "A coffee from you will surely be better than anything I can get at a hotel."

"Hotel?" Moira hung her coat on a hanger and looked at him questioningly. "Won't you go home?"

"No way!" Druidus slipped out of his shoes following her example. Barefoot, he went into the living room and sat down on the sofa. "The way my parents treated you this evening, I wouldn't be able to see them without another fight."

"Won't you tell them at least?" Moira put the regulator of her coffeemaker on three cups and woke the nerl.

"Don't make it too strong," she whispered to it.

Druidus folded his hands behind his head and stretched. "I think it's rather good for them if they fear something happened to me. It might bring them to their senses."

"What if they ask the Gendarmerie to search for you?" Moira took two mugs from a cupboard and put them on the table in the living room.

"Sabio knows how to reach me."

"You could sleep here tonight." Blood pulsed through her veins so strong, it roared in her ears, making it difficult to understand Druidus' answer.

"That's' really nice of you. I promise not to bother you."

"What if I want to be bothered?" Moira cocked her head, fluttered her eyelashes, and opened the topmost buttons of her blouse.

Druidus stared at her as if he'd never seen her before. He reached for her with one arm, and Moira realized with satisfaction that his hand was trembling.

"Moira!" His voice was husky. "Are you sure you want this?"

Instead of an answer, she took off her blouse. With one stride, Druidus stood beside her and pressed his mouth on hers. His kisses burned on her lips, and his hands burned her skin. Moira fought against losing control – in vain. Something like this had never happened in any of her relationships before. She panicked when Druidus' hands slipped under the waistband of her skirt, and she gasped.

"I love you so much." He whispered and hid his face in the curve of her neck.

Moira's panic drowned in a wave of love. She put both arms around his neck and kissed his forehead. "We should make ourselves a little more comfortable," she said.

Wordlessly, he picked her up and carried her into the bedroom. The calls of the coffeemaker nerl faded away unheeded.

Chapter 23

Druidus woke her with low music and an invitation for breakfast in the kitchen. "Your nerl was rather angry that I ordered coffee today. It took me a while to convince him."

Moira smiled. Her nerls had always been quite stubborn.

Druidus handed her the dressing gown. "Don't you think he's a bit big for a coffeemaker nerl?"

"It's the same with all my nerls. I had to get bigger living quarters for some of them already." Moira stretched and got up to go to the bathroom. "I wonder why they thrive so well at my place."

"They know you're someone special." Druidus kissed her. She answered in like, and they landed in bed again. The wake-up nerl's voice sounded angry as he sang his "Sortie du sommeil."

Druidus glanced at the clock and jumped out of bed. "Are you going to shower first or shall I?"

"You first." When Druidus was done, Moira showered faster than ever before, so they had enough time to enjoy a joint breakfast before they had to drive to work.

Since it was raining, Druidus dropped her at the entrance and drove on to his parking space. Moira entered the Gendarmerie and her footsteps echoed through the empty hall. In the corridor she met Sabio. He had shadows under his eyes and seemed floppy and tired. Wordlessly, he waved her to follow him into his office where he opened a safe set into the wall that she hadn't noticed before.

He took out the case with the evidence. "Could you take these to Excelsior? I have to finish another report."

"Sure." Moira took the case.

At that moment Druidus came in, shaking the rain off his coat. "Beastly weather!"

Sabio wiped his eyes and turned to Moira. "Your test is this afternoon, right?"

Moira pressed her hand on her mouth. "Dear me, the test! I completely forgot about it."

"Don't worry. You'll pass it," Druidus said.

"But I left my handicapped ID at home."

Druidus caressed her cheek. "We'll fetch it during the lunch hour."

Sabio smiled. "You'll be off duty until your test begins."

Moira was relieved. A free morning would be enough to fetch the handicapped ID, even without Druidus. She could take the evidence to the archive and get going right after. Sabio held her back.

"Since you've got time on your hands, would you mind visiting the nerlôpital unofficially this morning? Try to talk to the nerl you saved."

Moira nodded. "What shall I ask him?"

"If the doctors let you visit at all, I'd like to know if he'd heard anything."

Moira frowned. "Why shouldn't they let me visit him? After all, I saved his life."

"Suicidal nerls are usually not allowed to see anyone."

Moira pulled up her eyebrows. "Why should the little one try to kill himself? Shouldn't he be happy that he survived the loss of an arm?"

"You don't know much about nerls, do you? It really is a pity that Magical Theory is no longer part of the curriculum at schools." Sabio pointed to the chairs in front of his desk. He waited for Moira and Druidus to sit before he began to explain. "Listen. For the work nerls do for humans, they get the magical energy we can't use. They need this energy to live. To digest the magic they need their right hand, which they call the contract hand. Nerls who don't have a contract hand commit suicide sooner or later."

"But that's not what I saved his life for." Moira was horrified. "Is there no way to help him?"

Sabio shrugged. "I don't know. I'm no healer for nerls."

"In that case I'll have to talk to his doctors."

"I'll tell a patrol carpisto to fetch you at the entrance." Sabio reached for the parlebol. He looked as if he'd fall asleep any moment.

Moira felt pity for him. The burglary and the many murders burdened him and he had no one with whom to discuss his problems. She thanked him and got up. "I'll just take the evidence to Excelsior."

Druidus got up to leave the office before she could and took the case with the evidence. "I'll take it. You can go to the nerlôpital right away."

Moira frowned. "Are you sure you want to see your father right now?"

Druidus sighed. "With a little luck, he won't be there yet. He's late quite often."

"Don't let him harass you." She smiled at him. "At least he won't get rid of me with money."

His gaze grew solemn. "It's about time I talk to him. He has to understand that I'm going to live my life the way I want and that I won't let him or Mother determine it for me."

"Don't fall for his mockery." Moira offered her lips for another kiss.

When he came up for air, he said with a grin on his face, "I can always threaten him with the sword."

Moira's face fell. "That's not funny. Be really careful with the sword, please. No one knows what kind of spell it holds."

"I swear I'll not take it out of its bag." He kissed her one more time and walked down the stairs to the vault with the archive, and she left the building through the front door and entered the patrol carpisto that was waiting for her already.

She went to her flat to fetch the handicapped ID first, and then she went on to the nerlôpital. The ceiling of the entrance area was just about high enough that a human could move without crouching. Moira asked the nerl at the reception to announce her visit to the injured nerl's doctor and followed the receptionist's directions to the intensive care unit.

A healer hardly reaching up to her knee caught up with her in the hallway. "I'm really sorry but we cannot allow you to visit even though you're from the Gendarmerie. Gronk is traumati…" He stopped and stared at her. Then he grabbed her hand and dragged her along. "Come, hurry. Maybe it's good for you to talk to him after all."

Moira wondered about his sudden change of attitude but she followed without resistance. The healer pushed her into a windowless room that looked like a cave. Stalagmites covered walls and ceiling and the air was moist and cold. Somewhere water was dripping on stone. On a small mound of pieces of plate, Gronk sat and stared into space. Although the room was rather small, he looked lost in it. He didn't react when she greeted him.

"Get him to make a contract with you," the healer said. "With a lot of luck, it will help him. It's worth a try."

Hesitantly, Moira sat down on the ground beside the mound of plate. For a while she studied the armless nerl silently. The wound had already healed but Gronk's expression was anything but happy. When the healer had left, she said, "I know it's not a good time just now, but I have to ask you a couple of questions."

Gronk stared into space, motionless.

"The Gendarmerie depends on your statement. You're the only one who survived the bloodbath."

"Survived? Pah." Gronk spat and looked at her. "Piss off."

"I will stay here until I get a statement." Moira crossed her arms in front of her chest.

"In that case, you can wait until the dragons' world freezes over."

Moira remained silent.

"Go away. My word isn't of worth any more anyway."

"Why that?"

"I'm a dead nerl walking, a cripple who'll never grow again." Gronk slumped until his head rested on his knees.

His shoulders trembled, but his crying was so low, Moira couldn't hear it. She wanted to stroke his back, but she understood nerls well enough to know that she'd only make him angry. *If only I could help him.* She sighed. At that moment, she remembered how the nerl in the museum's archive had taken his payment out of her aura. After her visit, he'd been bigger than before. Also, all nerls working for her were bigger than average. *Maybe Gronk will grow despite the lost arm if he touches my aura.* She remembered that the archivist had moved his right hand over her arm. *If he can't move his arm over mine, I could move mine over his.* She bent forward and poked Gronk.

"Will you give me a statement if I can help you, even if it's just a tiny bit?"

Gronk moaned, tormented. "Why didn't you let me die?"

"So, how about it?"

Gronk sat up and looked at her with sad eyes. "If you really can help me, I'll tell you all I know."

"Deal." Moira reached out with her right hand and moved it over Gronk's armless shoulder. Waves and swirls surged through her, and she felt dizzy. *It's working.* She lost consciousness.

When she came to, Gronk stood on her chest lifting a cup of water over his head with both arms. Before she could say anything, he poured the water into her face. Coughing and spitting, she sat up.

"That wasn't necessary." She took the nerl who was clinging to her neckline and set him down on the ground.

Gronk beamed at her. "You healed me. Look! You really healed me." He turned in a circle holding out both arms. The right one was slightly shorter, and its skin was neither green nor knobbly – it had a decidedly human tinge to it – but it was an arm complete with hand. Gronk laughed, and it sounded like a fire in a fireplace. "Thank you, thank you, than you!" He clung to her arm and kissed her wrist.

When Moira had recovered a little, she said, "Now for your part of the deal."

Gronk climbed back onto his mound of plate. Satisfied, Moira noticed that it was too small for him now. The nerl smiled at her so merrily, all of a sudden he didn't look ugly at all.

Gronk sat down with his legs crossed. "What do you want to know?"

"Did you record anything before your injury?"

Gronk shook his head. "I hadn't been activated. But I heard a lot."

"Can you repeat it?"

"Not word for word, but the housemaid set an ultimatum for the master. She said that if he didn't manage to hold his wife away from her beloved, they'd both quit. The master wasn't very angry when he heard about his wife's affair, which surprised me a little. He sounded resigned." Gronk scratched his chin. "The housemaid left, and I heard sounds as if something was being opened. Maybe a box. And paper rustled. Then, there was this new voice. I had never heard it before."

Moira bent forward with anticipation. "What kind of voice was it? Can you describe it?"

Gronk pondered the question. "It was wonderful, harmonic, and silvery-bright like a glockenspiel. The voice talked to the master as if it were a slow-witted dog. After a while, Madame came to tell him she needed to go shopping. She screamed once, then everything fell silent. Even the silver voice didn't say anything. A little later, Mademoiselle was singing in the living room, and heavy footsteps walked over from the library. Her song ended with another scream. Yes, and then something shot through the lid of my box and my arm went up in flames. I can't remember anything else."

Moira thanked him. She had to endure many more thank-yous before she could leave.

In the patrol carpisto, she pondered Gronk's statement. *So, it wasn't a killing spree. There was someone else in the room. Who could that be?* She wondered whose voice one could call silvery-bright. *Probably not that of a human and surely not that of a nerl. Maybe it was an elf, a friend of Leclerque Bastide.* The assumption seemed sensible. *If one elf became an offender against all expectations, why not a second one? I should talk about this with Sabio.* The patrol carpisto stopped at the entrance of the Gendarmerie, and Moira got out.

Nearby, Excelsior exited a taxi. His suit looked as if he had slept in it. His hair and beard stood off in all directions. When he noticed Moira, he ran to her and grabbed her. His fingers dug painfully into her shoulders. "Where is my son? He wasn't with any of his friends. "

"Let go." Moira tried to break free, without success.

Excelsior shook her. "Tell me where to find Druidus! What did you do to him, witch?"

"Nothing." Moira remembered the night and forced herself not to smile. "He meant to take the evidence of last night's murder to your archive. But I can't say if he's still there or not."

Wordlessly, Excelsior let go and hurried into the building. Moira adjusted her clothes and followed more slowly. From the cellar she heard Druidus' voice before the fireproof door to the archive slammed shut with a reverberating thud. *Poor boy*, she thought. *Hopefully, Excelsior gets his temper under control soon.* She walked along the corridor to Sabio's office.

Sabio was still dictating a report into the funnel of a print-a-nerl. The nerl at the other end had difficulties wirting equally fast, but Sabio ignored its protest. When he saw Moira, he made a break. "That was fast."

Moira reported what Gronk had told her.

"So, we can forget about the idea of a killing spree. I guess a simple case of violence in a family would have been too easy." Sabio sighed, closed his eyes, crossed his hands behind his head, and leaned back. "I'm at my wits' end. Pete Huudien is the only clue we've still got, and we can't seem to find him."

"And the silvery-bright voice," Moira reminded him.

A gendarme knocked and entered the office. He bent nearly to the ground. "Commissaire Marten, Colonel Magique begs you to come to the archive vault. Druidus Van Steen is asking for you."

That didn't sound good. Moira ran. Undefined fear throttled her and made her heart beat faster. Since Sabio was sitting down, she had a head start. She flew down the stairs and through the open security door of the archive. Inside, she stumbled over Excelsior's head lying directly in the doorway. Only the wide back of the Colonel Magique stopped her. The empty gaze in Excelsior's dead eyes made her shiver. Where was Druidus? What had happened?

She freed herself and looked around. With wide open eyes, she stared at the scene in front of her.

Blood dripped from ceiling and walls. The sweet metallic scent of it made her gag. Druidus crouched on the ground holding Excelsior's body in one arm, the sword in the other. He rocked to and fro and whimpered.

A gigantic fist crushed Moira's heart. Her legs refused to carry her any longer, so she squatted beside him. Hesitantly she put a hand on his shoulder. "Druidus?"

Slowly he looked up and looked at her as if she belonged to a different world. His eyes were filled with fear and pain, but his face was motionless. He looked as if he didn't know her. "Can you find father's head?" He smiled, but it didn't look genuine. "He lost it." He giggled.

His low laugh set Moira's teeth on edge. She felt her breakfast rise in her throat and fought hard not to vomit. He must be under a spell. She squinted at the sword for confirmation, but the metal stayed dull. There was no trace of the light that normally indicated spells to her. But that was impossible, wasn't it? He couldn't have killed his father on purpose, could he?

"The boy is high," a gendarme said who stood beside the Colonel Magique. "I arrested a guy on a similar trip four weeks ago in the bar district."

At that moment, Sabio stumbled into the archive. Druidus looked up at him, his face expressionless. "I killed him, Sabio. Just me." Then he bent over his dad's body, hummed a melody, and didn't say another word.

Moira pressed her hand over her mouth to keep form crying. She was too weak to get up. Tears ran over her face, and her heart hurt as if someone had cut it in two. Steadfastly, she stared at Druidus. His face remained motionless as if chiseled from stone.

He couldn't be a maniac murderer. But what if? Had she slept with a murderer? He had confessed. Had he been playacting like his mother? Was that the reason Excelsior and Aparta tried to keep Druidus from having a permanent relationship? Did they suspect he was raving mad? Maybe they had even known for sure?

Moira's stomach cramped. Her breakfast wouldn't stay down much longer. Instinctively she got up and stumbled out of the archive. Beside the stairs, she vomited into a trash can until her body was empty.

Gently, Sabio put a hand on her back. "Something is terribly wrong here. Druidus would never do anything like this. I know him. Come, let the gendarmes do their job."

Moira straightened and looked at him. His face was pale as death. She longed to believe him, but what about Druidus' confession? Without resisting she followed him past their colleagues and up the stairs. Sabio talked soothingly to her, but all she caught was his promise to visit Druidus in prison together with her.

"Since you're an aspirant of the Gendarmerie, no one can keep you away," he said.

Moira clung to this thought like a drowning person to a lifeline. If only she could talk to Druidus, everything would be all right. He would explain what truly happened.

In the hall they met Aparta. Despite the chaos in her mind, Moira noticed the contempt in the woman's eyes as she glanced at her. With honey-sweet friendliness, the auralogist said, "Don't worry. The examination board isn't all that bad."

Moira ignored her. She let go of Sabio and collapsed onto one of the benches in the hall.

Aparta lifted an eyebrow and looked at Sabio. "What's wrong? Is she ill? Do we have to reschedule the test?"

Sabio didn't answer. He simply gazed at her in silence.

All color drained from Aparta's face. All of a sudden, her voice quivered. "Is something wrong with Druidus? Excelsior said he found him."

Sabio turned away and walked toward his office. "Please come with me. We need to talk."

Aparta grabbed his shoulders and barked, "Tell me right now what happened to Druidus!"

"He beheaded his father," Moira yelled. "Your son is a damned murderer!" Crying, she flung both hands over her face.

Aparta staggered a few steps backward, then she lunged at Moira. "That's not true!" Screaming, she hit Moira, who barely managed to keep her head covered. "My son would never do anything like that. Never! It's just not true."

"Don't you care that your husband is dead?" With her arms over her head, Moira's voice was dampened.

"He was an Idiot. But Druidus. My son. My little darling. He wouldn't do that." Aparta grabbed Moira's shoulders and shook her. "It's all your fault, damned slut."

Moira's head jerked to and fro. She didn't have the strength to fight back. In vain, Sabio tried to pull Aparta off. He needed the help of two more gendarmes to control the raging woman until Doc came running and injected a sedative into her arm.

He put his hand on Moira's shoulder. "Are you all right? Do you need a sedative as well?"

Moira shook her head. How could she be all right if the man she loved was a murderer?

"Fine." Doc took his bag and walked down the stairs to the archive.

Moira sat motionlessly on the bench in the entrance hall until an ambulance came to fetch the sleeping Aparta. Right behind the ambulance men, Franka and Tord entered the building.

"Poor thing." Franka hugged her friend and held her. Moira clung to her as if she wanted to squeeze her to death.

"Come, we'll take you home," Tord said.

At that moment, Druidus was led past them in handcuffs. He was staring at the ground. Franka let Moira go, turned, and spat at him. He didn't react. The gendarme leading him made a quick gesture with his hand, and the spit rolled off a temporary shield.

He frowned at Franka. "Don't do that again."

"Druidus." Moira walked toward the captive. As little as she trusted it, her heart insisted he wasn't guilty. "You didn't really kill him, did you? Tell me the truth."

Druidus lifted his gaze and looked at her. "Truth. I killed him. Just me."

His voice sounded apathetic, but his eyes were full of sorrow and tears. Moira reached out toward him. She trembled. "Why?"

The gendarme pushed her arm aside and dragged Druidus forward. "You're not allowed to talk to him."

A wave of despair buried Moira. How could she tell which one of Druidus' words or eyes was lying, if she couldn't talk to him? She felt as if someone had sliced her heart with a sharp knife. It became increasingly harder to stay on her feet. She faltered.

Franka put her arm around her. "Come, Moira, you need to rest."

Reluctantly, she allowed her friend to pull her along. When they entered Tord's rickety carpisto, she had an idea that didn't fit one bit with the turmoil of her feelings – a thought that seemed terribly funny. She giggled. *Now they will have to find yet another day for my testing.* Giggling mixed with sobbing. The whole way home, she giggled and cried and tears ran over her cheeks.

She was still laughing when Franka pushed her into her bedroom and took off her shoes and the spoiled dress. She only stopped when she lay in bed. Cover and cushion still smelled of Druidus. Moira threw them out, curled into a tight ball, and locked the world out of her mind. This, she had known how to do ever since her father had left. Franka's voice bubbled past her like the purl of a brook. After some time that seemed endless to her, Moira fell asleep.

Chapter 24

Moira stayed in bed letting herself go, hardly noticing Franka's caring attention. For hours on end she stared at the ceiling and tried to tell herself Druidus didn't exist. The longing for him cut into her heart like a knife. Several times, a healer Franka had called examined her, but no one could help. "There is nothing physically wrong with her. She should talk to a psychiatrist," he suggested, but Moira refused to leave the bed. In the evenings, she listened to Franka's atypically sad voice without grasping the meaning. In the mornings, she squeezed her eyes shut as long as she could. She was raw inside. *Why did you do that, Druidus? Life wasn't too bad the way it was. Maybe Excelsior would have changed his point of view later.* Angrily, she hit her pillow. *Why do I still love him?* There were no answers.

For two weeks, Franka endured Moira's emotional rollercoaster ride of apathy and tantrums. Finally, she lost her temper. "Stop acting like a child. For you, Tord and I moved the date for our wedding. We thought you'd come round eventually. I thought I could help you, talk to you. Instead, you're simply lying around not saying a single word." She put her hands on her hip. "And I wonder all the time, why? You hardly knew Excelsior van Steen."

Moira looked at her with red-rimmed eyes. "But I loved Druidus." She put her hands over her face. "I'm in love with a murderer. I'm so useless that I didn't even notice what kind of person he really is."

Franka sat on the edge of the bed. "That surprises me. Of the two of us, you've always been the better judge of character."

"He is… he is… I hate him." Moira dug her face into the pillow that still seemed to be smelling of Druidus despite having been thoroughly washed.

Determined, Franka got up. "You need to talk to someone who understands more about these kinds of things than I do." She went into the living room and Moira heard her use the parlebol. A little later, she returned and dragged Moira out of bed. She handed her a pile of clothes. "Get dressed and come."

Moira obeyed. She didn't care what happened anyway. Apathetic, she followed Franka and sat in Tord's carpisto. Silently they drove through town. Moira wondered how the sun dared to shine so brightly that even the alleys and backyards of her neighborhood looked friendly despite the rubbish and the rats and the dying, yellowish grass fighting for life in gaps and cracks.

Finally, Franka stopped in front of the P&OS building and helped Moira to get out.

Lavant Bellamie hurried toward them, pulled Moira close, and hugged her tight. "My sweet," he whispered. Then he looked at Franka. "Thank you for bringing her here." He took Moira's hand. "Come."

Moira shuffled after him through the entrance hall into the nerlift, along the long corridor on the fifth floor, through a threefold security door and into her father's living room.

He sat her on his sofa and handed her a glass of warm cocoa. "This used to help you," he said.

Moira sipped and put the glass aside. She pulled up her knees until they reached her chin and hugged her legs. "What am I supposed to do here?"

He scratched his beard. "Franka thinks we need to analyze Druidus' actions."

"What's there to analyze? Druidus sat with the murder weapon in hand right beside his decapitated father and he confessed to the murder." Moira fought against tears again. "He confessed twice."

"That's exactly what makes me suspicious. According to Sabio, he used exactly the same words each time. That's not normal." Lavant crouched in front of her and put one hand on her knee. "Sabio is convinced that Druidus is innocent. He even transferred so he could prove it."

"Innocent?" Moira raised her gaze and looked at her father. A twinkling of hope lit up the darkness of her heart. Was Sabio right? Could it be that Druidus wasn't guilty despite the evidence? She shook her head. It was impossible.

"There wasn't enough time for a brainwash, and you can't force a confession with magic."

"Not with legal magic, that's true." Lavant sat beside her and took her hand. "But there are enough inconsistencies to start looking for illegal spells. For one, we've got Druidus' curious confession. Add to that that none of the surveillance globes of the archive recorded anything – strange in itself."

"How so?"

"It seems that Excelsior van Steen turned them off. He came in, hugged his son fiercely, and said be had to talk with him about something important in private. That's why he deactivated the globes." Lavant shrugged. "I consider that rather suspicious."

Moira trusted Sabio's judgment and wanted to believe him and her father, but what options would be left if Druidus wasn't a murderer? "Excelsior didn't look like the kind of guy to commit suicide. But even if, why would Druidus accuse himself?"

"There are other possibilities." Lavant cocked his head. "Excelsior didn't seem all that pleased yesterday that Druidus had brought you."

Moira's eyes widened. "You're trying to tell me he attacked his own son? Just because he doesn't like his girlfriend?"

Lavant shrugged. "Stranger things have happened. Violence in upper class families isn't unheard of."

"In that case, Druidus would have acted in self defense." Moira put her feet on the ground and sat up straight. "There has to be some kind of proof."

"Sabio is working on it for Druidus' sake, and also because Aparta is pestering him. I've got the feeling the arrest of her son is more important to her than the death of her husband." Lavant leaned back. "That said, why should I wonder in an arranged marriage like theirs? For Excelsior, she never was more than a status symbol. I always wondered why she didn't keep a whole battalion of lovers."

Moira remembered how she had spied on Sabio and Aparta accidentally. "She wouldn't let everyone know, would she?"

Lavant nodded. "Excelsior once hired one of my men to observe her, but I haven't gotten a final report yet. Should there have been another man, she would have had a motive for getting rid of Excelsior too."

"Maybe Druidus is trying to protect her with his confession." Moira jumped up, completely rejuvenated. She felt full of energy and fresh. A heavy burden had dropped from her heart.

Lavant pulled her back down on the sofa. "There are more possibilities."

"What else?" Moira squirmed.

"Another person could have entered the archive, or the sword could have been carrying a homicide or a suicide spell. That would fit the killings at the Ramasseur's too. From all I read in the files, Madame Ramasseur would have had reason to have her husband kill himself. And a competing collector would have been an option. If that's the case, Excelsior would be a victim of his trade."

"I didn't notice any traces of a spell on the sword." Moira wiped her face with both hands. "Also, Druidus, Sabio, and Excelsior are experienced officers. They wouldn't activate a homicide spell, would they?"

Lavant smiled at her lovingly. "This kind of spell doesn't shut down automatically after use. Once they're active, everyone touching the weapon unprotected will be afflicted."

"Shouldn't Excelsior know that after all his years in the archive?"

Lavant nodded. "I didn't say I could explain all inconsistencies."

Moira breathed deeply and thought. *It's strange I didn't see any magic, but maybe these spells are so different that I can't spot them. One thing's for sure. If someone had bespelled the sword, it couldn't have been Madame Ramasseur. The gardener had said he took the parcel inside without her knowledge.* She sighed. "If there is a spell on the weapon, it must have been put on it before the Ramasseurs died."

"Maybe one of the burglars from the museum did it?"

Moira thought of Lif and Leclerque. "They're both dead."

"Except for Pete Huudien." Lavant leaned back again and crossed his hands behind his head. "As far as I know, Buds and Semra still haven't found him. And aside from his fiancée's statement there is no sign the two of them really meant to get married."

"Why would he put a spell on the sword?"

"To get rid of Lif maybe? It's possible he didn't know this kind of spell wouldn't deactivate."

Moira leaned back too and breathed deeply. The three options that allowed for Druidus' innocence gave her new hope. She considered it unlikely that Excelsior killed himself, but self defense wasn't out of the question. It was equally likely that Druidus surprised someone who beheaded the archivist and whom he wanted to protect – like his mother, for example. Still, Moira wondered if a dainty woman like her would have been able to lift the heavy sword. And why didn't Excelsior defend himself? On a purely physical level, he was superior to his wife. The most likely idea was the option with the homicide spell. She got up. "I have to help Sabio to prove Druidus' innocence."

Hope made it possible for her to see the world around her anew. A single portrait adorned the empty wall of the sparsely decorated room, a portrait of her at age six. A bunch of flowers stood under it in a vase. Moira bent down and hugged her father. "Thank you for waking me up," she whispered.

He returned the hug wordlessly. Then he got up too. "Come, I'll take you to the Gendarmerie."

"Let's go to the prison first. I need to see Druidus." Moira longed to tell her beloved that she believed in his innocence.

Lavant shook his head. "There's no use. Prison admin doesn't let anyone near him except for his lawyer and his mother. But tomorrow morning he's scheduled to appear at court."

"What? That fast?"

Lavant stretched. "The mayor has personally taken action to make sure the case is handled speedily. I think it's due to the hype the press makes about it."

"In that case, I'll be at court tomorrow too." Moira was sure that Druidus would be glad to see her. Surely he was waiting eagerly for Sabio to find proof of his innocence. "Let's go."

Chapter 25

When Moira entered Sabio's office, she was surprised to see Semra. "Where is Sabio?"

"He transferred to the archive." Semra held out her hand. "It's wonderful that you're back, Moira."

Only now did Moira notice the brass sign with "Commissaire Semra Jaman" written in dainty golden letters. "Oh, you've been advanced?"

Semra sighed. "Someone has to do the dirty work. I'd feel better if Sabio or Druidus would sit here."

Moira sat on a chair in front of the desk and explained the theories she and her father had come up with to Semra.

"Sabio and I thought along the same lines. Unfortunately we couldn't build a conclusive chain of events." Semra dug a file out of the pile of folders on her desk and handed it to Moira. "Doc's autopsy showed that, apart from Monsieur, the Ramasseurs died the same way as the homeless people before."

"The blood is missing?"

Semra nodded. "If you count five to six liters blood per person, there should have been twenty-five to thirty liters. I wonder where it all went." She bent forward. "By the way, the murders stopped since they took Druidus into custody. More than two weeks without new corpses. It gets you thinking, doesn't it?"

Moira fought to stay quiet. "I thought we agreed that Druidus isn't a murderer."

"I am only repeating the press' arguments. They say that he did confess to his father's murder, so why should it have been his first?"

Moira put the file back on the desk. "If it's only a question of no more murders, the reason could well have been Excelsior's death or that of Monsieur Ramasseur."

"We both know that the press earns its money with speculations like that. But as long as we don't have sound proof, there isn't much we can do." Semra stretched and yawned with her hand in front of her mouth. "Dear me, am I tired. How did Sabio survive this?" She smiled at Moira. "I'd appreciate it if you could work hand in hand with him. In his opinion, there is a homicide spell behind all the murders, because Druidus acted so strangely. Unfortunately our lab couldn't find one even with the most sensitive spell detectors."

"What do you think?" Moira asked.

Semra shrugged. "Difficult to say. But I really hope Sabio is right. All other possibilities are really hard to prove."

Moira got up. "I'd better go and help him right now."

Semra nodded. "Get him to rest, too, at least for a little while. Since he transferred to the archive, he hardly goes home any more. I fear he's close to collapsing."

At the door, Moira turned once more because she had remembered something. "Have you found a clue to Pete Huudien's whereabouts?"

"Buds found a couple of people who think they might have seen him near several of the crime scenes. But there's no trace of where he could be now." Semra dug back into her files. "Take care of Sabio, will you?"

"Done." Moira left. The closer she got to the archive, the slower she walked. Fear tugged at her nerves, and they vibrated like bowstrings. The gruesome scene was still too much alive in her memory. Her hands shook, and she felt cold. Reluctantly, she opened the door. She noticed with great relief that the crime scene cleaning crew had cleaned the room well. Not the slightest trace of blood was left behind. It didn't help her to cope with her memory, but it made it easier to enter the archive.

The archivist's workbench had been moved right beside the entrance desk, and Sabio crouched over a sheaf of paper lying on it. He looked up from his work and a smile brightened his sunken face. "It's nice to see you're feeling better. I worried about you."

Moira was horrified by his exhaustion. "May I help you?"

"Sure." He pointed to a wobbly pile of files. "Could you take care of these? I'm very busy with an invention to prove Druidus' innocence." His gaze hardened. "Or do you believe he's a murderer too?"

"No." Moira picked up the files. *But can I exclude you from the list of suspects? You would have had a motive.* She walked along the corridors and placed the files where they belonged. On the desk Excelsior had assigned to her lay another file. A note with Sabio's handwriting clung to it. It read, FIND FAULTS. SOMETHING DOESN'T FIT.

Moira opened the file. It held copies of every lab report connected to Excelsior's murder. Sabio had marked several places, for example, "No sign of homicide spell," "No Suicide spell detectable," "Fingerprints from four people verified: Pete Huudien, Monsieur Ramasseur, Excelsior and Druidus van Steen" and "Remaining blood in corpse and on scene: roughly four liters."

The last one had been underlined three times.

Only four liters? Moira wondered where the rest of Excelsior's blood had gone. He had been a strong man, and she would have expected at least six liters. She closed the file and returned to Sabio who was still bent over his construction plans.

"Sabio? According to the file, there were nearly two liters of blood missing from the crime scene. Do you think a third person took it?"

"You think Druidus wanted to protect someone?" He looked up at her. "I can't imagine why he'd do that. The only people close enough to his heart to do something so foolish would be Aparta and you. And neither of you was anywhere near the crime scene."

Moira remembered Aparta's reaction and was sure that she had been just as surprised by Excelsior's murder as anyone else. "How else do you explain the missing blood?"

"I don't know. I've been pondering this ever since the first murder with not enough blood on the crime scene." He yawned and rubbed his eyes. "Somehow all these murders are connected – the homeless, Lif Borson, Leclerque Bastide, the Ramasseurs and Excelsior. And the one thing that could explain a series of murders like this would be a homicide spell."

Moira frowned. "It should be illegal to put a spell on a weapon that forces others to kill."

"It is illegal. Doesn't mean it won't get done." Sabio pointed to a pile of weapons on a nearby shelf. "These are all weapons with one killing spell or another. And there's a whole bunch more, farther down in the archive."

Moira took a step backwards. Better to play it safe.

"Also, you're forgetting that the sword is an antique. Back then, people were less reserved with spells like this. I believe Druidus' only chance will be to prove there was a homicide spell." Sabio stretched, waved her over, and pointed at his plan. "With this gadget, it should be possible to focus magic with an unprecedented precision."

Moira stared at the lines and labels. It didn't make much sense to her untrained eye. "What's it for?"

"I will explain, but first I need to fill in your background knowledge." Sabio poured himself and Moira a glass of water and indicated for her to sit. "What do you know about Wild or Untamed Magic, also called Magie Sauvage?"

"It's all around us but useless to humans, right?" Moira wasn't sure if her answer was correct. She felt as if she was sitting for a test she hadn't studied for.

Sabio nodded and sipped his water. "Together with sunlight, plants use Magie Sauvage to turn water and air into carbohydrates. During that process, the magic changes. In the end, Unified Magic or Magie Généraliser is bound to the carbohydrates."

"Which can be used by humans," Moira said.

Sabio nodded again. "The amount of Magie Généraliser a creature can use depends on the species genetics and on the individual's personal talent. Unicorns for example use nearly one hundred percent, but humans only three to ten percent of this magic. The rest is released as Focused Magic or Magie Focaliser."

"Is that the kind of magic nerls need for their survival?" Moira was relieved she knew a small detail at least.

"Very good." Sabio looked at her with surprise. "Nerls digest Focused Magic, and the components rearrange into Magie Sauvage again, but that's not important for my gadget." He pointed to the dark blue, star-spangled safety coat and the pointy hat with the same design hanging beside his desk, ready for use. "With the proper safety measures, it's possible to amp up Magie Généraliser with a little bit of Magie Sauvage. It's very dangerous but worth the effort. Spells created like that are very durable and hard to trace."

Slowly, understanding dawned on Moira. "Homicide and suicide spells. Therefore the new invention."

Sabio tapped his drawings. "My magiskope should be able to determine and name even the smallest amounts of magic clinging to an object. I finished planning. Now, I need to build and test it."

With renewed vigor, Moira got up. "What are we waiting for?"

"We need living materials. Something best suited would be some sort of wood that's extremely flexible. A small tree or bush maybe."

"Semra has a bamboo plant in her office. I'll fetch it." Moira ran off.

When she returned with the plant, Sabio held a crying Aparta in his arms, trying to calm her. With a jerk of his head, he indicated for Moira to make herself scarce.

"It's not the end of days yet," he said.

"But the prosecutor demanded the death penalty!" Aparta's voice was hoarse from crying so much.

Sabio patted her back and signaled to Moira again to leave. She set the bamboo on the ground beside the door and withdrew. She only returned when she was sure Aparta had left. Sabio had already started to build his magiskope. The bamboo proved to be the ideal building material. It was soft enough to be twisted into different shapes and bound with twine, but strong enough to support the construction.

Moira realized she couldn't help Sabio right now. "What shall I do while you're busy?"

"Well, I should be working on destroying the cursed weapons. Would you mind taking care of that? The list with the numbers of the shelves we need to see to first lies in the topmost drawer of the reception desk." Sabio spoke without looking up from his work.

Moira found the list without problems. She crouched to pull out the arm-long burning box from under the desk. She stopped before her fingers touched the glass. "Sabio?"

"Yes?" He looked at her.

"Did you use Wild Magic for the burning box too?"

"Of course. Wild Magic can only be destroyed by Wild Magic."

"Can I still use it without trouble?" Pensively, Moira watched the multi-colored swirling of the glass.

"Of course. You just put the weapons in and activate it. The lid will close automatically."

"What I meant was, will the spell suffer if I touch the glass? You know how little magic and I get along."

Sabio smiled. "Don't worry. The spell is only triggered when the lid closes."

Hesitantly, Moira pulled out the burning box. Then she went to look for the first weapon on the list. It was a spear, and it lay in a shelf near Sabio's workbench, sparkling slightly.

"We'll need a much bigger burning box for this." She took the spear from the shelf.

"Moira, no!" Sabio shouted and jumped at her.

A tingle ran up her arm, spreading though her body in mere seconds. She pulled the spear aside before Sabio could grab it. He slammed into her, and she closed her arms around him without letting go of the spear.

Sabio smelled of coffee and ink. Moira leaned her face against his chest. The smell woke memories of a man she had once had a wild relationship with. She felt her nipples harden. *Why did I never notice that Sabio is really good-looking?* Unbearable longing made her pant. She pushed her free hand under Sabio's shirt and stroked the skin on his back.

212

"Moira, what are you doing?" Sabio fought her — without success.

The spear filled Moira with unknown strength. With the hand holding the weapon, she pulled his head toward her.

"Please, Moira, remember Druidus." Sabio stared into her eyes with plain fear.

She hesitated. Deep down inside, she knew that this compelling desire didn't mirror her true feelings. *It's the spear.* The thought shot through her fogged mind like lightning. She fought against the urge to kiss Sabio and rip his clothes off. With her eyes closed, she clung to Sabio. She gathered all her strength and concentrated on Druidus. Her breathing was irregular and fast, but she managed to recall his beloved face. She felt the tingling in her arm intensify. *I need to get rid of the spear.* With all her strength, she pushed against the spell coming from the weapon. A wave surged through her and washed away the desire. Finally, Moira understood that it was a kind of magic, too. Her own kind of magic, the one she wasn't supposed to have according to her handicapped ID. She laughed happily.

Without opening her eyes, she let go of Sabio and turned toward a wall. She gathered her churning magic and catapulted it out of her arm into the spear. The wood groaned. When Moira opened her eyes, the weapon lay on the ground, split in three parts. She turned back to Sabio. He was sitting on his chair, his back to his desk, staring at her open-mouthed as if she was from a different world. His face was pale as death, and he didn't seem to breathe. For a moment, Moira thought he'd died from a heart attack.

Then he breathed out audibly. "Dear me, Moira, what was that?"

"I forgot the safety gloves. Sorry."

"No, I meant that there." He lifted his hand and pointed to the splintered spear. His arm shook.

"Is it bad that I broke it? I thought we were meant to destroy it anyway."

Sabio got up, walked to her, and put both hands on her shoulders. Slowly, color returned to his face. "Don't you realize what this means?"

"I sure do." Moira beamed. "It means I'm not disabled, regardless of what the examinations say."

Sabio shook his head and looked into her eyes. "The doctors couldn't find magic in you. They were looking for the wrong kind."

Moira frowned. The wrong kind?

"Didn't I tell you a minute ago that a spell containing Wild Magic can only be destroyed with another one containing Wild Magic?"

Now, Moira understood. But could it really be Magie Sauvage? Was that the reason the clairvoyante had called her Katie Féroce? Moira's knees buckled. Sabio helped her to sit down on his chair. She looked up at him. "Magie Sauvage?"

He shrugged. "There is no doubt about it, although I haven't got a clue how you survive it." He picked up the pieces of the spear and weighed them in his hand. "No traces of a homicide spell any more," he said. "I was quite surprised to see that it affected you like a love spell." He walked to his workbench and put the pieces on the counter.

"Strange things have always happened to me." Moira told him about her driving school carpisto that hit the ground after she had accidentally touched the carpet, and about Mona Beth, who stuck out her tongue, and about the many small incidents that had turned her into a misfit as a kid. She put her hands over her face. "What am I going to do now? With this kind of magic I might be a walking danger to all those I care about."

"Why do you think that?"

Moira told him about the clairvoyante's reaction. "Somehow, Madame Suzanka noticed the Wild Magic in me. She was terribly afraid of me."

Sabio sat on the edge of his desk and observed her. "Well, I can't see anything unusual."

"It said on her sign that she could read auras, and Aparta de Frees said that my aura had a strange rainbow-colored quality to it. She thought it was a wrong setting on her machine. And there's more." Moira told Sabio about the seal on the stone urn that she thought could be a combination of Hern's and Wild Katie's sigil. "If the hammer and anvil belong to Hern, the rainbow would be Katie Féroce's. It makes sense, doesn't it?"

Sabio beamed at her. "That's incredibly interesting. We'll definitely have to examine your skills more closely soon. But first we'll rehabilitate Druidus, all right?"

The memory of Druidus' pending judgment the next day sent a pang through Moira's heart. She didn't want to think about it just now. Work would help. She got up, picked up the list of the weapons scheduled for destruction, and scanned it.

"We need a much bigger burning box. Swords, spears and lances won't fit in this one." She pointed to the arm-length box standing beside the entrance desk.

"I'll bring a man-sized box tomorrow. It's been finished for a week already but I didn't get a trailer for the transport until yesterday."

"In that case, I'll fetch the smaller weapons first."

"Please remember the gloves this time." Sabio took dark blue gloves from his workbench and flung them at her. "I won't stand another attack of love delirium."

Laughing, Moira set out into the oldest part of the archives, where daggers and pistols waited for their destruction, and where the victims' screams slept under the dusty covers of the files of enquiry.

When the shape of the magiskope was finished, Moira managed to convince Sabio to call it a day. Together, they walked up the stairs to the entrance hall.

Sabio yawned. "You were right. I need to sleep at once."

Semra left Sabio's former office and hurried after them through the hall. "Wait, Moira. We need to talk."

Moira stopped.

Semra put a hand on her arm. "I'm sorry, but I have to suspend you from work until further notice."

Moira stared at her. "Why?"

Semra blushed. "It comes right from the top, and there's nothing I can do about it."

"Didn't they give any reasons for the suspension?" Sabio asked.

"Bureaucratic buck-shit." Semra snorted. "The mandatory time frame for the performance test has passed. Moira is only allowed to work if she passes the test. I insisted they'd set another date as soon as possible."

Just when I finally discovered my magic. Moira hung her head. "I'll miss you," she said quietly, seeing as it wasn't a good idea to ignore an order from high up.

"Thanks for understanding." Semra forced a smile.

"Don't worry." Sabio patted Moira's shoulder encouragingly. "I'll make sure to finish the magiskope fast. I'm sure it will give me the desired results. Meanwhile, you could cheer up Druidus and give him hope."

Sabio was right. Druidus would surely be delighted to see her. Moira's mood improved considerably. Also, she could surely bust Druidus from jail with her newly discovered powers should Sabio against all expectations not finish the magiskope in time. Consoled, he said her farewells and went home.

Chapter 26

When she was ready to set out for the prison the next morning, Franka stood in front of her door, gasping for air from walking up the stairs. Moira let her in so she could recover.

"I never thought the pregnancy would make me unfit this soon." Gratefully, her friend slumped in a comfy chair.

"It's not the pregnancy, it's the chocolate." Moira smirked and she knew Franka wouldn't mind the joke. "What do you want here this early?"

"Your dad called me. I'm supposed to take you to court to see the summing up of Druidus' case."

Moira's eyes widened. "The summing up already?" She sat down on another chair with a thud. "Why do they hurry so much? In other cases it takes months before they set a first date at court, and this case is hurried through..."

Franka answered, still breathing heavily. "The mayor himself exerted pressure, and he's backed up by the press. He's convinced that Druidus is also responsible for the murders of the homeless, especially since they stopped ever since they arrested him."

"Rubbish. They cannot pronounce a sentence if the taking of evidence isn't finished yet."

"Officially, it is over."

"But Sabio isn't done yet."

"No one cares. They've got a confession in a seemingly straightforward case. All clues lead to Druidus and all tests they did showed the murder weapon wasn't cursed." Franka bent forward and put a hand on Moira's knee. "What if the evidence doesn't mislead? Druidus committed a murder that will cost him a very long time in jail, if he isn't executed. You should keep that in mind."

Moira's stomach cramped but before she could answer, the parlebol rang. Her nerl accepted the call, and Director du Mar's face appeared.

"You'll hardly believe this, Moira. Upon my question about weapons from Hern's time period, I got three offers. Three! How shall I proceed? What do you think?"

Moira didn't really want to talk to Du Mar at that very moment, but then she remembered that the discovery of the weapon's thief or their seller could put a different light on Druidus' case. In case of an arrest there would be someone who could say something about any kind of homicide spell at least. She longed to send Du Mar to Sabio, but the director had been very clear on the fact that he wouldn't work with the Gendarmerie. What else could she advise?

"Tell them to send you photos of the weapons. Insist on detailed pictures so you can compare them to your drawings."

"Great idea. I'll call you again as soon as I know more."

"Hopefully you'll be successful soon," Moira said and thought, *For Druidus' sake too.* She thanked the director and ended the call.

Luckily, Franka had recovered enough so they could finally set out. The backseat and trunk of Franka's carpisto were stuffed with cardboard boxes and books. Moira's conscience woke when she spotted a corner of delicate, silvery material hanging from a flat cardboard box. *I'm so tied up in my own problems, I completely forgot about Tord and Franka.* Her ears burned and she swallowed. The wedding was supposed to take place in a couple of days. "Is this your wedding dress?"

Franka beamed at her. "Spider silk! It's a dream. And the bodice is embroidered with rainbow pearls and magical Bonnechance-waterdrops. Your father bought it for us."

"Why does my father buy your wedding dress?"

"I think he's trying to endear himself to us, so I'll tell him about you. Of course I won't do that, but he's rather helpful with the wedding preparations."

Moira was ashamed. "Is there anything I can do to help?"

"No need to." Franka threaded her carpisto into the traffic running toward the city center. "Lavant supports us generously. I'm just hoping someone finds a way to prove Druidus innocent. I strongly believe that my wedding will have to be canceled otherwise because I'd be short of a bridesmaid." She concentrated on driving. The closer they got to court, the more difficult it became to find a way through the traffic jams. Often they had to wait for a long time or were redirected.

"Is it true you've been suspended?" Franka asked.

"How do you know?"

"Lavant knows it from Sabio. I didn't want to believe it at first." Franka took a turn into a side street. "Your father and Sabio agree that someone must have pulled some strings." She looked at Moira. "I don't understand why someone should bother to get an aspirant suspended. Why not Sabio?"

"It does make sense. With Sabio as supervisor, I would have been allowed to visit Druidus in jail." Moira remembered well how friendly Druidus' mother had chatted with the Director of the Gendarmerie. "Aparta wants to suppress every possible contact between Druidus and me. I'm only surprised that she thought of something this unimportant with all the worry about her son on her mind."

"She must hate you a lot."

Moira forced a smile. "Let's say we don't get along all that well."

For the second time, Franka traveled along a one-way street near the courts building. When she discovered a free parking lot, she used it. "I think we'll have to walk the rest of the way."

Moira joined arms with her and they walked. She was amazed at the big crowd of people waiting in front of the court building. Everywhere outside, broadcast vans of several senders held up the traffic. Countless people carrying baskets of rotten fruit seemed to wait for the accused. Moira followed Franka to the back entrance, and she noticed Aparta, surrounded by bodyguards, who was talking into several reporters' microphones.

At that moment, a barred van stopped in front of the staircase and Druidus got out, accompanied by four gendarmes. Involuntarily Moira stopped walking. The crowd greeted the captive with curses, insulting gestures, and smelly fruit. Reporters vied for his attention like starving vultures. Luckily, the gendarmes had been prepared. Reporters, fruit, and screaming slid off their protective shield. Untouched, they dragged Druidus up the stairs. Moira's heart went out to him when she saw him shuffle through the angry crowd inside the oval of the protective spell with unmoving features.

Franka pulled on her arm. "Come on, we need to hurry. Your father will not be able to keep our places for much longer."

Moira followed her. One of her father's employees pressed two Ident-cards into their hands and held the usually locked back door open. They thanked him and slipped inside the building. A throng of people waited in front of the hall of hearing. Gendarmes checked every visitor for weapons before they let them in. Impatiently, Moira and Franka waited for their turn.

Subdued chitchat echoed through the gigantic hall. It sounded like a swarm of angry wasps. Moira looked for her father. He had kept seats in the front row, right behind the barrier to the prosecutor. Moira would have liked better to sit behind the accused and his lawyer, but Aparta and several of her friends already sat there. Determined, Franka hurried to Lavant and chose a place so Moira could sit in the middle. Wordlessly Lavant squeezed Moira's hand.

Soon all the free places were occupied and the doors of the hall of hearing closed with a thud. When a side door opened and Druidus was led in, the murmuring died down. With his head lowered, he shuffled to the dock. The pink overall he wore hung like a sack from his wide shoulders. Moira felt like crying. She cleared her throat and squirmed in her seat to draw his attention, but he stared at the ground persistently. Only Aparta shot her a poisonous gaze.

Moira bit her lower lip.

"It's no use," Lavant whispered. "Ever since the trial started, he's been this apathetic. If it weren't illegal, you could think the Gendarmerie drugged him."

A gong resounded and everybody got up. The judge came in with his assessors, and the hearing began. Moira listened neither to the persecutor nor to the defendant. She concentrated on the monotonous ticking of the dicta-nerls, who wrote down every word, but her eyes focused on Druidus. She didn't miss the slightest movement. The lawyers talked without end. *They're probably trying to compensate for the short trial,* Moira thought. After two hours of this, the judge and his assessors withdrew to find a verdict. Immediately, the accused was led out of the hall, and the murmuring commenced.

"He didn't move," Moira said. "He behaves as if his body is paralyzed and his thoughts lost to the world."

Lavant nodded. "I know. He didn't turn to his mother once during the whole trial."

"I'm sure something is very wrong here. If only I had more time." She clenched her fists.

Lavant put his hand on her knee. "Whatever I can do to help, let me know. I've got employees for any job you can imagine. Magicians, trackers, muscles with persuasive power, strategists... one word and they'll all work for you."

For the first time since Druidus had entered the hall, Moira looked at her father. She smiled. "If I need them, I'll tell you." She closed her eyes, leaned her head against his, and waited for the judge to return.

It took much longer than she had anticipated, but finally the accused, the judge and his assessors returned in the same order as before. The audience fell silent when the head assessor got up to read the verdict. Moira's heart beat in her throat and blood roared in her ears.

"After significant contemplation and due to the existing expertise about the criminal responsibility of the accused, we deem Druidus van Steen guilty." The head assessor sank back into his padded seat. Deathly silence filled the hall. Not even the people's breathing could be heard.

The judge got up, and the audience with him. The defender pulled up Druidus who was the only one who didn't react. Moira's hunch that he wasn't himself grew to certainty.

The judge cleared his throat. "Druidus van Steen. Killing your own father without showing even a tiny bit of remorse is worse than anything I've ever encountered in my long career as a judge of this institution. Therefore, I sentence you to death. A fitting curse will be spoken in two weeks from today."

Druidus remained motionless, but Aparta collapsed. One of her friends caught her at the last possible moment. Moira, too, felt as if someone had ripped the ground from under her feet. When the judge sat back down and another assessor got up to read the reasoning of the sentence, the audience jubilated. Only when threatened with consequences did the clapping, calling, and trampling die away.

How can one rejoice at the death of a person? A tear ran over Moira's cheek. "I can't even say goodbye."

Lavant put his arm around her and pulled her closer. "You should go to the drinking fountain. Druidus stopped there every single day to drink."

Moira kissed him on a stubbly cheek. While the judged called the audience to reason again, she hurried toward the exit. Right beside the water fountain in a corner of the corridor was a nerlaroma. Between it and a decorative pillar, not even two steps away from the fountain, was a niche just big enough for Moira. Conveniently, the light above the fountain was broken, which would make it possible to get close to Druidus unseen. She was wondering whether her father was responsible for the broken light when the hall's doors opened wide and the audience left.

Moira pressed herself closer to the wall and waited. When most visitors had left the building, Druidus was led out. He walked over to the fountain. Immediately, the four gendarmes accompanying him formed a half circle around him. Except for one near Moira, they turned their backs to him and scanned the passing people. Druidus bent forward and drank. His eyes found Moira. There was a sadness in them that tied her tongue. She longed to jump from her hiding place, to hug him and flee with him, but she knew she wouldn't stand a chance. She blew him a kiss. He smiled weakly and straightened up without a word. She nearly missed the slip of paper he dropped into the fountain, but his gaze moved from her face to the fountain and back several times, so she saw it before he turned to the gendarmes. While he was led back to the waiting prison van, Moira left her hiding place and grabbed the note. Druidus had to have prepared it in jail.

A heart with Moira's and Druidus' names inside dominated the upper half. Below was a wobbly drawing of a sword or dagger. Pensively, Moira stared at the slightly soaked paper. Her father and Franka found her there.

Lavant gazed over her shoulder. "What does it say?"

"He drew a sword." She showed him the drawing. "It has to mean something. He seemed determined to make sure I'd find the note."

"But we know the sword was the murder weapon." Franka joined arms with Moira and they walked toward the exit.

Lavant shrugged and followed them. "Maybe he really is as disturbed as his lawyer tried to make out."

"No way, his eyes were clear. He knew exactly what he was doing. But I got the feeling he couldn't talk about the things he knows."

"In that case, he must have known that this would be his only chance to get a note to someone outside of prison." Lavant scratched his chin. "You are right, dear. He wouldn't have squandered this chance on something unimportant."

Despite her worries, Moira's heart grew warm. Druidus had only had this one piece of paper, and spent half of it for a declaration of love. She bit her lip again to keep from crying. She had to find a way to prove his innocence.

Franka had an idea. "Maybe he is trying to point to the owner of the sword."

"It's possible," Moira said. "Will you take me to the Gendarmerie? I want to talk to Sabio about it."

"Sure." Franka dug the key to her carpisto from the bottom of her oversized handbag and jingled them. Moira hugged Lavant farewell.

When they reached the carpisto, Franka unlocked it and said over the roof, "By the way, I found it great that you made up with your dad."

"Me too," Moira said and got into the passenger's seat.

Chapter 27

It felt like an eternity to Moira before Franka dropped her off at the Gendarmerie. She longed to finally do something for Druidus. Since she wasn't officially allowed to be here, she waited until the entrance hall was empty before she hurried into the cellar. As she had expected, the archive was open.

Sabio was just hanging the safety coat on its hook. "I thought you aren't allowed to come here," he said when he noticed her.

"No one can forbid me to visit my friend and mentor."

Sabio smiled. He still looked so tired that Moira feared he'd collapse any moment. The shadows under his eyes were nearly black.

"You need to sleep more," she said.

"I know, but there's so much to do. Since you're off duty, I'll have to destroy the weapons beside all my other work. And I needed to bespell a bigger burning box for that." He pointed to a glass coffin big enough to hold the well-padded President of the Gendarmerie Magique. "Add the work my magiskope still needs, and I hardly get home at night."

"Have you had a successful try with the magiskope?"

Sabio nodded. "I improved the magical focusing by seven percent. A few more adjustments and it won't miss the slightest trace of a spell."

Moira told him about Druidus' sentence.

He wiped his hand over his eyes. "I'm not surprised. All evidence points at him too conveniently, and with the confession…"

"But you only have to look at his eyes to see that something's not right. He behaves as if his body is under remote control. I'm quite sure the confession's not from him."

"Only those who know him well will notice things like that."

Moira showed the note to Sabio. "Can you examine it?"

Sabio nodded. He led her over to his desk where he stored his most important gadgets, including the magiskope.

Moira marveled.

He had managed to create a pentacle that rested half a cubit over the desk's surface on a support made of bamboo. Seemingly without support, a drop of water, a tiny flame, some smoke, a stone, and a lock of hair hovered between its spikes.

Sabio put the note under the magiskope. The magical symbols began to glow and the lock of hair sparkled with the colors of a rainbow.

After a few minutes, the magiskope spoke with a flat voice. "Paper made by elves, waterproof and tear-resistant, pen with run-of-the-mill lead, not bespelled. Inscription unclear. No connection to existing files."

Moira sighed. "I hoped Druidus had added a magical explanation."

"The note is from Druidus?" Sabio examined it more closely, while Moira told him how she got it.

He thought for a long time. "Druidus isn't stupid. He knows I'll do all I can to prove there was a homicide spell. So, the sword has to indicate something else."

"Maybe it symbolized the person behind the museum's robbery?"

"You think he wants us to find Pete Huudien? I'll request Buds' report on the current state of investigations immediately." Sabio yawned.

"You'd better lie down and rest for a while," Moira said.

"Later. I've got too much to do." Sabio went to fetch the report, but it didn't tell them anything new. None of the known informants had a hint of a trace that could lead them to Pete Huudien. And the other weapons hadn't shown up either.

When Sabio put the file on the desk, he faltered and bumped into the magiskope. It wobbled dangerously but didn't topple. Sabio breathed with relief and wiped his face with both hands. "You are right. I'm way too tired to work. I'd better get home before I start breaking things."

Discouraged and exhausted, Sabio and Moira left the archive. It was raining again. Before Sabio could fetch his carpisto, a taxi stopped in front of the entrance and ejected Aparta. Moira scurried behind one of the pillars supporting the porch roof before she could be noticed. Tears ran over Aparta's cheeks, and her eyes had swollen to slits from all the crying.

"Only a fortnight left," she whispered. "My son has only fourteen days left to live." She put her arms around Sabio's neck and let her tears run free.

Sabio looked as if a dragon had decided to roost on his heart. "I'm very close to a breakthrough." His voice was hoarse.

"You've been saying that ever since the trial started."

Sabio pressed his lips together.

Aparta looked up at his face. "There has to be something we must be able to do. It can't be too late."

"Don't give up hope. As long as he's not dead, the execution can be suspended to consider new evidence. All we need is proof..." Sabio's voice broke.

Aparta wiped away her tears and pushed out her chin. "Druidus did not kill Excelsior."

"He confessed."

"He was lying. Why don't you prove that there is a spell on the sword?"

"It's not that easy." Sabio sighed. "All specialists agreed that the weapon isn't cursed. It only tires the bearer. For them, the sword is nothing but a normal weapon. No better and no worse than any other weapon." He breathed deeply. "If my magiskope cannot find a spell either, we can only hope that the true murderer will speak up before it's too late." He put an arm around her shoulders and led her down the stairs away from the station. "I will examine the sword as soon as possible."

Aparta put her hands over her face. "You won't find anything anyway."

Moira pushed the thought away. Sabio's magiskope might confirm the experts' conclusions. It was unthinkable. She knew Druidus too well.

"If there is something, I will find it," Sabio said firmly. He led Aparta to his carpisto and held the passenger door open for her.

"I want to be there when you find it." Aparta got in.

"I'll call you in time–" were the last words Moira could understand before Sabio got in and left.

Bugged, she walked home through the rain. From the corridor outside her flat she could hear her parlebol ring. As fast as she could, she opened the door, ran into the living room and accepted the call. Too late. She swore. Too bad; she had forgotten to ask her parlebol-nerl to record the calls.

Although she wasn't hungry, she went into the kitchen. She was determined not to ignore her body's needs like Sabio did. She opened the fridge. Except for a moldy piece of cheese and cold cuts with a greenish tinge, it was empty. There wasn't even a ready-made meal in the fridge compartment. She looked at the clock. It wasn't too late to go shopping, and a short walk to the shopping center would prevent her from brooding over Druidus' fate. She grabbed her bag and hurried off.

When she returned loaded with food, the parlebol was ringing again. This time, she caught it in time. It was Director du Mar.

"Imagine, Moira, someone actually offered me a couple of daggers from the burglary. I will meet the seller tomorrow around noon."

Moira's jaw dropped. "Are you nuts?" The words escaped before she could help herself. Director du Mar looked hurt, and Moira apologized.

"What I meant to say is that a meeting like that is extremely dangerous. We'll have to assume that the person trying to sell the weapons to you might be the murderer of the homeless or at least an accomplice."

Du Mar frowned. "The newspaper insisted the murderer had been caught and sentenced to death. Surprisingly quick, if you ask me."

Moira pressed her lips together. She needed a while to compose herself before she could answer. "They've got the wrong person."

Du Mar paled. "But that would mean… dear me, I really could be in danger!"

Moira stayed silent.

"What are we going to do now?" he asked.

She thought for a while. Then she had an idea. "Can you come over and pick me up?"

"I'll be there as soon as possible." Du Mar reached for the keys of his carpisto beside his parlebol and ended the call. Moira called her father to prepare him for a visit.

Three quarters of an hour later, she sat in a plain beige and gray conference room of P&OS with Director du Mar and her father.

"Let me sum this up." Lavant smoothed out his notes and looked at Moira. "Your friend here lost a box with antique weapons to burglars roughly a month ago. Weapons from this box were used to kill Lif Borson and Bastide, as well as Druidus' father. Maybe they were also used to kill all those homeless people. And now, Monsieur du Mar arranged a meeting with someone who is most likely the true villain in all these cases or who knows the culprit at least."

Moira nodded. "I'm counting on your help. After all, you offered." She swallowed. It was the first time since her childhood that she had asked him for a favor. Would he let her down again?

"Why don't you get a special task force from the Gendarmerie?"

"First, Monsieur du Mar cannot work with the Gendarmerie at the moment because his wife obtained a temporary court order that forbids gendarmes to follow him. Second, no one will believe us because everyone thinks the murderer has already been sentenced to death." Moira counted off the reasons on her fingers. "Third, I've been suspended, and fourth, this inability to do something eats me up. If I can't help in any way, something that will take my mind off Druidus for a while, I'll go crazy." She looked at her father pleadingly. "Will you help us, please?"

Lavant woke a messenger-nerl. "Call all officers-in-charge. Alarm code one." The nerl shot off like greased lightning.

All of a sudden, Moira's heart was as light as never before. "Thanks," she whispered.

Lavant waved her gratitude aside. "A dagger from that burglary killed Bastide. I'm taking something like that personally, for crying out loud."

The next morning, Lavant's people hid around the storage building Du Mar had been given as the meeting place. Dressed up, they posed as drunks, homeless, prostitutes, lovers, and whatever else fit the shabby surrounds of the storage buildings. The limousine with Moira, Director du Mar, and Lavant turned into the seemingly deserted road at the appointed time. When Moira left the carpisto, she glanced around secretly for her father's employees but didn't discover a single one, even though she knew they were there. She joined arms with Lavant, who was playing Du Mar's role as a rich collector of antique art.

Since Moira had insisted on keeping him company, he had found her an expensive dress and high heel shoes, and decorated her with jewelry like a winter solstice tree. He insisted she wear a blond wig just in case the person they were meeting had been at Druidus' trial and had noticed her there. Moira had promised not to talk and to stay close to him at all times. She scuttled at his side toward the entrance of the storage building. Secretly she cursed the high heels, but she managed to walk without twisting an ankle. Her heart beat faster and she understood why Director du Mar had preferred to stay inside the limousine.

Lavant tried a small door set into the bigger gate of the storage building. It wasn't locked, so they entered. After the bright midday sun, Moira's eyes needed a while to adjust to the twilight inside. A few stapled wooden boxes on the left hand side looked lost in the gigantic hall. The room was two stories high and as wide as a football field. The three overseas containers at the far end also looked lost. In front of them several tables stood side by side and a long, bright Lumière Magique hovered above. Lavant was walking toward it purposefully when a distorted voice stopped him.

"Who's the woman?"

"My daughter." Lavant patted Moira's hand.

"Tell her to wait outside."

"Did you see the kind of people hanging around out there? I'm not going to leave my daughter there, all alone."

The voice stayed silent for quite a while.

"What's wrong? Do you want my money or not?" Lavant's voice faded into the vastness of the warehouse without an answer.

Finally a sigh echoed through the hall. "Fine, but tell her to leave her hands where I can see them."

"That's the spirit." Lavant walked through the hall with Moira on his arm. A darkly-clad, slim figure stepped out of the shade of the containers. He wasn't very big, and didn't seem very strong. A wide-rimmed hat hid his face in shadow.

Moira's gaze wandered to the items on the well illuminated table. On a white paper table-cloth lay knives, arrowheads, swords, bronze fittings of scabbards and bucklers, axe heads, and helmets made of bronze, all arrayed side by side. There was even a corslet. Moira's eyebrows rose when she noticed a distinctive scent that tugged at her memory.

Lavant nudged her with his elbow and lifted an eyebrow questioningly. She nodded. That was the pre-arranged sign that the weapons really were the ones they were looking for. While Moira wondered why the acerbic smell seemed so familiar, her father entered the oval of light cast by the Lumière Magique and stepped toward the dark clad figure.

"Merde," the voice said. The light flashed, and Moira closed her eyes, blinded by it.

"Go, go, go!" Lavant shouted.

Very nearly, Moira missed the low clink of weapons bumping into each other. Instinctively she pushed her dad to one side and flattened herself against the ground. Behind them, metal rang on stone and somewhere to the side hasty steps retreated. The strangely familiar scent faded. At all sides of the building doors slammed into the walls as Lavant's people stormed in with their weapons drawn.

Moira was sure the danger was over now, so she sat up and looked around. Beside her, her father got up. Behind him, a young man dressed up as a hustler stumbled to the side, seemingly without a reason. In falling, he grabbed for the air.

"Got him," he called.

But Moira saw a dark figure slip though the door at the last possible moment before fireballs ripped the frame apart.

"He had a camouflage coat. Those are really expensive." A woman took something from the young man's hand that Moira couldn't see and called out. "Boss?"

"Thanks." Lavant helped Moira to get up and they walked over to the two. Marveling, Moira caressed the invisible material.

"Search the area. Tell everyone not to touch the weapons. They might be dangerous," Lavant ordered. The woman and the young man ran off. Lavant pulled a messenger-nerl with a flight-gadget from the pocket of his jacket and threw him into the air. "Fetch Sabio."

The nerl flew away. Lavant turned to Moira and hugged her. "Your reaction was fantastic." He pointed to a dagger lying on the ground not too far away from them. "A blink of an eye later and one of us could have been seriously hurt or worse."

Moira was glad about his praise, but she was also annoyed that she hadn't thought of her newly discovered magical abilities. With them, she surely would have been able to arrest the guy. *Well, it can't be helped.* She walked over to the table and looked at the weapons more closely. Maybe Sabio would find fingerprints on them. She frowned. *I thought there were more weapons in the box. Where is the rest?* Her gaze fell on the containers behind the table. The middle one was missing the wire with the lead imprint of customs that was used to seal each container before transport. *Maybe they're in there.* She looked around but Lavant and his people were busy searching every inch of the hall. She walked to the container and lifted the grip of the closing mechanism. It had been oiled and she had no difficulty moving it. Carefully, she swung the door open. It was oiled too and didn't shriek, but something inside the container whimpered.

Moira flung the door all the way open so the light of the Lumière Magique would fall into the container. An open cardboard box with more weapons stood at the front end. Moira ignored it because a figure squatted in the far corner of the container.

The captive lifted his hands in a protective gesture. "Not again. Please, not again."

Moira turned and called her father, who turned toward her immediately. At that moment, Semra and Buds entered with a handful of gendarmes through a side door and stopped him. Moira signaled them to come and turned back to the person squatting at the back of the container.

She mumbled inconsequential but soothing words and walked closer. The stench made her gag. Near the right wall stood a bucket with feces, and right beside it a tablet with moldy bread and a spent candle. Moira covered her mouth with her hand and walked on. Her steps thundered on the metal floor. The person hugged his head with both arms and wailed. Moira crouched beside him and put one hand on his arm. "Don't worry. Everything will be fine. I'm with the Gendarmerie Magique." It was a little white lie but it wasn't the time for lengthy explanations just now. "Who are you?"

The man whimpered. Moira asked several times, but he only answered when she pulled her hand away.

"Pete."

Moira's eyes widened. "Pete Huudien?"

Steps echoed behind her and she looked up. Lavant and Semra approached her. Pete cowered even lower. He put his hands under his armpits, rocked his upper body while he whimpered.

"I don't want to. My head can't stand it any more." He sank to the ground on his side, curled up, and cried soundlessly.

Moira got up and stopped Semra and Lavant before they came too close. "We need an ambulance."

Semra nodded. "It's on its way. Who's that?"

"Pete Huudien."

For the first time since she had known Semra, the gendarma was lost for words. Open-mouthed, she stared at Moira, and her gaze wandered between her and the whimpering bundle on the ground.

"This is Pete Huudien?" Lavant raised his eyebrows. "He doesn't look like a mass murderer or criminal genius."

"True. And you shouldn't forget that he was locked up." Semra had caught herself. "The way he is now, we cannot interrogate him." She indicated for Moira and Lavant to leave the container. "Buds and his men will have to secure the evidence before he can be taken away. You'd better find his fiancée. Maybe he'll come round when he sees her."

"We don't need your people. We've got the situation under control," Lavant said, but Moira dragged him along.

"Come on." She pulled her reluctant father to the door they had used to enter the building. She didn't fancy getting told off for being at a crime scene. To interfere with investigations although she was suspended could cost her her last chance at an apprenticeship training position with the Gendarmerie.

Grumbling, Lavant told his men to withdraw. Swearing silently, he opened the door to the limousine for Moira before he got in himself.

Chapter 28

Director du Mar slipped to the front of his leather seat and looked at Moira expectantly. "And? Did you see my weapons?"

She nodded. "It will take some time before the Gendarmerie will release them though."

He leaned back and crossed his legs. "It doesn't matter, as long as they are safe and treated with care."

"They would have been in good hands with us too," Lavant said. "By the way, you should report to Commissaire Semra Jaman. She surely has a lot of questions for you."

"Oh, you're right."

Director du Mar had barely left the carpisto when Lavant ordered the chauffeur to drive off.

"Where do we have to go?"

Moira told him the address of Huudien's fiancée, leaned against him, and closed her eyes. She realized that the discovery of Huudien still didn't bring any relief for Druidus. The way they had found the nightwatchman, he couldn't possibly be responsible for all the murders. *I wonder who the guy was trying to sell the weapons. Hopefully Buds and his men find some good leads. Druidus doesn't have much time left.*

The carpisto stopped in front of the right house, and again Lavant held open the doors. When no one reacted to their ringing, he pulled out a bundle that he opened gently. Two rows of hooked wires adorned loops of soft cloth. Lavant examined the lock and chose a wire with flat sides. Carefully he threaded the skeleton key into the lock, and a little later the door swung open. They walked up the stairs to Rosina Ardappelen's flat where Lavant repeated the lock-picking. This door too didn't resist for long. Moira walked along the unlit corridor to the living room. It was empty and covered in dust. A new sofa and a table, both very dusty too, stood in the middle of the room. The dirty dishes in the kitchen were still untouched. Moira noticed that the stale food on many of the dirty plates had hardly been touched. The minidrac from the oven had vanished.

Moira remembered her last visit to Rosina Ardappelen. *Hopefully, she's not going to be in bed again.* Without hesitation she walked into the bedroom and opened the curtains. The room smelled of sweat, so she opened the window before she turned to the bed. Rosina lay with her eyes closed. Her skin was so pale, Moira feared she had died. Then Rosina breathed and her eyelids fluttered. Moira sat down on the edge of the bed. From the corners of her eyes, she noticed her father pull out his parlebol and return to the corridor for a better connection.

"Rosina?" Moira took one of the woman's hands. It was barely more than skin and bones.

Rosina's eyes opened slowly as if a terrible weight lay on them. Recognition dawned. When she spoke her voice was hoarse, as if she hadn't used it in a long time. "He is dead, isn't he? I felt it. Here." She put her free hand on her heart.

Moira immediately understood who Rosina meant. She shook her head. "We found him, and he's alive."

Rosina gasped and tried in vain to sit up.

"Don't get excited." Moira gently pushed her back into the cushions. "He's fine, considering the circumstances."

"I've got to see him." Rosina's eyes begged.

"Of course. But first you'll have to regain your strength."

"I tried to eat. I really did." Rosina breathed heavily but didn't try to sit up again. "But I couldn't."

"We'll take you to the hospital. You'll feel much better soon." Moira patted her hand. She understood Rosina's extreme behavior much better since Druidus' sentence had been announced. It was so difficult to concentrate on something as unimportant as food when you were caught up in your worries for a beloved person.

Rosina nodded weakly and whispered a word. "Pete?"

"I'll try to arrange for you to see him as soon as he feels better."

Rosina closed her eyes and sighed. She fell into a fitful sleep and woke when the ambulance men put her on a stretcher. Her eyes searched for Moira. "Stay with me."

Lavant's lips formed the words, "I'll follow," and he nodded.

Wordlessly, Moira walked beside the stretcher and squeezed into the ambulance. She tried to make herself as small as possible so she wouldn't hinder the ambulance men. Rosina was connected to a drip and received several shots. Luckily the ride to the hospital wasn't long. The patient was put into a hospital bed and wheeled into one of the examination rooms hurriedly. For the whole time, Moira held her hand. While they waited for a healer, she remembered that Rosina's fiancé had been taken to the same hospital. "Shall I have a look where they put him?"

Rosina nodded. Moira freed her hand from the cramped grip and left the room. Lavant leaned against the wall beside the door. When he saw her, his expression brightened. "Can we go now?"

Moira shook her head.

He sighed. "In that case, I'll wait in the carpisto. I hate hospitals."

Moira watched him go until the doors to the staircase closed behind him. Then she started looking for Pete. In the corridor she met a healer and a nurse.

In passing, she asked the nurse for Pete Huudien's whereabouts and got directions to the intensive care unit. She took the next nerlift, rode it to a higher level, and passed the doors to the OP-area. Two gendarmes stood in front of a room of the intensive care unit. Moira headed toward the door they protected.

"You can't go in there," the stockier gendarme said.

Through the window in the door, she saw Semra standing beside the patient's bed. "Could you inform Commissaire Jaman that I'm here?" She told the gendarmes her name and waited. The slim one went through the lock between corridor and room. When he returned, he held the door open wordlessly. Moira entered the lock. On the orders of a nurse sitting at a tiny table filling out paperwork, she donned a coat, a hairnet, rubber gloves, and a single-use surgical mask before she stepped through the second door into the room. She walked to over to Semra, who was dressed in the same way as she was, and said, "I think this is slightly over the top."

"Not really. He's so weak that the slightest infection could kill him." Semra didn't look at her. "Did you find his fiancée?"

Moira nodded. Carefully, she took Pete Huudien's hand and bent forward far enough so he could see her without moving his head.

"Monsieur Huudien?"

He opened his eyes but it took him a while to focus on her face.

"I murdered them," he whispered. "I murdered them all. Six people. T'was really easy." He closed his eyes again.

Moira lifted an eyebrow and looked at Semra.

She shrugged. "He doesn't say anything else."

Moira bent forward again and stroked his hand. "Monsieur Huudien. Rosina Ardappelen is waiting for you."

Pete frowned and murmured the name several times. Then his eyes flew open and he stared at Moira, but he was too weak to sit up. "The wedding."

"Your fiancée will visit you as soon as you feel better." Moira smiled at him, but Pete's eyes already gazed past her into the distance again.

"Six people. I murdered them all. T'was really easy."

Moira sat on a stool and looked at Semra. "Does he use the same words over and over?"

Semra nodded. "Just like Druidus. I already alerted the Gendarmerie's specialist for psychology." She pointed to the door. "Looks as if he's just arrived."

A big, broad-shouldered man entered. Above his surgical mask a pair of friendly, brown eyes glittered. He took Semra's and Moira's hands in greeting. "Would you mind leaving me alone with the patient?"

Reluctantly they left the room but waited in the lock. Through the glass door, Moira observed the psychologist talk patiently to Pete.

"Do you think it's possible that he'll discover something?" she asked.

Semra nodded. "I once had a case where the victim was brainwashed so she couldn't witness. The young woman spoke just as monotonously as Huudien, and repeated the same phrases all the time."

Moira leaned her forehead against the cool glass. She didn't dare to hope that Huudien's condition would have an impact on Druidus' sentence.

Semra seemed to know her thoughts. "Even if my suspicion regarding Huudien is right, it won't help Druidus at all. Several psychologists declared him sane."

Moira sighed. "It means we'll have to find out immediately who locked up Huudien."

"That's not all." Semra counted the items on her fingers. "We would need a confession from the culprit, an explanation of how and why he manipulated Druidus, and proof for the manipulation that's admissible in court."

"And all of that as fast as possible." Moira wiped her eyes. All of a sudden she felt more tired than ever before in her life.

The door opened and the psychologist came through. A machine beeped. The nurse got up, pushed past him, and walked to Pete Huudien's bed. The psychologist closed the door carefully behind her before he spoke. "I can only confirm your suspicion, Commissaire. His consciousness accepts the murders as if he had watched them from afar, but he knows details only the murderer could know." He spoke faster because the nurse was returning. "For me, there's no doubt that he killed the homeless. But by my reckoning, he wasn't master of his own mind during the crime. I'll have to talk to him several times more and record the meetings to construct a valid chain of proof for court."

"Will you be able to break through his blockade?" Moira asked. She thought it horrible to feel responsible for the death of so many people for the rest of one's life.

Semra made room for the nurse who had just stepped though the glass door.

"I'm optimistic." The psychologist hung up his coat and dumped surgical mask and gloves into the bin. "I believe Monsieur Huudien will be able to work off the events in a way that they will not burden him later."

Semra thanked him, and he left.

Moira took off her coat too. She was relieved, not only for Rosina Ardappelen's sake. Now she only had to find a way to save Druidus. She looked at Semra. "Can I come back to work again tomorrow, please?"

"Your suspension came from very high up. I don't think I can change anything." Semra took off her surgical mask. She closed her eyes and breathed a couple of times. "I wish Sabio would crawl out of his archive. I'm missing his bright mind everywhere."

"If you allow me to work with him so we can find proof for Druidus' innocence, he might leave the archive soon."

Semra shrugged. "It's worth a try. Fine, I'll talk to the personnel officer." She threatened Moira with her index finger. "But only if you don't get involved in anything like the storage raid again."

"Cross my heart." Moira beamed. Semra's promise was no guarantee that she could work again soon, but it was better than nothing.

The next morning, Moira's parlebol rang before she got up. She pulled the cover over her head and tried to cling to the dream she had been having, where she enjoyed holidays on a sunny beach with Druidus. But the parlebol didn't stop. Again and again, someone tried to reach her. Finally she was awake enough to remember that Druidus was waiting for his execution in jail. She felt as if someone had dumped a bucket of ice water over her, and she struggled to get a handle on her longing. The parlebol rang again. Moira blinked away her tears and swore.

Annoyed, she climbed out of bed and shuffled into the living room. Before she could answer the call, her door-nerl shouted. "It's Franka. It's Franka." He only stopped when

Moira told him to open the door. She reached for the parlebol, but it was too late. The caller had given up.

If it's important, they'll call again. Moira went into the kitchen, patted the minidrac, and made coffee.

When Franka stormed in breathlessly, the kitchen smelled strongly of the spicy drink. Tears ran over her cheeks. "I don't know what to do. I think he doesn't love me any more."

Moira tried to calm her, but Franka didn't listen.

"I'm so unha-ha-happy." Crying, she threw her arms around Moira's neck. "My wedding dress is ruined, too."

Moira patted her back and murmured soothingly until Franka calmed a little. Then she sat her down on a chair in the kitchen, handed her a couple of paper tissues and a mug with a lot of milk and very little coffee. "Now, all in good time. Why is your wedding dress ruined?"

"I put it on secretly this morning. Because it's so lovely. Then I heard Tord at the door. And since it's considered unlucky if the bridegroom sees me in my wedding dress before the wedding, I hid in the wardrobe." She blew her nose. "The skirt must have caught on something, because I heard it rip when I got out again. Oh, Moira, that's the worst omen for a wedding, isn't it?"

Amused, Moira shook her head. She had forgotten how superstitious Franka could be sometimes. "It's only a rip in a dress, and it can be mended. Did you bring it?"

"It's in the carpisto." Franka snuffled.

Moira went to the parlebol and called inquiries. When she got the address of an artist of invisible mending, she took Franka's arm. "Come. You can tell me the rest on the way."

When the carpisto rolled along the street Moira lived on, she made her friend tell her why she was so very desperate.

"Tord hides in old files all the time. He hardly eats or sleeps, and he doesn't talk to me. It's obvious he doesn't love me any more." Franka patted her belly with a hand. "He probably noticed how fat I got."

Moira laughed loud. "Your honey loves every rounded inch of you. He said that more than once."

"But the pregnancy…"

"…is hardly noticeable." Moira put a hand on Franka's arm. "He's probably got a good reason to lose himself in work at this moment."

Franka's lip trembled. "He doesn't. He's still off work till the end of the month. The flat is pure chaos because I can't unpack the boxes all alone, and we haven't even talked about where we want to travel for our honeymoon."

Moira pondered this. Sure, Tord loved his work, but she knew he loved Franka even more. He worshiped the ground she walked on and would never desert her. "Did you ask him what he's looking for so desperately?"

"Yes, but he only goes on about a Katie and a smith and documents from the ninth century, and I don't understand a word." Franka steered into a parking space and stopped.

Moira put her left arm around Franka's shoulders and hugged her. "You know what? When we've handed the dress to the mender, I'll come along and we'll unpack the boxes together. Maybe I can even get a few sensible words out of your boyfriend."

Franka hugged her. "You're the best friend in the world."

Chapter 29

Two hours later, they stood between half emptied cardboard boxes.

"Wow, that's kitschy." Moira held up an Aphrodite made of porcelain, with gilded hair.

Franka opened her eyes wide and reached for the hand-sized figurine. "Don't you dare to drop it. Tord's mother would kill me."

"She wouldn't. She likes you far too much for that." Tord came out of his study and stood beside Franka. "Do you know where we put the box with the parchments I hadn't looked at? I know exactly that I brought it along from the university."

"I put it on top of your filing cabinet."

"You're the best." He vanished into his room again.

"I think this will be my best chance." Moira handed Franka the statue.

"You'd better wait. He doesn't like to be interrupted when he's working."

Moira smiled at her. "I'll manage." She fetched a tray with coffee and cookies from the kitchen and entered Tord's sanctuary.

Her jaw dropped when she looked around. Books, magazines, manuscripts and overflowing boxes covered the floor in unstable piles. There was hardly enough room to reach the desk. She wondered about this considerably since Tord was one of the tidiest people she knew. *What's wrong with him?*

He only noticed her when she put the tray on the tiny free space on his desk. She didn't beat around the bush.

"Tell me, why are you neglecting my best friend until she shows up crying at my place at the brink of dawn?"

Tord jumped to his feet. "My angel cried?"

His wide eyes stared at Moira with so much horror, she had to laugh. "I know you love her, but she's doubting it at the moment."

"Why?"

"Do you wonder? You're bundled up in this room for days on end without telling her why. Franka believes you can't stand the look of her any more."

Open-mouthed, Tord fell back into his chair. His mouth opened and closed but he didn't utter a word. Finally, he said, "She's the most beautiful woman in the world to me."

"I know that." Moira pointed to the chaos. "What are you looking for anyway?"

"Well." He squirmed. "You know that Franka's biggest wish is to be your bridesmaid. And I thought I remembered an old text I have read some time ago which might prove helpful."

"Tord, what does an old text have to do with a bridesmaid?" Carefully, Moira pushed aside a couple of files, sat on the desktop with one leg, and looked into Tord's face.

He swallowed. "As you know, Hern's sigil is an anvil with a hammer vertically above it. He engraved it on everything he forged."

Moira nodded. She remembered all too well the stone urn with the eerie warning. It had held the same sigil with six semicircular lines above.

"Well, I remembered a text from a monk of the early Middle Ages who described the same seal but with an added rainbow. The monk's hypothesis was that the rainbow was Katie Féroce's sigil."

Although this confirmed Moira's own conclusion, it still wasn't a good explanation for Tord's strange behavior. "That's all very fascinating. Get to the point."

"I cannot remember how the united sigil was connected to a cursed dagger, but I do remember that many monks were murdered with this dagger. The author of the text was the last survivor, and he meant to throw the dagger into a moor. He described the effects of the curse in great detail, and many of his observations fit Druidus' behavior at court. I thought the document would probably help to exonerate Druidus somehow. But I'm searching like mad and I can't find it." Tord tore at his hair. "And Franka would be delighted to see you happy again. You would be happy if Druidus came free, wouldn't you?"

"Of course." Moira had to fight tears of emotion. Her voice sounded hoarse. "Why didn't you tell Franka?"

"It was meant to be a surprise."

"I think you should explain it."

He nodded, got up, and hurried to the door.

"And Tord." Moira blinked away the tears and looked at him as he stood waiting with one hand on the doorknob. "If you find this document, let me know immediately."

"For sure."

"Thanks," she said.

"I will find it. I promise." Tord left the room.

Moira had never anticipated how much she meant to Franka and Tord. It soothed her feelings, although she still longed for Druidus and feared for his life. She put her face in her hands, trying to control her feelings again.

When she recovered, she left the study. Obviously Franka and Tord had finished talking, since they were hugging and kissing in the corridor.

As a little tease, Moira said, "See? No danger of losing him. He's still glued to your lips."

Beaming, Franka wiped a strand of hair from her face and kissed Tord once more. Moira took a pile of cushions meant for the sofa in the sitting room, and left the couple alone. The parlebol on the sideboard rang, and Moira managed to talk Franka's answering-nerl into accepting the call for her. Director du Mar seemed relieved to see her.

"Dear me, you were hard to find."

Moira lifted an eyebrow. "You've been looking for me?"

"With the Gendarmerie's assistance, I will present the returned finds from the dig this afternoon around three. My wife would be delighted if you would accompany us."

"My friend just moved and I promised her to help unpack."

"It'll only be only half an hour at the most. I'd pick you up, too. Please do us the honor."

Moira gave in. "Fine, but only if you bring me right back afterwards."

"Of course."

Moira told him Franka's address and went back to work.

A quarter to three, she stood on the sidewalk in front of Franka's and Tord's flat, clean and with her hair washed, where Director du Mar picked her up like he had promised. When they entered the museum's entrance hall, Moira marveled at the number of guests.

Madame du Mar approached them, hugged her, and kissed her cheeks. "I am incredibly grateful."

"What for?" Gently, Moira freed herself. Madame du Mar's flowery perfume tickled her nose. "It was my father who helped your husband to retrieve the weapons."

Madame waved her comment aside. "I've never been very interested in all this old stuff. For a while now, Charles has been courting me again. He brings me flowers and takes me dining. I finally have the feeling I'm just as important as his work. And that's your doing."

Moira remembered the talk she'd had with the director what seemed like an eternity ago. "I'm surprised he followed my advice."

A bell rang. The guests hurried to the museum's right wing and onward through two open doors into a separate showroom.

Madame du Mar pulled Moira along. "He's just as attentive as when we got to know each other. If I can ever help you in any way, please let me know."

Moira didn't like the praise. Her eyes scanned the room where Madame du Mar had taken her.

The back was separated with a big, white linen curtain with a lectern in front of it. The rest of the room was filled with rows of chairs. Right at the front, she spotted her father.

"The places up front are reserved for us," Madame du Mar said.

Moira squeezed through the crowd behind her until they reached the front row.

Lavant grinned. "Well, sweets, how did you like our little adventure?"

"I'm fine but I would like to know who the seller of the weapons could have been." She made herself comfortable between him and Madame du Mar. "I'm hoping Buds and his boys found a couple of leads."

"I'm more concerned about the fact that he fled when he saw me."

Moira's head shot up. She hadn't thought about that yet, but her father was right. The seller of the stolen weapons had only fled when Lavant entered the circle of light. "Do you think he recognized you?"

"Possibly. After all, I've been in the papers more than once." Lavant pointed to the front. "Shhh. It's starting."

Director du Mar walked to the lectern amid a thunderstorm of flashes from the press.

"Dear guests," he began. "I don't want to keep you on tenterhooks for long. Today, it is a great honor for me to present to you the reclaimed pieces of our latest dig. For the next four weeks, we will showcase them the way they were found during the rescue raid. Voilà!" He pulled a cord and the white linen whooshed to the side, clearing the view for a diorama.

Moira felt as if she was back in the storage hall. She could nearly see the shadowy figure with the wide-rimmed hat in the background. Again, Madame du Mar's flowery perfume filled her nose. She slapped her forehead. *I forgot about the scent.*

A reporter lifted his hand. "What will happen to the exhibit at the end of the four weeks?"

"They will be cleaned and examined by archeologists specializing in finds from Hern's era. I very much hope that we'll be able to present them together with the other finds in a themed exhibit permanently."

"Do you know who burgled the museum?"

Director du Mar shook his head. "The Gendarmerie's enquiries are not over yet. Even if I knew anything, I couldn't give you any information."

The reporters pestered him with questions about the burglary for a while longer before they gave up. Soon, all questions focused on the pieces of the exhibit, their value, their restoration and presentation. Moira's thoughts returned to the acerbic, slightly sweet scent she had smelled when the weapon's seller had fled. She was fairly sure she had smelled it before, but she couldn't remember when or where.

Due to her brooding, she missed the end of Director du Mar's speech. Only when the guests and reporters got up and walked toward the exit did she catch herself. She got up, but Madame du Mar held her back. She sat down again.

The room emptied except for a handful of people, and the President of the Gendarmerie Magique walked up to Director du Mar and the lectern. Since he was known as a man of few words, Moira didn't wonder that he went right to the point.

"First, we want to apologize for the inconvenience we caused. We are especially glad that you still cooperated with the Gendarmerie Magique." He pulled a small box from his pocket and opened it. On dark blue velvet lay a star-shaped medal with a silver ribbon. "In the name of our mayor, I award to you the city's Ordre du Courage Civique. Your caution during the retrieval of the stolen items was a great help for the Gendarmerie, and we hope that the financial benefit that comes with the medal will help to restore the items to their former glory." He handed the medal and the box to the director. With a reduced voice, he added, "By the way, you may spend half of the money for yourself legally."

Everyone laughed. Director du Mar thanked him with a very short speech and invited everyone for a little snack in the entrance hall. Moira joined arms with her father, and they walked past the new Diorama together.

Lavant squeezed her arm. "Why did you slap yourself after the unveiling?"

Director du Mar approached them. He took Moira's hand and shook it while talking. "I can't thank you enough. Naturally, Ill give you part of the money. Without your help I would never have been able to get the weapons back."

Moira refused, but Du Mar didn't accept it. At least he let go of her hand.

"I'm especially glad that we discovered Pete Huudien. You won't believe how happy I am that my judgment of his character was correct after all."

Moira raised an eyebrow. "It was?"

"After the Gendarmerie had written the report, I was allowed to read his statement. He had nothing to do with the burglary. His mistake was that he was friendly with one of our cleaning ladies. I'm going to ensure his wedding will be the best he can have."

"But first Pete Huudien has to be cleared of the accusation of involuntary manslaughter," said Moira. "After all, he confessed to the murder of the homeless."

Du Mar scratched his chin. "I'm sure they won't press charges. Pete's psychologist is confident he had been brainwashed and thus wasn't responsible for his own actions. My lawyer will represent him."

"Good to know." Moira was glad for Pete. As unsympathetic as she remembered Du Mar's lawyer, he knew what he was doing.

Du Mar bobbed on his toes. "I'm looking forward to his face when he realizes that we'll throw his wedding party in the museum."

Moira laughed. "Whose idea was that?"

"Joes van Gro. He's going to pay for most of it. Well, since his copies became so sought after, he can probably afford it."

They kept talking for a while before the director left to find his wife.

"Finally." Lavant sighed. "Back to my question. Why did you slap yourself when the weapons were revealed?"

"I remembered something." Moira leaned her back against the glass of the Diorama. "Did you notice the scent of the guy who tried to sell us the weapons?"

"Sure. Acerbic Frisian with a tiny trace of ocean." Lavant scratched his head. "I told them when I made my statement, but I'm not sure it'll help the gendarmes."

Moira sighed. "I can't shake the feeling that I smelled it before."

Lavant lifted an eyebrow. "Together with the hasty retreat, it implies that both of us know the culprit. You should talk to Sabio about his as soon as possible. He's got a clever head. Maybe he can come up with an idea."

Before Moira could answer, Semra approached. "The President of the Gendarmerie Magique has interrogated me about your situation. He was impressed by the care you took when reclaiming the finds. I explained your situation as best I could, and pointed out that I need you urgently."

Moira opened her mouth to say something but couldn't utter a word. Excitement restricted her throat.

"He was very thrilled about how you handled Director du Mar's refusal to work with the Gendarmerie. That's why he ordered you back to work in the archive with Sabio from Monday on."

Moira couldn't keep back a squeal. She slapped both hands over her mouth and blushed.

Semra grinned. "No field work until you pass your exam."

Moira nodded, and watched Semra walk over to the Du Mars. Only two more days and she could finally start working again. She had to fight not to run off to Sabio right away. Instead, she hugged her father as tightly as she could.

"Are you trying to choke your old man?" he said, laughing. "Come on, let's celebrate this."

"I can't. I promised Franka to help her tidy away their belongings."

Lavant put an arm around her. "I'll help. You'll see, we'll be done in no time, and your friend and her book rat can join our little celebration."

Chapter 30

Lavant was right. With his help, the furniture soon stood where Franka wanted it, and they had unpacked most of the boxes before the early evening. For the visit to a most exquisite restaurant in town, even Tord unglued himself from his manuscripts.

Moira couldn't remember when the last time she had such a merry evening was. Now and again, the longing for Druidus overwhelmed her for a while. Then she would bite the inside of her lip and would force her thought away from him. Only two days over the weekend and she would be able to help Sabio find proof for Druidus' innocence.

Two days.

She could make it.

She was absolutely certain of that.

When she finally dragged herself into her flat, tired and full, she nearly overlooked the letter on the ground behind the door. She picked it up, wondering why it hadn't come with the regular mail. A note was scrawled on the front.

"This came today, thought you'd like to know. Sabio"

He must have slipped it through the gap under the door. She turned the letter over and looked for the sender's address. *It's from the Gendarmerie's examination board? I'd better sit down.* She only opened it when she was sitting in her favorite chair. Her fingers trembled, and she found it difficult to concentrate enough to read the official-looking paper.

Dear Madame Bellamie,

At the recommendation of Commissaire Sabio Marten, whom we consulted, your final test of your magical abilities will take place on Thursday seventeenth of Julander 3019 at 10:30 in the main building of Salthaven's Gendarmerie. Please report to the assigned administrator in room 15.2 one hour before the testing commences.

Sincerely

Moira didn't know the name of the secretary who had signed but she'd have liked to hug him. *They'll be so surprised.* She thought about her newly discovered abilities and tried to imagine the stunned faces of the testers when she used a kind of magic they didn't understand. She decided to start training early the next morning. She hurried to get into bed so she would be well rested. During the night, she dreamed she was walking along the beach in the moonlight, hand in hand with Druidus. She smiled in her sleep.

Right after breakfast, Moira went into the park in the city center. On Saturdays most visitors didn't show up before lunch, so she was free to test her magic. On an empty meadow in an out-of-the-way part of the park, she recalled the wavy feeling that was connected to her talent. It was there immediately but she couldn't remember how she had used it. Again and again she tried, but she didn't even manage to turn an apple into a pear. Toward midday, the park filled up, and she gave up, frustrated.

All afternoon she brooded over the question of whether she could do things differently. *Somehow I have to learn to control this darned talent. Katie Féroce did it.* She dug through the worldwide Infonet for hours on end without success, and her frustration grew with every minute.

In the evening her parlebol rang. It was Sabio. "Would you like to help me with the final testing of my magiskope? It's finally done."

Moira declined. She didn't dare to risk the President of the Gendarmerie changing his mind. "I'll be on duty again from Monday on."

"In that case, I'll wait with the testing. I need you there."

Moira could hardly believe it. "I'd love to be there, but wouldn't it be a waste of time to wait another day?"

Sabio laughed. "It doesn't make much of a difference if I test the gadget tonight or the day after tomorrow. I wouldn't be able to examine the sword this weekend anyway. Semra ordered me to take a day off. She threatened to arrest me if I didn't." He stopped and looked closer at Moira. His eyebrows rose. "Hey, why do you look so angry?"

"Oh nothing." Moira shook her head, but Sabio didn't give up so easily.

"Don't lie. What happened?"

Moira told him about her frustrating tries to use her magic or to find some information about it at least.

"I'm not surprised." Sabio smiled tiredly. "There is no one in the world who can tell you how to use Wild Magic because there is no one who can use it. All you learned about magic in school has been developed for Unified Magic. You will have to work out your own rules."

"But I tried everything I could think of."

"I can help you if you want."

"Tomorrow?"

"Since I'm not allowed to work, why not?"

Early next morning, Sabio rang at her door. Moira was ready to go, and so they left immediately.

"We'll go to a remote place outside the city, just in case your magic breaks free unexpectedly," Sabio said. "I know the perfect place."

Half an hour later, they got out of the carpisto on a gravel-covered parking area near a little forest. Birdsong filled the air, and it smelled of mushrooms and earth.

Sabio slung a small backpack over his shoulder. "We'll try a few techniques I learned at the Akadémie Magique. They weren't originally designed for the use of Wild Magic but I think they can be useful for you too."

In silence they followed a narrow trail. *It's so peaceful here.* Moira couldn't say why she hadn't been out of town more often lately. A myriad shades of green around her soothed her soul, pushing away the town's grayness. She felt refreshed already.

The path cut deeper into the earth and widened into a gully. A little later, Moira and Sabio stood in a depression with steep walls of nearly white sand.

"They cut out sand from here up to the year before last," Sabio said. "I sometimes come here with my nephew. You can use your magic without the danger of harming anyone." He took his safety coat and a foldable focusing hat from his backpack and donned them. "I will erect a shield over the sand pit that should neutralize Wild Magic for roughly five minutes. That will give us enough time to run should we get into trouble."

Moira swallowed. "What am I supposed to do?"

"As soon as the shield's up, you lie on the ground, close your eyes, and listen inside. When you think you've discovered your magic, describe the feeling to me." Sabio drew a pentagram into the sand and placed his magical symbols in the corners. With his back to her, he spoke the activation words of a safety shield.

Moira didn't wonder that it was unknown to her. Shields against Wild Magic surely weren't the stuff of a normal curriculum. A golden shimmer spread like a lid over the sand pit and covered everything, even the beginning of the gully. She lay down.

Sabio's arms fell and he turned to her. He frowned. "How did you know the spell was done?"

"It's plainly visible." She pointed to the golden shimmer.

"You can see the shield?"

"You can't?" Moira sat up, her hands digging into the sand behind her.

"Incredible." Sabio pushed his hat as far back as it would go without toppling. "What I wouldn't give to be able to see magic."

"I didn't know it was something special. I thought everyone can see the stronger spells."

"What does it look like? Can you describe it?"

Moira tried her best to find words for the glowing gold.

Sabio listened with fascination. "We'll examine that more closely soon," he said. "For now we'd better concentrate on getting you connected to your magic."

Moira lay back down obediently, closed her eyes, and felt inside. Immediately she felt the magic's rocking waves that made the cells of her body sing.

Sabio's voice was low. "Describe the feeling as best you can."

It was difficult for Moira to explain. It felt like telling a deaf person what a song was.

Sabio didn't interrupt her for questions. When she was done, he stayed silent. Only when Moira opened her eyes impatiently did he speak. "Were you able to use any magic at all in school?"

"Sometimes."

"Try to think about what might be there to block you. Try to be honest with yourself."

"What do you mean?" Moira didn't understand his directions.

"The use of magic is often dependent on how you feel. During my officer training course, I coached a couple of students and helped them develop their full magical potential." Grains of sand rubbed against each other as he sat beside her. His hand closed around her fingers. "There was a young woman whose theoretical strength in magic was way above average but she couldn't do anything more than the average magic user. Due to the pressure of her parents, she had agreed to marry an aspiring gendarme she hardly knew and who was much older than she was. When she finally admitted to herself truthfully that her heart belonged to someone else, she was able to use magic in a breathtaking way."

"Did she leave her fiancé?"

"It doesn't matter. The knowledge alone freed her magic."

Moira had a suspicion. "What happened to her?"

"She has been working independently for quite a while now. But once in a while, she still works for the Gendarmerie."

"And before that?" Moira was sure he was talking about Aparta.

"Up to the birth of her child, she was a member of the Gendarmerie's testing council."

Moira was silent. His voice sounded so sad, it had to be Aparta. She wondered if Excelsior had forced her to give up working after Druidus' birth, or if she had quit of her own free will.

"That's not important for your situation," Sabio said. "You'll have to find your own strength and weaknesses. Do you understand?"

Moira nodded, and Sabio seemed satisfied.

"You don't need to tell me your block. But you should answer all questions truthfully to yourself. When you're done, just squeeze my hand."

Moira nodded again, and Sabio began. "How do you get along with your father?"

Moira opened her mouth to answer, then closed it again. She pondered her relationship with Lavant and was surprised to realize she didn't have any problems with him any more. In the last few weeks they had grown so close as if he had never left. Warmth flooded her when she thought about him. She squeezed Sabio's hand.

"Are you in love with Druidus?"

The question caught her red-handed, and she didn't want to think about it. *What is love anyway?* She was close to giving the sign for the next question when she remembered Druidus' face at the water fountain. His dark eyes with the helpless, beseeching gaze tore her heart apart. Tears shot into her eyes. She let go of Sabio's hand, rolled to the side, pulled up her knees, and hugged them with her arms. Druidus' gaze didn't leave her. *Why?* In her mind, she screamed at him. *Why didn't we even try to flee?* She cried. *Damned, I miss you so much. I'd give my life to save yours.*

In the last few days, Moira had forced herself not to think about Druidus so much that her despair overwhelmed her now, and she had no resilience against it any more. Sobs shook her body, and she hugged her knees harder and harder. Anger, grief, despair – the feelings fought for her, and the battlefield was her body. For a long time she didn't register Sabio's hand stroking her back. But when she did, a soothing thought rose over the chaos of her feelings. *I'm not alone. Sabio will do anything to prove Druidus' innocence – for me and for Aparta.* Then she remembered Turd, who was looking for exonerative arguments too. Her sobbing ebbed away. Sniffing and wet from tears, she slowly returned to reality. She rolled onto her back again and looked at Sabio. "I love Druidus more than I ever thought possible."

"It seems like you found your weakness. Druidus is so lucky." A smile spread over his face, making it glow. "Well, let's see if you can do a simple spell now. Change the top-most layer of sand into a blanket."

As she had been taught in school, Moira tried to press the waves from her fingertips into the sand. She imagined that the sand was covered with a soft blanket, but nothing happened. She pressed her eyes tighter shut to concentrate some more. Finally. Something soft.

She opened her eyes, sat up and looked at the place she had just been lying. Sweat ran into her eyes and she breathed as if she had run for hours. She blinked the sweat away and looked closer. Where her hand had touched the sand lay a hand-sized square of fluffy fabric. No more. Moira's heart sank. "How can I help Druidus if I can't do something this easy?"

"Your magic works differently. At least you didn't fail completely. Don't worry. We'll find out what you need to do." He pushed her back into the sand. "Come on, we'll try something different. Find your middle. Find the place inside of you where your Magic feels strongest."

Moira obeyed and closed her eyes again. Awed, she realized how easy it was to follow Sabio's directions. The waves of her magic carried her to the right place. "It's right above my heart," she said.

"I should have known." Sabio squeezed her hand. "Very well, let's try the next step. Imagine your aura had a hole. A tiny one. Directly above your heart."

Moira was just about to imagine such a hole when she realized there already was one. She reached for the spot, and it felt as if she were using her hands even though she knew they were resting comfortably beside her body in the sand. This double perception confused her a little but she got used to her invisible fingers soon. She felt for the hole and found a needlepoint one in the middle of a depression. "I got one," she whispered.

"Let a little bit of magic escape. Only a few drops."

"Shall I try to make another blanket?"

"No, don't direct your magic for now. Don't worry. I'm with you."

Moira felt Sabio's warm fingers on her hand. With a racing heart, she pushed a single wave toward the hole. *Hopefully, it'll work*. The wave flowed back. Moira felt the sweat that made her dress cling to her body strongly. With her invisible hands, she pushed the wave again, stronger this time. A surge of magic shot from the hole in her aura. Moira opened her eyes and marveled at the column of glittering energy standing above her heart. The colors of the rainbow whirled around each other, but nothing else happened. Moira reached out with her invisible hands and touched the column. Warm tickling spread through her body from her heart. In a whisper, she described everything to Sabio.

"I'd love to see that." He sighed. "Point your magic to the branch over there. Try to turn it into an iron bar."

Wood to iron had been one of the easiest exercises in school, except for Moira. Reluctantly, she pushed her magic. It flashed. Blinded, she blinked to clear her vision. Beside her Sabio laughed. "That's fantastic!"

Finally, her eyes recovered and she could see again. She sat up and looked around. Where the branch had been now sat a rabbit, and its nose trembled. After a while, it hopped toward the forest. It flashed again as it crossed Sabio's shield, but a lot less strongly, and a lifeless branch fell to the ground.

"But I aimed for an iron bar." Disappointment cut through Moira's heart like a pointy arrowhead.

Sabio patted her shoulder. "You need a lot of magic to turn something unloving into a creature brimming with life. You will learn control later. For the beginning, this was spectacular."

Chapter 31

They trained some more. Sabio had a lot of things in his backpack that he made Moira turn into something else. Nothing came out the way it was supposed to. Cookies didn't turn into carrots but into soup – without a bowl. Wool didn't knot into a net but into a ball with bells inside. Instead of slipping open into neat slices, an apple grew wings and flew away until it hit Sabio's shield.

"I'll never get the hang of it." After an hour of training, Moira was ready to give up. "My magic is uncontrollable."

"I wouldn't say that. In Druidus' report he wrote that you created a nice explosion with your spell at the carnival." Sabio pulled another apple from his backpack and handed it to her. "Today, everything is still in one piece. Bon appétit."

Moira looked at him, surprised. *He's right. So far, it either worked or it didn't, but today I was able to control strength and direction of my magic easily.* A smile flitted over her face, and she bit into the apple. When they had eaten, she trained some more. At first, she still lay on the ground, but soon she sat and stood. She wasn't too determined to get the correct result as long as she could reduce and aim the magical flow in a way that it didn't have any side effects. After a while, she shook out her hands because her fingertips tingled. She magicked some more.

Sabio pushed back his hat. "You've been training for three hours now. Aren't you tired?"

"No." On the contrary. Moira felt as awake and fresh as she hadn't in a long time. Only the burning sensation in her fingertips got stronger, and she was thirsty. She took the water bottle Sabio had brought and drank.

"Incredible." Sabio shook his head. "I collapse if I have to do more than two unique and strong spells at a time. And they attributed to me more than average magic."

"The one thing that's a bit annoying is the burning in the tips of my fingers."

Sabio's eyebrows shot up. "Does it feel as if you accidentally toughed a piece of glowing coal?"

"I guess so." She opened and closed her hands several times but the feeling didn't subside.

Sabio beamed. "I've got a theory I'd like to test. Could you do some more magic and tell me when your fingers hurt so much you can't stand it any more?"

Moira obeyed. Finally, not only her fingers burned, but her arms up to her elbows felt the same.

Sabio took another apple from his backpack and put it into the sand a little to the side. "Imagine the tip of your index finger has a hole. Point it at the apple and push the burning sensation out of the hole. Try to use the burning to peel the apple."

Moira wondered about this order. Her previous attempts had shown that she wasn't able to do something like that. Still, she did as she was told. She pointed to the apple with her right index finger and imagined magic shooting out. Immediately, the burning in her arms subsided. She stared at the apple that had risen a hand's width in the air majestically and was turning. The peel sank into the sand in an even spiral. When the apple was peeled, Sabio stepped forward and caught it before it could land in the sand.

"You most definitely have plenty of Unified Magic. It is just so busy keeping your Wild Magic under control that there isn't any left to do the things other people do with theirs. Now, that you used up a considerable amount of your Wild Magic, you've got enough Unified Magic left."

Moira saw daylight. "That's why the auralogists got different results."

All of a sudden, the realization of her dream seemed close. "So, all I need to do before my exam is to lose enough of my Wild Magic to pass the test."

"It's not that easy." Sabio bit into the apple. "You've got the problem that you can't control the results of your Wild Magic yet. It's going to be rather difficult to get rid of a sizable amount."

Moira pondered this. "If we can't prove Druidus' innocence, I'll use it to bust him from jail."

Sabio sighed. "I couldn't allow that. You can't ignore laws simply because you don't like them."

"But Druidus isn't guilty."

"I know." He lowered his head and stared at his hands as if he'd never seen them before. "If everyone only kept to the laws they like, the world would dissolve in chaos. I will suffer terribly should we not be able to save Druidus, more than you might think. Still, I'll keep the law. It is right more often than not and it assures peaceful living together for everyone."

Moira was silent. A few days ago she would have agreed wholeheartedly, but since Druidus had been sentenced, she had reconsidered some things. Should Sabio's magiskope not exonerate Druidus, she would most definitely use her magic to free him. Somewhere in this world would be a place they could hide. Maybe Lavant would help her. But she'd better not tell Sabio.

Sabio got up and flung the rest of the apple into the forest. "It will grow dark soon. Let's call it a day and go back to the city." They packed their equipment and walked back to the carpisto.

The next morning Moira arrived well rested and full of zest in the archive. Her heart beat fast. Finally, they were able to do something for Druidus. She was there so early she had to wait for Sabio, but she didn't mind.

He came down the stairs with his coat flying and saw her immediately. "I'm glad you're here this early."

The door to the archive opened and he hurried in. He had hardly hung up his coat when he pulled her toward the magiskope. "This is the final test. The gadget focuses your magic so precisely that we won't miss the smallest spell. Look."

He pulled a small handheld mirror from his bag. When he noticed Moira's questioning gaze, he said, "It belongs to my niece. Her mother insisted on giving her a mirror that reflects her more beautiful than she is. As if she needed that. It was supposed to strengthen her self confidence." He grinned. "It wasn't my idea, and we fought a lot about that back then."

"Doesn't your niece complain that you're using it for testing?"

"She gave it to me especially for this. She's always been far more interested in inventing and engineering than in beauty." Sabio breathed deeply several times and then put the mirror under the magiskope.

"She probably takes after her uncle." Moira watched Sabio activate his invention. Hopefully everything would work all right. She knew that a lowly spell like the one on the mirror had been untraceable up to now.

Sabio teetered on his toes. He irritated Moira.

The magiskope clicked and rattled, then a flat voice spoke. "Handheld mirror. Marginal fair-appearance spell. No cross reference to current cases."

"It's working!" Sabio rubbed his hands. "I'm as happy as at the time when I got my stripes as Commissaire Magilis."

"Congratulations." Moira patted his shoulder. "It's incredible that the gadget compares the test object with the archived material automatically."

"That was the easy part. Shall we test a few cursed weapons?" Sabio walked to his worktable and donned the protective gloves. He picked up a crossbow from the table. Moira had to look closely to see the telltale sparkle of a spell. For some reason she couldn't see mixed magics as well as spells woven from one kind of magic. If she hadn't known it was a cursed weapon, she might not have noticed the glittering at all.

Sabio walked to the magiskope, and Moira realized how excited he was. Small pearls of sweat had appeared on his upper lip, and his breathing was fast and shallow.

She was as tightly wound up. Her heart beat so loud, blood roared in her ears. She held her breath when the magiskope checked the weapon. *Please, please, let this work.* Moira didn't dare to think of Druidus for a superstitious fear that things wouldn't work in that case.

Finally, the flat voice droned, "Crossbow. Small. Ebony and forged iron. No magical activities. Cross referenced in files..." It rattled down a long list of files.

Moira's heart sank, and she pressed her lips together to keep from crying.

Sabio's face mirrored her frustration. He looked as if someone had dumped a pail of cold water over him. "Why does the magiskope find the nearly untraceable spell of the mirror but fails with a really strong homicide spell? I don't understand. What did I miss?" He tugged at his hair.

Moira slapped her forehead. "Of course! Wild Magic."

"Sorry?" Sabio looked at her with raised eyebrows.

"You told me yourself that suicide and homicide spells contain some Wild Magic. I think you can only detect a Wild Magic enhanced spell with a gadget containing Wild Magic too."

Sabio stared at her, open-mouthed. Then he became elated. "Moira, you're a jewel. I should have thought of that myself." He put his safety coat on, pondering the magiskope. He scratched his chin. "I'd better go to the sand pit."

"What for?"

"To prevent accidents. Wild Magic is dangerous and I haven't developed a safe banning spell for this kind of thing."

"You could use my magic. Thanks to you I can control it enough to adjust strength and direction." Moira smiled at Sabio expectantly, waiting for an answer.

He took his time. Several times, he opened his mouth as if to speak but shook his head and closed it again. Moira suspected he was thinking of the mangled results of her former spells. Still, she waited wordlessly.

Finally, he nodded. "We'll try. Just in case I'll put up a dome-shaped security spell over you and the magiskope. You'll have to wind your magic carefully around all parts. Try to keep the other spells intact or I'd have to start from scratch."

Moira felt warmed by his trust. She grinned. "I can do that easily. I just wound a wreath for Franka's wedding."

"But not from Magie Sauvage, I hope." Sabio also grinned. He gathered the magical items he needed while Moira drew a generous pentagram on the floor.

A little later, she stood inside the glittering dome of Sabio's protective spell that only she could see, with the magiskope in her hand.

"What we are trying to do now has never been done before," Sabio said. "Please be careful."

Moira swallowed. Her hands were sweating and her throat dry. *Hopefully I didn't bite off more than I can chew.* She remembered the stone urn from Tord's dig and realized she wasn't the first to try. Katie Féroce and Hern had to have interwoven their magics too. She breathed deeply, closed her eyes, and felt inside. Her Wild Magic was there. This time she could even feel the other magic containing the Wild Magic in a layer of fire. Carefully she extended a thin thread of Magie Sauvage toward the magiskope. In her invisible fingers, the magic felt like a narrow ribbon. She kept her eyes closed to keep up the illusion. Very slowly, she wound the magical ribbon around the magiskope's first support. She felt the tingle of Sabio's spell and took great care to add her magic in a way that his spells weren't disturbed. It was very difficult. When she finished the third leg, she breathed deeply and wiped the sweat from her brow. "Only the pentacle left and I'm done," she said to Sabio. She didn't hear his answer.

Half an hour later, she opened her eyes and set down the magiskope. If she looked closely, it dazzled with sheen like mother-of-pearl. *Is that my magic?* She bent forward until her nose nearly touched the magiskope. Greenness overlaid the spells, making the gadget look like an exotic flower. Moira marveled. She hadn't thought it would look so beautiful.

"Are you done?"

She nodded absentmindedly and stretched.

"Let's test it again." Sabio deactivated his dome and carried the magiskope to his desk. Again, he put the mirror under it, and Moira stepped beside him. They waited breathlessly, and were rewarded. The flat voice told them the same as it had before.

Sabio sighed with relief. "You didn't damage the focusing. Very well done."

A load fell off Moira's heart. "Shall we try the crossbow?"

Wordlessly, Sabio donned his gloves and picked up the weapon. He looked into Moira's eyes. For a moment they looked at each other, then Sabio put the crossbow under the magiskope. He took Moira's hand and squeezed it gently. His grip grew stronger, but Moira barely noticed. Her gaze was glued to the rattling gadget, and she hardly dared to breathe.

Finally, the flat voice spoke. "Crossbow. Small. Ebony and forged iron. Self-cleaning ban. Strong homicide spell. Cross referenced in files..." The list of files followed again.

"It's working!" Moira threw her arms around Sabio's neck. In her mind's eye she saw Druidus in freedom. "We did it."

When she let go of him, he took her hands and kissed them. "Thank you. Thank you so much." He let go of her and took the crossbow away.

Chapter 32

At that moment the parlebol on his desk rang.

"External call," it announced.

Sabio walked to his desk, pulled the dark blue bowl closer and bent over it. Water splashed over the rim. He accepted the call, and Moira sat down on his desk to wait.

A glance on the glittering water told her Aparta de Frees was calling. Her blond curls hung lank into her face, tears ran over her face, and her eyes were swollen to slits.

Moira turned away.

"How much longer will you need?" Aparta asked. "Tomorrow, my boy will only have a single week left."

"I'm really close to solving the case." Sabio's voice was carefully optimistic.

Still, Moira felt a strange sadness beneath. She longed to hug him for comfort.

"You've been saying that for so long."

Sabio pressed his lips together. Moira was sure he would love to soothe Aparta's pain.

He tried to look confident. "We just had the deciding breakthrough."

Aparta's eyes widened. "We?"

"I couldn't have done it without Moira."

"But didn't I... Hasn't she been suspended?"

Moira realized that her suspicion had been right. Aparta had arranged her suspension. *Does she despise me so much that she deliberately hinders me although I'm working on exonerating Druidus?* She swallowed. *Maybe she believes I'm troubling Sabio when he collects evidence for Druidus' innocence.* She looked at Sabio and listened again. They had obviously talked about her.

"She is a burden," Aparta said. "You should use your valuable time to find something that will help Druidus. There has to be a spell on the sword."

"I'll be able to tell you tonight. And you should be glad Moira is allowed to work again. Without her help I would have had to spend years on this."

Aparta wiped away her tears and pushed out her chin. "All I'm interested in is finding proof of Druidus' innocence. He's no murderer."

"Still, there's the confession. It's not possible to disregard it that easily."

"Why don't you find the darned spell then? Or do you want to watch my only child getting cursed to death?"

Sabio sighed. "If the magiskope can't find a spell, we'll have to accept the inevitable."

Moira was surprised that Sabio managed to say this. Surely he wasn't comforting Aparta with these words. She clenched her fists. *And me neither. Druidus has to be innocent.*

Sabio's face looked as if chiseled from stone. "We will examine the sword again right away. If something's there, we'll find it."

"I want to be there," Aparta said.

"That's too dangerous."

"I will come whether you want me to or not."

"Aparta, stay home, if only to please me. I'll call you the minute we have a result."

"It's Druidus' last chance. I will come."

Moira recognized the granite in Aparta's voice.

Obviously Sabio noticed too because he gave in grudgingly. "Be here by eleven o'clock." He deactivated the parlebol and looked at Moira. "Fetch the sword."

Moira slipped off the table. "It's another hour till eleven."

"I don't intent to wait for her."

Moira wondered until she remembered that the examination wouldn't guarantee the result they were looking for. *Aparta with a nervous breakdown really would be the last straw.* She walked toward the shelves. "Where did you put it?"

"What?"

"The sword."

"Which sword?"

Moira turned. *How can he forget from one minute to the next?* She opened her mouth to ask, but Sabio beat her to it.

"Oh yes, that sword. I don't know." Frowning, he shook his head. "Why can't I remember?"

Moira shrugged and wondered secretly. So far, Sabio had never forgotten anything. "We'll find it. Don't worry." Searching, she walked along the shelves holding the evidence. She tried to remember if she had seen the telltale glitter of a spell on the sword, but she had been too focused on Druidus. She could barely remember how the weapon looked. *Drat.* After the third shelf without any swords in sight, she returned to Sabio.

"Try to remember where you saw it last," she said.

At that moment the door to the archive opened, and Semra looked in. "May I interrupt you, Sabio?" She smiled and pulled up her eyebrows questioningly. "The Committee for Safety Measures is here."

"Now, of all times! We've got so much to do." Sabio yawned and rubbed his eyes.

"It's truly important. A good part of our monthly pay depends on the fact that you can prove that Cursed Weapons can be destroyed without danger."

Sabio shook his head to and fro. "Can't they come back tomorrow?"

"They are leaving tonight." Semra cocked her head and fluttered her eyelashes. "Please, Sabio."

He shrugged. "Fine. Bring them right after lunch. We'll prepare everything for a demonstration."

Semra thanked him and hurried away.

Sabio bent to pull out the burning box from under his workbench. He looked over his shoulder at Moira. "Will you please fetch the trolley with the Cursed Weapons labeled for destruction?"

Moira nodded. The weapons lay on an oversized metal serving trolley and glittered to Moira's eyes like a mountain of jewels. She squeezed her eyes shut, pushed the trolley back to the hall half blinded, and placed it beside the burning box. When she opened her eyes again, her gaze fell on the clock above the door. *Only half an hour until Aparta arrives. Hopefully we'll find the sword before then.*

She looked at Sabio who pulled a small, black, disk-like box from a drawer. When he activated it, it hovered in the air as if hanging from invisible wires.

He noticed her gaze. "It's a recording box. It hovers in the air and records everything in the room – pictures and sound. It's one of the few magical gadgets that are admissible as evidence in court."

"You're going to record our test?"

Sabio slapped the box like an old friend. "As a security measure in case we have difficulties to convince the judges to re-open Druidus' lawsuit."

Moira was just about to go out again to search for the sword when the door swung open.

Aparta stormed in. "I had to come early. I couldn't stand the wait any longer."

Moira rolled her eyes and turned back to the shelves. Her gaze went over the trolley with the cursed weapons, and something on it caught her attention. A wide grin spread over her face when she recognized the sword. Half covered, it lay under a mace. "I found it." She pointed to it but left it to Sabio to pull it from the pile. After all, he was still wearing the safety gloves.

Aparta glared at her. "Don't you have anything better to do than to disturb Sabio?"

Sabio lay the sword on the table and patted Moira's shoulder. "She is a very good assistant."

Moira didn't listen to either. Her gaze was glued to the sword, and her eyes burned.

She couldn't see the slightest trace of magic on it. But it had to carry a spell. Druidus would never have murdered his father otherwise. She felt like crying, and reached out to pick up the weapon for closer inspection.

Sabio picked it up before her hands reached the hilt, and he showed it to Aparta.

Why did I do that? Moira wondered. *I know how dangerous a cursed weapon is.*

"Of course, I'll sign," Moira heard Sabio say. Irritated, she watched him lay the sword back on top of his work-table before he took off his gloves. He pressed his left hand on a sheet of paper Aparta had given him. A purple flame ran around his hand once and compacted into his initials.

Moira noticed that the paper glittered. Why does Aparta plant an ensorcelled paper on Sabio? She walked closer and examined it more closely while she listened with half an ear to Sabio's explanation of his magiskope.

At first glance, the paper looked like a petition to pick up Druidus' lawsuit once more. Moira narrowed her eyes and concentrated on looking past the obvious letters. Slowly, she deciphered the words of the hidden text.

I, SABIO MARTEN, CONFESS TO THE MURDER OF EX-CELSIOR VAN STEEN. I CURSED THE WEAPON DRUIDUS VAN STEEN USED TO KILL HIS FATHER. NATURALLY, I REMOVED THE SPELL BEFORE I SENT THE SWORD TO THE LAB FOR TESTING. PLEASE TAKE INTO CONSIDERATION THAT I'M DEEPLY IN LOVE WITH APARTA DE FREES, EX-CELSIOR VAN STEEN'S WIFE. I WANTED HER FOR MYSELF AND DIDN'T KNOW HOW MUCH SHE LOVED HER HUSBAND. BUT I CANNOT WATCH APARTA SUFFER ANY LONGER. ALSO, I APPRECIATE DRUIDUS VERY MUCH, SO I DECIDED TO BREAK MY SILENCE. DRUIDUS SHOULD NOT BE EXECUTED SINCE HE'S INNOCENT.

Underneath, verified by his signature spell, shone Sabio's autograph.

Moira pressed her lips together and snorted. *The backstabbing, lying slut!* She longed to take Aparta to task immediately. She called Sabio, and suppressed anger echoed in her voice.

"Yes?" He turned to her with raised eyebrows. "Why are you so angry?"

"Your beloved Aparta is trying to frame you. Listen." She read the letter to him. Every word drained some more color from his face. When she finished, he had to hold on to the table top to keep from falling.

"Aparta," he whispered. He stared at her and his eyes were wet.

"What else could I do? Druidus will be executed in one week." Tears ran over her cheeks, and she wrung her hands.

"It hurts that you don't trust me to find the truth. Didn't I build the best aura reading device of your profession for you alone?" He struggled to stand straight. His gaze practically stuck to Aparta. She covered her face with her hands, and her shoulders trembled. Sabio took a step toward her. He looked ten years older than a few minutes ago.

Moira longed to support him but didn't dare to walk over to him. This was something Aparta and Sabio had to work out on their own.

"If only you had asked, I would have signed this letter without cheating." Sabio blinked and his voice shook. "I love you more than my own life. It's been that way ever since we met."

"I didn't know what to do." Aparta sobbed. "He's my only child, Sabio. My one and only!"

Slowly, he walked up to her and hugged her. He murmured soothingly until she recovered. "Remove the spell from the paper," he said. "If my magiskope doesn't discover anything, we will hand it in together." His gaze met Moira's. "Will you betray us?"

She shook her head. If Sabio was prepared to forget about his principles out of love, who was she to judge him? Especially since she would get Druidus back that way. Also, she had been the one to disregard her principles a short while back. Suddenly, she had a stale taste in her mouth. Sabio's life for Druidus' – the swap seemed unjust. Hadn't she longed to become gendarma to find the truth and to make the world a little more just? She bit her lower lip. *The magiskope simply has to find a magical manipulation. I would never be happy again if Sabio sacrifices himself for Druidus.* The short trip to the worktable seemed unbearably long.

"We should examine the sword now." Her voice sounded hoarse, as if she hadn't used it for ages.

"Which sword?" Sabio looked at her with confusion, but remembered the weapon immediately.

That can't be normal, Moira thought. *It's impossible to think the sword had never existed twice in a row in mere minutes.*

Sabio picked up his gloves and started to take the weapons off the trolley that were piled above the sword. *Wait a second.* Moira frowned. *The sword was on Sabio's table just now.* Frowning some more, she put on safety gloves and lay the weapons Sabio handed her beside the burning box. *How did it get back into the pile? Sabio or Aparta must have stuck it there when I was busy with the letter. It's the only explanation. But why?*

Finally they reached the sword that Druidus had used to behead his father. Moira felt the cutting edge. Even through her safety gloves, she felt considerable strength spread from the gleaming blade. Her gaze wandered over the bright metal – silver, sparkling, smooth, and without rust. She yawned. *It's way too beautiful to destroy it.* She yawned again.

Sabio looked at her. "Maybe you should withdraw a bit before I pick it up." He pointed to the wire mesh between the work area and the entry desk of the archive. "I'm sure the mesh can prevent the worst should anything happen. It's covered with strong safety spells."

Moira put the sword on the table and walked over to Aparta. "Come."

Aparta crossed her arms in front of her chest. "Sabio promised I could be here."

"You can watch it from afar." Moira took her elbow and pushed her toward the entrance desk. She pulled the door closed, and the lock clicked shut. Intent, she watched Sabio. He picked up the sword, his eyelids drooped, and he yawned.

"Sabio!" Moira called as loud as she could.

"What?" His head shot up, and he put the weapon aside. Part of the blade landed under the magiskope.

"Something isn't right. You keep forgetting about the sword," Moira said.

"Which sword?" Sabio shook his head. "No, don't. I remember. Where is it now?"

Moira pointed to the magiskope working with a slight rumbling sound. Sabio pushed the sword a little until it lay properly under the pentagram.

A few seconds later, the gadget announced, "Weapon not catalogued."

Sabio, who had returned to his notes already, shot up. "Repeat that."

"Weapon not catalogued, two cross-references. File HnP 33/19 and file HmP 1/19."

Sabio shook his head. All of a sudden he was alarmed and wide awake. He tapped the recording box that still hung in the room twice to activate command mode.

"Replay the last minute," he ordered. The box obeyed. Sabio repeated the reference numbers of the files. "Well, well. HnP 33/19 and HmP 1/19."

Moira's fingers curled into the mesh, and she longed to hurry back to Sabio, but she knew she'd only be in the way right now. From the corners of her eye she watched Aparta, who stood just as close to the wire mesh as she did.

Breathlessly, Moira watched Sabio walk to a filing cabinet. When he knocked twice, two files flew out and landed in his hand. He lay them on the tabletop beside the magiskope and set the box back to recording.

"For the giving of evidence," he said in its direction, "the thirty-third homicide among natural persons in the year 3019 concerns a collector of antiques who slaughtered four members of his household with an antique sword before committing suicide. It was the case in which my colleague Excelsior Van Steen was supposed to catalogue the sword and destroy it afterwards.

"The only homicide of magical people in the year 3019 concerns Excelsior Van Steen, whose head was cut of with the same sword. I was forced to arrest his son Druidus as murderer since I found him on-site with the sword. He confessed, but I was, and still am, of the opinion that he had been influenced from outside. Unfortunately, I couldn't find proof for my theory. Druidus Van Steen was sentenced to death. The date for the execution is set for one week from tomorrow."

Sabio turned back to the magiskope. "Complete scan."

Moira held her breath. Her heart beat up to her throat. *Hopefully the result will exonerate Druidus. There has to be something even if I can't see it. Why else would Sabio forget about the sword all the time?*

It seemed to take the gadget an eternity to finish the scan. The voice of the magiskope crackled, sizzled, and hissed. "Saracen short sword. Inorganic life form."

Moira's jaw dropped, and she stared at the magiskope.

Sabio seemed surprised too. "Life form? Specify."

"Life form based on metal. Undetermined mode of life. Internal safety spell hinders detailed analysisssssss." The magiskope hissed, and sparks shot out of the wood. Hurriedly, Sabio deactivated the gadget. His hand wandered to the recording box.

Is he going to switch it off? Moira rattled the mesh. "Sabio. Wake up!"

Irritated, Sabio shook his head when he realized what he had been about to do. "What am I doing?" Pondering, he stared at the sword. "There is no doubt that this weapon can manipulate humans. We will have to find a way to show how this is done so we can prove Druidus' innocence. Does anyone have an idea?" He looked at Moira and Aparta, but both shook their heads. He scratched his chin. For a while they thought in silence.

Moira remembered that she had accompanied Franka and Tord to a lecture about Shamanic trances. She cleared her throat. "What if the sword is using a method that isn't magical, like hypnosis, drugs, or shamanism?"

"We can test that." Sabio turned to the recording box and activated the command mode. "Keep recording but activate answer mode too," he ordered. "Did you record anything that can be picked up by human senses but cannot be heard?"

"Positive," the box said.

Moira chewed the nail of her index finger and hardly dared to breathe.

"Make audible and replay," Sabio said.

For a single breath, there was silence. Then a semi-transparent picture overlay the room, and a silvery voice whispered, "Delete the recording."

A ghost like Sabio reached out for the recording box.

Moira slapped her forehead. "That is the silvery voice that sounds like chimes. Ramasseur's nerl told me about it."

"Stop replay," Sabio ordered. His eyes sparkled, and he grinned. "You are right. Finally, we have something that indicates that Monsieur Ramasseur didn't kill his family voluntarily and that Druidus was forced to kill his father. If we can turn it into irrefutable proof, the judgment has to be revoked."

Suddenly, Moira felt light headed and happy. They would really be able to prove that Druidus wasn't guilty. She breathed deeply several times.

Chapter 33

In her happiness, she reached her hand out toward Aparta. "Isn't that wonderful?"

Aparta ignored her outstretched hand. "It's not real evidence yet. The magiskope isn't admissible to court."

"But the recording box is," Sabio said. "And we know that this unknown life form can influence humans. I've got an idea." He tapped the recording box again. "Keep recording. Move non-audible tones to the audible spectrum. When you reach maximum recording time, start the alarm and fasten to the files HnP 33/19 and HmP 1/19."

The box confirmed the order and returned to record mode.

"Now, if the sword talks to me, we've got final proof." Sabio grinned like a wolf. He went to his coat rack and donned a helmet of alloy that would better protect his thoughts from hypnosis and similar methods than the pointy hat. He did without the coat, but put another pair of safety gloves over the ones he was already wearing.

Moira's eyes widened. "What are you going to do?"

"I'll put some pressure on this life form. Let's see what it'll do." Sabio walked to the table and set the magiskope aside.

"Be careful. It could be dangerous." Moira's voice trembled.

Sabio didn't look at her and didn't answer either. He opened the lid of the burning box and grabbed the sword's hilt.

"You can't just destroy it!" Aparta shrieked. "How are you going to prove Druidus' innocence without it?"

"You've got my confession, and it's already signed." He used his second hand too and lifted the sword inch by inch. According to his red face, it was incredibly heavy. "It won't help you. The burning box will destroy you whether you like it or not." Beads of sweat formed on his forehead.

"Put me down. Delete the recording," the silvery voice ordered with a cutting edge. This time, everybody heard.

Sabio grinned and his eyes glittered. "Your trick is not working any more. My helmet protects me. You'll have to think about something new."

Moira was sure the sword wouldn't give up so easily.

"Ouch!" Sabio yelled. "The little blighter cut me through the gloves."

The sword pulled up his arm. The air hissed around the blade as it shot toward Sabio's throat. At the last moment, he grabbed his right wrist and diverted the hit. The blade bit into a shelf and left a deep cut in the wood.

Merde. The sword is controlling his arm. Moira's gaze scanned the room. *How can I help? There has to be something I can do to help.* In one of the shelves at the front, she spotted an old-fashioned shield. Unfortunately, the shelves were on the other side of the wire mesh separation. Moira ripped out the drawers of the desk, searching for the key to the door.

Again, the sword dragged up Sabio's arm and tried to stab him vertically. This time Sabio was prepared. He clung to his right wrist tightly. The sword stabbed the table behind him instead.

The magiskope sparkled and broke.

"That won't help you." Sabio panted when the sword attacked again. "We can build a new magiskope any time. Also, the box records everything."

The sword shot up. Sabio pushed his arm to the side just in time to save the recording box. The blade shot down and sliced through Sabio's left thigh. He screamed.

At that moment, Moira discovered a bunch of keys. While Sabio fought screaming against the pain, she tried the keys with flying fingers.

Sabio ripped the sword from his wound and staggered away from the table toward the burning box. Blood ran down his leg, but the ache seemed to have given him back control over his arm. "Why are you doing this?"

"Blood," the sword whispered. "Blood is life. My life. Since the beginning of time."

It pulled up Sabio's arm again, posing as if for a victory. "Six thousand years of blood and war, war and blood. Until... Katie Féroce and Hern and darkness. Close to death. Then, a man. He loves me, strokes me, kills for me, bleeds for me. I drink."

"Was that Lif Borson?" Sabio took another step toward the burning box.

The sword ignored him. "Darkness again, waiting. Then, paradise. Enough blood every night. Finally, another man who cleans me and kills for me."

The homeless and the collector. Moira tried the second-to-last key. It fit. At last, the door opened.

Aparta pushed past her and walked toward Sabio.

"Then, a man who wants to destroy me. We fight. Like now." The sword lowered itself toward Sabio's chest, but he held it at bay with his free hand.

"His mind is strong. As strong as Katie's, as strong as Hern's, as strong as yours." The sword arced through the air and sliced through the tabletop. Moira pulled Aparta aside just in time.

"A man with the same blood comes in. His mind is less strong. He kills for me, and I drink. I will drink your blood too. And that of the women." The sword dragged Sabio toward Moira and Aparta.

"Aparta, run!"

The sword laughed triumphantly and forced Sabio's arm toward the women. "Blood!"

Sabio twisted to the side on his healthy leg. The blade missed Aparta by a hair's breadth. Instead, it grazed Moira's cheek, leaving a deep gash. She felt a fair amount of blood being sucked out of the narrow wound. She faltered.

Sabio swore. He held out his free hand toward Moira and Aparta and called a spell. The words echoed through Moira's head, rumbling like boulders. Her arms and legs froze. *I can't allow this*, she thought. *I have to help him.* She collected her magic, but Sabio's spell was stronger for the moment. Helpless, she was forced to watch him fight the sword for his own body.

"I won't let you kill Aparta or Moira." Sabio grabbed the blade with his left hand and pulled it close to his body. The cutting edge sliced through his gloves into his fingers, but he didn't seem to notice the pain. Step by faltering step he retreated. Blood ran over the blade.

Moira concentrated on the hole over her heart. Carefully, she let out some magic and threw it against Sabio's spell. Horrified, she noticed that the hilt in Sabio's hands was becoming slippery with all the blood. It became harder for him to cling to the weapon.

The sword rejoiced. It twisted in his hands and tried to break free. Sabio sweated, and the hilt slipped even more.

I have to get out of here. We can only defeat the monster together. Just like Hern and Katie. She closed her eyes and concentrated completely on her magic. She found breathing difficult but she forced herself to calm down.

Her pulse thundered in her ears, and only the sword's song of victory came through. With a strong, hard jerk, she shot out a gush of magic.

Sabio's spell fell off her. As a side effect, a tiny whirlwind appeared. It danced around Aparta and carried her perfume to Moira. It seemed strangely familiar, but she had no time to ponder it.

She stormed toward Sabio, who was leaning against the burning box with his right knee, trying to wipe the blood on his jumper. The sword had nearly cut through all the fingers on his free hand. More and more blood welled from the ripped vessels in rhythmic bursts, but it never reached the ground. Sabio moaned with the pain. He looked at her, and a sad smile flittered over his rugged face.

"Never let anyone bring you down, Moira. You are made for the Gendarmerie."

Moira reached for the sword, but Sabio twisted it away so she couldn't touch it. At his moment, Aparta woke from her torpor too.

Sabio's gaze focused on her face. "I love you."

Clinging to the sword, he fell backwards into the open burning box. Moira grabbed for him, but he slipped through her fingers. The burning box closed automatically and sealed itself. Inside, Sabio spoke the activating spell with a hoarse voice.

"NOOO!" Screaming, Moira threw herself on the box. The fire spell activated, swallowing man and sword in bluish flames. A small part of the heat hit Moira's face, and her eyes watered. *Idiot! Selfless, stubborn idiot.* She put her face on the warm glass and let her tears run free.

A hand landed on her shoulder and an acerbic smell reached her nostrils.

"He did it for us," Aparta said, "and for Druidus."

Moira didn't hear the words, but the smell tugged at her memory. It irritated her so much she lifted her head to smell it more easily.

Aparta walked to the recording box and examined it. "How do we turn it off? Surely, we don't need it any more."

Moira was close to answering when she remembered where she had noticed the aftershave-like perfume the last time. Frisian acerbic with a hint of ocean.

"You are behind all this." She threw herself on Aparta and punched her with both fists. She only hit glittering air. "You recognized my father when we tried to buy the antiques. That's why you ran away."

"Don't make a fool of yourself." With an outstretched hand, Aparta stabilized the shield that held Moira at a distance. "How could I get antiques to sell?"

Moira stopped. With her fists clenched, she stood in front of Aparta. Her brain worked at full speed. Finally, all of the details fit into the bigger picture. "From Bastide. He was a partner at the burglary of the museum, and he knew you from Excelsior's surveillance assignment. His files prove that."

Aparta's face contorted. "The little bastard tried to blackmail me. He meant to tell my husband about Sabio and me if I didn't sell his damned weapons." She steepled her fingers, and a fireball grew around them. With a fluid movement, she flung it.

Moira evaded it at the last possible moment. The shelf behind her splintered.

"The sword was the only interesting bit in the whole collection. It was an exhilarating pleasure to watch it kill the smoothie Lif." Aparta flung a second and third fireball, and Moira evaded them with great difficulty. She hid behind a couple of metal shelves.

I need a shield right now. She closed her eyes and concentrated on the tingling in the tips of her fingers. It was there, weak but clear enough for Moira to feel it.

One of the shelves burst into flame. Moira ran down the corridor deeper into the labyrinth of evidence and files. Aparta's flames followed relentlessly.

Moira pressed as much Unified Magic into the tips of her fingers as she could and held them over her head like a roof. Flames surrounded her, and countless screams of death faded when a shelf with ancient files charred. She stopped and turned.

Aparta stepped into the corridor. The recording box hovered behind her. Another fireball raced toward Moira, but it scattered on her shield. "Very well done. It seems you have some small magic after all. What a surprise."

Moira breathed hard. "You locked up Pete Huudien and forced him to murder the homeless."

"The sword and I were a great team."

Boiling hot rage swept through Moira. With the anger, the waves of her Wild Magic churned higher and higher. *If I have to keep up the shield for much longer, it'll break free and tear me apart. I have to distract Aparta.* She bent forward.

"How could you allow the sword to force Druidus to kill his own father?"

Aparta finally lost control. "My son. My sweet, little baby." Screaming, she jumped at Moira and clawed at her face with her fingernails.

Struggling, Moira protected her eyes.

Crazed, Aparta fought. "It's all your fault. Every idiot knows that it's the aspirant's duty to take the evidence down to Excelsior's archive. But you had to use my Druidus."

I was supposed to murder Excelsior? Surprised, Moira lowered her hands and stared at Aparta, open-mouthed. She could hardly believe it, and felt nailed to the spot.

Aparta stepped back and threw a silver ball that slammed into Moira's chest and burst. The stasis spell activated, and in a split second, Moira couldn't move any more.

Aparta laughed. It sounded shrill.

Struggling with all her strength, Moira tried to break free from the spell, but she had hardly any Unified Magic left. *I can't let the Wild Magic out on purpose. It would endanger all the people in the building.*

"This time, it will hurt. For a long time." Aparta lifted her arms and recited a death curse with a low voice.

Moira's heart nearly jumped from her chest. She wanted to run but not a single muscle worked. She couldn't even scream. The black shadow around Aparta's hands grew with every word she spoke.

Waves of Wild Magic churned through Moira's body and broke through the thinned-out protective walls of her Unified Magic. A giant surge of Magie Sauvage burst forth. Rainbow colors mixed in a wild whirl with the curse's blackness, thinned it, ripped it apart, and threw the fragments back at Aparta.

She dropped without another word.

Moira faltered. The stasis spell had vanished just like the chaos of burned, splintered, and toppled shelves. In their place, a world spread out like she had never seen before. A bright blue sky curved over trees that reached her hip. Grass, as soft and smooth as a carpet of velvet covered the ground around her and Aparta. Birds the size of her fingernails fluttered through the air, accompanied by elves as tiny as a pinhead. In the denser part of the forest, Moira discovered a fox, barely bigger than the nail on her thumb.

"Maximal recording time reached." The recording box blinked brightly and pulled Moira from her reverie. The box sped away. Moira grabbed Aparta's shoulders and dragged her after the box toward the archive's entry. The newly created world seemed to follow her, spreading with every step she took. Moira saw trolls, deer, reindeer, horses, dogs, and people. Sabio's worktable had vanished, and a veldt-like landscape spread around the burning box. The recording box hovered above it blinking with a bright red light. The two files hung from a clasp that had appeared on the side of the box. "Fly to the exit," Moira ordered after activating the command mode, and the blinking box obeyed.

Gasping, Moira followed it with the still unconscious Aparta. As the door in the mesh wire fence came closer, she noticed that there was still Magie Sauvage spilling from her. She gathered the last of her strength and closed all the holes in her aura. *Hopefully they'll stay shut.*

The door slammed open and Tord stormed in. "Don't touch the sword! It is..." He stopped abruptly and his eyes widened. "What happened here?"

Aparta moaned, and the pinkie of her right hand twitched.

"I'll tell you later." Moira searched the desk in the entrance area with flying fingers for another stasis spell. When she had found the silver ball, she pressed it into Tord's hand and pointed at Aparta. "Activate it fast, before Aparta regains her consciousness."

Aparta's eyelids fluttered. Wordlessly, Tord obeyed. Moira felt very relieved that he trusted her judgment.

Just as the silver shimmer of the stasis spell spread over Aparta, the door opened again. Semra entered with four magicians in long safety coats and pointy hats. They had slipped their hands into the sleeves of their coats and reminded Moira a little bit of vultures. She had to laugh.

"Moira! What happened?" Wide-eyed, Semra looked around, but Moira didn't answer. Her knees buckled and she sank to the ground giggling. She noticed that the recording box flew toward Semra with the two files.

Moira's field of vision narrowed with every second, and black dots danced in it. She wondered why the box and the files hadn't changed, and then she lost consciousness.

Chapter 34

When she came round, she lay on a stretcher. Semra and the President of the Gendarmerie Magique stood beside her. Tord held her hand.

"Franka will never forgive me for being too late." The whooshing of the Wild Magic in Moira's body nearly drowned out his words. She felt her magic search for a way out, and she needed all her strength to stop it. She clenched her fists, closed her eyes, and searched for the rest of her Unified Magic.

A hand touched her arm and made it even harder to concentrate. She opened her eyes.

The President of the Gendarmerie Magique shook her hand. "I am happy to see that you survived this chaos, and I'm very eager to hear your statement."

"Me too." Semra stepped up beside him. "Where is Sabio? And what is Aparta doing here?"

"The box," Moira whispered. "It's all in the box." She closed her eyes again and focused her energy on keeping her Magie Sauvage under control. Inexorably she slipped back into the blackness of unconsciousness.

When she woke the next time, everything around her was white and light yellow. It smelled of disinfectant. *Looks like a hospital*, she thought.

"Hello, beauty. Awake at last?" A nerl hopped onto her bed. It was the size of a two-year-old child and seemed strangely familiar. She frowned.

A thought surfaced. "I have to see Druidus." She tried to get up, but her body was too weak. With surprise, she stared at hands that couldn't even manage to lift the cover.

"Don't worry. Druidus is fine, and he sends his best wishes," the nerl said. He bent over the edge of the bed. "Hey, boys. She's awake."

Moira felt someone tug at her cover. Another nerl climbed up on it until a surprisingly big nerl entered through the door, picked him up, and set him on the bed.

Moira recognized the biggest nerl immediately. It was the museum's archivist. He had put Gronk on her cover, whose right hand had regrown wonderfully. She noticed that the skin of the new arm was still a mixture of the usual nerl-green and a well-tanned human skin. *Wild Magic seems to have side effects for nerls too*, she thought. Finally, she remembered where she had met the first nerl who was now sitting on her cover. "You're Grub, aren't you?"

The nerl nodded. Moira frowned. Slowly her brain began to pick up work again. Her gaze went from one to the next. She thought she could remember that Grub had been the size of a baby when they had examined the surveillance globes together. Gronk and the archivist also seemed bigger than before. "Is it possible that you have grown?"

Grub nodded. "You sustained us very well."

"You'll have to explain it properly. Can't you see that you're confusing her?" The archivist pulled a chair to the bed and sat beside Moira. "When you lost consciousness for the second time after the catastrophe, you also lost the grip on your magic."

Moira remembered the changes in the archive. "Not before?"

"You had everything under control before then." The archivist bent over her and put his hand on he shoulder. "Grub immediately realized what was happening, and suggested the usual deal to the President of the Gendarmerie Magique."

"Which deal?"

Grub hurried to answer. "For my help in analyzing the happenings, the collective of nerls was allowed to skim your magic as long as you weren't in control. It turned out we needed three nerls to do that or we would have grown too fast. Believe me. Thousands volunteered, but the elders chose us because you already know us."

"Thank you for organizing it so well. So many things could have happened!" Moira closed her eyes, relieved. She was so tired. Then she remembered something and looked at the three nerls again. "Didn't I have to agree to the deal?"

"The President of the Gendarmerie Magique did that in your place. As your boss, he could do that in a legally binding way, and believe me, it was urgent. It was the only way we could prevent uncontrolled changes," the archivist said.

"Well, except for the one doctor." Grub grinned. "He'll run around with a wing for quite a while yet."

I changed humans? Moira's eyes widened. "Will he return to normal?"

"Of course. Part of your magic evaporates after a while." Gronk pointed to his arm. "See? It is nearly green already. At first it was mostly pink."

"But it's still an arm, not a stump," Moira said.

Gronk didn't seem to be worried. "My doc thinks that the arm will stay when the color has drained. It was a strong spell."

"Does that mean the archive will return to normal too, one day?" Regretful, Moira thought of the countless tiny creatures and the incredible landscapes she had seen. "It would be a pity if everything turned back into piles of folders and shelves."

The archivist steepled his fingertips and tapped his hammer nose with his index fingers. "First, the change of the archive is based on the negation of a death curse. That was confirmed by analysis and by the record on the box." He lowered his hands, leaned back, and crossed his legs. "Second, you pumped so much Wild Magic into it that it should suffice for a couple of hundred years at least. By then, a magical balance will have established itself that will prevent the dissolution of the world. I think we can safely assume that the world you created will be there for good."

Grub crawled over the cover until he sat near her shoulder. "Do you know what I find absolutely incredible?"

Moira waited.

"Your control on the Wild Magic."

Moira's eyebrows shot up. "My control?" As far as she could remember, the Wild Magic had broken free full force.

The archivist seemed to notice her confusion. "You spared all the files and evidence that was still needed for the unsolved cases. Meanwhile, they have been taken to an unused room in the Gendarmerie's lab."

"Meanwhile? How long have I been out?"

"Not long. Only three days," Gronk said.

"Druidus!" Moira tried to sit up, but the archivist and Grub pushed her back into the cushions, and Gronk patted her hand.

The archivist picked up her other hand. "Don't worry. His execution and the lawsuit of Pete Huudien have been put on hold due to the new evidence. Both will be negotiated anew soon."

"In that respect, Sabio's sacrifice wasn't in vain," Grub said.

Moira's eyes filled with tears, and she felt guilty for not thinking of him right away. "He is–" Her voice shook. "He was the first colleague who believed in me."

"Shrompdonk." Gronk growled at Grub and jabbed him in the ribs. "Look what you've done."

Moira ignored them. She remembered Sabio's understanding for her reluctance to examine crime scenes, his conviction that she'd become a good gendarma, and she remembered the day in the sandpit. Magic tried to cool her heart that rubbed hot and sore in her chest. She rolled onto her side, pulled up her knees and cried.

A few days later Franka and Tord picked her up. The doctors and nurses had fixed her up so well, Franka didn't need to help her getting dressed. Moira was looking forward to getting back to her flat.

"I'm so sorry I was late that day," Tord said. "Maybe my findings would have kept Sabio from–"

"It's alright." Moira interrupted him. "It wasn't your fault."

"You miss him, don't you?" Franka lay her hand on Moira's shoulder. "You should know that we'll always be there for you."

Moira didn't answer. It would take her much longer to come to terms with Sabio's death, and she would always miss him, but the first wave of intensive grief was over. Silently she sat in the wheelchair that would take her to the exit. Hospital regulations. Franka insisted on pushing the wheelie despite her swollen belly. On the way down, she let her curiosity take over. "Will you have to testify against Aparta de Frees in court?"

"It depends on the judge." Moira hoped with all her heart that the box's recording would suffice. She didn't fancy seeing Aparta de Frees ever again in her life.

Lavant waited at the carpisto. Wordlessly he hugged her and left it to Tord to drive them home.

On the way, Moira stared out the window and watched the people attending to their business. Some wore colorful clothes, others gray or black and white. Now and then a spell sparkled. *That's just like life*, Moira thought. *Sometimes, its wonderfully colorful, a rainbow of life. Then it's sad and gray. But it hardly ever is black and white.* She turned to Tord. "By the way, what did you mean to tell me and Sabio back then in the archive?"

"I finally found the article I have been searching for. It was on the shelf with the fairy tales and legends."

"And it tells an interesting story that Tord didn't consider worth pursuing for many years because the source is questionable," Franka said. She shot Tord an exaggerated, angry look.

He smiled back timidly.

"What did it say?" Moira's curiosity woke.

"The monk I told you about …"

"The one where all the other monks were killed with a cursed dagger?"

"Just the one. He was convinced that the dagger wasn't really cursed, but a strange creature. After he dumped it into a moor, he searched the world for more daggers like this." Tord's eyes sparkled as he talked. "He tells of a stone pillar in a valley in India, that tells a story of Katie Féroce. It says that the sword Katie had chosen as a wedding present for her beloved had been alive. According to the stone pillar, it tried to force Katie to murder her whole tribe when they came for the wedding. But she fought it valiantly and saved most of the tribe that way. Finally, she managed to stun the sword with her magic for a small while. With help from Hern, she created an urn of stone that they sealed together. She died from her wounds after she had put her remaining strength into a safety spell that begged possible finders not to open the urn. She didn't want the sword, which she called Malice Animé, to ever force a human to murder others again."

"Maybe she even suspected how long the sword could survive in the urn," Franka said. "At least, this story teaches us not to discount something as humbug just because we don't have an explanation."

Moira smiled. She was happy to know the real end of Katie's and Hern's story, especially since it meant lots of awards for Tord. And the more awards, the better the pay from the university. It was a good feeling to know that Franka and the baby would be well provided for.

"By the way, we decided to delay the wedding until after Druidus' second trial." Tord steered into a parking space near her flat. "Franka thought she couldn't celebrate happily without him there. Also, she's still hoping for a double wedding."

Thinking of Druidus cheered Moira up and helped her to enjoy the festive meal Franka had prepared in her flat.

Two weeks later, Moira stood in a magic-safe room with the President of the Gendarmerie Magique, Semra, Buds and two Commissaires of the examination board. Everybody shot spells on Moira. She deflected them easily since she had used up so much of her Magie Sauvage that she could use her Magie Généraliser for the exam. She managed spells that would have been impossible before Sabio's training. *What a pity that the Magie Sauvage will grow back.* She deflected a fire ball from the President.

When the testing was over, Buds patted her shoulder. "Never thought you'd turn into something this good."

"Sabio always knew how to spot talent." Semra took her hand, beaming. "Well done."

The President of the Gendarmerie Magique smiled at Moira. "Please wait in the entrance hall for us. I don't think our consultation will take up much time."

Moira walked up and down the hall. She breathed as deeply and regularly as she could but it didn't help. Her knees shook, her hands sweated, and her heart thumped like it might have after an hour of combat training.

The entrance door slammed, and she spun around. When she saw who was approaching, her eyes widened and her legs felt as if someone had stolen the bones from them.

Luckily Druidus hugged her before she collapsed. "Thank you," he whispered. His voice was hoarse.

"I thought the new trial will only start tomorrow," Moira said.

"It has been rescheduled due to pressure from the Gendarmerie. Mother's confession sped the thing along, too. The only thing they're still discussing is the admittance of the magiskope as a legal item of evidence at court." He bent his head until his forehead touched hers. "You can't imagine how horrible it is to be locked inside your own body. I wouldn't have been able to stand it without thinking of you."

Moira shivered. "Did they break the sword's influence completely?"

Druidus held her closer.

"The psychologist thinks that I will remember the events for all my life. At least I don't experience them as if they were real. It's more like a film I watched. I remember all the details but there is no emotional connection. I think I'm thankful for that."

Moira leaned against him and breathed in his scent. It soothed her soul and for the first time since her father had left the family, she felt complete again. After a while she asked, "How about Pete Huudien? He had to kill many more people."

"His mental blockade is different. The psychologist said Pete could barely remember the murders any more already. I envy him." Druidus sighed. "His fiancée picked him up. As far as I know, they took the shortest route to a Marriage Registrar."

Moira kissed him. She pressed her lips on his as if this would be their last kiss. Tingling, more ferocious than Wild Magic, spread from her lips through her body. She closed her eyes and allowed her emotions to carry her away.

Someone cleared his throat, and Druidus let her go. Reluctantly Moira turned to the examination board. She clung to Druidus' arm, determined never to let him go again.

"What a pleasure to see you, Monsieur van Steen," the President of the Gendarmerie Magique said. "I truly regret the circumstances that led to your arrest. Hopefully you will be able to forgive us."

Druidus looked at him sternly. "Since there was no evidence for my innocence, you didn't have a choice. Thank you for the psychological help you organized."

"It was the least we could do for you and Monsieur Huudien."

Druidus pulled his face into a smile as if he struggled to remember how to do that. "Maybe I'll return to duty soon."

"You'll be very welcome. We always need an able gendarme like you. I'm looking forward to the day you pick up duty again." He turned to Moira. "Now, we don't want to keep you in suspense any longer. Surely, you're very excited already."

At the moment, there was nothing Moira was less interested in than the result of her exam. All that counted was that Druidus was back again. She leaned her head against his shoulder and he pulled her closer.

"Since there is no doubt about the fact that you have considerable magical abilities, there is no reason why you shouldn't continue your training with the Gendarmerie."

Semra congratulated her and added, "Since you already worked as a full assistant in the Gendarmerie, proving that you're good at working with the hard cases, you've been assigned to Murder Two – if you don't decline. You can do the minimum times at the other stations, and that should suffice for your education."

"You only have to sign here." The President of the Gendarmerie Magique handed her the Contract for Training. Moira hesitated for a brief moment. As a gendarma, she'd have to live in constant fear of losing someone she loved. Would she still be able to see the wonderful sides of life? She looked at Druidus, and their gazes met. His eyes promised love and security. Moira breathed deeply and signed.

Chapter 35

The cave was dark. It was so dark that the rat, despite its great night-vision, couldn't see a thing. It depended on its sense of smell. The tiny brain registered that a young male had passed this way a few days ago, but it had been long enough that the rat didn't feel the need to follow it. It sniffed at a stone which smelled of iron and something else. Hesitantly the rat rose, placing its front paws on the stone. Since its hip wasn't designed for standing on the hind legs for long, it sank to the ground after a while.

The stone cracked open, and the rat landed on something hard and pointy. A human would have recognized it as a tiny sword. A silvery voice mewed. Obediently, the rat picked up the sword with the right front paw. Walking on its hind legs, it left the cave holding the sword ready for a fight. It followed the trail of the young male and its nose vibrated with bloodlust.

The End

Thank you for reading this. If you liked the story, please leave a review on Amazon, Goodreads, Shelfari or any other platform. Thank you in advance.

You can find more stories by me on my homepage:
http://www.katharinagerlach.com

Glossar

auravaluation	=	examination of a person's aura to determine the state of health and the talents
Bonnechance waterdrops	=	drops of water held in shape with a spell bringing luck to the bearer.
carpisto	=	car-like vehicle powered by a flying carpet
chargerie	=	loading station for carpistos (see above)? often including a sales outlet for countless everyday spells
Charme Securité	=	safety spell
Colonel Magique	=	leader of the local Gendarmerie Magique ?
Commissaire Magique	=	officer of the Gendarmerie Magique ?
elf-net	=	net for stunning elves
gendarm, gendarme	=	male/female police officer
Gendarmerie Magique	=	police for magical felonies
homicide spell	=	spell that forces a person to commit murder
ID-panneau	=	flat pane of glass that can determine the identity of a person by examining their hand
Lumière Magique	=	magical ball of light
Magie Focaliser	=	Focused Magic
Magie Généraliser	=	Unified Magic
Magic Sauvage	=	Wild Magic
magiskope	=	gadget for determining the smallest amounts of magic
magicuter	=	computer powered by magic
Malice Animé	=	living evil
Maréchal	=	sergeant, rank below Commissaire ?
merde	–	French swearword
nerlôpital	=	hospital for nerls

parapluie spell	=	keep-me-dry spell, protecting against rain
parlebol	=	bowl that allows talking over long distances (similar to a telephone)
Sortie du sommeil	=	raise from your sleep (= Wake up)
stasis, stasis spell	=	magically constructed state where nothing can be changed by human interference; the spell freezes everything it hits in place
suicide spell	=	spell that forces a person to commit suicide
tapisrapide	=	high speed carpisto ?
traceball	=	ball-like tracking device for finding elves

More Books by the Author

For fourteen years, street urchin Paul's miserable existence has kept him safe from an ancient law that sentences all second-born twins to death. When he learns he is the younger twin of the mentally handicapped Crown Prince who's in danger of being killed for his disability, he agrees to play the role of the miraculously healed royal heir.

Paul struggles to learn how to act like a born ruler, but finds that his greatest skill, getting by unnoticed, is now his greatest liability. He knows if he is discovered, he will be executed like all second-born twins.

When a vengeful sorcerer threatens the kingdom, Paul is the only one who can oppose him. But using his unique talents will expose him. Now, he's got the choice. What is more important, his life or his family's and the kingdom's safety?

Urchin King is available at your favorite retailer.

Since Bryanna grows up in Scotland, she is familiar with hobgoblins, selkies and kelpies from the tales of her mother country. But she is very surprised when she starts seeing these creatures one day. Is she hallucinating? Before she can ask her father's advice, he is kidnapped by a woman whose scent seems awfully familiar. Instead of calling the police, Bryanna follows the kidnapper and lands smack-dab in the middle of the adventure of her life. It's just as well she knows the old legends and myths well. The world she lands in is murderously dangerous. And even if she survives the journey, she is fated to kill her father.

Scotland's Guardians is available at your favorite retailer.

Find out more on www.katharinagerlach.com. For information about new releases join the author's mailing list: bit.ly/KatharinaGerlachNewsletter (beware: bit.ly-links are case sensitive)